NEVER LOVE A LORD

Heather Grothaus

ZEBRA BOOKS
KENSINGTON PUBLISHING CORP.
http://www.kensingtonbooks.com

ZEBRA BOOKS are published by

Kensington Publishing Corp.
119 West 40th Street
New York, NY 10018

Copyright © 2013 by Heather Grothaus

All rights reserved. No part of this book may be reproduced in any form or by any means without the prior written consent of the Publisher, excepting brief quotes used in reviews.

If you purchased this book without a cover you should be aware that this book is stolen property. It was reported as "unsold and destroyed" to the Publisher and neither the Author nor the Publisher has received any payment for this "stripped book."

All Kensington titles, imprints, and distributed lines are available at special quantity discounts for bulk purchases for sales promotion, premiums, fund-raising, educational, or institutional use.

Special book excerpts or customized printings can also be created to fit specific needs. For details, write or phone the office of the Kensington Special Sales Manager: Attn. Special Sales Department. Kensington Publishing Corp., 119 West 40th Street, New York, NY 10018. Phone: 1-800-221-2647.

Zebra and the Z logo Reg. U.S. Pat. & TM Off.

ISBN-13: 978-1-4201-1244-3
ISBN-10: 1-4201-1244-9

First Printing: January 2013

10 9 8 7 6 5 4 3 2 1

Printed in the United States of America

Chapter 1

April 1277
Fallstowe Castle, England

With one step, it would all be over.

Sybilla Foxe swayed with the stiff breeze that shoved its way between the battlements where she stood more than one hundred feet above the ground.

Beneath her, six hundred of King Edward's finest were readying to make war against her, their torches and balefires blooming in the night, the creaking of wooden beams and the clanging of metal wafting up to her as discordant notes from a demonic orchestra. The conductor of the affair had only just arrived in an ornate carriage, driven to the fore of the company and rocking to a stop. As of yet, no one had emerged.

To either side of Sybilla—indeed, around the whole of the castle's impressive topmost perimeter—Fallstowe's soldiers crouched behind the protective stone merlons of the castle's tallest turret, their own torches snuffed. They were one with the shadows cast by the bone-white moon, round and glaring down on them.

Save for Sybilla, who stood in an embrasure, her arms outstretched so that her palms held her fast within the teeth of the battlement. She knew that her silhouette would be visible to anyone with a keen eye who looked in just the right spot. The wind came again, pushing her, buffeting Sybilla so that her spine bowed, her palms scraped against the stone. She was like the mainsail of a ship filled with a seaborne tempest, her rigging straining where it was lashed to landlocked Fallstowe. Her hair blew forward around both sides of her face, catching in the seam of her mouth. If she but loosed her stays, the wind would rip her away from the turret into the night, wildly, silently, without remorse.

Sybilla closed her eyes and tilted her face up. Now she was the carved figurehead on the bow of the ship, so free and fearless. She could feel the grit beneath her slippers rolling as her feet slid almost imperceptibly nearer the abyss.

With one step, it could all be over . . .

"Madam?"

The wind relented, and Sybilla sagged back between the merlons. Disappointment prickled along her jaw, causing her chin to tremble, her eyes to sting. She forced her reluctant arms to fold, stepping backward and down from the battlement and onto a mantlet, the large wooden shield ready to be put into service at a moment's notice. Sybilla turned calmly to face her most faithful friend—Fallstowe's aged steward—properly.

"Yes, Graves?"

In that instant, the air before Sybilla's face went white hot and flames flashed before her eyes with a blinding *whoosh*. A solid-sounding *thunk* echoed in the soles of her feet and both Sybilla and Graves looked down at the flaming arrow stuck in the thick wood of the mantlet, a hand's-breadth before her right foot. A parchment was tied to its shaft.

Sybilla looked up at Fallstowe's steward in the same instant that he, too, raised his eyes.

"Shall I fetch that for you?"

Sybilla forced herself to swallow. She had been closer to death than she'd realized.

Without waiting for her answer, Graves reached out one long, thin arm and jerked the now sputtering missile free before snapping the shaft in half and tossing the glowing ash of the fletching to the stones. The only sounds atop the turret were the wind, the barely discernible rustle of armor covering the backs of impatient soldiers, and the scratching of Graves's fingernails against stiff parchment.

Sybilla could scarcely hear them above the blood pounding in her ears.

At last Graves handed the missive to her. Sybilla held the curled ends in her hands, turning the page toward the bright moonlight. The page was covered with thin, scrawling characters, undecipherable in the night, but the ornate preface as well as the thick, heavy seal under her thumb were clear enough that Sybilla understood without reading the royal proclamation.

Edward I had come for her. The king meant to take Fallstowe, this night.

As if she had not already ascertained that fact by the six hundred armed men arriving by moonlight to camp beyond her moat.

She sighed and dropped the hand holding the missive to her side. "Thank you, Oliver," she muttered. Certainly Edward would have come for her eventually, but the king had no doubt been prompted to act by the message recently sent by Sybilla's newly acquired brother-in-law, Oliver Bellecote.

Sybilla hoped her younger sister, Cecily, was enjoying her wedding night more than was Sybilla.

Only a handful of months ago, the king himself had warned the youngest of the Foxe sisters, Alys, at his own court. Alys was now safely ensconced at bucolic Gillwick, with her husband, Piers.

It will come down to you, Sybilla. She heard the phrase in her mind, spoken to her so many times by her mother. She could still picture Amicia vividly, lying in the bed that was now Sybilla's, her useless right side both bolstered and half-hidden by pillows.

And it will end with you.

Sybilla wondered who the king had sent to lead the siege against her, and she called to mind the ornate carriage she'd seen arrive below. She turned her face toward the battlements again, just as another flaming arrow whooshed over the crenellation and sank into the wood at her feet.

Sybilla gasped this time, and she felt her brows draw together as she saw another parchment tied to this arrow's staff. She was becoming slightly irritated with this particular method of correspondence. The murmur of soldiers' armor was more insistent this time, and Sybilla knew they were anxious to act.

"My lady?" Her general rose from his position, obviously waiting for her to give the signal to return fire. His drawing hand hung at his hip, the exposed fingers in his glove catching the ivory moonlight as they clenched and unfurled.

"Hold, Wigmund," Sybilla cautioned him.

"It nearly struck you," the knight argued. "'Tis obvious

the thieves are aware of your presence—they think to avoid a fight should they fell you in advance."

"I know your men are eager. You will likely gain the battle you crave before the dawn has stepped both feet onto the earth." Sybilla looked back down at the arrow. "But I am as yet untouched. Hold."

"Madam?" Graves asked solicitously.

"I'll get it," Sybilla said, hitching her skirts up slightly into the crease of her hips in order to crouch down on the massive wooden shield. She untied the parchment, leaving the flames to flicker their little light while she unfurled the message and held it near the dying flame.

Shall we negotiate?

JG

Instinctively, Sybilla looked to the battlements, although from her crouched position she could see nothing but sky. Negotiate? She could see no points on which either side was willing or able to concede. The only information that might save Sybilla, and which the king couldn't already know, was what she had sworn to her mother while Amicia lay dying. And *that* she would never, ever tell.

Fallstowe might be taken, the Foxe family would be no more, Amicia's name would be synonymous with deception and scandal, but the greatest secret of all would be buried in a grave.

Most likely Sybilla's.

As if to emphasize the inevitability of her fate, another flaming arrow lofted over the battlements, this time pinning the hem of Sybilla's gown to the wooden platform.

The roar of armor shook the night as soldiers rose like a black wave to the battlements, even as Wigmund bellowed "Place!" and was answered by the echoes of his lieutenants repeating the order around the whole of Fallstowe Castle. The air trembled with a whiny reverberation, the audible tautness of hundreds of bowstrings.

Graves cleared his throat. "Won't you come away from the edge now, Madam?"

But instead of fear, Sybilla began to feel the familiar rumblings of anger. "*I said hold!*" Sybilla shouted up at Wigmund. "Hold your men!"

The general glared at her but relayed the command. He did not order the men to stand down, and Sybilla had not expected him to. She knew they would be pushed only so far, with or without her word.

Still, once they fired on soldiers of the king, their fates were sealed.

Sybilla tossed the earlier plea for negotiations aside and, without unpinning the still-flaming arrow from her gown, removed the latest message.

Last chance.

JG

"That pompous ass," Sybilla growled, her fury spreading like thick ice on a deep lake. "Wigmund," she called out calmly as she jerked the extinguished arrow free from the wood.

"My lady?"

"Bring your bow. Wrap and dip a fletching—I want to be certain it is seen."

Sybilla turned the dead arrow in one hand, using her other hand to place the most recent missive on the flat shield. With the coaled end of the arrow she scratched a short, crude message, and then tossed her makeshift writing utensil aside.

When she looked up, Fallstowe's general stood above her, his longbow in one hand and a single arrow in the other, its end bulbous and dripping with pitch.

Sybilla stood in one swift motion, still anchored to the wooden shield by the flickering arrow, the parchment crumpled in her hand. She seized the projectile Wigmund offered and then glanced at the general out of the corner of her eye as she tied her message to the arrow.

"I haven't the strength to draw a longbow, good sir; I shall have the one across your back."

If the general was surprised that Fallstowe's lady intended to send the message herself, he hid it well, ducking his head to remove his shorter weapon and holding it toward Sybilla. Before she took it, she bent at the waist and yanked the flaming arrow from her hem, quickly touching it to the primed fletching in her hand. Then she grabbed the bow and turned to the battlements once more.

"I shall be the only one to fire," she advised her general, and was satisfied as the command to hold made its way around the turret and away into the night.

Sybilla stepped into the embrasure and knocked her arrow, the bubbling pitch hissing, the heat from the flames rising up to warm her face. She knew she had only seconds before she was spotted. She quickly raised her elbows and lowered her weapon until she had sighted in on her target.

The carriage. A lone archer stood with his back leaning against the ornate conveyance, bow in one hand, arms crossed over his chest, as he conversed casually with another soldier. He paid Fallstowe no mind.

She drew the bow, her muscles quivering with effort. With no archer's glove to protect her, the flesh of the first two fingers of her right hand felt cut to the bone by the bowstring. Her shoulders and chest strained, but she no longer felt like stepping off the ledge into oblivion. In fact, she felt rather better.

Below, the archer's face turned upward, and she heard his faint shout of surprised alarm.

One more fight then, for posterity's sake.

Sybilla felt her lips curve into a smile, then she let her arrow fly.

Chapter 2

It seemed as though not a single candle was lit within the whole of Fallstowe Castle, implying that the entire household beyond the still, moon-washed stones was abed and unaware.

Julian Griffin was not so foolish as to believe that was true at all, and so he was willing to give the lady ample time to reply. At least another moment or two. It would disappoint him greatly to order the drawbridge fired, but it seemed unlikely that Fallstowe would simply roll over at this late date when faced with yet another royal decree.

Yes, very disappointing indeed. Julian had been very much looking forward to speaking at length with Sybilla Foxe. After the past year of research on her family—traveling both here and abroad—Julian had become fascinated by the enigmatic heiress of Fallstowe. He dropped his hand and the heavy curtain covering the carriage window fell back into place.

Any matter, he was here to perform his duty for the king, and in return he would be rewarded with a home and lands for himself and Lucy. Scholarly curiosity notwithstanding, that was his main goal.

His thoughts turned briefly to Cateline; how smugly pleased she would be if she could see him now, outfitted in one of her cousin the king's royal carriages, on the eve of leading a siege in the name of the Crown. How far he had come from the penniless noble she had first met upon his return from the Eighth Crusade. Julian had gained so much since then: a powerful friend and benefactor in Edward, the king's own cousin for a bride, authority in London, coin to spare. And most important of all, of course, was Lucy.

Julian sighed and moved the curtain back once more. He could hear his archer conversing with another soldier. Julian's eyes shifted, and he saw Erik standing a few feet away from the carriage, overseeing the erection of a war tent. Julian put his hand on the door latch, ready to remove himself from the carriage and set the siege in motion. Sybilla Foxe was not going to surrender.

Before he could open the door, he heard the archer's shout, and then the carriage shuddered as a loud crack emanated from the roof. Julian turned his face up and saw a distinct point in the satin lining of the carriage ceiling directly above his head, where only a moment before it had been flawlessly smooth.

"What wuzzat, milord?" Murrin gasped, coming aright from her slouch in the corner where she'd been sleeping. Her hands reached instinctively for the traveling cradle beneath her arm, although Lucy had not stirred.

"All's well, Murrin," Julian said. He pushed the door open and stood up on the frame in order to poke his head over the top of the carriage.

An arrow, flaming wildly, punctured the king's royal conveyance. Julian's face turned upward to the castle's tallest turret, and in the shadowed relief of the battlements, he saw a small figure.

A figure whose skirt was blowing wide in the wind.

Julian reached up and jerked the arrow free of the wood before hopping to the ground and closing the carriage door gently. When he turned, he was immediately surrounded by his officers and two soldiers bearing torches. None of the men said anything while Julian untied the wrinkled parchment and threw the flaming arrow to the ground. He unfurled the page, saw his own writing, and then turned the parchment over.

You alone.

It was unsigned.

Julian looked up once more at the figure still standing in the crenellations, and he knew the author of the message just as surely as if she had whispered the two words into his ear.

"Hello, Sybilla," he murmured through his grin.

"Shall we make ready, Lord Griffin?" Erik prompted, shaking Julian from his reverie so that he turned to address the armed man.

"Not yet, Erik," Julian said, handing the man Fallstowe's message. "It seems I've been granted an audience." He turned to the carriage door again.

"You're not actually going alone, though, are you?" Erik demanded incredulously.

"Of course not," Julian said easily over his shoulder as he opened the door. Then he spoke to the carriage's interior. "I'm sorry to disturb you, Murrin, but I'm afraid you'll have to ready Lucy and come with me." Julian turned back to his frowning officers.

"How many shall accompany us?" Erik asked, his blond brows drawn together ominously.

"No *us*, Erik—only Lucy and Murrin and I."

"Lord Griffin, perhaps that is unwise," Erik suggested, with obviously forced patience. As one of Julian's closest friends, it was oft difficult for him to retain professional deference before the other soldiers. "Who's to say that the viperous traitor won't cut you down once you cross her threshold? And then what will become of Lady Lucy?"

"I don't think we have to worry about that," Julian said, helping Murrin down from the carriage, the swaddled bundle that was his daughter held lovingly and securely in her arms.

"Blimy, milord," Murrin gasped, staring up wide-eyed at the castle. From within the embroidered coverlet, Lucy began to fuss, and Murrin bounced on the balls of her feet out of habit. "Shh, kitten. Shh."

Julian turned to his men. "Send the first runner with a message stating that I've begun negotiations. If you do not have word from me within one hour, send a second, fire the gate, and storm the castle."

"Julian—" Erik began.

But Julian turned away from his friend and general, staring once more at the lofty battlements. The figure was gone. But now, all along the crenellations of Fallstowe, balls of light burst into existence as, one by one, torches were lit. In less than a minute, Fallstowe wore a fiery crown, and the hundreds of shadow figures that were her soldiers stood looking down on the king's men.

It was a dangerous situation, yes. And in that briefest moment, Julian considered ordering Murrin to stay behind in the carriage with Lucy. But once inside, Julian had no intention of leaving Fallstowe until he'd brought the lady to heel, and he would not be separated from his daughter in the interim.

From what Julian had learned about the Foxe women, the heeling could take some time. Perhaps decades.

"Come along, Murrin," Julian said mildly, and began walking around the fore of the company toward Fallstowe's drawbridge.

"Directly behind you, milord," the nursemaid chirped.

The three stood on the road near the edge of the moat when the giant slab of wood began to lower with shuddering creaks. Once it had touched earth, Julian saw the flurry of activity within the bailey as the portcullis was raised. Scores of soldiers were falling into rank in two lines to either side of the barbican, forming an aisle of blade and armor through the bailey, up the steps of the keep, and through the open double doors. Red light from the torches bubbled together with shadows.

"Fancy," Murrin whispered.

"Quite dramatic," Julian agreed and then stepped onto the drawbridge.

They walked the predetermined path silently and swiftly, but still did not gain the steps of the keep for several moments. During his march, Julian was silently counting the well-armed soldiers keeping watch over them, and mentally calculating the total with the number of men he had seen atop the castle itself.

Julian came to the conclusion that Fallstowe had been more than ready for his arrival, and that troubled him. If it came down to a battle, it would not be a short one, and he'd seen enough bloodshed already in the Holy Land to last him three lifetimes.

Only one more battle, though, he told himself as he stepped into the heart of the Foxe family's lair. The doors shut firmly behind him, and Julian steeled himself not to turn around, even as he heard the thick beams set in place.

A thin, gray wraith stood at the top of a set of stone

stairs, his posture stiff and formal, his hands clasped behind his back as if in anticipation of Julian's arrival. Julian noticed the old man's brief and discreet glance at Murrin and Lucy.

"Might I have the privilege of announcing His Lordship's arrival to Madam?" the old man queried.

Julian felt a faint smile come to his mouth again. "You must be Graves. Your reputation precedes you, even in lands abroad," Julian offered with a tilt of his head. "Lord Julian Griffin for His Sovereign Majesty, King Edward, to see Lady Sybilla upon her most recent invitation. Also, my daughter, Lady Lucy Griffin."

Graves bowed, and Julian could detect neither approval nor scorn in the man's expressionless face. Fallstowe's steward was nearly a legend for his poor treatment of his betters.

"Won't you follow me, my lord?" Graves turned on his heel and made his way down the dark stairwell.

The corridor emptied into a hall so large, Julian reckoned it was as grand as any in the king's own home. The ceiling was high, dark, domed, supported by carved buttresses which wore skirts of balconies and catwalk pleats. Huge black-iron circles hung on thick chains, bearing hundreds of dormant candles. Stacks of planked tables and benches were piled to either side of the polished stone floor, murky gray with shadows.

The only lights were a series of standing candelabras around the perimeter of the hall, and one lit iron chandelier suspended directly above the lord's dais, where a table and a single high-backed chair rested, their occupant present and awaiting him patiently. She seemed very small from so far away, and it was quite ironic, considering the immense trouble she had caused the king.

Julian felt his heartbeat speed up in a way that no

thoughts of impending battle could inspire. In only moments, he would at last be face-to-face with Sybilla Foxe, the woman whose family he knew more intimately than his own. The woman whom many thought to be only a myth.

Ahead of him, Graves called out in a surprisingly robust yet still completely refined voice, "Madam, may I present Lord Julian Griffin and Lady Lucy Griffin?"

As Julian at last began to draw closer to the dais, his heartbeat did not further increase—in fact, it slowed until Julian wondered if time itself would stop. He had heard tales of Sybilla Foxe's unearthly beauty, her witch-like powers over the opposite sex, her frigid demeanor, but it was only when Julian was close enough to make out her features clearly, breathe the air around her, that he thought he might at last understand.

She lounged in one corner of her chair—which re-sembled more of a throne to Julian—her legs stretched out to one side beneath the table and her ankles crossed. One elbow rested on the arm of the chair, her forefin-ger along her temple. A pitcher and a solitary chalice sat on the table before her.

She wore a scarlet velvet gown which shimmered in the candlelight, the arms and bodice fitting, her chest partially bared by the deep U cut of the fabric. Her skin was alabaster, so white and smooth that it didn't seem to be made of flesh. Her hair, in contrast, was as dark as the underside of a grave, as were her eyelashes, which framed eyes of the most blazing aquamarine. Her lips, full and motionless, rivaled the brightest summer apple—so red, Julian almost expected them to begin dripping at any moment.

She was a sculpture, a study in color and nature—snow, coal, jewels, blood. Julian Griffin's heart stuttered to a start once more with his next breath, as if it had been startled back to life.

He shook himself inwardly. She was just a woman.

Julian reached the dais and stopped, bowing low. "Lady Foxe, it is a pleasure."

"Lord Griffin," Sybilla Foxe said, almost pensively, her posture not twitching. "Did you bring an infant to a siege?"

Chapter 3

Her dagger was neatly at her side, attached to her waist on a fine, gold chatelaine. In a blink, Sybilla knew that she could retrieve the dagger and fling it at the man standing before her table, who was foolish enough to enter her home with the intention of stealing it away from her. She would send the blade into his eye, and Julian Griffin would drop to the stones like a pheasant from the sky. Then she would have his body thrown from the top of Fallstowe into the midst of the king's soldiers as a symbolic beginning to what would surely be the most terrible siege in the history of England.

But he had brought an *infant*. To a *siege*.

Julian Griffin acknowledged her question with a self-deprecating tilt of his tawny head. "My daughter, Lucy. She goes everywhere with me. I hope you don't mind."

"I do mind, actually," Sybilla said. "Fallstowe is no place for children. Especially on a night such as this."

"Then I can do no more than apologize for my pre-sumptuousness," Julian offered mildly.

Sybilla thought he seemed very at ease, and that

increased her resentment of him. "What is it you want, Lord Griffin?"

"I believe you know."

Sybilla sighed grimly as she settled fully against the back of her chair, interlacing her fingers over her waist. "Fallstowe, obviously. I won't let you have it so easily, though. It's mine. My family's and mine, and I am more than prepared to fight for it."

"Lady Foxe, you must realize that you've brought this condemnation down on your own head," Julian began in a reasoning tone. "Edward has sent no fewer than six summonses—"

"There were eight, actually," Sybilla corrected him.

"*Eight* summonses to Parliament, as well as countless invitations to his private court. The goings-on at Fallstowe since Morys Foxe's death must be investigated."

"Why?" Sybilla challenged him. "My mother held Fallstowe legally under Edward's own father. Is that not enough for our king?"

"I think we might agree that Henry's methods of rule were . . . less than thorough," Julian offered.

Sybilla shrugged one shoulder. "My father was loyal to Henry III throughout the most tumultuous period of his rule. He stood with him against the barons. He was killed fighting alongside *Edward himself.* Regardless of Henry's head, or lack thereof, for administration, that sort of loyalty needs to be rewarded."

"Agreed," Julian said. "And mayhap it would have only taken you explaining your case to the king personally when he summoned you, for you to have avoided this lengthy rebellion."

Sybilla chuckled. "At the risk of sounding rebellious,

you, sir, are full of shit. Edward made clear that he was prepared to charge my mother with treason, and now that charge has been transferred to me by default."

"If your mother was who I suspect she was, then Fallstowe does not belong to you," Julian Griffin rebutted quickly, calmly. His words caused Sybilla's heart to creak in her chest. "The charges against Amicia Foxe will stand posthumously, and the demesne will be seized by the Crown. It's as if a purse thief stole a bag, but before dying, gave the coin away to a little beggar child. Although perhaps the beggar child is innocent, the coin still does not belong to her."

Sybilla felt her cheeks heat as she stared at the man. "I'm not stupid, Lord Griffin, nor am I amused by your infantile metaphors. If it was your intent and mission to take Fallstowe by force, why not attack upon your arrival? Why must I be forced into banal conversation with a man who thinks more of his intellect than is likely deserved?"

Julian's eyebrows flicked upward, and a little knowing grin quirked his full lips. "Come too close, have I? You have raised the king's ire, and he has requested that you be brought to him to stand trial for your repeated insubordinations. But Edward wants the truth, Lady Sybilla. He wants the truth and he has sent me to ascertain it."

"You are to ascertain the truth?" Sybilla said around a perplexed grin. "And just how, might I ask, are you to do such a thing?"

"I am to interview you, before our return to London."

"Interview me?" Now Sybilla leaned forward in her chair, unable to contain her outrage. "You expect me to converse amicably with you while your men wait beyond my gates, ready to strike my people down?"

Perhaps it was Sybilla's raised voice that caused it, but the swaddled babe chose that moment to send up an echoing and mournful wail. Sybilla's eyes went to the woman who held her, hoping that her scorn was clear.

"Beggin' your pardon, Lord Julian," the nurse said in a lowered voice. "Lady Lucy likely wants a change and a feed."

The man with the lion's mane looked to Sybilla. "Is there someplace Murrin might retire to?"

Sybilla was not prepared to show the man an ounce of courtesy. "There are a multitude of benches at her disposal in this very hall, Lord Griffin. I would not have one loyal to you loose in my household." Julian Griffin's tawny brows lowered, and so Sybilla thought to push him a bit more. A battle she could handle, but she did not want to talk to the man. Not now, and especially not at length, and most definitely not about her family.

"As a matter of fact—Graves?" she said over her shoulder.

"Yes, Madam?"

"Would you be so kind as to accompany Lord Griffin's servant? I'd not have her marking the corners with her scent."

Sybilla heard the sarcasm thick in Graves's answer. "How could I refuse such an honor?" When she looked once more to Julian Griffin, she was pleased to see that his face was dark with indignation.

"You needn't consent to the interview," Julian said with obvious forced patience.

"I needn't consent to anything," Sybilla parried, leaning back in her chair.

"As I said, Edward wants the truth. But he is willing to settle for Fallstowe, and your corpse, as an answer to his summons. So the choice is truly up to you, *my lady.* You may answer for yourself and take your sentence, or you can die, many of Fallstowe's good and loyal people with you."

"I could kill you where you stand, you pretentious, court-softened dandy," Sybilla whispered. "I just might, yet."

"I would have your lovely neck snapped before you could so much as lay finger to that pretty little dagger at your waist," Julian returned in an equally low murmur.

Sybilla felt her eyebrows raise, her heart pound, but she could not decide if it was in fear or anticipation.

"Care to try me?" she challenged him.

"I can think of nothing else that would bring me more pleasure at this moment." Julian inclined his head slightly, as if in deference. "Upon your first move, lady."

Sybilla's heart still pounded like thunder in her chest, and she remained absolutely still. Her eyes bored into Julian Griffin's, and his into hers. She felt oddly alive just then, and wondered what Julian Griffin's hands would feel like around her neck.

"Don't do this, Sybilla," he cautioned her, but his square jaw remained set. "Don't force my hand. The last thing I want is to kill you. Give me a chance. Give yourself a chance."

"You're being watched right now, you know," Sybilla said, and glanced up at the darkened balconies. "You have no chance."

Julian nodded once. "I saw the archers. But I promise I will reach you first. Even should they kill me after, Fallstowe will quickly fall without its head. Its heart. Many innocent lives lost. You can't want that."

"You are not faster than an arrow," Sybilla challenged him, surprised at her reaction to Julian's reference to her as Fallstowe's heart. Surely it was the other way around.

"Perhaps not," he acquiesced.

Sybilla let her lips curl in a smirk. But in the next

instant, her breath caught in her throat as the figure of Julian Griffin became little more than a blur of fine tunic. In less time than it took Sybilla to blink, he had sprung over her table, wrenched Sybilla from her chair, and spun her around before him, even as the *chunk-chunk-chunk* of arrows peppered her table like hail. Sybilla heard the frightened cry of the nursemaid in the shadows.

In her ear he whispered, "But then again, perhaps I am."

Sybilla gasped shallowly through her open mouth. She closed her lips and swallowed deliberately. "Well played, Lord Griffin," she said. She inched her hand down toward her waist as she continued to speak. "Perhaps the pair of us are more equally matched than we suspect."

He whispered into her ear again, just as her fingers touched the cold, empty sheath where her dagger had been only a moment ago.

"Or perhaps not so equally matched," he suggested, and her skin broke out in gooseflesh at his hot breath along her neck. She heard a clatter, and her glance caught the flash of candlelight on blade as Julian Griffin tossed her dagger onto the tabletop.

For an instant, Sybilla thought she felt the brush of his lips behind her ear and it made her eyelashes flutter closed.

"What shall we do now?" she queried lightly, all the while trying to ignore the tightening sensation in her midsection. "We seem to be at an impasse."

"I will release you, if you give me your word that you will entertain the interview I requested to its end. Then I will take you—and the evidence—to Edward. If I determine it worthy, I will do all I can to help you."

"If I refuse?"

"Fallstowe will be no more. As it is, should my general

NEVER LOVE A LORD

not hear from my own lips in less than an hour, he has been ordered to initiate the siege."

"You cannot think me to converse civilly with you in my home while hundreds of bloodthirsty soldiers wait beyond my door."

"Then I shall send them away."

Sybilla laughed despite herself. "You shall send them away?"

"This very night," Julian agreed, his tone solemn, quiet, his lips still near her ear. "Not even within sight of Fallstowe."

Sybilla hesitated.

"I swear it to you," Julian whispered. "Trust me, Sybilla. I have your life in my hands already. Trust me to preserve it."

She felt an odd catch in her throat at his words, and had to swallow quickly before giving voice to her doubt. "I trust no one but myself."

"Because you've never had me."

Sybilla's lips curved even as her eyes ached with unshed tears. She would not weep before him. "You think quite a lot of yourself, don't you?"

"I believe the arrows on yon table speak for me." His arm tightened around her waist almost imperceptibly. "Trust me. What have you to lose?"

She noticed that her left hand was lying atop Julian Griffin's forearm. Through the thick, quilted silk, she could feel his strength. Her fingers curled around his arm of their own accord, as if she would cling to him.

"Send them away," she said, her eyes staring into the black shadows down the length of her hall, swelling with tears until the little lights from the candles were tiny shimmering suns.

"You are as wise as you are beautiful," he whispered so

low that her ears barely registered the words. Then, louder, he said, "Call off your guards, else the moment I release you, I am a dead man."

Sybilla nodded. "Stand down!" she shouted up toward the darkened balconies. "There is no reason for alarm. I am unharmed and will remain so as long as you make no move to attack Lord Griffin. He is our guest now, and I order you all to *stand down.*"

Although there was no discernible movement from the upper-level shadows, Sybilla knew her command would be heeded. And yet Julian Griffin did not readily release her.

"Lord Griffin," she said in a sharp whisper.

"Hmm?" he breathed at her neck.

"You may release me now."

"*May I?*" he taunted low. "What if I don't wish to?"

Sybilla was finished playing about with Julian Griffin. Although his touch was eliciting a physical response from her, she would not continue to be handled by him in her own hall. He was fast, as he had already proven by his agile leap across her table; he was crafty, evidenced by his swift commandeering of her blade. Perhaps she had underestimated his abilities upon his arrival, but she would not do so again.

Julian Griffin needed to learn that, despite any physical prowess he might possess, he was ill matched in this battle.

Sybilla thought of the standing candelabra at his back, and brought the ornate arms and slender, flickering tapers clearly to her mind's eye while she remembered the feel of the wild wind atop Fallstowe's turret.

"Do as you wish," she stated mildly, with a smile on her lips even, "but it may prove difficult for you to put out the fire without the use of both your arms."

"What fire?" he asked in a bemused whisper. But in the next instant, he was shouting his alarm and Sybilla was free.

She took up her dagger at once before turning to see him slap at the small wave of flames rolling up his shoulder and back, and Sybilla struggled to keep her face serene as he turned in a circle to reach the extent of the fire, rather like a dog chasing its tail.

His impressive mane was now at risk, and Julian Griffin glared at her. "Could you help?"

Sybilla held out her palms, her golden dagger resting in one. "Shall I stab at the flames?"

He had no time to answer before Graves, ever dutiful, gained the dais, the slop bucket from beneath the table in his capable and ready hands. Fallstowe's steward tossed the contents of the wooden pail at Lord Julian Griffin, reducing the flames on his back to little more than hissing smoke.

Sybilla had never fought so hard against laughter in the whole of her life. There stood Julian Griffin, King Edward's own man, before her, no longer afire but now drenched with the remnants of the supper meal of hours ago: old mead, wine, and milk dripped from his hair; a chicken leg bone stuck to the front of his tunic; spongy crusts of bread tumbled slowly down his front like fat, furry caterpillars.

Graves set the slop bucket down on the floor with a hollow *thunk*. "Are you injured, Lord Griffin?" he asked solicitously.

The man swiped at his face with his right forearm, the only spot on his person not at the moment covered with either refuse or soot, and then addressed Sybilla.

"There was a pitcher at your elbow," he accused her.

Sybilla turned around and indicated the empty

tabletop. "Sorry, no." She continued as Julian frowned and leaned to the side to peer around her and see the evidence for himself. "You must have knocked it over on your impressive flight across my table."

He leaned down straightaway but was standing aright again in an instant. "It's not there. What did you do with it? And I am no closer than six feet from that candelabra. It is impossible that it could have touched me."

Sybilla raised her eyebrows. "What exactly are you suggesting, Lord Griffin? That I not only somehow managed to set you afire while you were holding me quite captive, but that I also made a pitcher and chalice to magically disappear?"

She thought he may have growled at her for an instant. But then he continued in a slightly more civilized tone. "I have heard of your talent for sleight of hand."

"Really?" Sybilla mused. "Is that what they're calling it now?"

He held her gaze for a moment, and Sybilla couldn't help but revel in the rush of triumph she felt.

"I'll speak with my general, command the troops to another location away from Fallstowe, and then return with my things."

"I'll have your rooms readied in your absence," Sybilla replied.

Julian Griffin nodded and began to turn away. Then he paused and addressed her again. "I would prefer a chamber on the lowest floor, if you don't mind." He did a double take as his eyes landed on the pitcher and chalice sitting on the tabletop—exactly where they had been when he'd entered.

"I'll most certainly see what we have available for you," Sybilla promised.

Then he was stalking back through the hall, beckoning to his nursemaid, who scurried after him like a little brown spider carrying an egg sac.

From behind her, Graves spoke. "The tower room then, Madam?"

"My thoughts exactly, Graves." Sybilla reached down and picked up her chalice and took a lingering sip.

Chapter 4

Julian was not at all surprised when, upon returning to Fallstowe with his and Lucy's things nearly an hour later, the old steward deposited Julian's daughter and Murrin in a chamber at the bottom of a seemingly endless spiral of stairs and then began leading him up. He had to fight against the grin which wanted to spread across his lips.

He had requested a chamber on the lowest floor. Therefore he wouldn't be surprised in the least if the steward popped a trapdoor once they reached the top of the stairs and showed Julian to Fallstowe's roof.

The circular stone room was small—only perhaps twelve feet across—but it was furnished in a manner befitting its relation to Fallstowe Castle. A wide, wooden bedstead jutted into the center of the floor, its mattresses appearing freshly made with a thick coverlet and numerous pillows. A small yet ornate table and two chairs were placed beneath one of the shuttered arrow-slit windows, a deep trunk beneath the other. A single candleholder on both the table and the trunk gave the room a cozy, private glow. A narrow wardrobe stood guard near the miniature hearth which was already ablaze with a modest fire. Upon sight of the small wooden tub set before the crackling flames, Julian wondered if perhaps he had judged Sybilla Foxe too harshly.

She had ordered a bath for him.

He strolled over to peer down into the water, tugging already at the gold buttons of his tunic, while two of Fallstowe's servants carried his own trunk into the chamber and set it at the end of the bed. The water was black, owing to the lack of proper illumination of the room as well as the shadows thrown by the fire, but Julian could imagine the luxury of sinking into the warm, cleansing haven. A small stool bearing a stack of woven linens and a rough cake of soap stood at the ready. The smell of soured milk and mead was bringing the bile to the top of his throat.

The servants had quit the room save for Graves, who now stood near the door, obviously waiting for Julian's attention.

"Will there be anything else this evening, my lord?"

"Thank you, Graves, but I am certain I shall be quite comfortable."

The old man bowed and then took his own leave, closing the door soundlessly behind him. Julian waited for a scraping of lock to reach his ears, but none came. He raised his eyebrows in surprise again as he removed his tunic and dropped it in a heap by the tub and made his way to the table beneath the window.

Julian flipped the latch on the wooden shutter and pushed it open, shivering once convulsively at the increased breeze brought into the room. He bobbed and turned his head, gauging the extent of his view before crossing to the other window and doing the same. He sat sideways on the end of the trunk, removing his tall boots while he watched the disassembly of his army.

Edward would likely not be pleased. And Erik had been furious at first. But the king had not sent Julian to Fallstowe because of his penchant for foolishness. In the midst of the commotion below, he saw Erik standing on the driver's seat of the ornate carriage that had carried Julian and Lucy to Fallstowe, a long, blazing torch in his hand. From the castle it appeared that the man was examining the conveyance to see that it was readied for travel.

Julian twisted around to seize the candleholder behind him and stood, leaning on the edge of the window and thrusting his arm and the candleholder through the square opening and waving it in an X fashion. He withdrew his arm and peered out. Erik was returning the X gesture with his torch. After a moment, the man climbed down from the carriage and resumed his duties of dismantling the camp.

Julian replaced the candleholder on the trunk and smiled to himself as he undid his breeches. When the soldiers were dispersing, a pair of men would be left behind with knowledge of Julian's location inside Fallstowe. He was very glad he had made it a point to ask Sybilla Foxe for a lower chamber.

He kicked his breeches to the floor and then strolled to the tub in his hose and undershirt, still grinning at his cleverness. As he removed his silk shirt, he brought to mind the memory of a panting Lady Sybilla trapped in his arms. Her body had fairly pulsed against his in her surprise and fury, and the smell of her skin, wafting up warmly from the curve of her neck, had been fragrant and sweet and at odds with her frosty demeanor. Julian had barely been able to think around the bawdy imaginings of what it would be like to take her in his bed.

Perhaps she was not the devil everyone in the land—including the king—thought her to be. Perhaps she was just protecting what was hers, what she thought her mother, and then herself, had earned. Perhaps her actions were brought about by nothing more than self-preservation, duty, and loyalty, and in that Julian could find little fault. After all, had he himself not done such things?

He shook off the comparison, though, along with his hose, and considered that Sybilla Foxe's acquiescence to be interviewed might have more to do with his presence than her willingness to stave off a siege against her people. It was almost as if he could feel her response to him as he'd held her in his arms.

Perhaps she might fancy him.

Julian stepped up to the tub. Because he was feeling quite triumphant, he leaned over and grasped the two sides with his hands and lifted both feet from the floor, swinging himself over and then lowering quickly into the water of the tub.

He was out of the tub faster than he had gotten in, and would have likely been distressed at the very feminine sounding shrieks emanating from his mouth as he hopped around the wooden tub, water flying everywhere, except that his capacity for self-observation was completely overshadowed by his desire not to freeze to death. He snatched at the stack of linens on the stool, toppling it, and then fell upon the pile of rags. They were all no bigger than the palm of his hand.

He kicked his way through the mess to the bed and pulled the coverlet from the mattress, wrapping it around himself, and then turned back to face the tub warily, panting.

The fire glinted off the recently disturbed surface of the water in the tub, and now Julian could clearly make out the glistening shards floating quietly in the water.

Ice. The bitch had filled his bath with ice water.

Julian lifted one arm beneath the cape-like blanket and sniffed. He quickly turned his head away with a grimace. He *had* to wash. He stomped to the overturned stool, righted it, and sat down at the side of the tub. Steeling himself, Julian threw off the coverlet, snatched up one of the ridiculously small rags and the bar of soap, and dunked both of them in the frigid water. He was not looking forward in the least to washing his hair.

And he no longer thought that Sybilla Foxe fancied him.

Sybilla lay in her bed, staring up at the canopy. She was completely exhausted. The last three days had seen her younger sister kidnapped, rescued, and wed—with Sybilla herself deeply involved in each event. She'd ridden hard to and from Hallowshire Abbey, organized the defense of Fallstowe in preparation for an attack by the king's men, nearly gotten herself killed on the battlements, and now had to contend with Edward's own emissary as a guest. Along with his *infant*. Dawn was two hours away, and yet her eyes would not close.

Why had she agreed to this nonsense? Why hadn't she simply given the command for her own men to open fire on Julian Griffin at first light?

Perhaps, she thought, it was because she knew that no matter how well prepared they were, they would not triumph. The king had a near endless supply of soldiers at his disposal, and even if Fallstowe's army struck down company after company, there would always be another to follow, until all of Sybilla's soldiers were dead or everyone within the castle walls had starved to death. She had precious few friends, and those she did claim would never sacrifice their own status within the realm by going against the monarch, especially if they suspected the grounds for the conflict.

So, in her eyes, she had been faced with seeing Fallstowe and her good people destroyed starting with this night, or agreeing to the unexpected interview, perhaps buying her more time to think of an alternative to surrender. For *that,* she could never do.

Escape? Perhaps to Bavaria, or Persia even. But not France. She could never flee to the land of her mother's birth. Fallstowe was unguarded as far as was directly visible, and Sybilla knew it would not be difficult to gather all the coin she could assemble and simply disappear into the night with old Graves, leaving the entire mess of Fallstowe behind her.

But then she would also be leaving her sisters, and their children. Her family. Sybilla would never again have a home of her own. And she could never, ever return to England.

Perhaps she simply wanted to tell someone at last, although she couldn't imagine confessing the sordid details of her family to Julian Griffin.

I will do all I can to help you.

Sybilla sighed and turned over on her left side, so that she stared through the bed-curtains which she had left tied. Her big windows were painted with night and diamonds.

She didn't believe him. She didn't trust him. He had something to gain from fulfilling his obligation to Edward, else he wouldn't have agreed to send his men away. Julian Griffin needed Sybilla's cooperation. Perhaps she would engage the spindly little nursemaid in some espionage of her own. Sybilla always felt better knowing exactly what she was up against.

If your mother was who I suspect she was, then Fallstowe does not belong to you.

How much did he know, and how had he come by that knowledge? Sybilla decided she would play with Lord Griffin awhile, talk a little if he wanted to talk. Tell some truths.

Upon that thought, it was as if she could feel the weight of her mother's body upon the mattress behind her, sense once more the crippled old woman's bitter and frightened urgency.

"Not all the truth, Maman," she sighed, hearing the sadness in her voice that she felt all the time but only allowed to manifest itself when she was alone. "I keep my promises."

The tension on the mattress behind her eased, but Sybilla's shoulders did not. She commanded herself to sleep, and eventually she did.

Sybilla was used to getting her way.

Cecily Bellecote sat straight up in bed from a sound sleep, a sob catching in her chest. In the chill air of the bedchamber, where it had been warm from lovemaking only a short time ago, she could feel the icy streaks of tears on her cheeks.

Oliver stirred on the mattress at her side. "Cecily? Are you all right? Does your arm pain you?"

Cecily tried to slow her breathing, gain control over the spasms that wanted her to wail. She covered her face and eyes with her hands, took a deep breath, and then wiped the wetness firmly away.

"No, my arm is fine. I don't know. A nightmare, perhaps." She glanced toward the bank of windows in their chamber and saw the sun rising.

Oliver was nestling his face back down into the pillow, his words stretched and sleepy by the yawn that seized him. "You've experienced quite a bit of excitement the past few days," he ventured.

"Yes," she agreed. "Of course you're right." She felt a gentle smile come to her lips at the thought that she was being comforted by her husband in their marriage bed. She turned her head to look down at him and something wet splashed onto the back of her hand. Cecily frowned at the water she saw there, and then brought her hands to her face again. She pulled them away and stared.

Her eyes were still leaking.

"Oliver," she whispered, "I think something's wrong."

He rose up again immediately, his eyes still full of sleep but looking at her intently. "The baby?"

"No," she said, but still laid one hand protectively over her midsection. She glanced out the brightening window again. "I think perhaps it's . . . it's Sybilla."

Oliver sat up fully in bed now. "What do you mean? That she is injured or . . . ?"

Cecily knew he didn't wish to voice aloud anything more dire now that they both knew the king's soldiers were en route to Fallstowe.

"I don't know," she said, and her words betrayed the frustration and confusion she felt.

Oliver got out of the bed and began searching for his pants. "I'll send a messenger to the men I left behind. Perhaps they—"

His words were interrupted by a rapping on the chamber door. Cecily met her husband's gaze for a solemn instant.

"Who calls?" Oliver commanded as he fastened his pants and strode to the door.

"Argo, my lord." The answer was muffled through the wood.

Cecily watched as her husband opened the door a bit, and she was glad that he had not admitted Bellemont's steward. She pulled the coverlets up to her shoulders and waited while Oliver murmured with his man.

"*What?*" he shouted suddenly, and then seemed to forget about decorum as he left the door swinging and marched back across the room to throw the curtains over the windows, leaving them completely open. He braced his hands on the windowsill and hung his head for a moment. "Perfect," he muttered. "Perfect!"

"What is it, Oliver?" Cecily asked, glancing toward the doorway and seeing only a sliver of the proper Argo's form.

Her husband glanced at her. "One moment, love." He strode back to the door, shared a few quiet words with Argo, and then closed the door once more. He sighed and leaned his back against the wood.

"Edward's men gained Fallstowe last night after we left."

Cecily brought a hand to her throat, almost afraid to ask. "Did they attack?"

"No," Oliver said. He pushed away from the door and began searching the floor around the bed, presumably for the rest of his clothing. "No, they did not. In fact, they are no longer at Fallstowe. They're here."

Cecily frowned. "Here? Whatever for?"

Oliver stood upright and shook out his white shirt.

"Apparently *Lord Julian Griffin* carries Edward's banner, and he is currently in residence at Fallstowe with *Lady Foxe*," Oliver emphasized.

"Edward's doorman at court, you mean? With Sybilla?" This was getting stranger and stranger. "But why would the man sent to take Fallstowe from my sister send his soldiers to Bellemont?"

"Because your husband is an imbecile," Oliver muttered. Then a bit louder, "It seems our king is prepared to accept my gracious offer of support. I am to rally Bellemont's soldiers and be prepared to descend upon Fallstowe at Julian Griffin's signal. In the meantime, we are to house three hundred of the king's men whose siege has been postponed. Half of the army that was at Fallstowe."

Cecily looked out the window once more. "But he's at Fallstowe? *Alone* with Sybilla?"

Oliver stilled his motions, facing her now with his boots in one hand. "I am obviously not the only imbecile in the land."

Cecily felt her lips press together in a thin line. "Oh my. The poor man."

Chapter 5

Julian groaned into his pillow in response to the polite rap on his door. It felt as though he had only closed his eyes a moment ago. In truth, the bit of hair beneath his cheek was still damp from his frigid bath.

He heard the door scrape open, and he raised his head slightly. Sweet yellow light streaked through the window to his left in a rectangular beam, signaling that dawn had indeed already come, as had the morning maid, bearing a heavily laden tray to the small table. She turned toward the hearth without a greeting and immediately set to work laying a fire.

Julian pulled himself upright and glanced at the table; whatever was inside the large silver tureen seemed to make up the bulk of his morning meal, although he was glad to see a corked flagon and cup. He shivered once violently. It would take hours for the small fire to warm him sufficiently.

"I would break my fast in the hall with Lady Foxe," he called out to the maid's back. "You may take the tray away."

The maid straightened but only glanced at him, an

annoyed expression on her face as she went about the room gathering up his discarded clothing and rolling them thoughtlessly into a tight bundle.

"Madam doesn't breakfast," the woman informed him curtly, and then turned toward the door.

"She doesn't eat?" Julian scoffed.

"Your daughter and her nurse are in the great hall at their own meal," the maid said, almost grudgingly, then walked to the door.

"The tray!" Julian called after her.

"Take it yourself," the woman muttered, and slammed the door shut behind her.

Julian pursed his lips for a moment and then nodded once to himself. He should have expected such a response. After all, he was the villain in this scenario—the evil lord sent to steal Fallstowe away from their lady. They didn't want him here.

He threw back the covers and swung his legs over the edge of the bed. He would likely have to make some changes in staffing, should this attitude persist.

But in the meantime, he *was* hungry. By the time he was dressed and to the hall, Lucy would be ready for a bit of play and then a morning rest, and she would not tolerate waiting on Julian to finish his meal. He would eat in his chamber quickly then, so as to have time to spend with that sweetness before engaging the lady of Fallstowe. He visited his trunk first and quickly laid hand to a suit of warm clothing, dressing in front of the hearth.

Then he went to the table and pulled out one of the chairs, sitting down and rubbing his palms together swiftly, blowing warm breath on them in preparation for loosing the cork of the flagon. It was straight wine inside, not watered, and it ran rich and red into the cup. Julian savored the first mouthful, filling his cheeks until they burned before swallowing the warming liquid. He gave a satisfied sigh and filled the cup to the brim once more.

Then he turned his attention to the tureen. He picked up the engraved eating knife with his right hand, lifted the lid with his left, and peered down.

An entire, shiny black eel lay coiled in a weak saffron-colored broth, bits of black seaweed half floating on the liquid and half stuck to the slick-looking body.

Julian made an audible sound of disgust. Eel at the morning meal. And there wasn't even any bread.

"Well, it's not my favorite," he admitted aloud. But perhaps it was still hot, and he *was* hungry. He reached into the tureen with his left hand, preparing to grasp the neck and remove the head with his knife.

The onyx body flashed in the morning light as the eel whipped its head around and snapped at Julian's fingers.

He shouted his surprise as he snatched his hand away, and then in the next instant brought his eating knife down, at last subduing his breakfast. The broth turned murky with bright red swirls of blood and the body writhed for a moment.

Julian stood abruptly, his chair falling back behind him with a loud crack. He glared at the tureen as he swiped his cup from the table and drank the wine inside it straight down.

He was becoming annoyed with Sybilla Foxe's hospitality.

Sybilla rarely left her chamber so early in the morn, but the idea that Julian Griffin presently resided under her roof placed her in such a foul mood that she was unable to tolerate her own company beyond a single cup of tea. After her hair was dressed and coiled atop her head, she dismissed her maids even though she was still in her silk wrapper. She felt the need for privacy as she dressed herself, choosing a gown the color of the darkest moss.

She stepped through the panel hidden in the wall behind her dais and was pleased that the hall was presently empty save for the Griffin infant and her nursemaid.

And Graves, of course, standing patiently near her chair.

Neither mistress nor servant spoke, each having determined long ago that banal pleasantries suited neither and were patently unnecessary between them first thing in the morn.

Sybilla sat down in her chair, and almost instantly a cup of her preferred tea and a small silver plate with toasted bread was set at her elbow. Sybilla nudged it away with the back of her hand, choosing instead to concentrate on the fidgeting girl seated at a table on the floor, who glanced furtively in Sybilla's direction several times.

At last she seemed to find her courage and nodded toward Sybilla. "Good morrow to you, milady," she offered solemnly.

"Nurse," Sybilla replied in kind. She glanced down at the infant, who sat on the girl's lap playing with what seemed to Sybilla to be a knot of trailing, colorful ribbons. "What is its name again?"

The nurse's forehead creased slightly. "Lucy, milady."

Sybilla nodded. "How long have you been Lucy's nurse?"

"Since she was born, milady. One hundred and twenty-six days." The nurse smiled down at the child, who was frowning and jerking the knot side to side in a very uncoordinated manner. It sounded as though there might be a small bell hidden inside the riotous cluster.

Then the nurse glanced up at Sybilla again while she absentmindedly stroked the baby's head cap. "She's beautiful, isn't she?"

Sybilla felt her nose wrinkle slightly but then turned her attention to her heretofore neglected tea. She picked up the cup and blew on the surface, speaking to the nurse over the rim. "Bring her to me so that I might see her properly."

The girl hesitated for only an instant and then rose, one forearm around the infant's middle and the other hand supporting its bottom, and Sybilla was reminded of how one might hold a piglet, if one was of a mind to do such a thing. It *was* rather round and pink.

The nurse walked up to the edge of the dais, and then, seeming not to know what else to do, grasped the baby under each arm and hoisted her up so that the infant's gowned feet kicked just above the edge of Sybilla's table.

Sybilla placed her cup back on the table and leaned forward in her chair, her hands on her thighs. She peered at the infant's face, and to her surprise, the baby's blue eyes seemed to peer right back. It was quite an appealing thing when viewed up close, Sybilla determined, and she wondered if the child resembled its mother.

"Good day, Lady Lucy," Sybilla said levelly.

The infant's eyes seemed to widen at the sound of Sybilla's low voice. It stopped the futile cycling of its legs for a moment.

"Bah!" Lucy Griffin replied, then proceeded to blow a stream of spittle between her pink lips.

Sybilla felt one of her eyebrows rise.

"What on earth are you doing, Murrin?"

The baby's head whipped around at the sound of her father's voice, and Lucy began once more to frantically kick her legs, as if she would run to the lion-haired man if only the insufferable nurse would put her down.

"Lady Sybilla wished to examine Lady Lucy," Murrin replied in a rather unsure voice.

Sybilla leaned back in her chair and picked up her cup once more as Julian Griffin strode toward them. Under one arm he carried a thick, bound leather packet, which he laid on Sybilla's table before turning to the nurse and taking charge of his daughter. He smiled down at the infant, and Sybilla could not help but catch her breath at the way his face was transformed.

"Good morning, my darling angel! Good morning!" he repeated softly and kissed each of the baby's cheeks and then her head through her small white cap.

Lucy reached up and grasped a handful of her father's hair. "Bah-bah-bah!" she shouted as she jerked forcefully on the lock.

Julian chuckled. "I should say so," he agreed. He turned his eyes to Sybilla, and she realized that she had been staring at him, studying him. The idea startled her nearly more so than his next words.

"Would you care to hold her?"

Sybilla's eyebrows rose slightly. "I beg your pardon?"

"Lucy." He bounced the baby on his forearm. "Most women cannot resist her prettiness, which is why, I assume, Murrin was dangling my daughter like a leg of lamb before you. Would you care to hold her?"

"No." Sybilla took a slow sip. "I'm not terribly tempted at the idea. You will find, I think, through our time together, Lord Griffin, that I am quite unlike most women."

"Oh, I'm already aware of that, Lady Foxe," he replied evenly, and Sybilla glanced up to find him now studying her.

Sybilla cleared her throat delicately. "I trust your first night at Fallstowe was enjoyable? How did you find your chamber?"

His lips quirked slightly. "In truth, I—"

Suddenly, Graves spoke from behind her chair. "Where *is* that boy?" he muttered. Sybilla turned her head to catch him disappearing through the doorway which led to the kitchens.

She turned back to see Julian Griffin also regarding Graves's hasty departure. The expression on his face was shrewd, thoughtful. But he shook it off and looked at Sybilla once more.

"Everything was as I expected it to be. Thank you," he said, with a nod of his head.

Lucy Griffin had apparently grown weary of their talk, as she chose that moment to voice her displeasure at her father's lack of attention. Murrin stepped to the lord's side, her arms held open.

Julian kissed the child more times than were necessary, in Sybilla's opinion, and then handed her over to the nurse. "Sweet dreams, my precious," he said, his hands trailing away from the baby as if loath to release her. "Papa shall come for you straightaway at noon."

Murrin made the silly motion of lifting the baby's hand to wave at her father, before giving Sybilla a quick curtsy and departing from the hall. Sybilla wanted to roll her eyes—it was simply nauseatingly sweet.

Julian turned his attention back to the leather packet still lying on the table. He reached for it and then used it to gesture toward Sybilla.

"Shall we begin the interview?"

Sybilla's eye narrowed. "What's that?"

Julian glanced down at the thick, ledger-like bundle, and then back at her. "Your life, Lady Sybilla."

She chuckled, disbelieving. "My life, you say?" She set her cup back down on the table. The tea was ice-cold now, although the handle had grown warm from her gripping fingers, which she placed on her lap beneath the tabletop, out of sight. "I daresay my life comprises more than a hand's-breadth of pages."

"My penmanship is quite fine," Julian countered. "I needed to keep my findings compact for transport."

"All the way from London?" Sybilla said snidely.

"No." Julian's eyes found hers. "All the way from France," he corrected her quietly.

She held his gaze, but in her chest, Sybilla's heart beat madly.

"I only returned the month before Lucy was born." He tucked the ledger under his arm. "Would you have us commence here in the hall, my lady?"

"No," Sybilla said, trying to keep the frown from her face, but she knew she had failed. She stood. "Let us retire to my solar, where we will not be disturbed." Sybilla turned to walk from the dais.

"Or overheard?" Julian offered from behind her.

Sybilla's steps did not pause. "That is correct, Lord Griffin. Although I am certain you and our king see my defeat as inevitable, I still have interests that I would protect from gossip."

"Your sisters, you mean." His voice sounded directly behind her, although she had not heard his quickening footfalls or thought them to have gained on her so readily. She added *stealthy* to her mental list of Julian Griffin's attributes.

"Yes," she said curtly. She glanced at him and found that he was studying her again, so she looked away.

"You cannot protect them forever, Sybilla," he said, and the genuine concern she heard in his voice caused her to glance at him once more. "From gossip, or perhaps more devastating, the truth. They will know eventually."

Sybilla laid her hand on the latch of the solar door, but instead of pushing it open she turned to face Julian Griffin, her hands anchored behind her back. Her heart was pounding. "And what exactly will they know eventually, Lord Griffin? That the king does not take loyalty to heart? That he would steal the home my mother held for him? That he would slander her? This they already know, I can assure you."

Julian Griffin was only a pace away from her, and he closed that distance with a single slow step, stopping to look down into Sybilla's upturned face. She could feel the heat of him through the velvet of her gown, feel the corner of the leather packet brush along the curve of her waist as he stood nearly against her. The door was at her back, but she would not escape him.

"And they already know that only a person of noble blood may hold lands and title for the king," he said in a low voice, his eyes searching her face. "I find myself intrigued by you, Lady Sybilla."

She blinked at his sudden departure from the topic of the king, and for a moment no words would come to her. "Most men do," she answered at last.

"It must be deliberate. Do you encourage their attention?" he asked, his voice going even softer.

"When it suits me." She took her back away from the door, standing so that the velvet of her bodice brushed Julian Griffin's tunic. She felt an atypical flush roll over her cheeks as she looked up at him. "Would it benefit me to encourage your attention, Lord Griffin?"

"I think it would," he said, his face drawing nearer to hers. "But mayhap not in the way you are seeking."

"Meaning you would not return to Edward reporting that Fallstowe is innocent."

He shook his head almost imperceptibly. His nose brushed hers. "I promised to bring him the truth." The breath of his words caressed her lips. "And we both know that Fallstowe is anything but innocent."

"Then I see no benefit at all to sleeping with you," Sybilla whispered, her body screaming at her to pull the man to her fully. "Be warned, Lord Griffin—some say I am a dangerous woman." She tilted her head.

"What a coincidence—I had danger for breakfast just this morning." His mouth was over hers now, his lips open, almost touching, and she took a breath of his hot exhalation . . .

"Is the door stuck again, Madam?"

In a rush of cool air, Julian Griffin pulled away from her and turned, revealing Graves standing disturbingly close behind him, a large meat cleaver dangling from one hand.

Sybilla thought it would have been quite convenient had the old steward decided to make use of the tool a second ago. Although she would still feel the unfulfilled ache gifted to her by the masculine and imposing Julian Griffin, at least he would be dead and no further trouble to her.

"No, Graves. The door is fine." She let her breath out through her nose, slowly, inaudibly.

"I say, old man," Julian offered, gesturing to the weapon in Graves's hand, "those must be terribly efficient for—oh, I don't know—killing the errant eel, or what have you."

"Do you suppose, my lord?" Graves asked, cocking his head as if extremely interested in the idea.

Sybilla frowned at the two men facing each other like

adversaries, although their conversation was completely benign—even nonsensical. One would have to go very much out of their way to find a live eel in this season.

"I shall be in the solar if I am needed, Graves. Please have a tray sent up."

"Tea, Madam?"

Sybilla could feel Julian Griffin's energy radiating from him like a smithy's iron. "I think perhaps something stronger is called for, considering the topics Lord Julian insists on prying into."

The imposing lord was still keenly regarding Fallstowe's steward. "Why don't you join us, old man? It's well known that you—"

"That won't be necessary," Sybilla interrupted. Julian turned his face toward her, a look of curious amusement causing his eyes to gleam, and causing the hair at the nape of Sybilla's neck to prickle. "Graves carries many responsibilities in the hold. I would not keep him from his work for something so pointless as to sate your—as well as our king's—interest in morbid gossip."

A tawny, quirked eyebrow was Julian Griffin's only response.

"When you care to join me, Lord Griffin . . ." She let the sentence dangle as she pushed the door open behind her and took her racing heart into the solar.

Chapter 6

Julian let his eyes follow Sybilla Foxe's lithe back as she ducked into the shadows of the solar beyond the doorway. He felt his nostrils flare with the lingering scent her passing left in the close corridor. He rejected his most base urge to follow close on her heels, barring the door after them both. Instead, he turned swiftly back to the old steward, who didn't so much as flinch at the sudden attention paid him.

"Will there be anything else you require, Lord Julian?" he asked, his dark eyes seeming far too young and sparkling to be set in a face so thin and lined.

"Yes, Graves," Julian said in a low but amicable voice. "You may stop trying to kill me."

The old man's pale lips actually twitched, a skeletal smile. "Whatever do you mean, my lord?"

"You know exactly what I mean," Julian said. "It's not going to work. Ice in the bath, live eels at the breakfast table—you must think me feeble to succumb to such frivolous threats. After hearing of your reputation, I expected more. I must say I am slightly disappointed."

"Too subtle?" Graves asked, his face pulling into a long

expression of forced concern. Then he glanced down at the small ax still dangling in his right hand before meeting Julian's eyes directly.

The old man said not another word, only turned on his heel and slithered soundlessly into the shadows. If Graves had intended to kill him outright, he could have performed the deed in countless ways since Julian's arrival. The old man must have ulterior motives for his rather juvenile actions; beyond encouraging Julian to depart Fallstowe, obviously. Julian watched the place where Graves had disappeared from sight for a moment more, and then turned to step through the open doorway after Sybilla.

He closed the door soundlessly behind him as his eyes searched the shadows for her. Sybilla Foxe stood at a large square window set in the stone exterior wall of the solar. Her silhouette was black against the bright gray gloom of day, only a small fire in the hearth to combat the quiet. Her chin was tilted down, her gaze seeming to go beyond the wavy panes and race along Fallstowe's lands all the way to the horizon. She seemed completely lost in her own mind—or perhaps somewhere far beyond that horizon her eyes so desperately regarded—and Julian wondered if she realized he had joined her.

"What prompted Edward to order you to France?" she asked suddenly, indicating that she had been acutely aware of his arrival.

Julian stepped more fully into the room, his eyes seemingly unable to look away from her any longer than it took to glance down while he slid his portfolio onto a small, three-legged table.

"He didn't order me to France." Julian continued his stroll toward her, as if drawn, and when she turned her face slightly to regard him, he was struck by the depth and clarity of her blue eyes, cut by the bright gray light which seemed to make them glow like sea glass.

He came to stand close at her side. Julian guessed not many dared invade Sybilla Foxe's personal space, whether out of respect or fear or awe. He was pleased to see the slight crease between her eyebrows as she was forced to lift her chin to regard him, her question clear in her eyes.

"I sought his permission to go," he obliged her mildly, and turned to mirror her posture, looking out over the pie-shaped sliver of bailey and then to the rolling hills disappearing in the fog beyond.

"Why?" she asked quietly.

Julian drew a deep breath and sighed. There was no reason not to tell her. "Because I knew that if you were so bold—or so desperate—as to deny our king, it was very unlikely that you would simply give me the information I sought unless I had already determined a fair amount of it as fact on my own."

He felt her turn her gaze back to the window. "I see. Like Edward, you sought to try me and my family in your mind."

"Not at all," Julian insisted. "Our king is not privy to all of my findings as of yet."

"Why not?" she demanded, looking at him sharply again.

"It would be unwise of me to report a plethora of unconfirmed ideas or half-truths."

"How noble of you."

"That has nothing to do with it."

"Of course it doesn't," she replied.

After a moment of tense silence, Julian turned away from the window and headed toward where he had deposited his portfolio. "Do you mind if I sit?" He picked up the thick leather packet and sat down on the settee, placing the portfolio on his thighs while he untied the leather string holding the bundle together.

A soft rap fell on the door, and an instant later a maid entered bearing the tray Sybilla had requested earlier. The somber-looking young woman set her burden on the table at Julian's elbow, poured two cups and left them on the tray, exiting the room without comment. Sybilla Foxe had yet to move from the window.

Julian opened the ledger, but before flipping through the leaves of parchment contained within, he picked up the cup nearest him and took a sip.

"Where would you like to start?"

"I hope you don't expect me to vomit the history of my family at your mere suggestion. Surely you didn't think it would be so easy once you had breached my gates."

"Very well," Julian conceded with a nod. "What if I tell you what I know. If I am incorrect in any of my findings, or if you wish to offer further comment, you may instruct me."

She turned to look at him over her shoulder, and Julian realized that she had crossed her arms over her chest and was grasping her elbows. For all of her bluster and strong words, she appeared wary, unsure.

She looked out the window once more. "Very well."

"Your mother, Amicia, came to this land from Gascony at Christmastime, 1248." Julian glanced up at her. "As part of the party of Simon de Montfort." At the last words, Julian saw Sybilla Foxe's slender throat convulse as if she swallowed.

"That . . . ." She cleared her throat, then said in a low voice, "That is correct."

Julian took a moment to consider her answer. He had not expected her to confirm this so easily. After all, this first admission was only the beginning thread to a much larger knot of yarn. He looked down at his notes briefly.

"She was received by Lady de Montfort at Kenilworth Castle, where she remained until February, when Simon returned to Gascony. She did not return to the place of her birth with him."

"Why would she?" Sybilla said. "She was married by then."

"To Morys Foxe," Julian filled in immediately, not wishing to interrupt the unexpected flow of conversation between them. "They met on these very lands, inside the Foxe Ring, if the stories are to be believed."

"They are," Sybilla confirmed. She turned suddenly and walked across the short span of floor separating them. She stopped near the table and retrieved a cup of wine. After taking a long drink, she regarded him, although her eyes did not give the impression that she was entirely present.

"I know the tale by heart—Maman told each of us over and over, from all our earliest memories. She had been out riding with Lady de Montfort and some others, enjoying a particularly mild and sunny day for winter, when she became separated from the party. She was a stranger to these lands and quickly became disoriented. Night fell. She was cold, frightened. A moon rose, so full and bright that it seemed it would fall upon the earth and crush it, and against that brightness, she saw the outline of the ruins and mistook them for a populated place."

"And Morys?" Julian prompted, held rapt at the melody of her voice speaking at such length. "I have been curious as to why he was out at the ruins in the dead of night, alone."

Sybilla shook her head slowly, looking to a point

seeming to be in a dark corner of the room. "Likely he was out enjoying the mild weather as well."

"At midnight?" Julian prompted with raised eyebrows.

She turned her eyes to him, and Julian could see the coldness taking over her features once more. "Fallstowe was his life. It is said that he knew each stone, even the youngest sapling, so precious was Fallstowe to him."

"Do you believe such a fantastic notion?" Julian prompted. "That he knew each stone?"

She stared at him for a moment. "Lord Griffin, I personally know not simply each stone of this hold but even every blade of grass that grows on Fallstowe land. If a bird should fall from the sky and land upon this dirt, I will feel the reverberation of its body in my own bones."

Julian held her gaze, not minding the frost there at all. In fact, it seemed to rekindle a flame within him not entirely doused from their encounter in the corridor.

"An inherited trait, do you reckon?" he asked quietly.

She didn't answer him, only took another drink of wine, her eyes over the rim of the cup sending warning arrows encased in ice. She lowered her cup and turned away, speaking to him next in a tone that conveyed that his comment was summarily dismissed.

"They met in the Foxe Ring that night. He gave her shelter."

Julian followed her with his eyes. He could do naught else. "And they were married very shortly after."

"Yes."

"A rather fortuitous match for your mother."

"Not only for Mother," Sybilla said lightly, going once more to stand at the window. "The house of de Lairne was quite powerful."

"I concur—the de Lairne family was powerful, and a

connection to them could have been a boon to Morys Foxe, and perhaps an advantage to the king of England as well."

"Precisely," Sybilla agreed. "My mother was Amicia de Lairne."

"Your mother was of the de Lairne house," Julian conceded. "She took the de Lairne name. But she was not of the de Lairne family."

Julian saw Sybilla Foxe go completely still. Julian paused a moment, too, wondering at the wisdom of revealing too much too soon. But it would come out any matter. May as well start at the beginning.

"She escaped Gascony with the help of Simon de Montfort after aiding him against the de Lairne house. From the moment she set foot on English soil, her life was one enormous lie. Amicia Foxe was never Lady de Lairne—she was Lady de Lairne's *maid*."

After a long moment, Sybilla turned and began walking swiftly toward him. "We're finished for the day," she said in a cool voice. Her face was the color of the fog beyond the square window. She did not slow as she neared the table, only set her cup down as she passed by. The clicking of her footsteps echoed behind Julian, and then he heard the scrape of the solar door opening. He did not hear it close, and so he craned his neck around to look over the settee behind him.

The door was open, and Sybilla Foxe was gone.

"I'm sorry," he murmured to the empty, dark room. "Sorry, Sybilla."

And he found that he was, because he knew it was to get much worse.

* * *

"Oh, come on, you stupid . . . you stupid"—Alys pushed against the hulking beast with all her might—"*cow!*" Her breath came out of her in an agitated huff when she realized her efforts were for naught. She stood aright and slapped the red and white rump.

"You know if I can't get you to the barn, Piers will never let me help again." The cow turned its head lazily, grass poking from either side of its wide mouth as it regarded Alys over its shoulder.

Alys gestured toward the cow with the thick limb in her right hand. "He told me to use this on you, you know. 'Give her a good whack,' said he. Is that what you want? Can't you just mo—"

"Moo-oo," the cow interrupted.

"Yes, *moo-oove*," Alys cried.

The cow lowered its head to the new spring grass and began to graze once more.

"Bloody good dairy wife I've turned out to be," Alys grumbled and turned to lean her aching back up against the cow's warm side. She rubbed her left hand over her growing stomach and looked down. "I do hope you're a boy." There was a prickling at her neck and Alys instinctively looked up.

Coming up the closest hill from Gillwick were two riders dressed in quilted leather and mail, weapons clearly at their sides, their horses wearing padded armor.

Alys felt her brows draw together. What would soldiers want with Gillwick? Alys thought she'd left all remnants of politics behind with Sybilla when she had married Piers.

Apparently the cow also heard the riders coming, and fickly chose that moment to move her great bulk toward the barn. It caught Alys by surprise, concentrating on the approaching riders as she was, and she gave a short scream while she windmilled her arms valiantly. She toppled backward into the great, cold, muddy wallow the cow had most recently occupied, the muck splashing up to her hair and face.

And certainly the riders reached her just then, trotting their horses through the gate of twisted gray limbs that marked the field, directly over to her.

This shall likely be very embarrassing, Alys reckoned, as she used her husband's stick to lever herself from the mud.

"You there, farm girl," one of the soldiers called out. "Where is your master?"

Alys raised her gaze slightly from where she had been trying to shake the larger blobs from her skirt. "My master, you say? He is in yonder barn. Who are you to ask after him?"

The other soldier looked Alys up and down in a rather personal fashion. "I'd like to get to know *you* a mite better, missy. No reason not to have a little fun with a heifer that's been had, eh?"

After a short, outraged gasp, Alys swung the thick stick Piers had given her as hard as she could, and an instant later, the mouthy soldier had landed on his head in the mire.

"Ho, there, girl," the other soldier warned, nudging his horse as if to approach her.

Alys swung around, brandishing her stick. "I am Alys Foxe, Lady Mallory, and if you take one more step toward me, I promise you will be dead before my husband has a chance to rip you apart."

The soldier halted his mount instantly, and 'twas only then that Alys noticed the royal insignia burned into the saddle leather. "Lady Mallory, my apologies. Are you harmed?"

"I will ask you only once more," Alys said, eyeing the second soldier warily as he flung off the mud and made several false starts at gaining his mount once more. "Who are you, and what do you want with my husband?"

A deep rumbling of many hooves on packed earth tickled deep in Alys's ears and she turned her head to once more regard the hill the soldiers before her had only just gained.

A wave of soldiers—a lake, a sea, it seemed—rolled over the land toward Gillwick.

Chapter 7

Sybilla sat in the big, round copper tub before her hearth, the steam from the water wafting around her like the fog along the moors. If her maids had thought the request odd, of a bath so soon after emerging from her rooms, they had not shown it. Sybilla had no desire to join the household for the noon meal, especially since Julian Griffin had said earlier that he would be about with his noble spawn. She needed time to herself to think upon what he had revealed to her. Time to plan. Time to remember.

She stared at her bed—Amicia's bed not so very long ago—and in the gloom of the shadows it seemed as though the coverlet shimmered, the bed-curtains swayed with an invisible breeze full of whispers.

'Tis terrible things I must speak to you of, Daughter. Shameful things. Horrid, wretched things.

Sybilla closed her eyes slowly, gently, deliberately.

"You're still ill, Maman," Sybilla said as she went to the bedside to pull the coverlet up over the old woman's arms. It

seemed to Sybilla that their lives had been full of naught but
wretchedness since her father's death, and Sybilla had no desire
to encourage the ill old woman's tired regret. "Let us not talk of
anything so dire until you are feeling well again."

Amicia craned her neck, sliding her face up the pillow to better
look into Sybilla's face as her daughter drew near, carefully tucking the silk cover around her mother. From this vantage point,
Sybilla could plainly see the drawn and droopy muscles of the
right side of her mother's face. This last episode had been her third
in as many years. Some days Amicia could do little more than
grunt, and she could no longer move her right leg or arm on her
own at all.

"I'll not be well again," Amicia slurred emphatically. "I'll die
this time. And you must know what I would tell you if you are to
save Cecily and Alys." Her black eyes bored into Sybilla's. "All of
Fallstowe. It will come down to you, Sybilla. And it will end
with you."

Sybilla felt her brows lower. "Maman—"

A knock sounded on the chamber door, and a moment later
Fallstowe's old steward, Graves, entered.

"Graves," Amicia said. "You're just in time."

"Am I, Madam?" Then he looked to Sybilla, and for a
moment she thought she detected a look of pity in his old black eyes
as he regarded her keenly. But then again, Graves seemed to do
everything keenly. "Are you well today, Lady Sybilla?"

"I am, Graves. Although Maman seems to insist that we have
a rather serious discussion, and I am trying to convince her that
perhaps another time would be better. For her health, you see."

To Sybilla's surprise, the old manservant walked to Amicia's
bedside and took a seat in the small upholstered armchair placed
there for visitors. Then he sighed and once more regarded Sybilla
with a melancholy expression of regret before addressing Amicia.

"Would you care to begin now, Madam?"

Amicia nodded once.

"I was born in Gascony," she said, letting her eyes roll to the bed's canopy; and just as Sybilla was about to tell her that she already knew that, Amicia added, *"At least, I think I was. I don't know who my parents were."*

Sybilla felt her heavy eyelids blink once, twice, a third time, and her head tilted slightly, as if she had just entered some strange dream. Perhaps this last seizing had affected her mother's memory now.

"Maman, you were born Amicia Sybil de Lairne. Your parents were Lord and Lady de Lairne."

"No," Amicia said. She let her gaze fall back to her daughter as she repeated in a whisper, *"No. I was left in the kitchens of the de Lairne château when I was only hours old. The cook found me tucked in a basket among the loaves and took me to Lady de Lairne. The lady decided that I looked strong enough that she would keep me."*

Sybilla swallowed. *"She adopted you as her own?"*

Amicia shrugged her left shoulder slightly. *"I grew up alongside their daughter, only a pair of months older than I. I was raised to be her companion. They groomed me from an early age. When I was old enough to carry a large pitcher and make a neat plait, I became her maid."*

Sybilla felt her legs go watery, and her first urge was to sit down on the edge of the mattress where her mother was propped on an army of silk embroidered pillows. But she suddenly found the idea of being so close to Amicia distressing—this woman she had thought she knew, but wasn't quite so certain now—and so she stumbled back a pair of steps to lower herself into a chair, the twin of the one in which Graves still silently sat.

"You were her . . . her maid?" she repeated breathlessly. *"You must have loved . . . your sister very much to have agreed to play such a lowly part."*

"She was not my sister," Amicia hissed, and her chest hitched unevenly for several moments while she fought to regain her

composure. She closed her wrinkly eyelids for a moment, and when she opened them once more, she seemed to have taken her emotions in hand. "You must understand this first part best of all, Sybilla: the woman everyone thinks me to be, Lady Amicia de Lairne Foxe—she doesn't exist. She never existed. The truth is a dangerous thing, ofttimes. Who I am, truly, is that upon which hangs the fate of this castle and of your sisters."

Sybilla had enough clarity about her to realize that this was the second instance in which her mother had mentioned the safety of Alys and Cecily, but Sybilla had not been included in the concern.

"And me as well, Maman?" Sybilla asked, distressed at the timid and weak sound of her voice in such a plaintive bid for reassurance. "It will keep me safe?"

"Oh, my darling," Amicia slurred. "I cannot save you."

Sybilla realized that the bathwater had gone frigid.

She blinked, and was relieved to note that the coverlet on the bed had lost its shimmery appearance and that the curtains hung motionless once more.

Sybilla stood with a great fall of water and reached for her robe. She stepped from the tub and swirled the quilted silk around her wet skin, belting it tightly as she went to her wardrobe.

So Julian Griffin knew the sordid fact of Amicia Foxe's birth. That was not good, but not completely unexpected since he had announced that he'd gone to France inquiring after Amicia de Lairne. Perhaps it was the best thing that he was here, conducting this ridiculous interview. Perhaps he did not know everything. Perhaps he could be persuaded to believe what Sybilla needed him to believe. Perhaps, perhaps . . .

But if he was determined enough to discover that much, what else does he also know? He doesn't seem a stupid man.

She dropped her head and sighed, her hands fisting in the material of the gown she had pulled from the wardrobe, a sage-green damask with a wide skirt suitable for riding.

It was as Amicia had warned her. This was the end game, and Sybilla would need all her wits and cunning about her in order to attempt to save Fallstowe. It was her only hope.

She *must* keep hold of Fallstowe.

After locking his portfolio away safely in the trunk in his own room, Julian went to the guest chambers afforded to Lucy and Murrin. He arrived just in time to take up his daughter from her crib. As usual, she woke gently, smiling, and making her little dove noises she had so recently mastered. He waved Murrin away when she approached.

"She must be a soaking mess, milord," Murrin argued. "At least let me change her before she soils your sleeve."

"She's not that wet," Julian argued mildly. "It can wait." He took Lucy to a low-backed rocking chair and sat down, perhaps needing to absorb a little of the baby's sweetness to chase away the sour mood his first official meeting with Sybilla Foxe had induced.

"It would be pert of me to ask how it went," Murrin said in an airy manner as she took to sorting through stacks of Lucy's clothes in a trunk. She paused and glanced at him over her shoulder.

Julian sighed. "Since your future depends on it as well as ours, it went better than I expected." He sat Lucy up on his knee, smoothed a hand over her impossibly silky, fine hair. The top of her head was so soft, so delicate. It never failed to humble him that this precious, tiny creature had come from him.

Murrin had given up all pretense of sorting nappies and now regarded him with an armful of forgotten clothes, her eyebrows disappearing into her head covering. "Will you arrest her today, then?"

"No, no." Julian frowned and shook his head. "I've not proven the king's suspicions thoroughly enough for just cause. I must go about this slowly, so as not to arouse Lady Foxe's ire any sooner than I must. Although we have been treated . . . cordially thus far." Julian tried not to recall the first night of his arrival at Fallstowe. "I daresay we are entirely at her mercy."

"Hmm," Murrin said noncommittally as she began to once more sort through Lucy's clothing.

Julian turned his daughter around so that she reclined against his chest, and Lucy began to pull up her legs to grab at her feet. He looked around the chamber, admiring the fine architecture, and the craftsmanship of the furnishings of even a guest room at Fallstowe.

"It's a fine chamber, isn't it?" he remarked, not really expecting much of an answer from the nurse. After all, she was used to more lowly quarters than this.

But Murrin stopped what she was doing once more and took a moment to appraise the room. She wrinkled her nose. "It's quite small though, isn't it? Lady Lucy would be much more comfortable in the family wing, I reckon." She looked back at Julian. "Do you think they've a nursery outfitted, milord?"

Julian shrugged. "It's unlikely. There's not been an infant in residence at Fallstowe Castle for many years, that I know of."

Murrin sniffed and then turned back to her chore,

pulling out a fresh gown and length of cotton nappy before replacing the stack in the trunk and turning to walk toward where Julian sat with Lucy.

"No matter, that. It shouldn't take any time to choose a chamber and have it made over." She reached her arms out for Lucy and this time Julian relented, having at last felt dampness on his leg. Murrin nestled the baby against her and touched a forefinger lightly to the baby's nose. "Perhaps His Lordship will have the stones whitewashed for us, eh, milady? Then you shall be the princess of Fallstowe Castle!" Murrin giggled softly and then turned away to cross the floor.

Julian felt a slight frown crease his brow at the idea that Murrin was already choosing living quarters for themselves, but he wasn't sure why. It wasn't as if he felt guilty about what the king had sent him here to do. If Julian was correct in his theories, formed from his exhaustive investigation into Amicia Foxe and her family, then he was nothing more than a champion for justice. Righting a wrong. Revealing a lie and a treason.

Evicting a woman from her family home for a wrong done through no fault of her own. A woman who has ruled Fallstowe with cunning and bravery greater than most men's. Whose reputation even now heralds her as a warrior, a sorceress, a protector, and monarch in her own right.

But Julian knew better than most that in every war there were bound to be casualties. Innocent lives destroyed for the greater good. The law was the law. And Julian owed Edward a debt that he was determined to pay.

Lucy *did* deserve a home such as Fallstowe. The best Julian could give her. Julian may not have been in passionate, romantic love with Cateline, but surely the love that was absent from his marriage had bloomed a hundredfold and in pure, riotous color for little Lucy Griffin, his world. His reason for living.

He rose from the chair to precede Murrin, who carried Lucy from the chamber, and headed in the direction of the great hall for the noon meal. Julian doubted very much that he would even catch a glimpse of Sybilla Foxe the remainder of the day, and that suited him quite well, he found.

He had a priest to speak to this afternoon, and a message to send north.

Chapter 8

Sybilla was rather surprised and a little unsettled when Julian Griffin was late meeting her in the stables that evening. She had sent him an invitation to go riding with her shortly after the noon meal, and she had definitely expected him to be seated upon his mount and waiting for her in the yard when she arrived, but it had been a full quarter hour before he deigned to make his appearance, strolling into the stables with Fallstowe's priest, Father Perry, at his elbow, smiling and conversing easily with the holy man.

"You've already arrived," Julian said with a lift of his tawny eyebrows. "I'm not late, am I?"

"Quite," Sybilla replied. "If you are too engaged in other business at *my home*, Lord Griffin, I shan't trouble you with an activity as mundane as touring Fallstowe's lands."

"No, no. Forgive me," Julian said, and his face conveyed sincere regret. "I fear that I was so immersed in conversation with your good priest that I simply became unaware of the passing of time. Certainly, I am looking forward to riding out with you."

Sybilla very much wanted to beg off their excursion now. She was nervous, a condition as foreign to her as timidity, but there was no other option.

"Your horse is saddled and waiting. Although we shan't see the entirety of the grounds, we will still miss the evening meal. I've had Cook prepare a satchel for us."

An easy, surprised smile came over Julian Griffin's face, and it caused Sybilla's stomach to do a neat turn.

"A picnic, then? Smashing. I haven't eaten on the ground in months, and the weather is fair."

Sybilla felt her lips purse petulantly at his enthusiasm, and she turned away until Julian had bid Father Perry farewell and quickly took to his borrowed mount. He was still smiling when she looked back at him.

"I shall follow your lead, my lady," he said, gesturing with a wide sweep of his arm.

Sybilla kicked her mount and rode out into the yard ahead of him at a trot, muttering under her breath, "I certainly hope so."

They rode southwest from the gate, away from the woods and the road and toward the wide, fallow fields quilted with hedgerows and timothy grass. Sybilla kept their conversation matter-of-fact as they rode past the agricultural industries of Fallstowe, and she explained the different crops the field master oversaw, the unique schedule of rotation for the fields, the more rare varieties the manor was attempting. To her surprise, he seemed more than politely interested, asking pertinent and intelligent questions and seeming fascinated with the topic of harvest yields in relation to the weather conditions of last season.

Sybilla looked at him curiously as they headed down

a rather steep ravine toward the north of the demesne. "Do you run a farm manor, Lord Griffin? You seem rather intrigued by such dry topics as silage."

His glance caught hers, but he did not smile at her attempt at humor, which did not surprise her greatly. Alys was the funny sister.

"No, I've never run a farm. Always wanted to, though. I lived on one for a time in my youth. I would that Lucy know such delight."

Sybilla guided Octavian through the shallow, muddy creek at the bottom of the ravine and turned to watch Julian Griffin do the same with his own mount. "Where is your family home, Lord Griffin?"

He seemed loath to still his horse beside Sybilla's, and even though Octavian was an enormous beast bred from mighty war steeds and dwarfed Julian's borrowed mount, the man did not seem diminished at all in the saddle.

"The city. London," he clarified brusquely before she could ask. Then he nodded up the hill upon which the sun was spraying its last, red rays from the far, opposite horizon, turning the new grass to rust. "That way, then?"

She answered him with a nod of her own, and he preceded her up the sharp rise. Her eyes followed him keenly, just as Octavian fell into step in his wake.

He did not have the air of entitlement that resulted from being royal, nor the aversion to his own family, if his daughter was any indication. He was not an active general in Edward's army, a professional man of war. But Lucy Griffin had been born at the king's home only months ago, when Alys and Piers had been in London.

His dead wife, then. Her name, her name—what was her name . . . ?

She topped the rise shortly after him and he silently let

her lead the way, although Sybilla kept Octavian at a slow walk while she searched the very air around them.

"Was Lady . . . Ke—" No, no, that wasn't it! "Lady *Catherine* fond of the country?" she asked, and held her breath.

"Cateline," Julian corrected her.

Sybilla winced inwardly. "My apologies."

"Think naught of it. It is a common enough mistake. She said ofttimes that she answered to anything closely resembling it." He gave a wry smile and Sybilla returned it, relieved. "But no—Cateline preferred the excitement of town, the shops and fairs. Especially the dressmakers' shops." Sybilla looked over to Julian when he paused, and she caught him looking back at the small, purple shadow that was Fallstowe at dusk.

His eyes came back to her, and the emotion in them was sincere. "She would have been very impressed by Fallstowe, though."

Sybilla directed her gaze over Octavian's head once more, not liking the uncomfortable sensation Julian Griffin's honesty provoked in her. Still, she pressed on, feeling as though she was on the verge of a very important discovery, like smelling the water on the air before a much needed rain.

"It is through her position that you are here, is it not?" she guessed boldly.

Julian was silent for a handful of moments. "In part, yes. I knew Edward years before Cateline and I met, however. We warred together."

Sybilla felt a surge of triumph course through her body, but outwardly she remained unmoved, as if she had known this all along. "The Crusade, yes."

"You seem to know almost as much about me as I do

about you, Lady Sybilla," he said, in a not entirely easy fashion.

"Oh, I wouldn't say that," Sybilla hedged, as her mind worked up a fire behind her eyes that mirrored the flaming burst of the sun at their back.

"You're just humoring me," he accused her. "You knew of Cateline, that she was a cousin to the king; that I had enjoined in the Crusade with him." He paused. "What else do you know?"

She gave him a smile over her right shoulder. "Lord Griffin, you flatter me. I daresay I could ask the same of you."

He shook his head at her, his mouth quirking once more. Sybilla's heart thundered in her chest, and she quickly brought her head around so as not to look at him.

He and his daughter were related to the king. He lived in the king's home. He had been sent on a mission quite dear to Edward's heart, and was trusted enough to command hundreds of the king's men at his whim.

I can help you, Sybilla. Let me.

"Have you never thought of marrying, Lady Sybilla?" he asked suddenly from behind her, and Sybilla's thundering heart came to a frozen stop, as the image of August Bellecote bloomed in her mind.

"I have, yes," Sybilla answered, struggling to keep her words from sounding choked as they scraped past her constricted throat. "I once gave it very serious thought."

"What happened?" Julian pressed. "I would think it to be the wisest choice you could have made, considering your circumstances. Not that it could have saved Fallstowe entirely, but—"

"He died, Lord Griffin," Sybilla interrupted him. "*I*

would think that you above all others could sympathize with that."

The sound of hooves rustling in the wet grass rose between them for a time.

"I'm sorry," he said at last. "Would I have known him?"

"We should eat if we are inclined to," Sybilla said, blatantly ignoring his question. The last thing she needed was Julian Griffin prying into the strange order of events surrounding Sybilla's secret marriage to August Bellecote.

"All right, yes," Julian said lightly, oddly unperturbed that she had declined to answer him. "Where shall we go?"

Sybilla brought Octavian to a halt and took a deep breath, looking around the shadowy landscape as if considering their options.

Which was exactly what she was doing.

"Well"—she took a deep breath and blew it out quietly before turning to face Julian Griffin—"I think I shall leave it up to you."

His lips quirked and he gave her an amused look. "Me?"

"Yes. We can either turn south, which will lead us to the husbandry barns where we might procure a table and afterward you might investigate the livestock . . ."

"Or?" Julian prompted.

"Or . . . we can proceed to the old ruins," she said lightly, and then added, "and the Foxe Ring."

He shouted his disbelieving laughter. "You can't be serious! I have the choice of seeing where sheep do tawdry things in the presence of grown men, or I can view the legendary Foxe Ring myself? Fallstowe's very beginning?" he said with a shake of his head. He laughed again. "This way, you say?"

Sybilla barely had time to nod before Julian Griffin

kicked his horse's sides and was galloping toward the Foxe Ring and a darkening sky full of emerging stars . . .

And the faint, round outline of a ripe moon peeking through the sheer curtain of a solitary cloud.

Julian reined his mount to a hard stop when the bones of the old Foxe keep and monolithic ring stood up suddenly in the night, like a mythical giant-king who had surrendered his crown of stones and laid it on the ground before him.

He huffed out a breath and smiled behind his foggy exhalation, trying to burn these first impressions into his memory for all time. The Foxe Ring. The legend come to life. The site where the biggest con in the history of England would be initiated, almost completely successfully, and Julian Griffin was close enough to touch it.

No sooner had that thought entered his head than he was swinging down from his horse and striding up the slight rise to the ring, marching into it as if it were a long lost lover to be captured in a running embrace. He reached the first stones—two uprights capped by a massive horizontal slab—and he placed both palms flat against the stones with a happy sigh. They were oddly warm and smooth despite their cold appearance. The comparison caused him to remember the woman riding behind him and he turned his head to look over his shoulder.

She was walking up the hillock with long, slow strides, leading her horse by limp reins, and Julian couldn't help but think that she appeared to be a woman walking to her own execution. If Sybilla Foxe knew the entirety of her family's sordid history, perhaps the Foxe Ring was not the fantastic place for her that most took it to be. His hands slid down and away from the stones and he turned to watch her unstrap the leather satchel from her horse's saddle. She paused by her mount's head, grabbed the bridle and whispered something into his cheek, then walked toward the ring.

She was simply beautiful. Unearthly so in the moonlight, and Julian could not help but feel a stab of jealousy for the man Sybilla Foxe had wanted to marry. He knew that tens of men had sought her hand, some even going so far as to petition Edward with the promise of bringing her to heel. The king had given his permission more times than Julian could remember, but not one had ever returned with any inkling of hope to win the lady. She was singular. Autonomous. Choosy about those with whom she kept intimate company, and the rumor was that once she had allowed a man into her bed, she refused to see him again in a personal capacity.

Julian wondered then just how many men that had been. And how a man went about joining that particular queue.

Sybilla stopped just beyond the ring, and her gaze went past Julian to the ruin behind him. After a moment, she looked at him. "My sister Cecily nearly died here, only days ago."

Julian frowned; all sporting thoughts of casually gaining Sybilla Foxe's bed vanished. "In the ring?"

"The ruin," Sybilla answered. "The floor's rotted out of the hall, and she was pushed into the dungeon by a jealous ex-lover of her husband's."

"My God. Has the woman been apprehended? Shall I send men to detain her?"

Sybilla stared at him oddly for a moment. "That won't be necessary. She's dead."

"Dead?" Julian felt his brows draw together. "Sybilla . . ."

"Again you flatter me, Lord Griffin," she said, a smile in her voice. "Rumor is that she leapt to her death, quite of her own volition. From a chamber at Hallowshire Abbey where she'd sought asylum. Strange, isn't it? I suppose the guilt of it got to her."

Julian wasn't convinced, but then his mind seized on a bit of information Sybilla had inadvertently divulged. "Your middle sister has married?" Julian asked, alarmed that there were important developments he was as yet unaware of.

Sybilla gave him a smile that seemed rather sly. "Did I forget to mention that? Forgive me. Cecily married Oliver Bellecote, Lord of Bellemont, five days ago. She carries his child."

Julian felt a prickle at the back of his neck. He'd sent soldiers to Bellemont, to accept Bellecote's offer of assistance to the king. And now he learned that one of the Foxe women had ensconced herself there as lady, and was pregnant with a noble child, no less.

"The king will not be pleased."

Sybilla chuckled then, and Julian found himself quite taken with the husky sound. "Lord Griffin, when has the king ever been pleased with any of the goings-on at Fallstowe?"

He couldn't help but return her smile. "Lady Alys has found herself a good match, has she not? I met Lord Mallory in London, quite briefly."

"Indeed," Sybilla agreed. "I think highly of Piers and his grandfather. Both brave and noble men, if ever any truly exist." Sybilla paused and then looked Julian in the eyes. "Alys shall bear Piers's child as well, you know."

The prickle at the back of Julian's neck grew to a nagging pain. "No, I didn't. So it seems that you are the last."

"So it seems," she agreed, giving him a single, regal nod of her head. Then her sly smile returned. "All four of them met here. In the Foxe Ring."

"As did Amicia and Morys." He couldn't look away from her. It was as if the moonlight was doing magical things to her eyes, her hair, her gown; making them shimmer and sparkle and glow. "Fascinating." He shook himself, and swung his hands together once in a clap as if it would break the spell. "Well then, since you've already said that there's no floor to be had in the old keep, shall we?" He raised his eyebrows and then turned and entered the ring, looking up and around him at the standing stones as he walked toward the center altar stone.

He stopped and turned to speak to Sybilla, but she was not there. A quick search with his eyes found her still caught in the moonlight, standing outside the ring. "Sybilla?" he called out. "Aren't you coming in?"

She walked slowly to the very perimeter of the ring, stood just beyond the stone he'd laid hands on. "Are you certain you want me to, Julian?" she asked, and he noticed that there was no smile on her face, no tease to her words. She glanced up at the sky and then quickly back to him, her blue eyes reflecting the moon like diamond wraiths, turning his guts to jelly. "The moon is full. As learned as you are on all things Foxe, and as eager as you were to gain the ring yourself, certainly you are aware of the legend."

"Do you believe in it?" Julian asked her, and realized that, although they were standing more than a score of paces apart from each other, they were both speaking in whispers. It didn't seem to matter—each word from their mouths was as crisp and clear as if they had been breathing gossip directly into each other's ears. "Do you believe that if the moonlight catches us both inside the stones, we are fated to be together for all eternity?"

She stood so still, she could have been carved from the same stones. Her arms hung at her sides; in one hand she grasped the satchel she'd brought containing a meal for them both to share. Her face was alabaster, expressionless, glittering with exquisite, flawless beauty.

"Do *you*?" she asked, her words barely breaching the air, and yet they seemed to Julian to echo around and around in his brain.

He shook his head slightly, but it was a heartbeat longer before he could bring his lips to form the words. "No." He swallowed. Then he smiled and made a spontaneous bow. "It would honor me greatly, Lady Sybilla, if you would join me in the Foxe Ring. There." He stood and spread his arms. "That is what I think of old superstition."

Chapter 9

Sybilla forced her mouth to keep hold of the slight smile she'd donned for Julian Griffin's benefit. If it slipped only the tiniest bit, she felt she would be overcome with terror, and she knew, perhaps better than anyone else, that one's outward appearance and demeanor were all that ever really mattered: how you presented yourself, what you said, your mannerisms. People took them at face value, and you either commanded or you were commanded.

So it counted for little that, as soon as she had stepped foot inside the ring of stones, she felt the moonlight hit her between her shoulder blades, just as surely and deeply as an arrow. It took her breath, caused her heart to skip a beat and then flail wildly in her chest. The roots of her hair tingled beneath her scalp; her flesh crawled with soft lightning. And still she drew ever closer to Julian Griffin, who stood beside the altar stone as if he had been waiting there for her for a hundred years.

The wind whirled through the ring, blowing the man's tawny mane behind him like a wild sail. One muscular leg was stretched to his side at an angle, and his hands were on his narrow hips. He regarded her with a smile but no hint of rapturous passion. Only perhaps excitement, or amusement. She searched his face for any sign that he felt even a fraction of the energy the stones were throwing off like waves, but he seemed unfazed.

She came to a stop immediately before him, so close that she had to turn up her face to look into his eyes. He looked down and his smile became undeniably amused. She could smell him now, the warmth of him coming from his thick, rich clothing, but it smelled not of prestige or money—it only smelled like . . .

The tang of mead on your tongue.

The crispness of autumn leaves crushed underfoot in a deep wood.

A stone fished from the bottom of a stream and held to your face in the sunlight.

Skin warmed by a fire's smoke.

The wind over—

"Sybilla?" he asked quietly, and his amusement was clear in his tone.

She started, and realized she had continued to search his face for a sign, any sign, while being drowned by her senses.

"Yes?"

His smile grew infinitesimally wider and his shoulders gave a minute hitch. "Are you all right?"

"Of course. I'm fine," she said, and although she'd meant the words to come out terse and scoffing, when her voice echoed back to her ears it was breathy, weak, and sounded confused. "Are you . . . all right?"

"Ravenous, actually," he said. Then he moved and reached for the satchel hanging forgotten in her dumb hand. "If you'll allow me, I'll just get us set up here." Her fingers fell open and he quickly turned to set the leather bag on the stone. "You don't mind, do you?" he tossed over his shoulder.

"No," she answered, and then blinked several times. At last she forced herself to move, turning her head to look up at the stones, the moon glowing above them, as if to make certain she was actually where she was.

Foxe Ring, yes.

Full moon, yes.

And nothing had happened.

She turned her gaze toward Julian Griffin's back and felt her eyebrows lower. He was making gruff little sounds of happy anticipation, and Sybilla found herself growing fantastically annoyed. When she could command her feet to become uprooted from the loamy soil, she walked to stand at his side before the stone he was busy setting as a table.

"Your cook is quite capable," he said. "She's thought of everything."

Sybilla glanced at the brown oilcloth, where Julian was sparking life to a candle as thick as her forearm. As the flame bloomed, it tickled the glazing of a stout crock, its lid strapped tight with leather bands; a hunk of light-colored bread; and a corked flagon. A moment later, Julian had pulled two small wooden cups from the satchel.

She looked back to his face when he rubbed his hands together in anticipation and then turned to perch one hip on the edge of the stone. He was back on both feet again in an instant, a look of bewilderment on his handsome face.

Finally, Sybilla thought.

"I don't know what's come over me," he said in an annoyed voice, and then gave a short bow before gesturing to the stone. "I've completely forgotten my manners in the face of such a feast. Please, my lady, sit."

Sybilla felt her eyebrows rise.

She drew an inaudible breath and then, holding her mouth tight, placed her hand in Julian Griffin's offered palm while he assisted her onto the stone. Her skin burned where he touched her, but an instant later the contact was broken as he reclaimed his own seat and reached for the crock, working straightaway at unfastening the leather straps.

In only a moment the lid was free, revealing a half of a roasted bird in a savory broth, surrounded by caramelized root vegetables and swirls of limp, new greens.

Julian hefted the crock with one hand and held it toward her. "My lady? Have you your eating knife?"

"Go on," Sybilla said tersely. "I find I'm not at all hungry at the moment." Julian shrugged and brought the crock back to the oilcloth in front of him even before Sybilla could add crossly, "It must be the air."

He pulled the leg of the bird away easily and bit into it, leaning over the crock. "Mmm," he mumbled, and then chewed thoroughly. Sybilla watched his throat as he swallowed, her stomach clenching, and at the same time hoped he would choke to death.

"This is quite good. Delicious, actually. Tarragon?" he asked, raising his eyes to her face as he swirled the bone in his mouth and finished off the leg.

"I've no idea, I'm sure," she snipped.

"Lovely. Majestic," he said, and then popped a bit of

turnip into his mouth. A moment later, he said, "I'm glad you've realized that it's in your best interest to conduct our business in a more friendly manner. Your cooperation may hold sway with Edward."

"Friendly manner?" Sybilla repeated. "You think because I haven't killed you yet that we're friendly now?"

He gave her an indulgent look, as one might give a small child who vowed to run away from home due to poor treatment, before pulling a hunk of thigh meat free and setting it between his teeth with relish. Sybilla felt a bit of her discombobulation evaporate at his condescension. Her eyes narrowed.

In the next instant, Julian Griffin's eyes went wide, and harsh hacking sounds emanated from him. He grabbed at his throat with one hand and gained his feet, beating on his chest with his other fist.

Sybilla watched calmly until a moment later, when the lord fell into a fit of wild, wheezing spasms. The corners of her mouth turned down with disappointment, and she reached for the flagon and cup.

"I beg your pardon," he rasped as he regained his seat.

Sybilla handed him the cup of wine and then poured one for herself. She brought it to her lips but paused before drinking.

"All right, then. Go on. Tell me what you know," she said quietly, and then took a drink.

Julian had drained his cup and was wiping at his brow with his sleeve. He rested his wrist on his knee, the cup clasped loosely in his fingers, and regarded her.

"I'm not certain you're prepared for that," he said, and his face held no trace of condescension.

"I'll not have this hanging over my head any longer, Julian. Edward has sent you here to do his bidding. I would know the details of what I have been charged with so that I might have time to gather evidence to disprove it."

"You think I would charge you falsely? I can assure you, what I know as fact is bolstered by witnesses, documents. The things I have pieced together on assumption, I have done with much forethought, but I would not hand you over to the king based on my own theories, unless they could be substantiated."

She said nothing, only held his gaze.

"Sybilla, I—" He broke off abruptly, reached for the flagon, and refilled his cup. After taking a drink, he regarded her for a long moment before beginning again. "I have come to admire you greatly these past few months."

"You can't admire someone you don't know," Sybilla pointed out.

Julian nodded in acquiescence. "I admire what I do know of you then. What I have learned, and yes, what I have seen thus far in my short time at Fallstowe."

"Are you attempting to flatter me into a stupor before getting to it, Lord Griffin?" she snipped. "Because I find I am in no mood to play your court games. Either tell me what you know and get it over with, or this is finished."

"Finished? What do you mean?"

"I mean," Sybilla said coolly, "that we will return to Fallstowe, you may collect your daughter and your servant, summon your minions, and have at the siege."

"I'm not leaving now that I'm in, Sybilla," Julian answered quietly, but his tone was every bit as cool as Sybilla's had been. "Surely you don't take me for that kind of fool."

"Then it will be your general who leads your men in your name," she said pointedly. "Get on with it, Lord Griffin."

His head bobbed slightly as he stared at her, obviously considering his options. "All right," he said quietly at last.

He set his cup deliberately on the oilcloth, and the flame from the candle seemed to want to dip inside and explore the shadow of his wine.

"Your mother was serving as the de Lairne lady's maid in Gascony when Simon de Montfort was appointed to that post by King Henry III. The barons were not giving Simon his due, and so your mother saw a means to thwart her employers—the ones that had saved her from a life of poverty as an infant—and perhaps better her station at the same time. She conspired with de Montfort to bring the de Lairnes to heel, and in exchange, after his triumph in Gascony, Simon agreed to allow Amicia passage on his return to England."

Sybilla said nothing, but inside she quaked at the accuracy of Julian's information.

"She was quite adept at playing the part of a noble lady—she knew the manners, the way to walk, to talk, to carry herself. When she arrived in England, she was a guest at Kenilworth and a favorite with Lady Eleanor de Montfort, the wife of Simon and the sister of King Henry III, who took an unusual liking to Amicia and allowed her to stay, even when her husband returned to Gascony. Lady de Montfort even went as far as to encourage the ruse, introducing your mother as Lady de Lairne to her peers, boldly flaunting her about as if it were a great game.

"And while your mother enjoyed the attention and luxury she received at Kenilworth, she was no fool. She was in serious trouble. Very serious. And she knew that it was only a matter of time before Lady de Montfort grew bored with the novelty of her and—" Julian paused. "I'm sorry, Sybilla. I—"

"Go on," she demanded curtly.

"And she was pregnant," Julian finished. He gave her a moment of silence. "With you."

Sybilla wanted to drop her head and close her eyes as the reality of her situation crashed onto her like a weight of stone, but she would not allow a display of weakness now. So instead she looked away from Julian Griffin, through the stones and into the blackness of the night-hidden hills.

"It was a soldier from de Montfort's army, on the return from Gascony," Sybilla said calmly, as if speaking about some historical fact from long ago, and yet she could hear her mother's voice in her ear just as clearly as when she'd first found out. "Oddly enough, he was her protector. Had she not given herself to him, she would have been at the mercy of the baser men. She would have been raped daily. Probably would have died before gaining England, which would have suited de Montfort at the time, I can only imagine."

She looked back to Julian and saw sympathy on his face. In a way, it was a relief. He continued the story that Sybilla already knew too well.

"She was in serious trouble," he repeated. "And she had heard of the legend of the Foxe Ring. She became separated from de Montfort's hunting party, but with purpose, desperate to find the old ruins and try it. When she found Morys Foxe about the ruins, she took her shot, not knowing that she was about to seduce the greatest ally of de Montfort's enemy."

"The king," Sybilla supplied.

"Your mother was rumored to be a beautiful woman.

Young. Morys Foxe was neither beautiful nor young. Perhaps it was the romance of the legend—"

"It wasn't," Sybilla said bitterly.

Julian was quiet for a moment. "What I *don't* know is if she ever confessed to Morys that you were not his child. For all intents and purposes, he claimed you as his own."

Sybilla looked away again. "It doesn't matter. Even if Edward insists on declaring to the land that my mother was a fraud, without a single drop of noble blood in her veins, he has no proof that I am not of Morys Foxe's issue, and neither do you. King Henry awarded Fallstowe to my mother after"—she paused—"after Morys died at the battle of Lewes, defending the Crown against the English barons and de Montfort."

"He died because once again de Montfort called on your mother to pay more debt," Julian answered. "He threatened to out her, to out you as illegitimate, cast a pall on Morys and your sisters. She gave in, and Morys was killed." He paused. "It's treason, Sybilla. Your mother committed treason against the Crown. Against her own husband."

Sybilla said nothing. She could say nothing over the sounds of her mother's wails inside her head.

"But she tried to make up for it, didn't she?" Julian pressed, a note of intrigue or something Sybilla could not name in his voice. "She got her revenge on de Montfort the very next year, at Evesham, when she brought Edward word of de Montfort's son's unguarded army at none other than Kenilworth Castle, a place your mother knew well, and where she was welcomed. Because of her intelligence, Edward surprised de Montfort at Evesham under his own son's banner, and the reign of Simon de Montfort was no more."

Sybilla found that she was shaking her head ever so slightly and so she stopped. "You can't prove any of this," Sybilla said.

"But it's true, isn't it?" She sensed Julian turning more fully toward her.

"No."

"You're lying," he accused her, bitterness high in his voice. "You're lying to save yourself."

"No," Sybilla whispered this time. She turned her head to look at him.

"Then tell me where I have gone wrong," he insisted, and his gaze was so intense, so sincere, Sybilla felt for a moment that she might just tell him.

But then she saw her mother's weak body, lying in bed in the days and hours before her death. Heard Amicia's pathetic weeping alternating with shrill and slurred demands.

Don't you see now what I have done? You are the fairest, the richest, the most feared in the land. You have Fallstowe at your command and under your protection. Fallstowe and your sisters, Sybilla. Think of them! If you are to keep them, you must do as I say, and if all must be lost, you must take our secrets with you. There is no cause for Alys's and Cecily's lives to be ruined as well. Do not dare to dishonor the proud memory of the man who was your father.

"My mother . . . was a brave woman," Sybilla said. "And now I must be the brave one."

"Your mother as good as threw you to the wolves," Julian declared flatly. "And that is why you think you must be brave, why you have adopted such a demeanor as to make yourself intimidating, untouchable. It's because Amicia feared anyone to know the truth, and now you fear it, too."

"If I am not brave, Lord Griffin—" Sybilla queried, tilting her head and giving him a curious look, "if I am not brave, what can you promise me? That Edward will be so impressed by my forthrightness that he will give me Fallstowe? Lay the past to rest? Continue to take my money graciously and leave me in peace with my people, to run Fallstowe as I see fit?"

"He will take back Fallstowe, on the grounds that it was entrusted to your mother on a false and treasonous basis," Julian admitted. "But if you cooperate—"

"If I cooperate," Sybilla interjected loudly, "he will what? Entomb me in some nunnery with a stipend? Strip me of my title but allow me to marry a shopkeep? Or perhaps he will at last give his temper free rein and have me imprisoned, hanged? Beheading is too good for someone of my station, after all. I should not be afforded such dignity for daring to thwart him for so long."

"If only you would allow me to—"

Sybilla slid from the stone, her action cutting off whatever Julian Griffin was about to say. "My mother worked her entire life to ensure that my sisters and I would have the lives that we now enjoy. I will not dishonor her sacrifice by running to London and grasping at Edward's robes, begging for mercy."

"Your mother was a servant who did what she did to better her own station in life. Her loyalty was always for sale. She was not noble, in any sense of the word. She got her husband killed and she used you," Julian accused her, his brows drawing together. "She's still using you."

In two strides, Sybilla was before Julian. She raised her hand and slapped his face as hard as she could.

"Do not speak of her in that manner again, Lord

Griffin," Sybilla warned, surprised to hear her voice shaking, mimicking the trembling in her body.

He had moved from the stone before Sybilla's eyes could register it, grasping her by her upper arms and giving her a shake.

"I did not do these things to you, Sybilla," he whispered harshly. "And it is through no fault of your own that you are in this situation."

"It's charming how you think me so innocent." She mocked him, her eyes searching his face, her skin aching where he touched her. "Have you not heard the tales of Lady Sybilla Foxe, who has sold her soul to the devil?"

"I have heard the tales. But the only devil I believe you sold your soul to was a frightened old woman. I am not cowed by you. I am not indebted to you. And if you strike me again, I will turn you over my knee."

"I dare you to try it," Sybilla hissed.

His fingers tightened around her arms and he pulled her up against him, his mouth hovering over hers.

"You don't tempt me, either," he said in a low growl.

"Obviously," she smirked.

He let go of her then and stepped away. Sybilla could see that he was moved, regardless of his staunch denial. It was as if the air between them was alive.

"I'm not innocent, Julian," Sybilla said, noting the breathiness of her own voice. "I know what you say is true: Edward will not allow me to keep Fallstowe after you confirm that my mother was a fraud. So you tell me: What would *you* do? What would *you* do if someone showed up at *your* gate, poised to report to the world that the life *you* had was not real? That Lucy was not your daughter in truth? That each battle you fought and survived meant nothing. Your home was to be stolen away from you. Your marriage deemed invalid. Everything you had ever had, or loved, or worked for, would be taken from you forever because it was *the law*."

She paused for a moment. "Would *you* go quietly?"

"No," he answered in a low voice. "No, I wouldn't."

She rushed to him again, but this time, instead of striking him, she laid her right palm boldly against his chest, over his heart. "Then tell Edward that he is *wrong*. Tell him you found nothing of import, nothing that would confirm his suspicions. Don't let him take Fallstowe from me, from my family. You said when you first arrived that you might be able to help me, so help me, Julian."

"I won't lie to him, Sybilla," Julian said. "Especially since there are things you aren't telling me."

"What can I offer you?" she pressed. "What do you want? Money? My body?"

Julian grimaced. "Don't lower yourself like that."

"However much Edward has promised you, I will give you in kind."

He shook his head. "That's impossible. You must understand that even if Morys had lived, you could not retain Fallstowe. He would have seen you married off and away from here. Tell me what I need to know and come with me to London. It may not be pleasant, but Edward is fair. You may not come out of it any worse than what you would have, had the man who claimed to be your father lived. He'll likely dower you."

Sybilla let her hand slide away and stepped back, appalled at the tears in her eyes. "You don't understand. I gave my word."

"I, too, gave my word," Julian shot back. "My future is at stake here as well, Sybilla. Not just mine, but Lucy's."

"Then we are at an impasse," she said quietly.

"No. We're not. I will tell Edward all that I know, with or without your input."

She raised her hands slightly and then let them fall. "You may as well kill me now, then."

Julian approached her once more and took her shoulders. "I don't want to kill you, Sybilla."

"Then what do you want?"

"*I want you to tell me the truth,*" he gritted through his teeth. Then he paused. "And I want to kiss you."

"I thought you weren't tempted by me."

"I lied."

Chapter 10

Her blue eyes sparkled with cool surprise as she looked up at him.

It was true. He did want her. He had wanted her since the first time he had laid eyes on her in Fallstowe's great hall, sitting in her throne-like chair and receiving him as if she were royalty presiding over a court.

He wanted her because of her beauty, of course, but for so much more as well. Her bravery. Her determination. Her intelligence. Her deliberate defiance of everyone and everything that would try to defeat her, including Julian himself.

"Are you going to kiss me?" she asked, cocking her head to the side and looking at him in an interesting manner.

"I don't think so," he said, shaking his head slightly but seemingly unable to tear his gaze from hers. "Not until you trust me. I won't take anything that is not offered to me completely, and in good faith."

One of her slender eyebrows rose. "You think me to trust you when it is you who will tattle on me to the king?"

He made certain her eyes were trained on his. "Yes."

After a moment, Sybilla Foxe gave a huff of disbelieving laughter. She then turned her face away.

"We need to trust each other," he reiterated. "Edward doesn't expect me back straightaway. Think upon your options. If you decide that I am your best hope, you will tell me what you know, and then we will formulate our plan to present to Edward."

She looked back to him and her eyes narrowed. "What are we to do in the meantime?"

Julian shrugged, then looked about the ring as if considering it. "We enjoy our time at Fallstowe. You may go about your daily responsibilities as before—"

"Why, you're too kind," Sybilla snipped.

"And in your spare moments, you can better get to know me. And Lucy. A baby should be a novelty to you."

"I don't care for babies, actually," she said airily. "Noisy, smelly things. Always needing tending."

"You said yourself that you once very seriously considered marriage, so I fail to see how the prospect of an infant could be that very different from caring for a grown man."

"Indeed." She at last gave him a wry smile. Frosty around the edges, yes, but it was genuine. Genuinely Sybilla, and it was perhaps the first time that night that Julian had truly seen her.

But now he needed to move away from her lest he go back on his word and kiss her as he wanted to.

He stepped back and let her go, moving to the great fallen down stone in the center of the ring to begin gathering up the remnants of their supper. But in a moment, he felt her hand upon his arm, turning him to face her.

He was quite taken by surprise when she framed his

face in her palms and stood up on her toes, pressing her lips to his softly, lingeringly.

She sank back down on her heels after a long moment and her eyes fluttered open. Julian could not draw a proper breath.

"You intrigue me, Lord Griffin," she said musingly. "And you frustrate me. I feel I shall enjoy your company at Fallstowe."

"My lady," he said in a raspy voice.

She gave him a small smile and then stepped away, turning to blow out the candle.

He followed in her wake back to Fallstowe, enjoying watching her astride her great beast, Octavian. The moonlight lit them both, like a charcoal drawing on the landscape, sometimes blending horse and woman together with the very land of Fallstowe. Julian's conscience shouted and stomped in impotent rage.

That damned Foxe Ring. Was it a magical place? For surely he could not be now working out in his mind how he could keep Sybilla Foxe. They didn't know each other. They had been at odds from the first by their very natures, let alone because of what Julian had been sent to Fallstowe to do, and what Sybilla was sworn to protect.

He should simply tell her straightaway that Edward meant to reward Julian's successful investigation by giving him the title to Fallstowe. It was the honorable thing to do.

But then if he took her to bed, he would never know if she wanted him or wanted to keep some part of her demesne. He would never know her true feelings, of that he was certain. She had been trained well to do what was necessary, without regard for emotion.

Wasn't that the very gist of his and Cateline's limited

friendliness? Edward had made the match by touting Julian's exploits in battle, making him the famous warrior who had saved the king's life. It had made for quite the entrance into London's elite, and had given Cateline the prestige she'd always craved. But she had never loved him. The only times they'd made love were after feasts where Julian had been the toast of the gathering, women throwing themselves at him, men seeking his counsel, and Cateline well into her cups. They'd had nothing in common. She'd never wanted his conversation, his companionship.

Cateline had not been an evil woman; only a woman not in love with her husband.

Julian watched Sybilla Foxe sway in the moonlight. Was she an evil woman? He didn't think so. Quite the opposite, actually. She seemed to be a woman full of deep passion but with no outlet for it save Fallstowe. Her mother gone, her sisters off with families of their own. Who would be left to love Sybilla Foxe, and to be the recipient of all that passion when her only love, the grand castle, was taken from her?

I'm not innocent, Julian.

She wasn't stupid, either. So whatever it was she thought herself guilty of, it could not be more dire than what her mother had done.

Perhaps he could not love her. Perhaps he could not save her. But perhaps he could.

The Foxe Ring had not worked its magic with Sybilla and Julian Griffin.

Sybilla had not had high hopes of the legend being any more than fantastical nonsense, but she *was* in the very fist of desperation. If he was such an admirer of history as he appeared to be, she had hoped that the romance of the place might sway him to do her bidding, or at least encourage him to retreat a bit from his position.

But it had failed her. To the very end, he had seemed steadfast in his intention to report his findings to Edward, and to insist that she come to her senses and lay her soul—and her family's misdeeds—bare to him.

She sighed and threw the coverlet back. It was pointless to lie in bed when sleep was as far away from her as her dead mother. Although perhaps Amicia was closer than Sybilla cared to admit, which was why she found the choking tangle of sheets so unbearable.

Any matter, she rose from the bed and sought her quilted wrapper in the black room, the red coals of the banked fire and the white-lit panes of the window her only points of reference. White light, red light. Good, evil. Which one had Amicia been?

Which applied to Julian Griffin? To Sybilla?

She slipped her feet into her dyed leather slippers and left her room, uncertain of her destination.

Sybilla was not at all startled to encounter Graves in the private corridor leading to the secret door in the wall behind her table in the great hall. The man was a wraith, all knowing, and it didn't surprise her that Graves had sensed an unsettled soul roaming about his domain.

"Trouble sleeping, Madam?" he asked solicitously.

"A bit, Graves, yes," she answered. Graves was the only person under heaven that she felt she could be completely honest with at all times. After all, he already knew all of her secrets, and probably a few more that Sybilla herself could only guess at.

"Might I prepare you a toddy?" he offered as she drew near him.

"Only if you'll join me," she said, passing him and pulling at the silent and seamless door that would lead to her table.

She halted before the door was even a quarter of the way open, easily hearing the echo of quiet voices in the cavernous room beyond. She held up her left hand, signaling Graves to silence, and then slowly pulled the door open a bit more, searching the shadows for the midnight speakers.

Julian Griffin was pacing slowly in the aisle created by the rows of planked tables, his daughter perched upon his chest, her chubby forearms laid on his shoulder. The nursemaid, Murrin, sat at one of the benches, but her head was laid atop her arms on the table, a piece of sewing forgotten in her lap.

"Lord Griffin, Madam?" Graves asked in a whisper behind her.

Sybilla nodded.

"Is he stealing the fixtures?"

Sybilla felt herself smile and she shook her head absently. She turned her face slightly to direct her whisper over her shoulder. "He's walking the child. The nurse is asleep."

"Didn't we give them a *room?*" he muttered crossly.

Sybilla understood Graves's frustration. She didn't like strangers in her home either, even one as handsome as Julian Griffin.

Especially one as enigmatic and unnerving as Julian Griffin.

She couldn't take her eyes from him as he moved slowly through the shadows of the hall, speaking in a deep, soothing voice to the infant, who was happily chewing on one fist then the other. He seemed quite happy and at peace for such a late hour. They both did.

Would it have been so terrible had the Foxe Ring legend proved true for them? Sybilla thought no. Perhaps he was not overly wealthy, with lands and title to boast of. But he was closely connected to the king, and since he admitted to making London his home, he was likely well received and respected. He was of such repute as to have commanded a royal match, after all. If the Foxe Ring had worked, and Julian took his information to the king, if Sybilla begged for mercy, would Edward allow a match between them?

Sybilla didn't know how deep Julian Griffin's feelings for her could run without the magical workings of a legend. It meant little to her that he had admitted a desire for her body—even a prostitute could claim to be desired. Soon she would be without her title, without her money, her power—disgraced. Fodder for gossip. Doors closed, invitations ceased. Nothing to recommend her.

Her eyes followed him closely, marveling at him, up and about in the dead of night, his infant in his arms, while the dumb nurse slept through her duties.

Sybilla wondered what it would feel like to be comforted in those arms. Possibly heavenly.

She blinked and frowned.

"Are we to stand in the corridor all night, Madam?" Graves asked.

Julian Griffin turned on his heel and presented his back to the slice of room Sybilla could see through the doorway. He began walking slowly once more toward the stairs at the head of the long room, and Sybilla backed into the corridor, pushing the door shut before her.

She turned to Graves. "I think I shall beg off a drink, Graves. I feel I might be better able to sleep now."

The old man stared down his nose at her with narrowed eyes.

"What?" Sybilla demanded, moving past him.

"What?" Graves echoed.

She ignored him, making her way back to her rooms alone, the image of Julian Griffin still pacing running through her mind.

Chapter 11

Julian stared at the door in the early morning darkness of the corridor. Even if he had not done his own investigation of the private wing to determine where Sybilla Foxe's chamber lay, he could not have mistaken it. The door was carved with a fine and intricate design, and its thick coat of black paint marked it as unique from the other doors in the wing. He studied the markings as best he could in the meager light provided by the sconce on the wall behind him, running his fingers over it in spots.

Leaves of some sort, a long blade—a stylized sword, perhaps, but with a tip that ended in the shape of a serpent's head. There were words or symbols half-hidden in the design, in a language Julian did not recognize.

Was it a protective spell? The Foxe family motto? A warning?

Julian frowned. If he had heeded all the well-intentioned warnings he'd received in his lifetime, he would likely be long dead on some battlefield by now. He raised his hand and knocked twice, his call firm yet not demanding.

"Come in." Her voice called to him immediately from beyond the door.

Although he had been informed by several members of the staff that "Madam" did not take breakfast—in fact, Julian had not seen Sybilla Foxe eat a bite in the days that he'd been here—he was certain that she was up with the sun. And he was right.

He pushed open the door and stepped inside, unprepared for the sight that greeted him.

Sybilla was perched in a tall-backed upholstered chair cocked at an angle before a wide table set beneath an enormous bank of windows. Her knees were drawn up, her feet tucked beneath and to the side of her bottom, one arm around her knees, her other hand propping up her chin as she stared out the windows. Her long, dark hair was in a single plait, snaking over her shoulder and unfurling beneath her arm at her hip.

The peachy sunrise was just a suggestion, its glow seeming to illuminate the silk of her sheer, ivory dressing gown, the lace of it pooling around her bare ankles. It seemed as though she had donned the matching wrapper as an afterthought, for it hung off one narrow, delicate shoulder, her skin taking on the shy blush of the dawn.

She looked very young just then, much younger than her score and eight years. Young and innocent and very much alone.

Julian wanted to walk up behind her and cup his hand around the back of her neck beneath her braid, knead the muscles there where he knew they would be tense and aching. He wanted to lean down and whisper into her ear that it would be all right. He would do his best for her. She didn't have to be afraid . . .

But he didn't know that he could promise her any of those things with certainty.

"I hope I didn't keep you too long last night," she said quietly, still looking out the windows.

"No, but Lucy seemed determined to see the sunrise."

Her head whipped around, her light eyes wide, and she instinctively reached for the slipped shoulder of her robe. "I thought you were Graves," she said in a tight tone, so unlike the voice she'd used just a moment ago, full of concern and caring in those few short words. "What are you doing in my room, Lord Griffin?"

"I don't wish to disturb you," he said, quietly liking the way she had sought to protect her modesty when she'd discovered it was he who had come to visit and not some dusty old steward. It was quite at odds with her reputation, but then Julian was very certain that she was reputed to be many things that she was not. "I plan to start the servant interviews today. I thought you might like to know before I commence, rather than find out midway through the day. I don't want you to think I am doing anything covertly."

"An open book, are you?" she smirked halfheartedly, and then dismissed him by turning her gaze once more toward the windows. "I don't know what you're hoping to find by interrogating the kitchen maids. A good recipe for sausage, perhaps. Go on, though. I don't care."

Julian frowned, because it sounded as though she truly didn't care. "I'll not be speaking so much with the kitchen staff. Only those who were here while your mother yet lived. I have a list of names." He paused. "Graves is included, of course."

He saw her shoulders hitch and heard her little breath of laughter. "You have a list of Fallstowe servants? By name? You're quite thorough, Lord Griffin."

"I try to be." He could have left her then, now that he had told her what he planned to do. He should have, really. But he found his feet taking him to stand at the foot of the massive, carved blackwood bedstead that dominated the room. It was surrounded by the thickest scarlet-and-gold embroidered draperies he'd ever seen. The mattresses and coverlets and pillows seemed too plush, too decadent, as if made for luring a soul to sin. The furniture itself seemed too large, farcically so, and certainly much too imposing for a woman of such delicate stature as Sybilla Foxe. Julian had the odd and disturbing image of the bedposts gnashing her willowy body, devouring her, the bed's mouth of mattresses and coverlet tongue swallowing her up whole and with relish.

He thought of the rumors of her lovers. How many men had pleasured Sybilla Foxe in this bed?

"Is there anything else, Lord Griffin?" she said wearily. "You seem very interested in my belongings. Would you perhaps care to go through my wardrobe and catalogue my underthings?"

"Only if I might have something to keep," he responded cheekily. He looked over his shoulder, and although she continued to gaze through the windows, her lips curled in a small smile, perhaps in spite of herself.

Julian looked back to the evil piece of furniture. "Did you have this made yourself?"

"It was my parents'," she said, but a moment later corrected herself quietly. "Morys and Amicia's. He had it made for her shortly after they were married."

"The carvings on the post resemble those on your chamber door," he remarked.

"Mm-hmm," she responded.

"What do they mean?" he pressed.

She turned her head, but instead of her eyes finding

him, her gaze seemed to be focused within the heavy draperies of the bed. Her expression was tight, cold, filled with resentment. She turned back to the window.

"Ask her yourself," she said coolly. "She's not let me get a decent night's sleep since you arrived."

As soon as the words were out of her mouth, Sybilla regretted speaking them. Not that she was fearful of his incessant questions, but because it increased the tremendous wailing coming from the bed.

"Your mother, you mean?" Julian Griffin asked almost hesitantly.

"That is precisely who I mean. Apparently your presence is keeping her from her eternal rest," Sybilla said snidely. Then she closed her eyes and gave a brief sigh at the assault on her ears. It felt as though her hair should be blowing back away from her face, so loud were the furious screams.

"Don't you feel guilty?" She turned to gauge his reaction and found him considering her thoughtfully.

"Your mother's spirit is haunting you," he said flatly.

"Yes." She met his eyes, something inside her daring him to believe her.

"That's quite an odd thing to say, Sybilla."

"It's quite an odd thing to experience, *Julian*," she retorted.

"I can imagine," he said mildly, and turned back to the bed. Sybilla could have fallen from her chair when he raised his arms and waved them at the offending piece of furniture, as if trying to corral an out-of-control horse.

"Hah!" he called out menacingly. "Get from here, you wretched woman, and leave your daughter in peace."

Sybilla snickered lightly at his attempt, but then her

face went slack as the chamber fell instantly silent. She looked to the bed, and there was no haze, no rippled shadow.

"Did it work?" Julian said, his voice full of good humor.

It was obvious when he looked at her that her own face conveyed great surprise.

"Yes," she whispered. "She's gone."

His eyebrows drew together and he regarded her intently. "You were quite serious, weren't you?"

Sybilla could barely nod. "Very," she choked out.

"Sybilla," he began hesitantly. "Sybilla, are you frightened of this room? Of . . . of your mother?"

She stared at him, considering his sincere expression, the pained deliberateness of his words. She could sense no intent to use trickery or maliciousness.

And yet, she could not trust him.

"No," she said. "Of course not." She swallowed. "Haven't you heard? All we Foxe women are witches. We're used to this sort of thing."

He seemed unconvinced by her flippant explanation. "Are you a witch?"

"Perhaps," she answered quietly. "Perhaps I am."

"Would you like to come with me?" he asked, as if the thought had just occurred to him.

"I beg your pardon?"

"For the interviews. Would you care to accompany me?"

Sybilla gave him a sideways look. "Wouldn't that somehow defeat the purpose, if the lady of the manor hovered over the servants as they were asked questions?"

"Would you interfere?" he asked.

"No," she answered honestly. "None of them know anything of import. Save for Graves, but I can tell you now that you could take him a million miles from me, from Fallstowe, and he would still not divulge whatever morsel of information you seek, did it not please him to do so."

"I'll leave you to dress then," Julian said promptly and turned on his heel, speaking to her as he crossed to the door. "We shall meet in the great hall in a half hour." He paused with his hand on the latch and gave her a grin over his shoulder as his eyes quickly swept her form in the chair.

"Unless you need me to stay—for assistance, of course."

Sybilla did not want to return his smile, but it was across her mouth before she could properly fight it back down. "I think I can manage, Lord Griffin."

His smile lingered on his face, just as he lingered at her door for a moment longer, and then he was gone. Leaving her sitting with that damned amused smile pulling at her mouth.

But then the sound, like the slow, building wails of some poor beast in the throes of birth, wound up from within the bed once more.

Julian Griffin had somehow managed to chase Amicia away, but she was back now, and she was apparently extremely unhappy with her eldest daughter.

Sybilla shot from her chair and stomped to her wardrobe, throwing the doors open, and ripping through her gowns.

Although Julian had spoken truthfully when he'd said there were few of the cook's servants he needed to speak with, there were still one or two, and he chose to begin in that fragrant, humid room both for the surety of the staff's presence as they prepared the morning meal for the castle inhabitants, as well as the delicious warmth the cove-ceilinged chamber provided.

He'd hoped to catch them off guard, perhaps surprising them into candor, but he needn't have worried—Sybilla Foxe's appearance in the kitchen threw the entire population into an immediate uproar.

He was surprised at her obvious contrition, and he wondered yet again where the legendary taskmistress of Fallstowe was, for surely this woman could not be she.

"I apologize for disturbing you," Sybilla said in a low voice to the short, red-haired cook. She looked around the room at the owl-eyed servants, who were either staring at her stupidly, frozen in mid-task, or frantically engaged in some little job as if their lives at the castle depended on its completion in the lady's presence. "All of you, please, don't let me keep you from your duties. I'm only accompanying Lord Griffin, as he wishes to speak with some of the staff and is unfamiliar with the warren that is Fallstowe."

"Was yer tea fitting this morn, Madam?" the cook asked sincerely, her eyes searching Sybilla's face. "The bread crisp enough for you? Here now—you've nothing to drink! Hobie! Hobie, get off yer lazy duff and fetch Madam a fresh cup!" The cook's eyes flicked daggers at Julian. "And one for our guest, *His Lordship*, as well." She enunciated his title as if she were pronouncing a foreign phrase for the word *arsehole*, the consonants cracking like whips.

"I don't require anything at the moment, thank you," Julian said.

"As you wish, my lord," the woman said quickly, then dismissed him, turning her attention back to Sybilla. "What does he want from us, Madam? Is he to see us all jailed by the king? What shall we do if you leave? We'll not carry on if—"

Sybilla opened her mouth to answer the woman, but Julian beat her to it. "I'm not here to see any of you jailed. I need only to ask you some questions about your time at Fallstowe, and only a pair of you from the kitchen, as it were." He looked down at the list in his hand and spoke the names, then raised his gaze, waiting for the mentioned persons to step forward.

No one moved, save for the young man who was handing Sybilla a steaming mug wrapped in a soft-looking linen cloth. She thanked him quietly and then blew on the surface of the drink before taking a sip, the only person in the room who was not currently staring daggers into Julian.

He'd not received this kind of loyalty from the men in his outfit while engaged in battle, and Julian was struck again by the thought that Sybilla Foxe's roots ran very deep into the heart of Fallstowe. Regardless, though, he was here to do his duty, and he would not be denied by servants.

He cleared his throat pointedly and repeated the names.

The cook spoke. "The first girl isn't at her duties today. She's come down quite ill, I'm afraid."

Sybilla's concern was immediate. "What is it?"

The cook seemed relieved to focus her attention on her mistress. "I don't right know, Madam. She began feeling poorly yesterday, and this morn when she reported to work, she had such ghastly black rings about her eyes, coughing and retching, I sent her back to her cottage right away."

Sybilla's frown was sincere. "Was she fevered?"

The cook nodded. "I believe so, milady. Gray as could be and wet as a rag."

Julian felt his own grimace. "It sounds like one of the lesser plagues to me. It's gone round London lately. Terribly catching." He met Sybilla's eyes. "You'd do well to keep her from the castle and see if she improves."

"Has anyone else shown symptoms?" Sybilla asked the room at large.

"None else here, milady," the cook offered.

The serving lad, Hobie, spoke. "One of the chamber maids was coughing a fit before the supper last eve. I've not yet seen her today."

"Which girl?" Sybilla asked.

Hobie shrugged. "I forget her name." Then he glanced at Julian. "'Tis the one takin' care of their rooms."

Sybilla set her mug down on the large center worktable and then looked to Julian. "Forgive me, Lord Griffin, but I'm sure you understand that this requires my immediate attention."

"Of course," Julian said. "Can I help you in any way?"

Sybilla seemed as though she'd been about to say something else, but closed her mouth and looked at him oddly for a moment.

"No," she said. "Thank you." Then she turned to address the kitchen at large. "If Lord Griffin asks anything of any of you, I expect your full cooperation. Answer his questions honestly, with no fear of reprisal from me or the king. You are not being tried or charged with anything. You are innocent. But if you perjure yourself to an envoy of the Crown, you will be held accountable. I wish no harm to come to any of you, so please accommodate his requests. Do you understand?"

The crowd mumbled their assent.

Sybilla turned to Julian. "Excuse me, Lord Griffin."

Julian bowed along with the rest of the staff while Sybilla Foxe swept from the room. He wanted to follow her.

Instead he turned back to the glowering mass of red, sweat-dampened faces regarding him with obvious hostility.

"All right, then, let's get on with it."

Sybilla hesitated at the bottom of the long, spiral staircase. She looked down at her gown; she was a wrinkled, dusty mess. Her head pounded, her muscles ached. The supper meal had passed more than an hour ago, and she had only just now come from seeing that the last of the eight servants showing signs of sickness had been ferreted out and were well tucked away from the castle and cared for.

Sybilla longed for Cecily, who, up until a few weeks ago, had been Fallstowe's resident angel and healer, and Sybilla made a mental note to draft a letter right away, seeking the middle Foxe sister's advice.

She was in no way presentable enough to address Julian Griffin, but she felt it her responsibility to inform him of the goings-on of the day, considering that he had foolishly brought his infant with him. And she didn't care one whit what he thought of her appearance, any matter.

She stood at the bottom of the stairs a moment longer, and then turned on her heel and knocked upon the narrow door of the guest chamber at the bottom of the stairs instead.

Informing the nurse would suffice.

The door opened straightaway, and Murrin's pale face appeared in the seam of the door and jamb. The young woman's eyes widened a bit before she gave a quick curtsy.

"Lady Foxe, good evening," she said, surprise making her quiet words bright. "Is there something you require of me?"

"Yes," Sybilla said, wondering for an instant at the silence of the room and the absence of the babe from the nurse's arms. The child must be already abed. "Please inform Lord Griffin that sickness has indeed been found at Fallstowe. The maid who was taking care of your rooms has been touched. She has been removed, however, and a healthy girl will take her place in the morn."

"Oh, mercy," Murrin gasped, looking up and over her shoulder as the door opened wider. "Did you hear, milord?"

Julian Griffin's imposing physique soon filled the doorway, the yellow candlelight from the room spilling out around him and the lumpy bundle he held high on his chest. Julian frowned down at Sybilla, one large hand easily supporting Lucy's backside, the other resting on the door. His topaz eyes swept her from head to toe. Murrin disappeared behind him into the chamber.

Inside, Sybilla grimaced. So much for avoiding him.

"I heard," he said in a low voice. Then his eyes met Sybilla's. "Did it keep you engaged all the day, Lady Foxe?"

Sybilla nodded. "We can only hope for the best now."

"How many?" Julian pressed.

"Eight." She fought the urge to fidget.

"I'd see one or two of them tomorrow, with your permission, of course, to ascertain if the symptoms match what I saw in London."

"Of course. Do as you will." Sybilla paused. "Goodnight, Lord Griffin." She turned to go.

"Wait," he called out, louder than he should have, apparently, for the bundle on his shoulder began to squirm as Sybilla turned quickly back to him. He held up a finger toward her, patting the child's rounded back and making shushing noises.

He turned back to the room and Sybilla could see him carefully hand the baby to the nurse. He murmured something and then turned back to the doorway. As he stepped into the corridor and pulled the door shut behind him, Sybilla saw Murrin's perplexed expression.

"Sorry to keep you," he said in a slightly louder voice. "I'm sure you must be fatigued. But I have something for you."

Sybilla felt her eyebrows rise. "Something for me?"

Julian nodded and gestured toward the stairs. "Would it trouble you very much to come up? It's in my portfolio." When Sybilla hesitated, Julian spoke again. "You're tired, I understand. I'll bring it to you in the morn."

"No," Sybilla heard a voice say, and then in surprise realized that it was her own mouth forming the words. "I'm fine. Lead the way, Lord Griffin."

Julian smiled as he held his hand toward her, and Sybilla placed her fingertips in his palm. He led her lightly to the stairs.

"After you, my lady."

Chapter 12

She did look tired, and Julian felt a pang of guilt as she preceded him up the long flight of stone steps. Perhaps at first glance one would not be able to tell—her posture was still regal, relaxed; her steps light and agile. But Julian had seen it in her face—the worry, the intensity of her gaze mirroring the thoughts in her mind. Her gown was pressed into creases behind her legs, as if she had spent much time squatting, and little tendrils of black hair had escaped from her coif, coiling against her neck where they had dried like discarded snippets of silken thread.

They didn't speak as they made their way to Julian's tower room, the *shush* and scrape of their shoes taking them farther away from the business and worry of Fallstowe proper—far below now, it seemed—with a rhythm that was not unlike the opening beats of a song.

Julian felt a ripple in his stomach. A quickening of his heartbeat, as her scent rolled back on him with each swish of her skirts. He felt his desire for her grow. And he cursed himself for a fool, both in the feeling of want and the idiocy of inviting her to his chamber alone.

He was to deliver her to the king.

He wanted to protect her.

She had ignored lawful summonses and held property not belonging to her.

Fallstowe was her home.

She didn't care for babies.

Julian wanted to hold her in his arms.

At last they reached the landing, and Julian stepped around Sybilla and opened the door to his room. He told himself it was only his wild imaginings that saw her hesitate once more before stepping over the threshold.

"I've not been up here in years," she mused quietly, looking around the room as Julian started to push the door shut. He thought better of it, and pulled it flush with the wall instead.

Her eyes flicked to the conspicuously open door, but she did not comment on it. "Does it suit you?"

He shrugged and gave her a smile as he crossed straight to his trunk, fishing his ring of keys from inside his tunic. "It's rather unique that the chamber so well reflects the weather beyond the walls." He went to one knee before the trunk, moving the candelabra to the floor before handling the lock.

She chuckled softly and walked to the far window, ducking her head to peer through the slats of the shutter. "A kind way of saying that it's cold, I understand. It's why my fa—" She broke off. "Morys often spent many hours up here alone, going over his accounts. He said it was because no one dared climb all those steps to disturb him, and he could feel the air while still being removed from the constant demands of the castle."

Julian pulled the hasp of the lock free and laid the

keys and forged piece aside on the wooden floor with a soft clatter. He glanced at her while he raised the lid.

"Did he know he wasn't your father by birth?"

Sybilla was quiet for several moments, so that Julian did not think she was going to answer. He turned his attention back to the depths of his trunk and reached for the thick leather packet resting inside.

"I don't know," she said quietly. "He certainly behaved as though I was his daughter."

Julian paused, his portfolio resting on his bent knee, and looked at Sybilla. She seemed absorbed by the narrow view through the window.

"She told him nothing of her past, did she?"

Sybilla shook her head, her coif barely moving. "She said he hadn't cared. She let him believe what he thought was true about her birth and her family. He asked her once if she fancied visiting her home, and she told him that there was no place on earth she would rather be than Fallstowe. Perhaps it was the one time in her life that she could be completely honest. He never asked her again."

Julian scooped up his ring of keys from the floor and then took the packet in his hands and gained his feet. He walked to the side of the bed and placed the portfolio on the coverlet, working at the closure. He tried to keep his tone light.

"It's one instance in which you are very much like your mother, isn't it?" he asked. "There is no other place on earth that you would rather be, either."

She turned her head to look at him then, Julian catching the slight movement from the corner of his eye.

"I would forsake heaven itself for it," she said quietly. "Although perhaps for different reasons."

He made no further comment while he opened the

leather flaps and searched through the pockets inside for the small item he sought, while he thought that Amicia Foxe surely did forsake heaven for the mess she had left behind her. Surely she would rot in hell for how and whom she had deceived.

His fingers touched ornate carving, but Julian let the piece rest now that he had located it. He stood aright and let his eyes linger on Sybilla's face. She didn't look away in false meekness, nor take offence at his appraisal. She only looked back at him with her startlingly blue eyes.

"You're in a lot of trouble, Sybilla," he said evenly.

She nodded, no exasperation or sarcasm on her face. "I know."

"I want to help you."

"Unless you are prepared to lie for me, you can't help me." She tilted her head slightly, and Julian felt the floor undulate under his feet, as if she was some sorceress and he was caught in the sights of her spellwork. "Would you lie for me, Julian?"

"No," he said. He blinked, and the floor was once more still beneath his boots. "Still, you can't say with surety that I could not be of some help to you. But you don't trust me yet, I know."

"Why would I trust you?" Sybilla said reasonably. "Before you came to Fallstowe with your army, I knew you not. Not the first thing about you."

Julian decided the time had come. He reached back into his portfolio and withdrew his gift to Sybilla Foxe. Holding it down by his thigh, he began to traverse the room, stopping halfway across the floor before the hearth. She would need the light to see what he'd brought her.

"That's not entirely true," he said. "You knew of the aid I gave to your brother-in-law while he was at court battling for his own home. By association, I aided your sister Alys."

Sybilla cocked her head, conceding the point. "So you are filled with charity. Is that what you are offering me? Am I your next pathetic mission of mercy?"

"There is nothing pathetic about you," Julian said, feeling his frustration take form on his face. "But you will never know what could be if we don't take the truth to the king together. Not to boast, but he does regard my opinions."

"Really?" Sybilla gave him a smile, more than a little crafty and so full of effortless sensuality that Julian felt it stiffen his very spine. "And what exactly is your opinion at this moment, Lord Griffin?"

"That you have been badly played and left alone to suffer the consequences of actions you are not responsible for."

Her smile faded slowly and was replaced by a look of faraway sadness, as if no one could ever reach the place where she was so alone.

"Then I am sorry to inform you that your opinion is erroneous."

He shrugged, then raised his hand, holding out his gift. "Here."

She hesitated, looking at the small oval in his hand from a distance for a moment before coming across the floor to meet him in front of the fire. Her fine brow creased as she raised her hands to take the item. She looked at it, blinking, then raised her face.

"It is a portrait of two children," she said quizzically. "Cecily and I? But I've never seen it before."

Julian shook his head. "It's not you and your sister. It's your mother and Lady Sybil de Lairne."

* * *

Sybilla's gaze dropped back to the small oil rendering in her hand, her chest tightening, her vision going damnably blurred as she tried to focus once more on the two aged and peeling faces in her hands. The frame was thin but ornately carved, and blackened around one side as though it had only just been rescued from a fire. A loud buzzing filled her head, a scraping like a blade across a sharpening stone, and Sybilla had to squeeze her eyes shut very tightly to lessen it.

"Sybil was my mother's middle name," she said faintly, hearing the confusion in her own voice.

"No," Julian said. "It was yet another thing she assumed."

Sybilla looked up at Julian. She saw that he was regarding her intently, studying her face, his gaze almost palpable in the way it brushed her cheeks, her lashes, her hairline.

"Where did you get this?"

"From Sybil de Lairne."

Maman, what does my name mean?

Sybilla? Why, it means little Sybil, of course.

Just like you?

Who else, my sweet?

"Sybilla?"

Julian Griffin's voice startled her out of the memory, which had once been so welcome. Now, like custard that had been left out, the edges were crusty, curdled. The consistency off, runny, quietly and slowly decomposing.

"Sybilla, are you all right?"

"Why did she give this to you?" Sybilla asked, ignoring his inquiry as to her state. She wasn't at all certain how much longer her legs would support her, and she had to know. "And why do you now give it to me?"

"The answer to both questions is to show you the truer nature of the woman you are killing yourself to protect."

"I don't understand," Sybilla said, frowning around the jumble of thoughts, memories, suppositions shoving at each other to form a queue in her mind.

"Lady de Lairne loved your mother very much," Julian said. "They were raised together and Sybil considered Amicia her sister, no matter that your mother was given a servile position in the family."

She was not my sister!

Sybilla winced. "That makes no sense."

"Why? Because of what Amicia did to the family?" Julian took a casual step closer and glanced down at the portrait Sybilla clutched in her hands. Her fingers ached with it. He pointed to the darkened edge of the frame. "See that soot there? Lady de Lairne's mother—the very woman who saved Amicia from certain poverty and orphanhood-sought to burn the portrait after Amicia's betrayal was learned. But Sybil rescued it, refusing to believe such a horrid thing of her sister. Her mother thought better, though."

She was not my sister!

Maman, what does my name mean?

Sybilla? Why, it means little Sybil, of course.

"But . . ." Sybilla's voice trailed off. She was in no state to try to decipher this terrible riddle, and especially not in front of Julian Griffin. She swallowed. Took a deep, hard breath, and stiffened her mouth before looking up at the imposing man still watching her closely. "Thank you, Lord Griffin."

His eyebrows quirked. "Thank you?"

Sybilla sighed shortly. "Thank you *very much*," she said pointedly. She drew the portrait to her chest and then made to step around Julian. "Now if you'll excuse me, I find that I am very tired after the day's events. Good night."

He stopped her with a firm hand about her upper arm. "Sybilla, wait—"

Sybilla threw her arm up with a short, primal scream, startling her own ears, and Julian Griffin was tossed against the stone wall surrounding the fireplace, his boots leaving the floor for an instant.

"*Don't touch me*," she said in a low, cold voice.

He stared at her, not with shock or fear or loathing for what she had just done, but with alarmed concern.

"You're not alone, Sybilla," he said quietly. "I'm right here. You can tell me."

Sybilla walked straight through the open doorway, and her feet seemed to skim the stairs as she descended, the door's slam echoing round and round the spiral corridor as the voice screeched in her ears.

You stupid girl! You stupid, stupid, stupid girl. What have you done?

Chapter 13

It was a new moon, the sky overcast with thick clouds and the layers of blanketing smoke from the campfires, blocking out even the meager light the stars could have offered. She slithered quickly through the blackness between the tents and glowing red coals sheltered by awnings, wrinkling her nose against the smell of smoke, horse, and unclean men. Every score of steps she would stop, ducking between oilcloth shelters as soldiers quickly passed by her, talking in low, troubled voices. Each time, she would squeeze her eyes shut and hold her breath until they were gone, praying that she could control the sobs whirling in her chest, praying that no one would discover her, capture her.

If you are caught, I don't know what they will do to you. Terrible things.

Sybilla was frightened.

But she was a patriot, like her father; and like her mother's friends the de Montforts, although her father had never had much of a kind word to say about the family at Odiham and Kenilworth Castles, and Sybilla didn't know why. It seemed Lord de Montfort and Sybilla's father both wanted the same things for England. United. Lawful. At peace.

She would do her part then. Her father was a leader of men, getting too old for battle, but once this civil unrest was at an end, he would be at Fallstowe nearly all the time. Sybilla could sit outside his tower room on the topmost step while he worked at his ledgers, waiting for him to call for her. She would not have to help tend the little girls, Cee and Alys. She would be busy learning to run Fallstowe. Her father would teach her; he'd promised. And Morys Foxe always kept his promises.

Sybilla dared a peek around the sidewall of the tent. No one was coming, and from here she could clearly see her destination—the largest shelter in the encampment, one of the flaps was pulled back revealing a triangle of lighted interior. She looked both ways again, took a deep breath, and then ran toward the tent.

She ducked inside with a gasp, drawing a startled frown from the man seated inside on a folding chair pulled up to a cot he was using as a makeshift table.

"What in the bloody hell?"

"I know a way through," Sybilla whispered. "I know the unwatched way to Lewes. I can tell you how to go . . ."

Crying, crying, wailing—echoes all through the great stone room.

Her father was dead. Dead at Lewes.

"Oh, what have we done, my daughter?" Amicia whispered bitterly into Sybilla's hair. "What have we done that we are now so betrayed and alone? He'll come for us now, unguarded as we are. All these years, to come to this end."

Sybilla felt as though her body had turned to icy stone. She could not weep, even silently like her mother. She could not comfort Amicia nor be consoled by her. She could not ask how they were betrayed or who was coming for them. She didn't care.

It was her fault. Morys Foxe was dead and it was somehow entirely her fault.

* * *

Sybilla's eyes snapped open, finally shaking loose the grip of the nightmare, but she made not a sound in her bed.

She was not alone in her chamber.

Sybilla heard the rattle-scrape again, coming from her table beneath the bank of windows, and she strained her eyes to try to make out the wooden surface, awash with the glow of the moon beyond the glass. She thought she saw a glimmer, and then something crashed to the floor.

Her eyes narrowed. She threw the coverlets aside and soundlessly swung her legs over the edge of the mattress, the cold air patrolling the floor like sentries swirling around her bare ankles, investigating her. On the floor just beyond the bedpost, Sybilla could make out the edge of something rounded. With a scrape so quiet she might have mistaken it for her own breath, it started to slip out of sight toward the foot of the bed.

Sybilla's brows lowered. "I think not, Mother," she said, and slid off the bed. In three steps she was around the piece of massive furniture, staring down at the miniature portrait Julian Griffin had given her hours ago.

It was stuck against the edge of the thick rug, wiggling in short jerks toward the hearth, where small flames occasionally perked. The shadow covering the center of the rug was dense, inky, rippled around the edge.

Sybilla leaned down and swiped up the miniature with one hand, ready for the ear-splitting wail that followed her action.

"No!" Sybilla shouted. "It's mine! He gave it to me and you can't have it!"

The shadow seemed to boil for an instant and then began to roll awkwardly toward her, clumsily gobbling up the space between them. Sybilla turned her back to it and walked to her table, determined to ignore it, even when the mumblings started in her ear.

When Sybilla refused to acknowledge the garbled warnings, the mumbles deteriorated into the screams once more, and Sybilla sat down in her chair, pulling her feet beneath her and pressing her wrists to her ears, her right hand still clutching the portrait of two girls little more than babies.

In a moment though, the screeching ceased, and it was as if the voice had squeezed beneath Sybilla's wrist to whisper in her ear.

I gave you everything! I gave you Fallstowe! And you are going to hand it over so easily, so prettily, so nicely! Can you not trust me?

Sybilla dropped her hands to curl together between her chest and her drawn-up knees, the portrait resting over her heart. It was pointless to try to block her out.

She stared at the moon-drenched curtain wall in the bailey beyond her window. "Why?" she whispered. "Why, Mother?"

The voice stopped. The chamber fell silent.

"Why would you name me after a woman you hated so? I only did everything you ever asked of me. Have I not kept my promise?"

There was no answer, still.

Sybilla unfolded her hands and dropped her face into them. She had obeyed her mother in everything. Listened intently, performed the duties charged to her. She had kept Amicia's dreadful secrets, carried her burdens, looked after her other children, retained possession of the castle. All at the expense of her own soul. She could call no one friend save her two sisters and old Graves. She was wanted by the Crown, and Sybilla knew now that she could not win that trial. Even the Foxe Ring had failed her.

And still her mother's ghost drove her like a dumb beast.

Maman, what does my name mean?

Why, it means little Sybil, of course.

Sybil de Lairne had loved Amicia like a sister. The family had thought enough of the child to have her portrait made with their blood daughter. She had been raised with the manners and lessons of the nobility. And still, Amicia had hated Sybil de Lairne enough to try to destroy the entire family.

Maman, what does my name mean?

Why, it means little Sybil, of course.

She was not my sister!

Sybilla raised her face from her hands. "After all I have done," she whispered aloud, wonderingly. "After all you have made me do, all I have forsaken for you. How could you hate me so when I was only a baby?"

Sybilla felt a hot track on her cheek and she reached up with a frown. Wet. She was crying.

She thought of sheltered, perfect Cecily. Indulged, wild Alys. And then there had been Sybilla. Older. Reserved. Cool. Yearning more for her father's attention than that of her busy mother. More lessons for her. More responsibilities. More discipline, in the name of being the oldest, an example. Her sisters had never lacked for their mother's love.

Sybilla thought now that she had never had it.

And now she was alone, crying unlike she had since she was a very young girl, and haunted by a woman who held her in the grip of a deathbed promise. Alone, and unwanted by anyone who didn't have something to gain from her. Power, money, notoriety, sex. Not one person wanted her just because of her.

Julian Griffin does, a voice in her mind said to her. And that voice sounded like Sybilla's own, only younger, gentler, with something resembling compassion.

Julian wants you, and he can make her *go.*

The moonlight seemed to echo the words with its glow across her table, the lead hatching of the panes growing thick and long, like ancient standing stones at some forgotten ruin.

Go to him. Go to him. Go to him . . .

"Yes," Sybilla sobbed, nodding, and uncurling from her chair. "Yes," she repeated as she stumbled across the rug toward the door, the portrait still in her hand but forgotten now.

She couldn't stop long enough to don a robe or her slippers, crashing into her chamber door, struggling with the latch while her shoulders shook and she wept. She did not care about the icy air of Fallstowe in the dead of night as she half ran toward the rear staircase, weaving around corners, reaching out a hand to catch herself against a stone wall.

At last the steps were in sight, and Sybilla threw her body at them, clutching at the railing and half dragging herself up the long spiral, stumbling, crawling, then running as best she could until her lungs could no longer keep up and she collapsed at the top of the flight. It was so cold, like being out of doors in a snowstorm. Her eyes were blinded by tears when she stretched out her arm to lay her shaking palm against the wood of Julian Griffin's door. It slid down the old, oiled wood, her fingernails leaving little soundless grooves.

But he heard them any matter. Before she could try to draw another choked breath into her convulsing body,

Julian's door swung open with a frigid blast of air up the stairwell behind her.

She looked up and could see only the burst of twinkling light that was his fire filtered through her tears, and then his shadowy outline.

"Sybilla," he said in a low, alarmed voice. And then in the next instant, he was crouched at her side, his arms strong beneath her back and knees, lifting her from the cold, stone step and close against his bare chest, so warm and solid.

Her arms went around his neck as he turned back through the doorway and Sybilla sobbed into his shoulder as he kicked the door closed behind them both, leaving the tiny portrait lying forgotten on the stairs.

She clung to him like someone rescued from a rushing, flooded river, her body seeming frail and slight, limp, and so cold. And she was crying, pressing her damp face into his shoulder, her labored inhalations pulling at his skin.

Julian did not hesitate—nay, he did not even think twice about it—when he took her to his bed, kneeling upon it carefully and then twisting to lay Sybilla down. Her arms did not relent and so he stretched out beside her, still holding her close against him. He pressed one palm between her shoulder blades; the other cradled her head, stroking her hair.

This was unlike any Sybilla Foxe he had heard tales of. Unlike any Sybilla Foxe he had seen during his time at Fallstowe. Here was no ice-cold matriarch, no notorious demigoddess, no traitorous villain. This was a woman devastated, lost, so defenseless and defeated that she could not hold her head aright. Julian could almost feel the pain seeping out of her chest in the area of her heart and leeching into his flesh. He could almost hear the rending sound that gentle organ was making behind its thick fortress.

He held her closer.

"Shh," he whispered against her hair, and then pressed his mouth there at the crown of her head. She smelled of sunshine on a winter's day, like a steamy exhalation around a melancholy smile. Her hair was soft and clouded like silk, the vague scent of her particular soap lingering there like a nosegay of dried flowers forgotten in the snow. "Shh. Sybilla, it's all right."

"She hated me," she choked out against his chest, her words hot and wet with tears and emotion. "My own mother hated me."

Julian had no response.

It was several moments before her sobbing quieted to the occasional hiccough. "You don't understand," she said in a raspy whisper, and Julian imagined that her throat must be raw. "She named me after . . . *her.* After . . . *Sybil.*" She pulled away slightly to look up into Julian's face, and he was struck breathless at the beauty of her, the raw emotion spread across her face. Her eyelids were pink, the lashes black and spiky, like tiny weapons. Her nose and cheeks flushed atop her ivory skin.

"She denied her as her sister," Sybilla clarified. "She spoke of her so . . . so coldly. As if she was a stranger. Only she never told me her name. But now I know—she named me after the woman she considered an enemy."

Julian frowned. "But she let you assume you were named after her, and she never revealed that Sybil was not part of her given name. Surely you must take that as some sign of her consideration for you."

Sybilla put her cheek against his chest once more, gently this time though, without the desperation of before. He could no longer see her face, and Julian didn't like it.

"It was a little joke to her, I think," Sybilla said in a low voice, a dark voice. "It makes sense now. She took the name Sybil out of practicality, to lend authenticity to her stolen identity as a lady. She took a family name, that of a woman who had everything my mother wanted—money, status, privilege. Those things she did eventually gain. Then when I was born, she gave that name to me."

"I fail to see the humor in that particular joke," Julian hedged.

"I was a reminder of her past, the time before she was a lady. Morys Foxe would be my father, though, legitimize my birth in a way that no one could go back in time and do for her, no matter how she schemed, whom she married. So I was to be known as a lady, but Mother knew the truth all along—I was no lady. I was just like her. And she gave me this name to remind her of it every day."

Julian was silently rocked by such an insight, and infuriated at this new information about Amicia Foxe. Infuriated at himself for introducing this new pain to her.

"It means nothing," he said, pulling her minutely closer for emphasis. "You are who you are. She could not change it then, and she cannot change it now." He hesitated for a moment, and then said, "For what it's worth, Sybil de Lairne seemed a lovely, lovely woman."

"Of course she is," Sybilla huffed. "How could she be anything but, to have saved a memento of a woman so quietly wretched and not to have sought her out through the king? She could have destroyed my mother at any time. My mother likely knew that."

"Sybil asked me if I had met you," Julian said, stroking Sybilla's back now. "Of course I hadn't yet, but even she had heard the tales of your boldness and success. We compared stories." He felt a smile come to his mouth. Was this a dream? Was he truly comforting Sybilla Foxe in his arms? In his bed?

Her voice was uncharacteristically hesitant. "Was she appalled?"

Julian frowned, looking down at the curve of her cheek, the crescent of her ear—all of her that he could see. "Appalled? No. She was quite pleased and intrigued, I daresay."

"I would think it to be an embarrassment to her."

Julian took hold of her shoulder then, and held her slightly away from him so that he could look into her eyes. "How could you say such a thing? Sybilla, how could you think yourself to be an embarrassment to anyone?"

Her eyes searched his hungrily, helplessly, and it was in that instant that Julian realized how frightened Sybilla Foxe actually was. How frightened she had likely been for so long, and how alone.

"You," he said slowly, emphatically, "are a *legend*. You are amazing. Tremendous. Brave. Strong." He paused, swallowed. "I would be *honored* to even call you my *friend*, to proclaim that I *know* you. I would shout it from the very top of Westminster, and I would be the most envied man in England. In the *world*."

Julian was surprised when her chin flinched, her eyes filled with tears again. He had not wanted her to cry.

"Oh, but wait," he said quickly, pulling a disappointed face. "There is one person you have likely embarrassed deeply."

Her brow crinkled into a frown, but her eyes held their wetness at the brim without spilling over. "Who?"

He leaned his face close so that the tip of his nose

barely touched hers. "The king, I'm afraid. I've seen him face a score of wild rebels alone in a foreign desert, and yet he can't bring one tiny woman to heel in his own country. Quite humiliating for such a manly monarch, wouldn't you agree?"

Then Sybilla Foxe actually giggled. And Julian felt such relief, even as her mirth caused a rogue tear to roll down her cheek.

"I'm not a tiny woman," she objected.

"Oh, you give the impression that you are quite intimidating," Julian said. "But there's really almost nothing to you. Quite small, actually."

She gave a short gasp of outrage.

"No, really, see?" He ran the back of his fingers down her face. "This jawline—delicate." Down her throat and over her bare shoulder, where he encircled her bicep. "Your arms, strong, but slight." Down to the curve of her waist, stopping just shy of the crest of her hip. "Your waist, fragile. Vulnerable. Your legs, so shapely, and yet you come only to my shoulder when you stand." He was whispering now. "I daren't go on."

"Why?" she whispered back, and he could see a familiar spark in her deep and glistening eyes now. A glimmer of the Sybilla he had known since coming to Fallstowe.

"Because I want to so very much," he choked, and skimmed his hand back up her side and to her arm, where he let the pads of his fingers swirl against the perfect satin that was her skin. "And I don't wish to become a regret to you, Sybilla."

Her gaze never wavered from his as her palms came to the sides of his face. Slowly, keeping him pinned with the ethereal blue of her eyes, she moved her head toward his.

And then her lashes fluttered against her cheeks as she slid her open mouth onto his lips.

Julian's eyes were open when Sybilla pulled away from his mouth. She looked up at him, their eyes little more than a hand's-breadth apart, and she knew her desire had to be washed plainly over her face.

"Holy God, woman," he rasped. "Sybilla, you must know, I cannot in good conscience take you when you have been so recently distraught." The words seemed to dangle between them in the humid chill of the room.

"But?" Sybilla dared, looking at his mouth, unable now to look away from it, hungering for the taste of him on her tongue once more.

"But I am at your mercy," he confessed, and even as he spoke he drew her even nearer to him, until her flesh was pressed against him, into him. "I beg you, have pity on me."

His plea seemed anything but helpless, the fire in his amber eyes warming the skin of her face, and Sybilla could not slow her heartbeat. She didn't want to. And she knew fully that it was not Julian Griffin who was at anyone's mercy now.

"Pity you?" she said, unable to stop herself from reaching out her tongue and tasting him once more, just the slightest flick. "Julian—oh, Julian—how could I pity you when I can't stop thinking of the things I want you to do to my body right now?"

She felt his sharp intake of breath before he said, "If they are even a shade of the things I want to do to your body, perhaps you should have pity on yourself."

And then he rolled over on top of her, covering her chilled body with his own, pressing her head back into the mattress as his mouth descended on hers. Sybilla was lost in the hunger his kiss stirred in her, a deep, primitive want unlike any she had ever felt for a man before. It was vulnerable, frightening, consuming, and because she was so afraid of this cavernous depth of passion, she entered headlong into it, meeting it on the battlefield of Julian Griffin's bed.

"Love me now, Julian," she demanded in a mumble against his mouth when he drew away for a gasp of air. His right hand found her breast, stroked it too gently, making her squirm into him.

"Now?" he said in a taunting whisper. "Oh no, my lady. Not yet. Not for a while." He kissed her hard, with a closed mouth, and only for an instant before drawing away completely and getting up from the bed.

Sybilla had no time to voice her outrage at his departure before he had seized her ankles and dragged her to the edge of the bed. Then he leaned over and lifted her from the mattress, throwing her over his shoulder. She gave a shrieking laugh.

"Julian! What are you doing?" His body turned with a jerk into a semicircle and then she was flying back through the air, bouncing as she landed on the sheet of the mattress, the coverlet still in his hand billowing up from the bed.

"What few clothes you are wearing will be off of you in a moment, and I don't wish for you to catch cold." His grin was pure sin and Sybilla caught her lower lip in her teeth and bit down as she watched him. He looked so delicious, she wanted to sink her teeth into his chest.

"My clothes?" she teased as he crawled onto the bed toward her. "Why, whatever for?"

"Because . . ." He reached her, pulling the coverlet up to their shoulders and then sliding his hand down her stomach. Down, down . . . He kissed her lightly. "I'm going to make love to you." He kissed her again, and his hand slid into the junction of her legs. He pulled up firmly. "And make love to you." Again he kissed her, and then he spoke against her mouth while he dragged up the hem of her thin gown to touch her bare skin. "And make it, and make it, and make it."

Sybilla cried out in the back of her throat as he tortured her, and then her hands found his skin, and she sought to absorb him with her palms against his chest, his broad, sculpted shoulders. He was so warm, golden, as if he radiated sunshine, his muscles rounded and hard, the goodness of his body dripping like honey onto her skin.

She could barely hold on to her peak as he drove her, and so she ran her own hand down his front, into the loosened waistband of his pant, opening it until she had him firmly in her grip. The conflicting sensations of velvety softness and iron-hard length were heady, and when Julian Griffin gave voice to his own moan, Sybilla took her chance.

"Love me now," she demanded against his jaw, and tightened her fingers for emphasis before sliding her palm against him. "Now, Julian."

Then his hand was gone from between her legs, and in a moment the fingers of his right hand gripped her cheeks. He leaned close to her face, staring into her eyes. Her knees were open beneath the heavy coverlet, her gown around her waist.

"No," he growled. His fingers tightened as he shifted his hips and she felt the length of him high up on her thigh, so close. "You may be used to getting your way, Sybilla Foxe, but not here, not with me. You asked for this, and I will oblige you, lady, but I will do to you what I please, when I want to do it." He moved his hips again, and the tip of him touched her.

He spoke against her lips, puckered in his grip. "Do you understand me?" And then he was almost in her.

Sybilla let go then, going over the edge, her body grasping for him, her hips arching as she cried, "Yes, Julian."

And when she was back from her journey over the edge of the world, his touch gentled. He moved over her, stroking her face, kissing her lips so softly, licking her, murmuring his praise. Then he slid into her aching flesh, still pulsing around him, and he began to push her toward oblivion again.

And again.

And again.

Neither one of them saw his chamber door open slightly in the small hours of dawn. They didn't see the still shadow that was the brief witness to their continued passion. And they did not see the door shut again slowly, silently.

Chapter 14

Julian knew he was smiling before his eyes even opened. And he also knew that Sybilla Foxe would not be next to him.

He turned his head on the pillow and opened his eyes. He was alone in his bed, but he could still smell the scent of her on the linens where she'd lain. Where she'd loved him, and let him love her until nearly dawn. He sighed and looked back to the beamed ceiling.

This was a dangerous game, for both of them. He'd never wanted a woman more in his life, and now that he'd had Sybilla Foxe, he felt that his hunger had grown rather than been satisfied. He wanted her at his disposal, wanted access to her thoughts, her feelings, the innermost sanctum of her soul where the true woman dwelt, forgetting the tales and the rumors and the vivid portrait painted by gossip and history.

But he was here on a mission for his king, his friend, and upon the successful dispatch of his duties, Julian would be rewarded with the one thing that Sybilla Foxe held most dear—what she was willing to sacrifice heaven for: Fallstowe.

And what would Edward think, should he discover that Julian had become intimate with the accused? Julian knew one of the main reasons Edward had selected him for the mission was the assumption that Julian would not be swayed by the Foxe matriarch's legendary wiles. He'd just lost Cateline four months ago; he had an infant daughter to think of. He would not risk returning a failure and jeopardizing his and Lucy's future.

Would he?

No. No, if he returned a failure, they all lost: Edward would withdraw his offer of Fallstowe and likely turn Julian out, and Sybilla would lose her home any matter. The monarch was out for blood now, and he would not be denied any longer. But . . .

Could there be a future at Fallstowe for Julian, Lucy, and Sybilla? Could Sybilla trust him enough to let him be her witness to the king, to lay bare all the information the king sought, and then counter the king for the castle and the lady? Perhaps if he told her that Fallstowe would fall to him. Perhaps she would see that there was a chance to retain her home.

But then Julian would never know. He would never know if she had stayed only for Fallstowe.

Does it matter? he asked himself angrily. You cannot keep it from her any longer, especially now. If she chooses Fallstowe, she also chooses you. Sybilla is not Cateline. You no longer need a woman to legitimize you. Instead of marriage saving you, you would be saving Sybilla Foxe.

But there was Lucy to think of. Sybilla Foxe would become his daughter's mother, and Sybilla had been very forthright in her feelings toward offspring. Julian would not have his daughter subjected to the disinterest of an ambivalent maternal figure. Lucy needed love. She

deserved to be loved, thoroughly, madly, completely, for
who she was.

So did Sybilla Foxe.

Julian sighed again and then threw the covers off his
body, sitting up and swinging his legs over the side of the
bed with a groan. He felt muscles he hadn't remembered he possessed. One half of the louvered shutter
on the window across the room stood open, and Julian
saw the bright countryside beyond.

It was a new day. A new life, perhaps.

He got up and washed and dressed quickly, making
his way down the long spiral stairs and through the
corridors to the great hall. Murrin was sitting at one of
the common tables with Lucy, and they seemed to be in
easy conversation with one of the maids, a woman
standing between the tables with a bucket in her hand,
her hair wrapped in a banded coif. When the servant saw
Julian approaching, she bobbed a curtsy and quickly
took her leave.

"Good morning, darling," Julian said, and Lucy's little
capped head immediately swiveled to the sound of his
voice, a happy squeal coming from her. She pushed at
the table top with her heels as if trying to stand, her little
fists pumping the air. Julian took her from the table,
swooping her up in the air before bringing her back to
sit high on his arm.

Then Julian looked at the nursemaid, who had stood
when he took charge of his daughter. "Good morning,
Murrin. How did she do last night?" he asked, noting the
woman's pale face and shadowed eyes.

"Good morn, milord. About the same as before, I'm
afraid," the woman answered, trying to stifle a yawn. "I
almost expected you again last night. 'Tis well that you
weren't awakened by her cries."

Julian felt a pang of guilt. He couldn't very well confess that he'd actually gotten very little sleep because he had been entertaining Lady Foxe in his bedchamber.

"It's most likely that she's getting used to the strange surroundings," Julian said mildly, smiling into Lucy's face as she smacked at his cheek. "I'm certain she will become accustomed to it right away." He looked back to Murrin and noticed the woman's pinched brow and flushed cheeks. "Are you feeling unwell, Murrin?"

"I'm fine, milord," the woman said, her eyes darting to the side. "Only weary. I'll have me a good rest when Lady Lucy takes her morning lie-down."

"Very good," Julian said, but he continued to look at the nurse closely. "You will tell me, though, if you begin to feel ill. A sickness is making the rounds through Fallstowe's staff, and we can't have Lucy catching it. I'd have to send you back to London."

"Oh!" Murrin gasped, her face slack. "Lord Griffin!"

"It would only be a precaution," Julian assured her. "The king's doctors would have you well within a fortnight. I don't know what resources Lady Foxe has at her disposal here, and I would not tax her already burdened hospitality. You would return, of course, as soon as you were recovered. I don't know what Lucy and I would do without you."

"I understand, milord," Murrin said stiffly, lifting her chin as if already willing herself against illness.

"And now, Lady Lucy, will you do me the honor of accompanying me through Fallstowe in search of the lady of the keep?" He looked from the baby to the nurse. "She said yes," he said in a mock whisper. At Murrin's smile, Julian turned toward the main aisle. "I'll have her returned when she is hungry. Seek your own rest, Murrin."

"Yes, milord."

He was nearly to the short flight of steps leading to the main doors when old Graves seemed to materialize out of the shadows.

"Can I be of assistance, Lord Griffin?"

"Good morning, Graves," Julian said. "I still need to speak with you privately about the matter I've brought in trust from the king, old chap, but it can wait until later. Actually, now I'm looking for Lady Sybilla. Do you know where she can be found?"

Graves cocked one sparse eyebrow. "Isn't that my job, my lord?"

"Yes." Julian waited, and the man simply stood there, staring at him like a dusty old statue. "Graves?"

He blinked solicitously. "Yes, Lord Griffin?"

"I want you to tell me where Lady Sybilla is."

The old man's eyes narrowed. "You didn't hear my knock this morning, did you, my lord?"

Julian frowned and, against his will, swallowed. "No, I must not have." Had the corpse come to his chamber this morning? Had he encountered his mistress there?

"Did you also not hear me inform Madam that there has been more sickness discovered in the castle and that she was needed right away?"

Hell. Bloody hell. "No. I didn't."

"Perhaps a lack of trousers affects my lord's hearing?"

Lucy obviously took offense. "Bah!" she said loudly at Graves, and then ducked her face against Julian's shoulder.

"Is that so, Lady Lucy?" Graves asked with interest.

Julian had had enough of the servant's evasiveness. "I'll return Lucy to her nurse and go to her at quarantine."

Graves frowned. "Are you feeling ill, my lord?"

"No, Graves, I'm quite fine. I only wish to see if I might aid Lady Sybilla."

"Then my lordship would be better off to seek Madam's solar."

"Is that where she is?" Julian nearly shouted.

Graves sniffed. "Where else would she be this time of the morning?"

Julian growled at the steward and turned on his heel to head back through the hall. Murrin was already gone from the table, and so he and Lucy had no audience save Graves when they ducked through the hidden door behind Sybilla's table.

"Let this be a lesson to you, my darling," Julian murmured as he stepped into the corridor. "That dusty old man? The perfect example of loyalty gone very awry."

Sybilla was tired.

She sat in one corner of an upholstered couch, her fist against her temple as she perused the open ledger on her lap that chronicled the roster of Fallstowe's staff, food stores that had been consumed, and deliveries of goods, trying to make sense of the sickness that was rapidly eating its way through the castle.

Four more this morn. It could be nothing. It could be the plague that Julian had mentioned seeing in London. Sybilla had instituted the precaution of ordering the soldiers to sequester themselves, though. They could not very well defend themselves if all of Fallstowe's fighting men were abed with disease.

She sighed and closed her dusty-feeling eyes. Was it in her mind to defend herself still? Against whom—the king or Julian Griffin?

He had saved her last night, from her own bed, her own horrible thoughts, and for a few short hours, from her own life. Her body, fatigued though it was, still felt the electrifying charge of his lovemaking. It was as if she had been touched by lightning and her skin still crawled with rolling white light.

She'd had him now. It was over. She should feel satisfied and ready to move on with a plan to extricate herself from this most dire situation. The only problem was that she had no plan now. Sharing her body with Julian Griffin seemed to have exploded any sense of autonomy she had ever possessed. She found herself wondering what he would do, what he would tell the king. Although he'd said he wouldn't lie for her, he had promised to stand by her, help her.

How? The truth he had was devastating, and would only ensure the king's judgment upon her. And what Sybilla knew, she had promised to never tell.

If she told now, she would be like *her*. Like Amicia.

Sybilla had not been very surprised that Graves had managed to locate her in the early morning hours in the tower room. And she had not been surprised when he had failed to make any mention whatsoever of her presence in Julian Griffin's bed. Graves was very familiar with Sybilla's encounters with the men she chose. And he was also very familiar with her habit of singularity.

Graves knew that Sybilla would not be revisiting a night of passion with the king's envoy. There was no need to mention it, and certainly no need to chastise her over consorting with the enemy.

Is he your enemy? she asked herself suddenly. *Could he not become your ally?*

Before she could explore that mad notion further, a swift rap sounded on the solar door. She had no time to bid her visitor enter before the door opened and Julian Griffin stepped into the room, his infant in his arms.

She tried not to notice the skipping of her heart.

"Good morning," he said with a slow smile, pushing the door only partly closed behind him.

Sybilla closed the ledger in her lap and set it on the far side of the table, then reached for her cup of tea—ice-cold now, but it gave her hands a task.

"Good morning. Lady Lucy," she said, acknowledging the child before she took a sip.

"I had the pleasure of encountering Graves in the great hall. He told me that there have been more victims to sickness." He walked to the far end of the couch and took a seat, setting the child on one thigh. The baby weaved drunkenly on his leg, staring at her interestedly.

Sybilla returned her cup to the table. "Yes. Many more and I shall have to quarantine the entire castle." She met his eyes directly for the first time, and was unsettled by the intimate way his gaze regarded her.

"Why didn't you wake me?" he asked. "I could have helped you."

"It's not your responsibility," Sybilla said coolly.

Julian frowned. "That's an odd thing to say after last night."

Sybilla laughed, but there was no humor in it. "Why? We shared a bed together once. Now you somehow have a role in the keeping of my home? My home for the time being, any matter."

"I thought perhaps we might consider each other friends now."

"Lord Griffin"—Sybilla sighed and mustered all of her aloofness—"thank you for your comfort last night. I apologize for my state—I was under a great deal of duress from the information you presented me with yesterday. Your company helped to distract me from my own darkness, and I do appreciate it. I hope, though, that you don't take it as a sign that we are now fast allies."

"Then what are we, Sybilla?" Julian asked, and moved Lucy to sit between them on the couch when she squirmed.

"I don't know." She looked down at the child, whose little face rested against the plush upholstery, turned up toward Sybilla, regarding her with wide eyes. Sybilla had the urge to reach out and run a finger over the curve of that soft-looking cheek. "You must resemble your mother, Lady Lucy," she said softly.

"She does," Julian admitted.

The child suddenly lunged toward Sybilla with a little squeal, toppling halfway onto Sybilla's leg. She managed to catch the baby before she rolled off the couch onto the floor. The child's middle was plump and firm, and much more substantial than she'd seemed when swaying atop Julian Griffin's arm. Sybilla had caught Lucy under the arms, and since Julian did not reach for her right away, Sybilla pulled the baby onto her own lap and held her slightly away. She wasn't certain how to proceed.

"That's a lovely vision," Julian said with a stupid smile.

Sybilla frowned at him. "You can have her back at any moment."

"No, I think I rather enjoy watching the two of you."

Lucy discovered the string of pearls around Sybilla's wrist and began hinging her fingers back and forth over the small round jewels. A little coo of amazement came from her, and Sybilla was struck by the sweetness of it.

"Do you fancy jewels?" she asked.

"Pah-pah-pah-pah," Lucy replied.

Julian laughed. "Another thing she inherited from her mother, I'm afraid."

Sybilla could not help the slight, bemused smile that came to her mouth as she watched the baby's continued delight with the bracelet. She suddenly pulled the child against her stomach and brought both her hands together around the child, slipping the pearls from her arm. She looped them back on themselves, making a double strand, and then carefully fit Lucy's chubby left hand through the bracelet.

"There you are, then," she said. "You may have them."

Lucy squealed shrilly and then began jerking at the costly piece. "Pah! Pah-pah-pah!"

Julian seemed quite surprised. "That's very kind of you, Sybilla, but I think that perhaps an item of such value is a bit of a flamboyant toy for a child."

"They were my mother's," Sybilla said, continuing despite herself to be enchanted by the baby's every movement with the bracelet. "Lucy fancies them. I find suddenly that I do not." She looked at Julian. "You gave me a gift. I have nothing to give you. So this will have to do, I'm afraid."

"Thank you," Julian said, and his amber eyes seemed ablaze with something Sybilla could not name. "Sybilla, what if we were to marry?"

Her breathing stopped. "Marry?" she repeated, as if she had never heard the term before. "Each other, you mean?"

Julian laughed. "Yes, each other. Perhaps we could convince Edward—"

"That because I married someone with a title that he would allow me to keep Fallstowe? That's unlikely, I think."

"Not impossible, though," Julian said mildly.

"I do doubt the king would allow me to marry anyone at all of the nobility once you expose what you have discovered about my mother," she said. "And even if he did, there is very little likelihood that he would allow me to retain Fallstowe. So what then? You take me from my home to wherever it is you live in London? To host feasts and shop at the fairs?"

He stared at her for a long time. "Would that be so terrible a life?"

"As opposed to prison or death?" she asked. "I suppose not, but one never knows. We are hardly familiar with each other."

She thought he might be offended by her remark, but he laughed instead. "The time for you to shoulder all has come to an end, whether you want to admit it or not. You will need someone to take care of you."

"I can take care of myself," Sybilla argued awkwardly, bringing her attention back to the baby. She noticed that her knees had begun to bounce the child gently without her permission.

"I don't think so," Julian said. "Not anymore. And certainly not like I could take care of you."

The way he said it, so confidently, so intimately, made Sybilla's stomach flutter, and she felt like a silly fool for it. Then when he slid down the seat toward her, laying his arm across the back of the couch behind her, making a little nook for her and the child on her lap, her arms broke out in gooseflesh.

"Come to my room again tonight, and let me convince you."

Warning bells went off in Sybilla's mind. "I don't think that's possible," she said stiffly. "Haven't you heard? I don't carry on relationships. You may take your child now, please."

When he didn't move, she looked up into his face reluctantly. He was not smiling, only staring intently at her.

She swallowed. "Don't pursue me, Julian. I am poison."

He shook his head only slightly, moving his face nearer

hers. "I don't think so," he repeated in a whisper, and then he kissed her softly, his lips lingering against hers.

"Bah!" Lucy shouted, seemingly delighted, and slapped her father's cheek soundly.

Sybilla could not help her chirp of laughter. "Well said, Lady Lucy. Appalling behavior, I agree."

"Beggin' your pardon, milady, milord," a voice said, startling Sybilla's attention to the door where Murrin stood, her face ashen, dramatic, black circles beneath her eyes. "I don't mean to interrupt, but Lord Griffin bade me tell him right away if I was feeling poorly."

Julian stood up instantly. "What is it, Murrin?"

Sybilla saw the girl force a swallow from across the room. Her eyes were wide, wild. "I think I've fallen in with the sickness, milord," she said weakly. "I've already packed my things for London."

Chapter 15

It did not take long for Julian to see Murrin off. Sybilla had, at first, insisted that the nurse stay on in Fallstowe's makeshift sanatorium with the rest of the sick victims, but in the end she relented to Julian's cautious wishes.

That in itself gave him hope.

Even Murrin had obviously surrendered to the notion that she would be better off away from Lucy while she recovered from whatever was going around, citing that if she stayed on at the castle, Lucy would pine for her—and for the milk she provided. And so Sybilla had efficiently and without argument arranged for transport and guards for the nursemaid's journey to London, and then spent the remainder of the day securing a source of fresh, rich sheep's milk for Lucy.

"It is the best thing for her," Sybilla had informed Julian crisply. "My mother did not nurse me, and yet I thrived as a child."

Julian had wanted to ask if Amicia's lack of maternal attention was due to a physical impediment or otherwise, but in the end decided against it. It didn't matter at this point. And yet he did wonder how her other two daughters could have such devotion to the same mother they shared with Sybilla.

Sybilla had furthermore procured one of her own lady's maids—a woman who had raised four children who were now of age to work outside of the cottage—to tend Lucy, and installed her in the little chamber at the bottom of the stairs.

It bothered him more and more, the rumors of Sybilla Foxe's nature: vicious, heartless, brazen, cold. Yes, she did give that impression superficially. And perhaps her thought processes were more logical and analytical than most females, but if anyone dared to know the woman more than superficially, they could not help but see her compassion, her attention to detail, her devotion, her deep sense of responsibility to all in her care.

Sybilla Foxe was not content to ride her wave of privilege and notoriety. She did not give a bloody damn what other people thought of her. She did things as she saw fit, to the benefit of those who depended on her—nothing less would do. She did not want to be taken care of, and Julian thought the reason for that was because she had never been taken care of.

Groomed, perhaps. Girded. Tempered for battle. But never cared for, looked after, treasured, loved. Maybe Morys Foxe had loved the girl—his firstborn who was, perhaps unbeknownst to him, not of his issue. But he was long dead. Had been gone for so long that whatever gentleness or respite he had offered Sybilla was buried and forgotten, like the accounts he'd examined in the little tower room years and years ago. An old, worthless memory.

That was not entirely true, though, he argued with

himself. Sybilla's sisters loved her. Old Graves worshipped her. All of Fallstowe adored and respected and were bent on protecting her—the people and the edifice itself, it seemed. Of all the staff he had spoken to, from the kitchen to the stables to the old priest, not a cross word had been uttered. Nothing that could be considered anything less than praise.

So, more than whatever warped sense of honor she felt she owed the despicable woman who birthed her, Julian suspected that Sybilla fought as hard as she had, evaded him more craftily than any thief, in order to hold on to the one thing that brought her true, unconditional love: Fallstowe. It was her child, her lover, her beginning and end, the legacy she would leave behind like gold dust on the pages of the tomes of history yet to be written.

He shook himself from such romantic musings when Lucy took the skin she had been drinking from and threw it to the floor with a clatter. He chuckled down at her and set her up on his shoulder.

"Sorry about that, darling," he said, standing up from where he'd been sitting on the edge of the mattress, and bouncing on his feet as he patted her back. "Preoccupied."

She cooed her forgiveness, her fist finding her mouth, and she laid her head down on his shoulder. Julian hummed a meandering tune while he paced his chamber.

Perhaps he had mentioned the idea of marriage between them too soon—he hadn't planned on bringing it up, and had in fact been quite surprised when the words had come from his mouth. But they were running out of time. After Julian had conducted his last interview with old Graves, he would be bound to return to London with his evidence.

A knock sounded on his door, and Julian hoped beyond hope that Sybilla Foxe would be waiting on the small stone landing. He crossed the chamber, and could not contain his smile at the sight of her in a thick, embroidered robe, a tray between her hands.

She'd come back.

"Oh," she said coolly, her eyebrows lifting only slightly as her gaze lighted on Lucy's limp form over his shoulder. "I apologize. I would have thought her to be in her own bed by now."

Julian opened the door wider and gestured to the small cradle he'd moved from the nurse's chamber downstairs.

"She is yet uneasy with the woman you've provided," he explained, motioning with his head for her to come in. "I thought perhaps she would sleep more soundly in my room this night. I'm sure she'll warm up to her on the morrow."

"I've brought you a drink." Sybilla set the tray down on the trunk near the bed, and Julian could not help but notice the two chalices next to the decanter. She straightened and turned, her posture stiff, her expression enigmatic. "I'll leave you now so as not to disturb the child. Good night, Lord Griffin."

"Don't go, Sybilla," he said, reaching out and grasping her elbow with one hand.

She looked down at her arm where he touched her, and quickly up into his eyes, as if he were some beggar grasping at her hem for a coin.

"There's no need," he continued, not caring at all about the icy look she gave him. "I'd like it very much if you'd stay and keep my company, talk with me."

"So you can further interrogate me?" she accused him, and frost all but fell from her lips.

He shook his head with a smile, because he knew his mirth would goad her. "No. We can talk about anything you wish," he said. Then he released her arm and walked to the cradle, carefully lowering Lucy into it and tucking the blankets around her. He gave the side a gentle push, and the little woven basket began to sway. When he turned back to the room, Sybilla had not moved, but her expression conveyed her suspicion.

"Anything I wish," she stated flatly.

"Yes." Julian gave her another smile as he passed her on his way toward the tray. He uncorked the decanter and picked up a chalice. Pouring a generous draught, he turned back to her and held the cup out. "Anything you wish." She reached out a slender arm and took the wine hesitantly, prompting Julian to add, "As long as there will be no shouting involved." He waggled his eyebrows toward the cradle.

"Well, knowing us, I can't very well promise you that, can I?" she said, and then took a drink.

Julian chuckled. "Touché."

The corners of her mouth twitched faintly, and she turned her back to him and walked toward the hearth. "Tell me how you came to be married to the king's cousin." She glanced back over her shoulder warningly. "The truth."

"I would admit to nothing less," Julian said easily and set about pouring a drink for himself.

"My family name is an old one, some saying it can be traced back to the time of Camelot," he began as he made himself comfortable by leaning up against the post of the bed. "Old and noble, but for the last several generations, not very wealthy. By the time I was born, the family manor had long since been taken over by creditors, and my parents were renting a small house in London. I enlisted with the king's men for the Eighth Crusade, hoping to earn enough spoils to afford my family a better life."

"Did you?" she asked mildly.

"No. In fact, I returned poorer than when I left, if you consider the cost of outfitting and the injury I sustained."

Her head turned quickly toward him and he saw her quick appraisal. "Not permanently, I gather."

"No, all I bear now are scars," he admitted. "But some of them are quite deep. Especially the mental ones I carry."

Sybilla nodded as if she understood. Perhaps she did. "But what would then prompt Edward to promise his relation to such a penniless knight?"

"I made a good soldier," he admitted without pride. "I fought well—as if I had nothing to lose and everything to gain. It served me well. Served the king even more, when I intervened in an attempt on his life."

"So you saved him."

"Him and a score of his men," Julian clarified. "Divine providence, right place, right time." He waved the chalice. "Whatever you wish to call it. From that day on, I traveled with him. When he was called back to England to take the crown, I led his company."

"But could he not simply give you your home back?"

Julian shook his head. "No. The manor had been lawfully claimed, the debts too old at that point to be repaid. And both of my parents had died while I was on the Crusade. There was nothing left to return to, really."

Sybilla's forehead wrinkled slightly. "I'm sorry."

He shrugged, liking the soft look of her in her robe before his fire.

"So then what happened?" she asked.

"He held a feast in my honor, detailing in the invitation my feats of daring and bravery." Sybilla laughed softly, and Julian joined her. "It was rather embarrassing. I don't think the king expected me to garner the interest of one of his unmarried cousins—it had never occurred to him. But he was agreeable to it."

"As were you?"

Julian nodded. "Certainly. Cateline was comely, young, wealthy, well connected. It was a fortuitous match for me, and gave her somewhat of a reputation, marrying the king's champion, a wild and ruthless knight."

"Did you love her?"

Julian paused, looking down into his chalice as he swirled the wine in his cup. "I loved her for Lucy," he said simply, looking up at her again. "I didn't dislike her, if that's what you mean. But was our marriage a raging love affair? No."

"Shame," Sybilla said, and then took another drink of her wine, watching him over the rim of her cup.

"I'd not change any of it," he confessed, and looked pointedly toward the cradle where Lucy slept on.

"And so now the king trusts you enough to secure Fallstowe for him," Sybilla said, beginning to walk slowly toward him, considering him thoughtfully. "I assume he will pay you handsomely."

"Yes," Julian conceded.

"And you will secure a home for yourself with the proceeds of my crucifixion." She stopped near him, only two paces away perhaps. "One like Fallstowe?"

"Exactly like Fallstowe, I hope," he said. "Does that sway you? If I were to be lord over a manor such as this?"

Sybilla shrugged one shoulder. "I'm beginning to think that I might be able to tolerate you elsewhere, if need be."

His guts twisted then, the closest thing he felt that he could expect so soon from Sybilla Foxe in the way of admission of gentle feelings. He stepped toward her slowly, carefully, and took her chalice. Then he turned and placed both cups on the trunk. He walked directly to her, placing his hands at her waist and pulling her against him.

"If need be?" He cocked his head and looked down into her face.

"I'm still waiting on you to convince me further," she said in a husky voice, and then glanced at Lucy's cradle. "Unfortunately—"

He began shaking his head even before she finished. "Doesn't matter," he said, and grazed her temple with his lips. "I can convince you very quietly." Then he kissed her mouth deeply.

She pulled away from him after a moment, her blazing blue eyes finding his. "But I am not so certain that my acceptance would be as quiet."

"There's only one way to find out, isn't there?" he said, and then bent down to scoop her up into his arms and carry her once again to his bed.

A strange noise woke Sybilla, and she frowned before opening her eyes. It sounded almost like some sort of animal, mewing and yowling, and so she squeezed her eyes shut all the more tightly and snuggled against Julian Griffin's warm flank, his chest rising and falling easily with his deep, rasping breaths.

There it was again, more insistent this time, and it

sounded as though it was in the very chamber. Then her eyes snapped open.

The baby. Lucy. She was crying.

Sybilla rose up on one elbow to behold the room, only faintly illuminated by the small, weakening fire in the hearth. Julian did not stir, and a glance at the cradle near the stone fireplace rewarded her with a glimpse of a little fist waving over the side.

She looked at Julian's face and saw that he was clearly lost to a deep sleep.

Sybilla frowned. The baby had quieted, but Sybilla was uneasy. What if the child had awakened in the night, ill like her nurse? What if she had no further energy to cry out once more, alerting her caretaker that she was unwell? Children commonly died in their sleep. Could she in good conscience roll over and close her eyes?

She carefully extracted herself from the covers, swung her legs over the side of the bed, and reached down to grasp the neck of her thin gown from the floor. She slipped it over her head, the ice-cold silk bringing out gooseflesh on her skin. Then she stood and cautiously, silently, tiptoed toward the little basket, holding her breath.

Lucy Griffin had one of her feet in each hand and was quietly blowing little bubbles of spittle. Her eyes widened as she caught sight of Sybilla peering over the edge of the cradle.

"Bah! Pah-pah-da!" she said excitedly.

"Shh!" Sybilla frowned. "You'll wake your father. It's still night. Go back to sleep," she said sternly.

The baby's miniature brow crinkled, her chin dimpled, her bottom lip turned out.

"No, no, no!" Sybilla reached hesitantly to lay her hand on Lucy's stomach. "Don't cry, it's all ri—my God!

You're soaking wet!" she hissed. She reached up to lightly grasp the baby's hands and feet in turn. "And frozen through."

Sybilla glanced over her shoulder at the bed, where Julian slept on, oblivious. Then she turned back to the child, who had managed to seize one of Sybilla's fingers. Sybilla twisted her hand to extract herself from the little creature's clutches and then reached in with both hands to lift Lucy from the cradle.

Once she had freed the child from the little bed, though, Sybilla had no idea what to do with her. Lucy dangled from Sybilla's outstretched arms, kicking her feet inside her gown, and seemed quite happy to take in the view and chew on her fist. Sybilla looked around the room for some indication of the baby's cache of clothing, but could see nothing.

"We've got to get you out of this wet gown," Sybilla whispered. "But I've nothing to put you in." She didn't want to wake Julian because . . . because if she did, and Julian took charge of the infant, there would be no further reason for Sybilla to remain in the chamber. She would be forced back to her own dreaded, screeching room, or the solar, or the great hall. His warmth and the quiet lost to her.

She spied her quilted robe on the floor near the foot of the bed. Walking toward it, she caught a wrinkle with her toe and kicked it up onto the mattress.

"Shh," she whispered as she laid Lucy down on the silk and began searching for the numerous ties holding the baby in the gown. "You really shouldn't wet in your bed," Sybilla said, her words little more than breath. "It's too cold by far, and it should be quite smelly in the morning, I would guess."

"Pah-pah-nah," Lucy explained.

"That doesn't matter in the least," Sybilla argued in a whisper. "Ladies don't do such a thing. Aren't you embarrassed?"

"Nah-nah-nah."

"Of course you aren't," Sybilla said grimly, pulling the gown at last over the child's head with not a little effort and tossing it across the room with a grimace. Then she looked into Lucy's eyes. "You're a baby, I understand. But you must try to do better, all right?"

Lucy began blowing little bubbles.

Sybilla's eyes narrowed, even though she was quite charmed. "Cheeky one, aren't you?" She surveyed the ties holding the baby's swaddle round her backside, and tried to undo it whilst touching it as little as possible. The soaking wet nappy went the way of the gown in short order, and then Sybilla pulled the sides of her own quilted wrapper around the child and picked her back up, this time holding her against her chest as she had seen Julian and the nurse, Murrin, do.

"Well then," she said against the tiny cup of Lucy's ear. "What are we to do now?"

To her surprise, Lucy reached out a chubby arm back toward the bed.

"Bah-bah."

Sybilla felt her mouth pull down in a frown. "I don't know about all that," she said. "I'm only just now getting used to sharing it with him."

And then Lucy laid her head down on Sybilla's shoulder, tucking her stubby little appendage back inside the robe. "Bah-bah," she repeated, this time around a yawn.

Sybilla brought her hand hesitantly to the baby's back and stood at the side of the bed for a long time. She watched Julian sleeping; she felt the warming weight of his daughter in her arms, here in the odd place of the tower room.

Then she carefully drew up her knee, gaining the mattress awkwardly. She laid the thick cocoon of silk and wool and baby on her pillow near Julian's shoulder and then she stretched out alongside Lucy, drawing the covers over the three of them.

Lucy's eyelids were drooping even as the baby stared at Sybilla, and Sybilla folded her arm beneath her head, as there were no more pillows, and stared back at the child as Lucy surrendered fully to sleep once more.

There was an uncomfortable, catching sensation in her stomach as Sybilla, too, closed her eyes and slept.

Chapter 16

Julian decided that he would have to have a serious discussion with Sybilla Foxe, addressing her reluctance to wake in the same bed with him.

He'd slept later than usual, and when he finally roused himself, it was to encounter an empty chamber—not even Lucy was present, although evidence of a very wet night for the baby was obvious from the gown and nappy crumpled up on the floor near the crib, as if they'd been hurled there in a heap. The nursemaid Sybilla had appointed was obviously well versed in such duties, as to have retrieved Lucy so quietly and efficiently.

Oddly enough, there was a wet spot in the center of Julian's mattress as well, near his elbow, and Julian chuckled darkly to himself at the idea of asking Sybilla Foxe if she was of the habit of drooling in her sleep.

She'd come to him again last night, of her own volition, not driven there by the phantasm of her mother's memory. Even with Lucy in the room, with whom Sybilla was decidedly still uncomfortable, she had stayed.

I'm beginning to think that I might be able to tolerate you elsewhere, if need be.

He would tell her today. He must. They needed time to address how they would both approach the king, and how they were to present the evidence Julian held, in the best possible light. And Sybilla must understand that if she possessed information that would aid their plight in any way, she must release it. She could not continue this mad and pointless loyalty to a woman who had used her so. Her mother's memory could not harm her. Julian would not allow it.

But right then, he wanted a draught and to see his daughter, and so he dressed and once again trod quickly and lightly down the spiral stairs that he was actually becoming quite fond of.

Right away he saw the nurse Sybilla had secured for him, carrying a stack of linens and little white gowns through the corridor. "Good morn, milord," the woman smiled, with a little curtsy in her stride. "Madam's in the hall."

"Thank you, Nurse," Julian said. "But where is Lady Lucy?"

The woman frowned in a perplexed manner and then gave him a little smile. "Why, she's with Madam, of course, milord. Where else would she be if not at your side?"

Julian turned in a half circle but then froze, his head tilted to the side as he experienced a moment of befuddlement. "I'm sorry, but you're saying my daughter is with Lady Foxe?"

The nursemaid's eyebrows rose and she regarded Julian with an air of suspicion. "Yes, milord. That is what I'm saying, precisely."

"Voluntarily?" Julian pressed.

Now the nursemaid's eyebrows drew downward with growing disapproval. "Lady Lucy was insistent that

Madam not leave her, but I do believe the arrangement is quite mutual, if that's what you're asking after." The nursemaid sniffed. "Since it was her ladyship who came to breakfast with the girl, I assumed you were quite aware of the situation and approved."

Julian blinked. "Madam came to breakfast?"

Then the nursemaid did crack a little knowing smile. "I believe they shared a bit of porridge."

A huff of laughter escaped Julian and he shook his head.

"Go on," the nurse said gently and flapped a hand at him. "See for yourself. Although I wouldn't interrupt— Madam's about her business at the moment."

Julian nodded absently. "Thank you." And then he turned, half in a daze, toward the archway that would lead him to the hall.

He paused there, his eyes taking in the line of serfs and villagers queued up in the main aisle. Some carried baskets and bundles of goods, and one man held a goat on a woven lead. It seemed a score of children ran about the common tables playing catch-me and hoop, and several women with kerchiefs covering their heads sat on the benches, sampling from platters of sliced breads and pitchers of milk while they gossiped. There was a happy buzz in the air, and the sight was unlike anything Julian had ever imagined seeing in the heretofore luxurious and perfect hall. It was almost like a village fair.

Then his eyes found Sybilla. She was seated on her throne-like chair at her table, Graves standing just behind her and to the side, aloof to the goings-on, as usual. A clerk of some sort sat near her right elbow, a selection of open ledgers spread out before him.

On the table as well, within Sybilla's curled left arm, sat Lucy, happily tossing and jerking on what seemed to be a string of . . . rubies? The baby squealed and flapped her arms up and down, as if at the wash, and the clatter of the heavy stones rang against the hard and shiny tabletop. Then he saw the twinkle down her front—several necklaces; gold links; fat, tear-shaped emeralds; pearls; topaz—the strands so long and weighty that some were worn across her chubby body, draping over her shoulder like a sash. Each wrist was laden with rings of hammered gold, some falling up to her elbows as she played.

A tiara, which looked to be made of diamonds, sat far back on her head cap.

"My God," Julian breathed in disbelief. He had never seen so many costly jewels in one place before, outside of the king's royal outfit, and now his baby daughter was bathing in them, at Sybilla Foxe's side, while she held court.

"It matters not," she was saying to the two men before her table. "You didn't finish the job, and so you don't deserve payment."

"I did half of it, though," the younger man argued petulantly. "He could pay me for half. I need the coin, milady."

"He didn't hire you for half a job," Sybilla said without sympathy. "If you are in such need of coin, quit wasting my time and go finish what you promised to do. When you have completed your task, if your employer thinks the work is worthy, I'm certain he will pay you the agreed-upon amount. That is all."

"But, milady," the man began to whine.

"Who is next?" Graves called out, effectively dismissing the pair of men.

The old chap with the goat hobbled up to the table

and handed the lead to the servant boy who stepped forward from the end of the table.

"Good day, Irving," Sybilla said, glancing at the old man as she adjusted Lucy's slipping crown. "How is your leg?"

"Much better, milady, and I thank you. I'm here to repay you as I promised. You saved our lives this winter, with that Fallstowe buck to freshen our nanny after we lost our'n."

"Irving, I'll not have your only kid," Sybilla said coolly; one who didn't know her might have taken her tone for scorning. "Especially since it is a male and you are still without."

"No, milady, no—your buck was a good'un and give us twins," the old man said with a smile.

"Be that as it may, I do believe that we are quite run over with billies at the moment. Is that not so, Graves?"

Graves closed his eyes, a long-suffering gesture that was perhaps supposed to be taken as a blink. "Where would we put another goat, Madam?"

"My thoughts exactly," Sybilla said dismissively. "Please take him out, Irving, lest he befoul the floor."

The old man bobbed a bow before the table, his smile shining in his knowing eyes. "Of course, Lady Sybilla. Sorry to trouble you with it."

Julian found himself smiling, too.

"Who is next?" Graves called out, a sigh in his voice.

But then Sybilla turned her head suddenly, and her gaze landed on Julian. The corners of her mouth lifted hesitantly, as if she was unused to making such a gesture so early in the day.

Julian looked pointedly at Lucy for a moment, placed

his hand over his heart, then held his palm toward Sybilla.

Her smile widened briefly before she addressed the hall. "A short recess, while I attend to other business. We shall resume within the half hour."

The queue dispersed to the tables and the clerk rose and departed Sybilla's side with a bow. Julian gained the dais and sneaked up behind his daughter, dropping a kiss on the side of her neck and causing her to squeal in delighted surprise.

He looked down at Sybilla with a smile as she withdrew her arm from around Lucy, allowing Julian to pull his daughter from the table with copious clanking and tinkling of jewels.

"Good morning, poppet," he said to Lucy, kissing her again just because he couldn't help it, and noticing that she smelled faintly of Sybilla's personal cologne. "I see you've found a playmate. A wealthy playmate."

"You should be ashamed, Lord Griffin—your daughter has absolutely no toys. Not one thing to amuse her could be found in her chamber this morn."

"That's not so," Julian argued. "She has a doll. I think."

"If you mean that knot of rags, you should be doubly mortified."

Julian laughed. "Perhaps she is getting old enough for a true toy, but, Sybilla, you can't allow her to play with your jewelry."

She frowned at him, obviously offended. "It's mine. I shall do with it what I wish."

"A diamond tiara, Sybilla?" he said. "Really? Is that appropriate for a baby?"

"It suits her." She looked at him levelly now. "I was

going to sit her in a great trunk of gold coin, but thought perhaps that would pose a choking hazard."

He threw back his head and laughed then, from his very toes it seemed. "How is it possible that I find the two of you here in this state?"

Sybilla shrugged and then took the chalice of wine presented to her by a kitchen boy. "I supposed Lady Lucy feels she is indebted to me for rescuing her from certain death by drowning in her own clothes last night and placing her in bed with us," she said lightly, and then took a sip from her cup.

"You got up with her in the night?" Julian said softly, completely amazed.

"I could no longer stand the incessant wailing," Sybilla said.

Julian was baffled, bemused, and completely encouraged. "So that's why the mattress was wet!"

Sybilla looked up at him and blinked through her frown. "What? Did you think it was me?"

"I did." He laughed. He felt drunk with hope. "Or perhaps the both of us."

She gave a short huff. "That's disgusting."

Julian only laughed again. And then kissed his daughter's cheek once more, although this time she tried to dodge him.

A soldier approached the table just then. "Milady, a message has arrived for Lord Griffin."

"As I am not Lord Griffin, perhaps you would do well to address the man."

The soldier bowed and then made a quarter turn, holding a wax-sealed parchment toward Julian. "My lord."

Julian took the note. "Thank you." He looked down

at it and noticed the seal was of a religious house. The bishop's response to his query then. Good.

Sybilla did not show the least bit of interest in the missive. "I really must see to my duties the remainder of the morning," she said, setting her cup aside and straightening in her chair.

"We shall leave you then," Julian said with a bow. He turned to Graves, who had not so much as glanced toward Julian during the entire exchange. "Would you mind assisting me in stripping my daughter of her wealth, old chap?"

"How could I refuse?" he grumbled and was soon looping strand upon strand of precious jewels upon his wiry arm.

"Perhaps tomorrow we shall search for earbobs," Sybilla said, looking coolly up at Lucy.

"Bah-pah-pah!" Lucy shouted.

Sybilla quirked an eyebrow at Julian. "Bad Papa?"

"That is not what she said," he denied with good humor. "Shall I see you at the noon meal?"

"More likely at supper. I am besieged today."

Julian nodded. "Very well, darling. Until tonight, then. Wave good-bye, Lucy."

He ignored Sybilla's widened eyes as he left the dais and the hall. He would be certain to call her darling more often.

Sybilla searched nearly all of Fallstowe for Julian before the evening meal. Lucy was readily located in the small chamber at the bottom of the stairs with Sybilla's maid. The two seemed to be getting on much better now, and Sybilla was more pleased than she would have dared admit at the baby's delight upon seeing her. She took several moments to hold and bounce the child, slipping a jeweled brooch onto the little ties of the baby's gown, while she inquired as to the whereabouts of Lucy's sire.

He was not in the stables or the chapel or the tower room; neither the hall nor Sybilla's own solar. She sighed irritably as she made her way toward her own corridor, intending to change into a fresh gown before returning to the hall for supper. He would most likely turn up there any matter.

She heard the terrible crashing before she saw the jagged square of light falling through her doorway and onto the stone walls of the corridor. Horrible, shattering sounds of rending wood, accompanied by the grunts and labored breathing of a man at work.

Her brows lowered as she increased her pace toward her room, and then shot upward as she saw the black ruin that had only hours ago been her—very locked— door.

An ax had been taken to the carved slab, crudely chopping out the latch and then, as if for spite, applied to the center of the intricate design, leaving raw-looking, yellow gouges in the lacquered door. And then she shifted her gaze through the doorway and saw the worst of it.

Julian Griffin swung the long-handled ax from over his head, sinking it deep into the already ruined mattress of her bed. Thick batting was vomited out in great clouds over the shattered posts, the bed-curtains tangled in them like skirts around raised legs. The tall headboard had been hacked to pieces, only a jagged sliver seen above the rent cushions.

"What are you doing?" Sybilla shouted.

The blow of the ax effectively severed the footboard,

and as Julian twisted and jerked the head of the ax free, the bed gave up its last support, collapsing in the middle with a screech that seemed to sound eerily like Amicia Foxe's distressed cries.

Julian stood aright at last and turned to face her. He dropped the head of the ax toward the floor, his chest heaving with his breaths. He glared at her, his amber eyes so dark they seemed to flame, and Sybilla got the distinct impression that he was a dangerous man in that moment.

"*What are you doing?*" Sybilla repeated.

He reached into his tunic with his free hand and jerked out the now wrinkled and creased message he had received earlier in the great hall and held it out to her.

"What?" she said, unwilling to move toward him. "What is it?"

Julian flung the parchment to the floor between them. His eyes seemed to blaze even more brightly with the first words he had spoken to her since she had entered her destroyed chamber.

"August. Bellecote," he growled out succinctly.

Her breath caught at the top of her throat. "Is dead," Sybilla said.

"You married him," Julian accused her.

Sybilla neither denied nor confirmed. She didn't know who the message was from. Surely not the bishop who had married her and August by proxy. Sybilla's current poor standing with the king could spell only disaster for the powerful holy man if Edward found out he had helped her try to retain Fallstowe. He would not confess his involvement voluntarily.

"He is dead," Sybilla repeated. "And I would advise you not to take such a rumor as truth lest you have the bishop's own testimony to witness for you. It could be quite devastating to your case against me with the king."

"Don't evade me," Julian sneered. "I'm not stupid, Sybilla. And *this* testimony"—he gestured to the missive on the floor between them—"is likely more damning than one from the bishop's own pen, I'd reckon. It's from a man who has intimate knowledge of the series of events that led to your sister Cecily marrying Oliver Bellecote."

"I beg your pardon?" Sybilla asked, confused.

"The bishop's own secretary, Vicar John Grey."

Sybilla's eyebrows rose. "The bishop's secretary now, is he? That was fast. Good for him."

"You slept with him, didn't you?" When Sybilla only sighed and considered the ruination of her bed, Julian continued. "I suspected as much by the way he displays both fear and **awe** of you. The manner in which he praises your cunning and yet rues ever seeing you again."

Her face whipped around to regard Julian. "Why? Because that's how you feel about me now?"

"No," Julian ground out. "I would only hope that the woman I have come to know would not practice her wiles on a priest in Holy Orders!"

Sybilla rolled her eyes. "For the hundredth time, it's only a courtesy title."

Julian threw the ax to the floor with a flaming curse. "You *did* sleep with him!"

"I daresay you knew of my scandalous reputation before taking your charge from the king. I had you in my bed within a fortnight, didn't I? Don't pretend ignorance."

"Did you love none of them? Not even one?"

She lifted her chin. "I admired each for some characteristic or another," she said. "But no, I did not love any of them. Of course not."

"*Of course not?*" Julian repeated incredulously. "Do you know how that makes you sound?"

"Like a man, you mean? You . . . you hypocrite! You, who confessed readily that you didn't even love your own wife!"

"That's not the same thing in the least."

"It is exactly the same thing! Would you rather I *had* loved them?" she demanded. "Loved all of them? Would it please you to think that what I am beginning to feel for you I have felt many times before for other men?"

"Perhaps then I could be assured that you at least knew what the emotion meant!"

Sybilla felt her head draw back even as his face took on the immediate expression of regret.

"I'm sorry, Sybilla," he said, taking a step toward her. "I didn't mean that at all."

"That is the very reason why I purposefully didn't love any of the men I've had," she said quietly. "Why I never entertained them more than once—not even August, the man I married by proxy. Our union was never consummated—he died en route to Fallstowe after receiving confirmation from the bishop. The marriage is invalid. But there is no evidence that will ever be found to prove it even happened in the first place—I destroyed all the documents personally. Are you happy now, Julian? Are you quite satisfied? I know what it means to love—to truly love. The cost. The consequences. August was willing to pay them. I never was."

"Until now?" Julian prompted. "Until me?"

Sybilla did not answer his question, only looked at the splinters and crude spears that had once been bedposts, the exploded mattress that had once been her bed—her mother's bed.

"I was crazed with jealousy," he admitted in a low tone. "I knew you were no innocent, and yet—I couldn't bear the thought of it, Sybilla. There will be no more men. Not in this bed, and not in any bed you occupy in the future. Only me." She glanced up at him, and he repeated. "*Only me.*"

"I can't believe you did this," she said softly. And then she turned away from him again. "I'm leaving first thing in the morn for Bellemont," she said in an even, expressionless tone. "Some of the ill have begun to recover, but a dozen more have contracted it in the meantime. Cecily has great knowledge of healing—she will best know how to treat the sick."

"I can't let you leave Fallstowe, Sybilla," Julian said with a wary frown. "If the king found out, if you decided to never come back—"

"I'll go where and when I please," Sybilla hissed, and even she could almost see the icy blue sparks glinting off her words. Even after she had all but confessed her feelings for him, he did not trust her to return. "No one commands me! Not you, not the king, no one! I must do what I must do for my people, and I will do it. You cannot and will not stop me."

"I *can* stop you," Julian argued quietly.

"Try it," Sybilla challenged him. "Try it, and I will bring hell down upon your head."

"You don't mean that."

She stared at him. "Try it," she repeated simply.

"I may not have come to Fallstowe with the intention of protecting you," Julian said. "But that is my intention now, and I fully expect to succeed, even if it's yourself I

must protect you from. You"—he glanced at the bed—
"or the ghosts from your past."

"Perhaps we shall discuss it when I return," she said,
and turned to walk to the cleaved and shattered door.

"Dammit! It's not safe for you to go alone. I'll meet
you in the stables at sunrise," he called after her. "Wait
for me there. *Sybilla!*"

Sybilla did not pause as she quit the room, nor did she
reply. She feared even the slightest response would set
loose the torrent of sobs clawing at her chest.

Chapter 17

He should have known she would already be gone.

It was not yet dawn when Julian marched into Fallstowe's quiet and humid stables the next morn, but the hands were already alive with work, spreading bedding, forking out waste, feeding and organizing and oiling leather accoutrements. Julian knew when he saw the busy activity that Lady Foxe had been early in their presence. He threw his riding gloves to the dry, dusty floor with a curse and then forgot them, turning to stare out the wide-open doors into the still dark stable yard, his hands on his hips.

He could follow her to Bellemont. Likely should. But he feared the outcome of that pursuit would not be desirable for either of them. Sybilla would be even more furious with him than she was at the present time, and there was no telling how she would retaliate if backed into a corner. There would be plenty of his own men at Bellemont to subdue her, perhaps return her forcefully to Fallstowe, but at what cost?

At that moment, Julian felt like the stupidest man alive. He didn't know what had come over him yesterday after reading John Grey's response to his query. He must have read it a thousand times in the span of a few hours. Read it, reread it, his mind turning the innuendos and veiled answers to his questions into a maelstrom of jealousy and confusion, until his rage was such that he could not stop until he found an outlet for it.

As Amicia Foxe was already dead, he'd chosen the next best subject—the symbol of her hold over her daughter, the symbol of the men Sybilla had had before him. And he had destroyed it.

Foolish, selfish, stupid act! Rash to the extreme, when Julian had always prided himself on his logic and clear thinking. He had destroyed her personal possessions in a most terrifyingly violent manner.

And then he may as well have called her a whore. He didn't know where that had come from. He certainly didn't view her in that light, and the logical part of his brain was well familiar with the tales of her romantic escapades. They didn't matter. They were in the past.

Sybilla had been right when she'd called him a hypocrite. How many women had he known before Cateline? He cringed at the nameless faces that flickered through his mind in a blur, the memories of dark, winesoaked nights over some tavern, in crude field tents and luxurious brothels. At least Sybilla had chosen her companions with some eye for their character. Julian could not claim even that. He was ashamed. Sorry. Angry. And confused.

Could he love her already? Surely that couldn't be it. Romantic love—the type that was meant to last forever and ever—it took years to cultivate. To know a person, to grow to love them, despite their flaws. Perhaps even because of them.

Didn't it?

But when he tried to envision his future, his and Lucy's future, Sybilla Foxe was there. He couldn't imagine not seeing her every day. Even the thought of it gave him the uncomfortable feeling of not having sufficient air to breathe—his chest tightened, his throat constricted. And to think of never seeing her again—ever?

She could be a wonderful mother to Lucy—the best sort. For she had already been a victim of the worst. Already she had begun the process of attachment, practicing instinctual habits such as fetching the crying baby from her bed in the middle of the night, ensuring that she was dry and warm and comforted.

And, of course, there were the jewels.

Julian felt a smile crack the rusty corners of his mouth.

He'd meant to tell her about Fallstowe yesterday, and instead had perhaps driven her away from him. How would she react now when she found out? Would she return from Bellemont still so angry and hurt that the possibility of a future with him—anywhere—was erased from her mind?

Should that be the case, Julian knew that he would lose. For she would fight him and the king to her last breath to stay at Fallstowe—or to keep Julian from having it. Either way, Julian would never see her again.

"Do these belong to you, Lord Griffin?"

The dry, put-out tone seemed to scrape at Julian's spine, and although he knew who the speaker was, even before turning to face the old man, he was rather surprised to discover Graves had been lurking about the shadows of the stables in the small hours before daybreak.

The old steward held forth Julian's riding gloves, and Julian took them.

"Yes, thank you, Graves. I must have dropped them."

"Perhaps it was when you threw them to the ground, my lord?"

Julian glared at the steward for a moment, and then resigned himself to the man's insufferable presence for the immediate future.

"I'm glad you're here—you're the last member of Fallstowe's household that I have a need to speak with. It's fortuitous that Lady Foxe is away for . . . the time being, so that perhaps you will have more time to accommodate me."

Graves stared at Julian with an odd intensity. "Why do you think I was waiting here for you, Lord Griffin?"

Julian stared back. This he had not expected. "To kill me, perhaps? Bury my body before the lady of the keep returned?"

Then the old steward actually smiled. But he denied nothing. "Where would you conduct your interview, my lord?"

Julian made a sweeping gesture with the hand holding his riding gloves, toward the open stable doors. "Lead the way, old chap."

Sybilla rode hard away from Fallstowe for the first half hour, to give her a good head start in case Julian Griffin revealed himself to be so dense as to attempt to follow her. But once she was safely into the cover of woods, the sky lightening almost imperceptibly, she slowed Octavian to a walk, letting him amble to a ropy stream and drink his fill.

In the predawn light, the wood filled with timid chirps from the most ambitious of birds, the wind slipping through the new leaves, stirring smells both green and brown, Sybilla thought about her flight from Fallstowe.

True, she was going to Bellemont to pick at Cecily's knowledge of illness, but before yesterday afternoon, she likely would not have. Whatever was going around Fallstowe was nothing more than a simple weakness of body due to the changing season, and it was entirely possible that Lucy's nursemaid, Murrin, had recovered before reaching London. No, this trip was a spontaneous escape, used to afford herself a bit of sanity, quiet, to think upon what was happening to her life. She'd had to get away from Julian Griffin before he consumed her, and upon seeing the wreckage he had created of her chamber, her choices had been to either flee or be pulled under forever.

He had been jealous of August. Of John Grey. Of the other men, likely many fewer than was rumored or that he suspected. He had been insane with jealousy.

No more men . . . only me.

Had he meant it, though? The words had sounded strange coming from him, and Sybilla now knew why: the very idea that she would ever take another man to her bed that wasn't Julian Griffin had immediately struck her as ludicrous. His presence at Fallstowe was now taken for granted. It was as if it was his home. His and Lucy's.

Could Sybilla be a mother? She didn't know.

And even if he loved her—or could come to love her for what she was, and what she was not—Fallstowe would be closed to them both after the king's hearing. And should the king allow them to marry, where would they go? Could she love him, love anyone, outside of those gray stone walls?

Could she love him? Did she already?

He was committed to do the job the king had sent

him to do, and although it made Sybilla's future uncertain, she respected his honor. He kept his word. So did Sybilla, and so she understood. He was still willing to vouch for her before the king. Perhaps Julian Griffin's opinion was held so dear by their monarch that he could be swayed, should Sybilla also stand before him, contrite and ready to surrender the only home she had ever known. The place and the people she had literally risked her life for, time and again.

Were Julian and Lucy Griffin worth Fallstowe?

She went deep into her mind, trying to speed up time so that she could see the baby at five years, ten, a score. See Julian, his tawny hair growing wheat colored, lines at his eyes forming like the spines of a fan when he grinned. To see them both every day, to have them both be hers—belong to her, in name and in truth. Honestly.

Yes. Yes, she thought that perhaps they were worth it.

No man had ever taken such passionate liberties with her before, shown such unyielding anger in the face of what was simply her life up to the point when he had sent flaming arrows over Fallstowe's battlements. Perhaps he was strong enough to be her man, forever.

Her chest swelled with the very idea of it; her eyes blurred for a moment.

She nudged Octavian back to the road toward Bellemont. Regardless, Sybilla needed to inform her sister of the dire state of things within the family, so to speak. If the worst happened, at least Cee and Alys would know most of the truth.

Most of it was all Sybilla was willing to tell.

Julian had expected Graves to lead him to Sybilla's solar, or the great hall, or even Fallstowe's small chapel,

so he was somewhat surprised when the old man's un-
foreseen swift if stiff gait brought them to the chamber
in which Julian had so recently vented his jealous rage.

Nothing had been tidied, the aftermath of his fury
still lying raw about the floor, like some forgotten battlefield claimed and then marched over by a conquering
army. Julian saw the destruction with new eyes, and he
was ashamed. A weaker woman than Sybilla Foxe would
have been terrified by what he'd done, seeing what he
was capable of. Instead it had been she who had felt the
need to defend herself. The sight of jagged splinters of
varnished wood rising haphazardly and threateningly,
the dusty quilting exploded, chastised Julian.

This is the dangerous path you have made, he told himself.
Tread carefully.

Julian stopped just inside the ruined door, while the
ancient steward stepped matter-of-factly over the chaos
to stand before Sybilla's wide table, staring out the bank
of windows over the glowing mist veiling the rising sun.

"Will you betray Madam to the king?" Graves asked
musingly.

Julian bent down to pick up a burst embroidered
pillow. He held it between his hands and then tossed it
in the general vicinity of the bed. "I will take the evidence I have found to Edward. It is the duty I swore to
undertake."

"So that is a yes?"

"I am hoping that Lady Sybilla will place her trust in
me to protect her."

Graves looked over his shoulder, glancing at the floor.
"As you demonstrated to her here?"

"No." Julian sighed. "No, this was an exercise in very
poor and rash judgment on my part. Uncharacteristically
so, although I'm certain you don't believe that."

The ancient manservant neither denied nor confirmed. "What do you wish to know, Lord Griffin?" he asked in a resigned tone.

Julian regarded Graves's slim, erect posture, his skeletal hands now clasped behind his back, the hair on his head like cobwebs. Perhaps even more so than Sybilla, Fallstowe's steward was an enigma.

"Why is it that you only speak in questions, Graves?"

He sniffed. "How else is one ever to learn anything, my lord?"

Julian smiled and then, although he felt it was a further desecration to avail himself of Sybilla's furnishings, he was fatigued of a sudden, so he dropped into an upholstered chair near the door. He should have journeyed to his tower room to fetch his portfolio, but decided that it would have likely been a wasted trip. He would get no revelatory answers from the fiercely loyal man—especially when the interview would need be conducted with dueling queries.

"Was Amicia Foxe of noble blood?"

"You don't already know the answer to that question, my lord?"

"I do." Julian sighed. "I believe I've worked through the mystery surrounding Amicia's installation as Lady of Fallstowe so many years ago. Perhaps I was only trying you to see if you would tell me the truth."

"But you truly desire knowledge about the lord's betrayal at Lewes, do you not?"

Julian stilled. "Which lord? Morys Foxe or the king?"

Graves cocked his head. "Does it matter?"

"Not really, no." Julian watched the still man closely, and drummed his fingers on the arm of the chair. "Did Amicia Foxe commit treason by leading Simon de Montfort's men to the king's soldiers at Lewes?"

"Would you believe me if I told you the answer was no?"

"That's impossible," Julian spat. "All the evidence I have points to her. Witness accounts, descriptions, timing of events, opportunity, Amicia's fondness for the de Montforts, her indebtedness to Simon himself. Rumor is always based at least some small part of it on truth. It could be no one else."

"Lord Griffin," Graves began slowly, carefully, "what do you suppose would have been Lady Foxe's fate had it been she who traveled in the dark of night to the barons' camp, betrayed her king, and then was apprehended?"

Julian held his palm up. "De Montfort would have given her up, certainly. Her past would have been discovered. She would have been definitively outed. Stripped of her title, humiliated, likely put to a common traitor's death."

Graves nodded. "And after all that she had already risked, the great and awesome ruse that she had perpetrated, the spoils and respect she had won; after all that you have come to learn of her character to this point, do you think it likely that she would so blatantly and fearlessly wager her life—the lives of her entire family, Fallstowe itself—in such a brazen undertaking?"

"The evidence I have, Graves—it could be no one else."

"Couldn't it?"

Julian was becoming frustrated. He was getting no answers. "Listen, old man—I have taken it apart piece by piece and then put it back together again, a hundred times—a thousand. A young, beautiful, raven-haired woman who was obviously known and trusted by de Montfort was seen at the enemy camp, seemingly instructing a small group of generals over a map. It is common knowledge that Amicia Foxe was Morys's junior by a score of years, and tales of her handsomeness were widespread even at the time of their marriage. That night, she was dressed in common garb and would have been taken as nothing more than a camp follower, save the one anomaly that set her apart from a common prostitute: the jeweled dagger she carried under her cloak. She wielded it before a pair of soldiers who approached her as she was leaving the camp, supposedly offering to see her safely away. But I presume it was more likely that they were seeking to enjoy her charms before battle. Amicia did nothing more than brandish her weapon and warn them away with words, but both men reportedly died on the trail that night from mysterious internal injuries. It marked the woman in the soldiers' minds as a sorceress, and thus the legend was born."

Graves had nodded throughout Julian's rapid-fire condensing of the facts he held. "Let's review, shall we? You say it was a handsome, young, dark-haired woman, carrying a jeweled dagger, on a desperate mission, who very swiftly and mysteriously dispatched a pair of ne'er-do-wells who threatened violation of her person?"

Julian frowned. "Yes."

"How young do you think Lady Foxe would have been at that time, Lord Griffin?"

"Do you mean Amicia?"

"Do I?"

Julian opened his mouth to insist that, yes, of course, that's who he meant, but no words came to him. His heartbeat slowed, slowed, nearly stopped as the evidence towering above him tilted, swayed, and then came down around his heart.

He didn't want to hear the next question Graves posed to him, quietly, emphatically.

"Have you not heard how closely Madam resembles her mother?"

Sybilla, on the night Julian arrived at Fallstowe, the jeweled dagger at her hip.

Her knowledge of warfare, the ways of the king, and her knack for thwarting him.

Her assertion that Julian could not save her, that she could not save herself. That Amicia was not a traitor.

The odd happenings in her bedchamber, the way she had seemingly thrown Julian against a wall without so much as touching him.

Are you a witch, Sybilla?

Perhaps I am.

Julian tried to shove his way through the roiling implications in his mind to reconcile the dates, the years past.

"She could have been no more than fifteen," Julian managed to choke out. "No—no, that's . . . it's not possible."

"Why?" Graves asked, and then turned to face Julian. "Why is it not possible that a girl, so desperate to please her mother—naively convinced that she would be aiding her father, her country—would not visit a family friend to give him assistance?"

"Sybilla . . ." Julian swallowed, all his grand ambition for bringing the truth to light before the king, in the faith that good would triumph, crumbling like a grand statue that was revealed to be formed from nothing more than old, dried mud. An illusion. A crude rendering of the truth.

Julian felt as though a crushing weight had descended upon his chest. "Sybilla is the traitor."

So shocked by this remolding of facts was Julian that he didn't notice Graves had come back across the room until the old steward was standing near the door.

"Is there anything else you wish to ask me at present, Lord Griffin?"

"No," Julian said in a strangled voice, and then cleared his throat. "No, Graves, I think you have given me quite enough to think about."

Graves stood there a moment longer before saying, in an unusually hesitant and sympathetic tone, "Loyalty can ofttimes be completely relative, wouldn't you agree?"

Then he was gone from Sybilla's chamber, leaving Julian staring dumbly at the destroyed room. At Sybilla Foxe's destroyed life, dealt by Julian's own hand.

Chapter 18

There were soldiers camped outside of Bellemont. The king's soldiers.

Sybilla urged Octavian quickly from the road into a small dip in the rolling countryside leading to the Bellecote hold, considering this surprise.

Julian had vowed that he would send his men away, and he had. Of course he would dispatch them to Bellemont—Oliver Bellecote had vowed his support of Edward's campaign against Sybilla and Fallstowe, and so it only made sense to have the bulk of Julian's men camped at a location where ready aid was at hand. But the brief glimpse of tents and armaments she'd seen before departing from the main road to Bellemont had seemed too few to accommodate the hundreds of men who had appeared at Fallstowe initially.

Where was the rest of Julian's army? She frowned and pondered. Likely Gillwick. Yes, Julian was keen enough to shield Sybilla's retreat on all sides, and to be well-informed should either of her sisters attempt to give her aid.

Why hadn't Cecily or Alys sent word to her, though?

For a brief moment Sybilla thought very hard about swinging Octavian back to the wood and returning to Fallstowe. She wasn't certain if any of the men camped outside Bellemont's walls would be on the lookout for her, or what scenario was playing out within the hold itself. But no sooner had the idea of flight occurred to her than she dismissed it summarily.

She must speak to her sister. And nothing or no one was going to stop her.

Sybilla closed her eyes and took a deep breath, turning her face up to the bright midday sun, trying to soak as much warmth and light into her body as she could hold. When she righted her head and opened her eyes, her vision seemed to dance, the green countryside around her to sparkle with gaiety and contentment. She relaxed her mouth and deliberately created a smile on her lips. Then she drew up her hood over her hair, adjusted her skirts in a dainty manner, and kicked at Octavian's sides. She had to stop the beast twice before they crested the rise, chastising him for his accustomed aggressive stomp, and then patted the warhorse's neck in praise as he reluctantly adopted and maintained a light, prancing trot.

Octavian so hated playing the dandy.

It seemed the better part of an hour before Sybilla actually rode through the sea of soldiers to arrive at Bellemont's gate. And as she had suspected, a young man bearing the king's colors stepped directly into her path, waving her to a stop.

Octavian snorted threateningly, and Sybilla could feel the warhorse's shoulders bunch in anticipation of a charge.

"Shh" she whispered fiercely. "Easy. Easy. Hold, boy."
She brought Octavian to a stop, and the soldier approached, his arm outstretched, obviously thinking to
take hold of the horse's bridle.

Octavian tossed his head threateningly.

"I wouldn't do that!" Sybilla called out with a laugh.
"He is terribly ill-mannered and hasn't yet learned not
to bite."

Thankfully the man halted his reaching hand, giving
Octavian an uneasy look.

She let her smile shine down on the soldier's upturned and wary-looking face, trying to summon the
sunshine she had saved and pour it out with her words.
Warm. Friendly.

"It's a wonder I manage to ride him at all, really, he
frightens me so," she tinkled in self-deprecation. "Don't
tell anyone, though."

"It seems a woman of such beauty should not be
forced to ride such an unruly monster. Good day, milady,"
the soldier said, his face bearing a slightly confused expression even as his mouth wanted to smile back up at
her. "What business do you have at Bellemont?"

"Good day to you, as well, kind sir. I've come to see
Lady Bellecote."

"I see. Your name, if you please?"

"Oh, she's quite expecting me," Sybilla said, flapping
a hand at him and then giving him a wink. "Although I
dare say Lord Bellecote shall not be pleased, as it will
mean hours spent speaking of such things as tiny gowns
and nappies. I know the way. Just open the gate for me,
if you would."

"I can't do that, milady," the soldier said, but he winced
as he said it, as if something in his head pained him.

NEVER LOVE A LORD

"Whyever not?" Sybilla asked, putting on a look of hurt confusion.

"I . . . have my orders and they clearly state that—" He broke off, wincing again, this time even bringing his fingertips to his temple.

"Yes?" Sybilla said, looking at him so very closely and with deep, deep concern. "Your orders state . . . ?"

"I seem to have forgotten," the man said bewilderedly.

Sybilla laughed uproariously. "Oh my! That does happen to me all the time!" She leaned down slightly and said in a conspiratorial whisper, "I won't tell anyone. Now, let me pass."

He nodded as if in a daze. "Yes, of course." But then he halted, holding up one finger. "But I do recall that I am not to allow anyone to enter on horseback. I'll need to take your mount until you are ready to take your leave of Bellemont."

"Nooo," Sybilla said gravely. "I can't let you do that, good sir." Sybilla leaned down once more, and she was no longer smiling, putting on the act. "He would stomp you to death as soon as you laid a hand to him."

The man's eyebrows rose.

Sybilla stared at him. "He is trained to kill you. And I would let him. *Now, open the gates and let me pass.*"

The soldier backed three paces away from Sybilla and Octavian before signaling the men on either side of Bellemont's plain but sturdy wooden gates. In a moment, the bailey was revealed to her.

Sybilla nudged Octavian's sides, jerking on the reins when he made to rear. Fighting the beast into his previously submissive prance, she rode through the gate, blowing a kiss to the still perplexed-looking young man.

She rolled her eyes once she was safely inside and the gates were closing behind her.

"Edward, Edward." She sighed. "You never learn."

She could have absconded with the whole of Bellemont once through the gates, Sybilla discovered, for she saw only a handful of Oliver's own men and none of the king's inside the bailey. Two little peasant girls were playing in the dirt near the steps that led into the hold, and so Sybilla dismounted there. She crouched before them and gave each girl a shiny coin in exchange for their promise to stand watch and tell anyone who approached that the horse belonged to the lady of Bellemont and was not to be put to stable or touched in any way.

At their eager acceptance, Sybilla rose and strode to Octavian, grabbing his muzzle to pull his head down so that she could look in his eyes while she rubbed his forelock roughly.

"Babies, Octavian," she whispered, and glanced at the girls. "Careful."

The horse tossed his head free and sidestepped a pair of paces away from the girls before dropping his head to pick at the new grass growing along the side of the steps, his reins trailing after him.

"No riding, girls," Sybilla warned the urchins.

"No, milady!" they piped excitedly, having forgotten all about their game now, watching the passing townsfolk with wary eyes.

There wasn't a doorman, and so Sybilla let herself into the shadowy entry, pushing back her hood. It had been years since she'd stepped foot inside Bellemont.

Before her mother had died. When August first began trying to win her.

And won her he had, although what a poisoned prize she had turned out to be.

Sybilla paused, closed her eyes, and dropped her head for a moment. She had to swallow twice before she had composed herself enough to venture farther into the castle, seeking the great hall. It was midday. Everyone would either still be at luncheon or just quitting it.

In the great hall, she gasped a quiet breath when she saw the small group of people knotted together at one of the common tables, their heads leaning toward each other, their faces wearing similar masks of intense concentration as they conversed in low tones.

Oliver and Cecily on one side, Alys and Piers on the other. Sybilla's sisters were reaching across the table, clasping hands with each other.

Sybilla placed a palm against the stone archway and leaned there, drinking in the sight of them. Oh, she hadn't realized how much she'd missed them both! Her throat constricted as she watched them, and she remembered that these were the same two little girls that had so long been in her charge, even up until months ago, weeks ago, when they were no longer little girls, but grown women.

Alys, who would dance around in the cook's apron, tucking dandelions into the rising mounds of dough and pinching anyone who told on her.

Cecily, who had a lovely singing voice but was too shy to ever perform, and who would burst into tears at the slightest hint that she had disappointed anyone.

Alys, who had kept what she'd thought was a kitten in her chamber for nearly a fortnight before anyone discovered that she had actually been spoon-feeding thinned porridge to a rat.

Cecily, who'd been convinced that babies came from wishing for them in the well and then drawing them up in the bucket, which was why they were always so wet and messy for days after they were born.

Now they were grown and away from her, away from Fallstowe, and both to be mothers themselves before the year was through. They had their own families now, their own homes. Sybilla loved them both so, and she missed them more than she could ever say, standing alone in the shadows, watching them.

They would not like what she had come to tell them. And Sybilla didn't want to. But, like most things in her life, she had no choice.

Cecily turned her dark head just then, as if Sybilla had called her name. Maybe she had; Sybilla couldn't honestly say. But in an instant, Cecily had popped up from the bench and was running across the hall toward her, her arms outstretched. Sybilla heard Alys gasp from the table.

"Sybilla!" Cecily cried, and the relief in her voice was obvious. "Oh, thank God, thank God!"

Sybilla smiled and stepped from the shadows, catching her sister and clinging to her just as tightly as Cecily hung on.

"Cee," Sybilla whispered, "it is so good to see you."

Cecily pulled away only enough to clasp Sybilla's face in her palms and kiss both of her cheeks. Then she looked into Sybilla's eyes. "We've been so worried, you have no idea! How did you get through the gates?"

Sybilla smiled. "I rode Octavian."

Cecily's eyes narrowed, but her smile was indulgent.

"Yes, well, don't tell me then. I truly don't wish to know, any matter." Cecily took her arm and the sisters began walking back toward the table, where Piers and Oliver were now standing.

"Hello, Oliver," Sybilla said lightly as she approached. "I take it the king doesn't know you're for me now rather than against me."

"I can better keep an eye on them this way," Oliver admitted, and then took Sybilla from his wife's grasp and also kissed each of Sybilla's cheeks. His eyes held deep concern as they searched her face. "All right, Sybilla?"

"I'm fine," she said, and pulled away to face the table. "Piers, I'm rather surprised that you would have Alys away from Gillwick in her cond—" Then Sybilla noticed that her blond youngest sister had her head buried in her arms on the tabletop and was sobbing until her shoulders shook. Sybilla frowned. "Alys?"

Then Sybilla's littlest, most troublesome sister raised her tear-streaked face and scrambled over the bench to throw herself into Sybilla's arms.

"Sybilla! Oh, Sybilla," she wailed. "I am so, so very happy you are here! Truly! I—I . . ." Her words were hiccoughs as she struggled to form them around her emotions.

Sybilla glanced at Piers Mallory, Alys's husband, and he shook his head while making a sweeping motion over his stomach, as if mimicking Alys's maternal condition.

Alys continued, "I have worried myself sick that they had disposed of you! But, Sybilla, how could you?"

This mysterious accusation startled Sybilla. "How could I what, Alys?"

"I know we didn't know him very well, but he seemed

such a good man! And he aided Piers when no one else would! And surely there was another way you could have ended this—the poor man had just lost his wife! Oh, poor, poor Lord Griffin!" she wailed.

"Alys, what are you talking about?"

The little blond woman pushed at her flowing eyes with the heels of her hands for a moment. Then she sniffed and looked at Sybilla mournfully. "You're here, smiling at all of us, and so Julian Griffin must be dead!"

Sybilla couldn't help the laugh that burst from her. It obviously startled everyone gathered around her, for they exchanged quick, wary glances with each other.

Save for Alys, who had now put on her angry face. "It's not funny! He has a baby, Sybilla!"

Sybilla truly tried to stanch the laughter which seemed to well from her toes, but her little sister's outrage at the idea that Sybilla had actually murdered Julian Griffin was just too much. She made her way to the table all had so recently been conversing over and sat down, touching her fingertips to her eyes.

"Alys," she chuckled, then blew out a cleansing breath. There, that was better. "Lord Griffin is not dead."

Alys frowned. "He's not?"

And then Oliver placed a hand on the tabletop and leaned forward incredulously. "He's not?"

"No," Sybilla stated firmly.

Piers Mallory sat down across the table. "Then where is he?"

"Presumably still at Fallstowe." She looked at Alys pointedly. "With his baby, I might add."

Cecily sat down at Sybilla's right side. "He brought a baby to a siege?"

"He did."

Alys sat down on Sybilla's left. "That cad!" she exclaimed.

Sybilla chanced a glance at Alys's husband and caught him rolling his eyes.

"What's he going to do?" Oliver asked, sitting down across the table, next to Piers. "Has he given you any clue?"

"Yes. Actually he's told me exactly what he plans to do," Sybilla said. "He's been researching Mother—all of Fallstowe, really—for quite some time. He'll take the evidence he's found to the king."

"And then?" Piers pressed.

Sybilla shrugged. "From what I gather, the king is to pay him quite handsomely for his investigation."

Everyone at the table was silent for a long moment, staring at Sybilla.

"That brazen son of a bitch," Piers growled.

"Sybilla," Cecily said hesitantly, laying her hand on Sybilla's forearm. "You know this, and yet—are you very sure that you *haven't* killed him? Perhaps it was . . . an accident?"

"I did not kill Julian Griffin," Sybilla stated flatly. "As a matter of fact"—she paused, then lifted her chin slightly—"I'm becoming quite . . . fond of him." She looked at the shocked faces around her. "And his daughter. Her name is Lucy, which isn't horrid, I don't think."

"Sybilla," Alys whispered, her brown eyes as big as cartwheels, "Julian Griffin is—"

"No." Sybilla stopped whatever Alys was going to say by shaking her head and holding up a palm. "I don't have much time, and I came here to tell Cecily something very important. It is a miracle that you are here as well, Alys. It will be so much better that I can tell the both of you at once."

"But what Alys is trying to say—" Cecily began.

"No, Cee," Sybilla interrupted again. "It can wait. I don't want to tell you what I've come to tell you, but it can no longer be avoided. After I've said it, we may talk about Julian Griffin, if you wish, but not before." She paused, lowering her voice. "If I wait much longer, I fear I won't be able to get it out."

"Wait!" Alys said, sitting up straight on the bench and frowning crossly. "Why were you coming here to tell Cecily and not to Gillwick to tell me?"

"Because Cecily is older than you," Sybilla said.

Alys's frown deepened. "So?"

Cecily leaned forward to speak around Sybilla. "And Bellemont is closer than Gillwick."

"So?" Alys insisted.

"Alys," Piers finally begged from behind the hands rubbing his face. He looked at her with a pleading expression. "I love you so, my darling. Would you please shut up and let Sybilla tell what she has to tell?"

"Oh!" Alys said, as if just remembering that there was news to be had. "Of course. Yes. Sorry, Sybilla. Go on."

Sybilla looked at Piers Mallory. "You, sir, are my hero."

The stocky man shot her a weary grin.

Then Sybilla drew a deep breath and laid both of her hands on the tabletop, palms up. Her sisters immediately took hold.

"You both know that there have been rumors for many years about Mother. And they have grown to the point that the king believes he has grounds to take Fallstowe away from us." Sybilla swallowed. "Away from me."

"Yes," Cecily said gently. "We've heard the rumors."

Alys squeezed Sybilla's hand. "But it's just that the king can't stand the idea of a lady holding so rich a prize as Fallstowe, isn't it? It doesn't matter whether the woman was Mother, or you."

"I don't think it is entirely that the king was against Mother's ruling Fallstowe because she was a woman," Sybilla said. "But because she was never a lady to begin with."

Chapter 19

It was so silent in the hall immediately following the tale she told of Amicia Foxe's enormous ruse that Sybilla could hear her own heart beating. And now three of the faces regarding her did so with mouths agape, eyes wide, complexions pallid.

Save Piers Mallory. But Sybilla suspected that the news of her mother's play to nobility didn't surprise him in the least after what he'd been put through by his own family.

Alys was the first to break the silence, of course, although the point she chose to touch upon was not what Sybilla expected.

"So I'm only half noble?" she said, her eyes still wide.

Sybilla shrugged. "It would seem so. Yes."

On her right, Cecily huffed a mirthless laugh. "I scarcely can believe it," she said, and then hurried to reassure Sybilla by bringing her other hand to her sister's forearm. "But I do believe you, of course, Sybilla. It's only, well . . . but I suppose that does explain a lot about Alys's personality, though, doesn't it? Forgive me, Piers."

"No offense taken, Cee," Piers assured her mildly.

"Me?" Alys screeched. "Me? At least I waited until I was married, *Saint* Cecily!"

Cecily glared at her younger sister for a moment but then looked to Sybilla, her brown eyes heavy with sympathy. "But one would never know it from Sybilla, would they? Completely noble, to her core."

Sybilla stared at Cecily, willing herself not to weep yet. She opened her mouth, but as usual, Alys began speaking once more.

"Yes. And it's not as if that gives the king complete grounds to seize Fallstowe, any matter. Nobles marrying commoners might be unusual, but it's not completely unheard of. And while Mother had no noble blood to speak of, she is no longer the head of Fallstowe—you are, and you are absolutely Papa's girl. Like him in so many ways." Sybilla felt the tightening in her chest increase as Alys regarded her with such sweetness. "You always were his favorite."

Sybilla could not look at either of them, so she dropped her gaze to the tabletop, the tears pushing heavily on her eyes causing the wooden surface to blur and rise toward her.

She felt Cecily's hand tighten on her arm. "Sybilla? What is it?"

"I—" She tried to begin, but the word came out as a croak, and so she was forced to stop, swallow. She closed her eyes and a tear slipped from beneath her lashes, feeling white-hot against her cheek.

"I'm not Papa's girl, though," she said hoarsely, her eyes still closed. "Morys Foxe was not my father."

Oliver's voice was hushed with shock. "What?"

"Oh, Lord have mercy," Cecily whispered.

"Sybilla!" Alys demanded, and shook Sybilla's hand,

prompting Sybilla to look at the stunned woman. "What do you mean?"

"I mean that Mother was pregnant when she arrived in England," Sybilla said. "My father was a common soldier in Simon de Montfort's army. So you see"—she pulled her hands away gently to tend to her wet face—"I am actually completely common. And once Edward finds out . . ." She shrugged again.

"That's why we always thought she favored you," Alys said wonderingly. "She was readying you for this day."

Sybilla nodded. "And it's why she bade me see the pair of you married well. She knew that if the truth was discovered, there would be little recourse for me, but you and Cecily would be safe."

"That . . . that"—Cecily seemed to struggle to find words for a moment—"that bitch!"

Sybilla turned to look at her usually reverent sister, unusually shocked at the foul accusation toward a woman Cecily had loved very much.

"She may as well have thrown you to the lions!" Cecily accused her, her face a mask of delicate fury unlike anything Sybilla had ever seen from her.

"No," Alys argued meekly, shaking her head. "No, Mother loved Sybilla best—she would never put her in such jeopardy."

"Then why didn't she see that Sybilla was *first* to marry?" Cecily demanded, and then shot to her feet, as if her anger would no longer allow her to sit. "I will stop praying for that woman's soul, for surely she resides in hell this day."

"Cecily," Oliver said softly, and rose to stand at his wife's side, turning her into his chest, where she clung and began to weep loudly.

Alys still seemed quite subdued with shock. "But . . .

but surely Edward would not punish you for something which you have no control over, not when you've done so well by him at Fallstowe."

Cecily pulled away from Oliver, her anger still pulsing through her tears. "Perhaps not, but he's pushing the old bone that Mother somehow aided Simon de Montfort at Lewes, isn't he?"

Sybilla nodded. "Yes," she said quietly.

"But that's ridiculous," Alys insisted. "Papa was killed at Lewes! Mother may have been capable of and done things that none of us thought her able, but she loved Papa. She did not betray the king at Lewes." Alys turned to Sybilla. "Did she, Sybilla?"

"No," Sybilla said, even more quietly than before. "No, she did not."

Piers spoke then. "You're completely sure of that? You have proof?"

Sybilla nodded, cleared her throat. "I am completely sure."

"See!" Alys said, triumph in her voice. "I knew it!"

"Mother didn't betray the king or Papa," Sybilla said. "I did."

Oliver Bellecote sat down on the bench near his wife's hip. "Fuck me," he breathed.

"Sybilla," Cecily whispered. "That can't be true."

"It is, though," Sybilla said on a sigh, better able to control herself now that the bulk of it was out. "In my defense, I was not quite sixteen, and not at all sure of what I was doing that night. I thought I was . . . helping."

"That's what she led you to believe, wasn't it?" Piers suggested. "Amicia."

"It doesn't matter," Sybilla said. "It was I."

Cecily slapped the table with her palm. "It does matter!"

"It matters very much, Sybilla," Oliver said gravely.

"You were only a girl, coerced into what you did with no malice or ill intention of your own. For Christ's sake— your own father was killed in that battle!"

"He wasn't my father, though," Sybilla reminded him lightly. "And Amicia did not think him to be in the thick of the fighting. She never expected him to be endangered by what she had set in motion."

"I remember," Alys said softly. "I remember the night we received word that Papa was dead. How distraught everyone was, Mother included." She turned to Sybilla, confusion in her eyes. "Except you. You never wept. I remember thinking that was when you became so . . . cold. But it wasn't that you didn't care, was it?"

"It was that you had realized what you had done," Cecily supplied. "What she had persuaded you to do."

"I thought I had killed my father. I didn't know all the truth until the months before she died."

"The king is a reasonable man," Piers said suddenly, although his attention was focused on the tabletop, as if studying it, contemplating its nature. "He is just."

Sybilla took a deep breath, focusing her thoughts. "Although Julian is under oath to take his evidence to the king, he has also promised me that he will stand up on my behalf. He's . . . he's offered me a life after all this is over. A life with him and Lucy."

No one gathered around the table spoke. They only stared at her with wild shock. And so Sybilla expounded.

"But he doesn't know about Lewes yet. He still thinks it was Mother. Perhaps if I tell him—"

"No!" Cecily shouted, and stepped toward Sybilla, grasping her by her shoulders. "No, you mustn't tell him! You mustn't tell him that!"

"I have to, Cee!" Sybilla insisted.

"What do you mean, he's offered you a life?" Oliver asked, staring at her intently. "He wants to marry you?"

"He's mentioned marriage, yes," Sybilla said calmly, with a nod. "I don't know where we would go. I don't care, really." She paused, looked around the table at the wary and concerned faces regarding her. "I think I'm in love with him. With him and his daughter."

Cecily brought her hands to her mouth. "Oh my God."

To Sybilla's left, Alys once more laid her head upon her arms and sobbed. "Oh no! All these years she's waited! It's not fair! It's not fair!" she wailed.

"Sybilla," Oliver said carefully. "I don't know how it's happened that you've come to trust a man you barely know, let alone love him. You've always been so cautious, so careful. I . . . don't know. But there is something you need to know about Julian Griffin before you tell him anything more. Something I learned from his own general the morning after his army arrived at Bellemont."

Cecily's hands still covered her mouth, making her words barely audible as she stared, motionless, at Sybilla. "Don't tell her, Oliver."

"I must," Oliver insisted grimly. "Sybilla, the handsome payment Edward has promised Julian Griffin is Fallstowe itself."

Alys's continued sobs filled the cool air of the hall. Sybilla stared at Oliver Bellecote as if he'd just told her that the sun would never shine again. She could think of nothing to say. She didn't wish for him to repeat it—she'd heard him clearly, understood his words completely.

One like Fallstowe?

Exactly like Fallstowe, I hope.

His endless questions. His intense interest in the

grounds and industries. The way he walked about as if . . . as if it were already his home.

It *was* already his home.

He had tricked her. Tricked her into letting him in, telling him what he wanted to know. Tricked her into his bed. Tricked her into loving him.

And the entire time, he was stealing Fallstowe out from under her.

Sybilla stood slowly, calmly. "Thank you for that information, Oliver," she said coolly. She felt she had come back to herself suddenly, as if she had been away for weeks and weeks, and had now come home. The coldness, the lack of emotion, the betrayal: old friends, all. And she was once again in familiar surroundings inside her own icy heart.

"I'm sure you understand that I must be away immediately. I have some things to tend to at the keep."

"Sybilla," Cecily said, stepping toward her with her hands out. "Don't leave now. At least stay the night here at Bellemont. Give yourself time to think, to plan what you will do. You're in no state to make the journey back now."

"I will not have him in my house," Sybilla said, and her voice was low, guttural, spoken between clenched teeth.

Piers stood now. "Cecily is right; you're in no shape to ride now, Sybilla. It's too dangerous."

From behind her on the bench, Alys reached up to grasp her hand. "Please don't go, Sybilla," she said, weeping softly. "I'm so afraid for you."

"Stay here, where we can protect you," Oliver offered.

"I don't need your protection," Sybilla said quietly.

Cecily stomped her foot. "You are not going! I won't allow it!"

Sybilla let her eyes flick to the double doors of the

hall, and they blew open with a great crash, as if on a mighty gust of wind. All heads turned to look at the calamity just as the sounds of heavy hooves clomping on stone echoed in the hall.

In moments, Octavian's great, grey, muscled body pulled itself through the doors after his charging hooves. He clattered surely down the stairs and galloped toward Sybilla, his mane flowing out behind him.

Cecily screamed as Oliver jerked her out of the path of the horse and Octavian whirled to a stop before Sybilla, standing between her and the people gathered there, his breaths whooshing out of him, stirring and heating the air.

In a blink, she had pulled herself into the saddle and fished up the reins. She turned Octavian in a tight circle, looking down on her sisters clinging to their husbands.

"I love you all very much," she said, and she realized that her frigid tone belied her warm words. "You will know when it's over."

Then she kicked Octavian's sides, and the warhorse lurched forward once more toward the doors of the great hall even as her sisters shouted protests. The horse devoured the stairs in two leaps, and the two little serf girls, who had come to stare through the doors in amazement, leapt away from the opening just as Sybilla and Octavian burst from the keep.

She urged him through the bailey toward the solid, closed gates, faster, faster, leaning over his neck and driving him.

"Go, boy," she whispered. "Go!"

A high-pitched squeal rang out through the bailey as Sybilla and her horse drew ever nearer the gates. Then the wooden slabs bulged, shuddered, and seemed to fall from their hinges as one, sending up a great storm of dust as the king's soldiers scattered and Sybilla and Octavian thundered over the breached gates.

Octavian had never run so fast—perhaps no horse ever had, or ever would again. But the king's soldiers would later report seeing nothing more than a cloud of dust and then a sparkling white light race down the road away from Bellemont, like a shooting star.

A dying star, bright with its own fate as it raced to bury itself in the earth.

Julian spent the rest of the day in Sybilla's solar with Lucy. He dismissed the temporary nursemaid, and tended his daughter himself all the day. He fed her, played with her, tucked her into the deep cushions of the couch when she wished to sleep. He wandered about the room, considering each furnishing in great detail: the shield and crossed swords over the fire, once belonging to Morys Foxe; the hammered and oiled urns; the carved arms of the chairs; the tapestries of a million threads in a hundred different shades; the rugs—dense, bright costly; even the fine panes of expensive glass set in lead squares. Items that had surrounded Sybilla the whole of her life. He took no luncheon, and only picked at the supper tray that was sent.

The nursemaid finally came for Lucy, suggesting gently that the hour grew late, and perhaps 'twould be best if the wee lady retired for the evening. Julian relented, shocked at the blackness outside the window, barely recalling that a servant had come hours ago to lay a considerable fire in the hearth. He kissed his daughter, held her close despite her indignant squawk, and then turned her over to the kind-eyed matron.

When he was alone, he stood before the warming blaze, his hands clasped behind his back as he stared at

Morys Foxe's intimidating weaponry suspended over the mantel, which held a collection of delicate-looking, fired and glazed vases. The irony was not lost on him. Sybilla Foxe—so beautiful, so cunning, so capable—was a traitor to the Crown. Once Edward found out, Sybilla would be put to death, Julian was certain of it. It would not matter to the king that Sybilla had been unaware, at the time, of the gravity of the crime she was committing. It would not touch his heart that the only man Sybilla had ever known as father lost his life in the battle that followed her treason. A crime had been committed, a most serious offense, and the perpetrator would be held accountable.

And Julian would be lauded as a hero of England, awarded the spoils of Fallstowe, where he could raise Lucy in the manner befitting a princess.

Julian picked up the vase in the middle of the mantel, directly under the shield, and admired it, turning its smooth surface in his palm. It was quite valuable, beautiful. Unique. And then he hurled it into the fire, enjoying the smashing sound it made on the stones, the shower of dangerous sparks sent rolling from the white-hot logs.

He would not do it. He would not sentence the woman he loved to certain death. The woman who he knew somehow in his heart would pour out more love upon his daughter than even he could summon. The woman who had changed the course of the history of a nation, thwarted a king, played a man's game better than any man, and lived through it all with her heart still intact.

At least, Julian hoped it was still intact.

How foolish he had been not to have heeded her warnings that he could not help her. How prideful he was to think that he could somehow right whatever it was

that was wrong in her life. He could not protect her from
the dead; from the past, which was even now reaching
up like hands from a grave to grasp at her ankles.

His time at Fallstowe was nearly over. The king would
send for him soon. But now Julian planned to be far
from Fallstowe when the summons came, Lucy and
Sybilla Foxe with him.

Whether she went willingly or nay.

Chapter 20

It was the middle of the night. She had come straight back to Fallstowe lands from Bellemont, although Fallstowe had not been her initial destination. She'd gone instead to the Foxe Ring, where she had laid herself down on the flat center stone in the moonlight while Octavian meandered about the ring. She had lain there for hours, watching the stars spin and slide across the sky, watching the moon flicker and glow in its misty shroud. She let the cold of the rock seep into her body, her bones, as her mother's voice whispered to her.

I told you not to trust him! You can trust no one but yourself!

"Not even my own mother," Sybilla breathed. "You used me to save your own skin."

It wasn't that way at all! I knew you could take care of yourself; you were the only one who could! If only you had heeded my direction from the start and obeyed me! You always disobeyed me!

"I disobeyed you once, and it saved England," Sybilla

answered. "You were a liar, a traitor, a betrayer, even unto your own."

No!

"You loved Cecily, you loved Alys, but never me. I was disposable. A weapon you forged and wielded."

I loved you best of all, don't you see? Why can't you see? You were the only thing in this world that was truly mine, that truly belonged only to me! Only you could do the things such as I have done, been as strong, as cunning! You were my child, alone! I trusted you with my life, with our legacy!

"I am ashamed of you," Sybilla said, her voice catching. "Ashamed of myself, how I defended you to everyone, deflected the rumors. The true reason I kept your nasty secrets is that I knew that if I told, I would be just like you. No loyalty. No honor. And I am nothing like you."

You are exactly like me. You are *me. We are one.*

"No."

There will come a time when you will see that what I say is true. When you love someone so much that it does not matter what happens to yourself or anyone else. You will lie or steal or kill to see them safe. I loved you, loved your sisters, loved . . . others in that way. There will come a time, and you will see.

Now Sybilla felt as though she had been formed from ice as she made her way through the darkened passages of Fallstowe from her ruined chamber. She had traded her damp and dirty gown for one of sheer, white silk, which tied at the chest and claimed simple, billowing sleeves with drawn satin ribbons. Her hair was undone, brushed down her back. Her bare feet made not the slightest whisper on the icy stones; her breathing was shallow, silent.

She came to the foot of the spiral staircase and paused, looking up for a moment.

He had come to Fallstowe knowing everything he did about her, knowing the castle would be made his if he turned her in to the king. He had fooled her into trusting him, into making her almost believe that he could love her, help her. He had played to her every weakness, and she had believed him. Most likely Julian Griffin would only have laughed at her after handing her over to Edward, smirked while she was dragged away to the gallows.

She began to climb the steps. The jeweled dagger in her cold right hand felt light, warm, alive. With each riser she gained, slowly, numbly, a different memory flashed through her mind, spanning years, going both forward and backward in time.

The way Julian had held her, threatening to snap her neck, the night he'd arrived at Fallstowe.

The weeks after Lewes, when she'd found her mother weeping bitterly over some letter she'd received.

Lucy's warm body snuggled next to hers while she'd lain in Julian's bed.

Morys Foxe stealing her away from her lessons to go riding through the demesne with him.

Julian Griffin destroying her bed in a rage.

Amicia's face, tears leaking from her useless eye, her clawlike hand grasping Sybilla's so tightly as she'd slipped away from this world.

Alys, always laughing.

Cecily's sweet smile.

All of them gone from her now.

The chamber door was cracked open a bit, and it made not the slightest creak on its hinges as it swung open slowly, seemingly of its own accord. Sybilla stepped through the doorway, the chamber nearly as dark as the stairwell save for the little glow from the fading fire. But Sybilla was beyond the light then, full of darkness herself, and so she could see quite keenly the shape of Julian Griffin in the center of the bed.

She seemed to float over the floor to the end of the bed, then stopped there, watching him sleep. Her fingers unclenched, shifted, then curled back around the hilt of her dagger.

No more men . . . only me.

I must protect you.

The image of him grew blurry for a moment and Sybilla blinked, sending a tear down her cheek.

As if he had heard the whisper of wetness sliding over her skin, Julian Griffin's eyes snapped open and he sat upright in the bed, his left arm braced behind him.

"Sybilla," he whispered. He seemed not the least bit surprised to see her there. His gaze swept down her body, stuttering as it caught sight of the weapon in her hand. He brought his eyes back to hers. "Have you come to kill me?"

She nodded, only the slightest downward movement of her chin.

He shook his head, his eyes continuing to bore into hers as he slowly threw the covers from his legs and swung his feet over the side of the bed.

"No," he said.

Sybilla could only whisper, "Yes."

"No," he repeated, standing up from the bed, completely nude. "I can only guess at what you were told at Bellemont. It's Fallstowe, isn't it?"

"You lied to me," she said, her voice trembling.

"No," he said again. "I asked you to marry me."

"You didn't mean it. Stop talking."

"I did mean it," he said, his face stony as he took a step toward her. "I still mean it. I will marry you tonight if you'll agree; even now, knowing that it was you at Lewes."

Sybilla blinked, and she felt the iciness of her heart fracture the tiniest bit, like the pattern on a moth's wings.

He continued to step toward her, slowly, cautiously, but purposefully. "We are leaving Fallstowe; you, me, Lucy. As soon as can be arranged. We will go abroad, to a country where Edward can never reach you."

"You would not give up a prize such as Fallstowe," she said bitterly.

Then he was upon her, Sybilla shrieking as he seized the dagger in her hand and wrenched it away from her, twisting her wrist painfully. He jerked the weapon free and threw it to the shadows, then grabbed her roughly, pulling her against him despite her struggle.

"*I don't want Fallstowe without you,*" he shouted into her face.

Sybilla stilled in his arms, but she did not look at him, instead keeping her gaze upon his collarbone.

"I love you, Sybilla," he said, a touch of anger in his voice. "Yes, the king has promised me Fallstowe, and no, I didn't tell you. Would you have let me stay had you known? No," he answered himself.

"You could have told me later," she accused him. "When you asked me to marry you."

"And then I would never have known if it was me you wanted or this damned pile of rock!" He took her shoulders and held her away so that he could look into her face. "I was going to tell you anyway, the day I received the letter from John Grey, the day you left for Bellemont. I couldn't keep it from you any longer; I didn't want to."

"That's a convenient excuse, isn't it?"

"No, it's not," he growled, shaking her. "It's rather inconvenient that I am giving up a certain future for myself and for my daughter because any future we would have without you in it is not worth living."

"I don't believe you," she insisted, and the cracks around her heart widened.

"Fine. Don't believe me. Don't believe me while you are packing your things. Don't believe me while you are gathering all the coin you can lay hand to. Don't believe me when we reach the docks and hire a ship in the night to take us across the Channel. Don't believe me as we race together across the Continent, the three of us." He took her face in his palms. "But let's do those things quickly, so that once you do start to believe me, we are far, far away from here."

And then he kissed her, long and deep and hard, and Sybilla felt her hands reaching for him, grasping at his arms as she kissed him back, her heart breaking open and tears spilling from her eyes as white heat overtook her flesh.

Julian pulled away slightly to speak against her lips. "I love you, Sybilla. I love you so, and I will do everything in my power to protect you, to keep you with me. Please, please, now will you trust me?"

She nodded, the movement jerky and hesitant, feeling as if she would burst with this foreign weight of emotion inside her.

"I love you, too, Julian Griffin. I never wanted to, but I do." And then she instigated the next kiss, pushing him backward as she walked toward the bed.

He fell onto the mattress, pulling her with him, and then turned until she was beneath him. He was inside her in an instant, loving her the way she needed to be loved—firmly, completely, quickly.

They lay there in the dark afterward, both drifting off to sleep, Julian's hand curled around her face behind her ear. But then Sybilla blinked her eyes open and felt a frown come to her brow.

Something was wrong. Something was missing.

Chapter 21

He was alone again when he awoke, but neither surprised nor alarmed by it. He was beginning to become familiar with some of her ways, and it gave him a bit of peace in the midst of what they were to undertake.

There would come a day, he was certain, when they could lie about at their leisure, together. But today was not that day, and they would likely not realize that fantasy for many weeks. Time, now, was of the essence.

Julian found Sybilla and Lucy in the hall, his daughter perched on the lady's hip as she bent her head over a ledger and traced the page with one finger, turning her face slightly to inquire this or that of the clerk at her side.

As if she sensed his arrival in the hall, she turned to him. "Good morrow, Lord Griffin," she said coolly. "I've located the accounts you asked after."

"Good morrow, my lady," he said, and joined her on the dais, catching on and playing to her charade instantly.

"Very well. May I?" At her nod, he pulled the thick book toward him.

"Thank you. That will be all for now," Sybilla told the clerk. "You may come and fetch your work in an hour."

Then the clerk left them. Lucy was reaching for him, so Julian straightened and greeted his daughter with a noisy kiss and a toss into the air. Then, not bothering to glance about, he snaked an arm around Sybilla's waist and pulled her to him, pressing his mouth to hers firmly.

"Good morning," he whispered.

She glanced away from him, a small smile threatening her mouth, as if she had gone suddenly modest. "Julian, please." She disentangled herself and turned her attention back to the ledger. "This page is what we have on hand at the present," she explained, running her finger down an impossibly tiny line of scratch marks. Her fingertip stopped near the bottom. "The total sum."

Julian leaned forward, bracing Lucy's back with his hand. He squinted and blinked at the tiny numerals and then drew his head back to look at Sybilla.

"That's what you have on hand?" he asked incredulously. "Are you certain?"

"My clerks are thorough," Sybilla said with a slight frown. "Is it not enough?"

Julian huffed a laugh. "It's ten times more than what we require."

Sybilla lifted her chin as if he had offended her. "Perhaps it is ten times what *you* require; however, I have no intention or desire to live in poverty."

"I don't think that will be a concern," Julian said. "However, I don't know how we will transport it all."

Her brow creased. "I don't know, either. Perhaps we

can take what would fulfill our immediate needs, then have Oliver secure the remainder for us."

"That is a possibility," Julian said, pleased at the easy way they seemed to be flowing through the details. "I would be ready to away in the morn. Can you send directions to him by then, with assurance that he will do as you ask?"

"Without doubt," Sybilla said, and the tone of her voice put to rest any concerns Julian might have had. "I'll need to inform Graves this afternoon. I've not seen him since I returned, and he will need time to pack what he wishes to bring."

Julian paused. "I beg your pardon?"

"What?" She closed the ledger and looked at him expectantly.

"Graves is coming with us?"

"Of course," Sybilla said simply and set about locking the thick leather straps about the accounting book. "It would seem quite strange for a family to be traveling to the Continent without any servant at all, would it not?"

"Yes," Julian admitted. "But, Sybilla, he's 110!"

She frowned at him. "He is not. We may need his . . . unique skills, and I would not leave him behind to deal with the aftermath of our departure after he has so faithfully served this family."

Julian had to admit she was right. It was no secret what Graves meant to the family, and he would be interrogated without mercy as to the goings-on of the last month at Fallstowe.

"Fine," he said easily. "Come to think of it, I've not seen him myself since yesterday. Do you think he can be ready by this evening?"

"Yes," she said. "He's quite efficient. I will employ the brawnier of the stable hands to load our things once night has fallen. They have little interest in what goes on outside the stable walls, and their curiosity will not be engaged. We shall meet in your chamber at midnight."

"Mmm," Julian said with a smile and drew her near once more. "That sounds promising." Lucy obviously took the lady's proximity to mean that she was being transferred, and threw herself happily at Sybilla, who laughed and awkwardly caught the baby before drawing her head against her cheek.

Then she did give Julian a smile. She opened her mouth to speak but was interrupted by one of the gate guards entering the hall and striding toward them. Sybilla slid from his embrace and stepped a respectable distance away.

"Milady," the man said, stopping before the dais with a bow. "Lord Griffin's men have returned."

Sybilla's head turned swiftly toward him, and Julian did not bother with trying to hide his shock.

"Erik, you mean?"

"Sir Erik, yes, but also the soldiers. All of them," the man clarified stiffly, glancing at Sybilla. "They said you were expecting them."

Julian could feel Sybilla's wariness from where she stood. "No, I told him I would send word in a month, not to come before then." He looked to Sybilla. "I wasn't expecting them," he said in a low voice, knowing how this must look to her. "I can't deny them, though—it would greatly arouse suspicion, and we aren't ready."

Sybilla regarded the soldier with tense resignation.

"Open the gates, give the soldiers entry. Bring Lord Griffin's general to him."

"At once, milady." The soldier bowed and then was away again.

Julian turned to her, ready to receive the storm of her accusations, but she was grim, determined, even as she rubbed Lucy's back in comforting circles. "If all the men are inside the walls, perhaps there will be fewer to see us leave." She jiggled the baby on her hip and looked into her face. "Isn't that right, Lady Lucy? They shall never see us."

"Nah-nah-nah!"

Julian stared at Sybilla for a moment, speechless. "Thank you for believing me."

She stared back, then shrugged as if it were nothing. "I keep my promises. They were coming in, any matter. Better at my request than not."

The men must have been waiting just beyond the doors, or else they came running at being granted entrance, for in the next moment, Erik and one other man Julian was only vaguely familiar with entered the hall, a pair of Sybilla's guards following them closely.

Erik did not look happy, and so Julian called out to him. "Ho, Erik, what brings you here without my summons? And who is this in your company?"

Erik's jaw was set, his words spoken between clenched teeth. "This is not my doing, Julian."

The stranger stepped forward. "Lord Julian Griffin and Lady Sybilla Foxe?" he demanded.

"Yes," Julian said, his patience wearing thin. "And just who the bloody hell are you?"

* * *

The man pulled a rolled parchment from his vest and unfurled it, clearing his throat before reading aloud. "It is hereby proclaimed that Lord Julian Griffin is wanted by the Crown, Our Sovereign Lord, King Edward, under charges of aiding and abetting a traitor to the Crown, and conspiring to commit treason."

"I beg your pardon?" Julian shouted.

The man turned to Sybilla, who was now holding Lucy close to her face, breathing in the simple scent of the child while her heart pounded in her chest.

"Lady Sybilla Foxe, upon grounds of treason, espionage, and insubordination to the Crown, you are both hereby placed under arrest. It is my duty to accompany you to the king for your immediate trial." The man rolled up the parchment and looked at them both. "How do you answer?"

"How do I answer?" Julian demanded. "Fuck off, is how I answer! Erik, what is the meaning of this?"

"'Twas Murrin," Erik answered stiffly, his eyes only flicking to Sybilla. "She was only pretending at being ill, Julian. She thought she was protecting you and Lucy. Perhaps she is."

"Murrin?" Julian repeated incredulously, and then his brows lowered further as he caught Erik's insinuation. "You don't know anything about it, Erik."

Then the nagging sensation that something was missing, which Sybilla had felt since last night in Julian's bed, found its answer. The miniature portrait of Amicia and Sybil de Lairne. She'd had it in her hand the first night she'd come to Julian's bed, but she'd never seen it again and thought she had simply misplaced it. But the next day had been when Murrin came upon Sybilla and

Julian and Lucy in the solar, when Julian had suggested marriage to her.

The solar with the door that had been open at the time.

Murrin had left Fallstowe that day.

"How do you answer, Lady Foxe?" the man demanded of her.

"I'll answer you naught, you lowly hoof-scraping," she said, pleased when the man's frown turned threatening. He began to reach for his side. "If you take one step toward me whilst I hold this child, I will cut you from your tiny little cock to your Adam's apple, wherefore shortly thereafter you will have the unique experience of holding your own guts in your hands. I will give my answer to Edward and to him alone. If he wants me so badly, then he shall have me."

"You'd better watch your tongue, lady," the man growled, although his face had paled.

"And you'd better watch your back," she informed him coolly.

It must have been at that moment that the man felt the sword point between his shoulder blades, for his eyebrows rose and he held his hands out to his sides in a gesture of surrender. Erik stepped away, drawing his weapon.

Graves leaned to the side slightly so as to address Sybilla from around the king's man. "Spot of trouble, Madam?"

"Unexpected guests, Graves," Sybilla said, jostling Lucy, who had begun to cry.

The threatened soldier spoke loudly, his fear evident in his words. "If you kill me, all the lives in this hall are forfeit!"

At her side Julian spoke low. "Run?"

Sybilla considered it. But she knew they were surrounded by soldiers who were no longer under Julian's command. They were inside the gates, the keep surrounded. If they ran, and if they were caught, they would both be killed on sight.

Sybilla felt Lucy's weight most heavily in her arms.

There will come a time when you will see that what I say is true. When you love someone so much that it does not matter what happens to yourself or anyone else. You will lie or steal or kill to see them safe.

There will come a time, and you will see.

"I will go willingly," Sybilla answered.

"Sybilla, no!" Julian hissed.

"But," she said, ignoring Julian's protests, "the child will not. There will be none to care for her. She shall stay with her nursemaid."

"I will not leave Lucy," Julian growled. He stepped toward Sybilla, pulling his daughter from her arms.

The guard still at the mercy of Graves's sword argued. "This is some ploy. The child goes, as well."

"What do you think her to do, you cheese-headed oaf? Incite a rebellion? She's an infant. And as none of your proclamations place *her* under arrest, she is in no better hands than here at Fallstowe."

"No, Sybilla," Julian said. "I can't—"

"Julian," she said in a low, cool, calm voice. "I have trusted you. Would that you show me the same courtesy."

"She's my child," Julian pleaded in a cracking voice.

She looked at him then, clutching the baby in his arms, his face a mask of fury and fear.

"She was to be my child, too," she breathed. "You will see your daughter again."

She saw Julian swallow. Then he hesitantly nodded.

Sybilla looked back to the guard. "If you agree that the child shall remain at Fallstowe to be cared for, I will go willingly to London, and none of your men will be attacked. If you refuse, I will send up the battle cry." She paused. "You may have a bloodless victory, or fantastic carnage. Your choice."

The man frowned furiously at her, but then nodded. "Very well. I give you my word. Call off your man and send for the child's nurse."

Sybilla nodded toward her steward, and Graves lowered his sword and took a step away from the man.

"Nurse?" she said pleasantly, pointedly.

Graves stepped forward, both hands clasped over the hilt of the sword still hanging in front of him. "You called, Madam?"

"What kind of nonsense is this?" the soldier demanded. "You expect me to believe that this old corpse is a baby's nurse?"

Sybilla raised her eyebrows at the man. "Would you agree, sir, that it is a fact that Lady Lucy's original nurse, a girl named Murrin, is no longer at Fallstowe?"

The man frowned. "Yes, that is true, I suppose, but still—an old man?"

"Graves is the most trusted servant Fallstowe has ever known." She looked to Graves and hoped that the love she felt for him was evident in her eyes. "There is no one better to protect Lord Griffin's child in his absence." She nodded toward Julian. "Go on, Graves," she ordered softly.

It took the old man a moment to walk to the dais steps and gain the platform. Then he laid his sword down carefully upon the lord's table and turned to Julian, his wrinkled and knobby fingers outstretched.

"Would you come with me, please, Lady Lucy?"

The baby stared wide-eyed at the old man and shrank back against Julian for a moment.

"Graves . . ." Julian said in a choked voice, and then halted as if unable to speak further.

Sybilla barely heard the old man's query to Julian.

"Think you this is the first precious daughter placed in my care, Lord Julian?"

Julian kissed Lucy's head firmly three, four times and then handed the baby to the old steward.

Graves turned away, the baby still regarding him with wide eyes. "Let us go find a nipple, shall we?" he said soothingly, and his eyes met Sybilla's when he passed her.

Sybilla hoped he would hear her. *Send him after me tonight.*

He nodded once at her, the motion so slight that no one save Sybilla would ever have noticed.

And then he was gone.

Julian turned to face the hall aggressively as the king's man stepped forward with chains. Erik refused the pair offered to him, obviously intended for Julian.

"Never," Erik said, his chin lifted. "Not under the threat of death."

Sybilla did not look at Julian again as her dagger was removed from her side, the cold bite of chain fastened around her ankles and wrists.

There will come a time, and you will see.

The time had come. And Sybilla saw.

Within moments, the men who followed Erik had laid hands to Julian's trunks and his thick leather portfolio, filled with the history he'd collected about the Foxe family.

He and Sybilla had waited in the hall, both shackled in a primitive manner on opposite sides of the room. She would not meet his eyes. And she spoke not another word to anyone.

Outside the hall, though, the bailey was in pure chaos.

Word had spread quickly from the household that Madam was being taken from them, although Fallstowe's soldiers made no move to attack the tight ring of the king's men who made a living corridor for the prisoners to walk through.

The servants and villagers felt no fealty to the king's men, however, and they pushed against them in a mighty, furious wave, shouting obscenities, hurling eggs and dung at the royal soldiers. Sybilla did not acknowledge them with the slightest glance, only walked calmly between her personal guards—one to each side and one to the fore and aft. Julian noticed that none of the men dared touch her.

Likely very wise.

Julian followed, an officer to either side of him. At the end of the avenue of soldiers, a strange, fortified conveyance waited, with a soldier posted on each side of the open door. It was a wooden carriage of sorts, but the planked sides had been bolted over with close strips of thick iron, the windows barred. A team of six sturdy horses had been harnessed together tightly to pull the monstrosity. Julian had to laugh out loud when he saw the crucifixes fastened to each face of the imposing-looking rolling dungeon.

Then Sybilla did glance over her shoulder at him. "Flattering," she said with a smirk.

"No talking," the man to her left shouted, and made the mistake of shoving Sybilla's shoulder roughly.

She did nothing more than pivot her head quickly toward him, but in the next instant the man was lying on his back in the dirt. Fallstowe's citizenry went mad, pelting the man with rocks and manure until he cried out in a panic and was helped to his feet by his fellow soldiers.

Sybilla ignored it all, stepping up into the carriage awkwardly, no man daring to give her assistance after what had just happened to their comrade.

The soldiers quickly moved to shut the door, even as her skirts slid inside, and Julian watched as a series of three locks along the seam of the doorjamb—all as big and thick as his own fist—were latched with loud clicks. Then a chain was dragged through two loops across the width of the door itself and secured.

Julian was afforded his own mount, although he would have much preferred accompanying Sybilla in the ridiculous wheeled prison. The chains around his ankles were removed, but his wrists were left bound. It was more than he expected, especially since Erik had already departed for London, ahead of the massive wave of soldiers, leaving Julian without his friend.

They rolled through Fallstowe's gate and over the drawbridge in a sea of soldiers that seemed to be a mile long; one small woman the remote island in the very middle of it all.

Julian saw two men astride some distance away, watching the passing mob of boots and swords and banners. He looked closely.

One of them had the blocky silhouette of Piers Mallory, Lord of Gillwick; the other, Julian could only assume, must be Oliver Bellecote.

Julian did not signal to them in any way, only turned his head forward and rocked in the saddle. He trusted

Sybilla, and so he would trust these men that she had deemed worthy of her sisters. They would be completely loyal to her—Sybilla would accept nothing less, and she gave nothing less to those whom she loved.

For some reason, that realization stirred an uneasy feeling in Julian's stomach.

Chapter 22

Sybilla's conveyance was abysmally loud and uncomfortable, but that suited her. The jarring motion of the racing carriage made it impossible for any of the guards riding alongside to keep a clear watch over her through the tiny, obstructed windows, and the outrageous clamor masked the sounds of her exploration of the carriage's interior construction.

Even the floor was sheeted over with hammered metal, bolted to the frame and impervious to any tool she might have been able to procure; which, of course, she hadn't. The window frames were solid, reinforced. The door didn't so much as shudder as the carriage careened over the rutted road. The roof, she had seen upon entering the vehicle, held no hatch.

The benches to the front and rear of the carriage were upholstered, though, and so Sybilla began prying at the tacked edge under the front cushion, a lip of perhaps two inches, using her fingernails to pick at the material until she had pulled a small strip of it loose. She poked a finger into the hole and felt through the scratchy straw and woolen batting until she found the bench frame beneath. Wood, with a small gap where the seat and front facing met.

Sybilla smiled and rose to her knees on the hard metal floor. She hooked the fingertips of both hands under the lip of the bench and pulled with all her strength. The seat did not budge, and as the carriage hit a particularly deep hole, Sybilla was thrown onto her shoulder.

She grimaced and pulled herself aright again, this time sitting on her bottom. She turned her right hand palm up, and laid it under the bottom edge of the lip, and then curled her back to fit the cusp of her right shoulder against the back of her palm. She braced her feet against the opposite bench and threw herself upward against the seat. It creaked, almost imperceptibly on her first try, and so she did it again. And again. The three smallest fingers of her right hand felt as though they would shatter.

Perhaps it was after her tenth go at it that the seat bench lifted; sturdy, square iron nails pulling halfway from their moorings. Sybilla gave a huff of relief and quickly gained her knees. She peered through the gap created and was shocked to see the carriage's front axle turning beneath her. Wasting no time, she once more grabbed the lip of the bench with her fingertips and pulled.

The seat pulled free easily this time, like opening the lid of a trunk, and Sybilla was rewarded with the sight of the brown dirt road spinning away beneath the carriage, dust and rocks tumbling furiously. One such rock chose that moment to hurl itself through the bench opening, whizzing past Sybilla's face and missing her eye by a breath. It clattered around inside the carriage for a moment like a wild arrow, then fell to the floor near her left calf. Sybilla lowered the bench seat most of the way with one hand and picked up the rock with the other.

It was a wonder it hadn't killed her. Oblong, the length of her palm, the rock could have been a rough-hewn end for a primitive spear, its edges thinned and chipped by years and years of hooves and wheels. She turned it over in her palm and looked at it for a moment, then slid it behind the rear upholstered edge of the opposite bench, between the seat and the back wall.

Then Sybilla lowered the seat bench back to its usual placement and climbed upon it.

Now she would wait. Wait, and try not to think about anything at all.

The whole of Edward's army departed Fallstowe. Oliver was surprised they hadn't left at least some soldiers behind to secure the castle for the king, but Piers had suggested otherwise.

"Fallstowe folk would have seen them all dead before the last man crested yon hills."

Alys's husband was right, of course. With Sybilla gone, it would be no great task to return the king's army to Fallstowe and overthrow any of the men who—now leaderless—thought to resist. Sybilla *was* Fallstowe. Without her, there was nothing to fight for.

And Oliver wanted to fight.

He and Piers gained entrance to the gates without incident, the fighting men and villagers obviously relieved to see them. Oliver and Piers put them off, though, making their way straight to the hall, seeking the one who would know what Sybilla wanted them to do.

They found him not in the hall but in the kitchens.

While the cook and the maids laid their heads upon the massive center workbench and sobbed, Graves sat in a little wooden chair by the hearth, calmly feeding an infant from a bladder.

Oliver halted in his tracks, Piers following suit, and both men simply stared at the old steward. In a moment, Graves deigned to look their way, and a slight smile cracked his dusty old countenance.

"She's a beauty, is she not, my lords?"

"My God," Piers said. "Is that Julian Griffin's child?"

Graves sniffed. "Who else would she belong to?"

"What's she doing here?" Oliver demanded.

"Can't you see that she's having luncheon?"

Piers turned to Oliver. "This is no good."

Oliver grimaced and nodded. "All right, you old badger, what is it we are to do to rescue Lady Sybilla?"

"Do, Lord Oliver?"

"Yes, do. Sybilla has obviously been taken against her will to the king."

"Has she?"

Oliver growled. "Well, I'm fairly certain she didn't plan it thusly."

The old man raised his eyebrows and shrugged, returning his attention to the infant who was regarding Oliver and Piers quite warily from the corners of her eyes.

Then Piers spoke, in his calm, thoughtful manner. "She already has a plan."

"Doesn't she always?"

Oliver was frustrated to the extreme. It had been enough of a struggle for him and Piers to leave Bellemont without their pregnant wives. If they did not resolve a way to rescue Sybilla Foxe, and quickly, they might as well not return to Oliver's home at all.

Piers spoke again, and Oliver admired the man's careful way of holding his tongue while his brains did their work. Oliver would have to try that in the future.

"What does Lady Sybilla need from us?"

Graves was silent for so long that Oliver did not think he would answer. The child's feeding bladder was empty, and so the old manservant removed it and expertly placed the baby on his shoulder, patting her back as if it was his sole duty in life to care for children.

"What do you know of Madam's character?" he asked musingly.

Oliver was not amused. "I'm not playing your little game, Graves."

"Strong willed," Piers said immediately. "Faithful. Cunning."

Graves rewarded Piers's answer by pointing at him with one gnarled finger. "And when the pair of you and your wives were in the most dire of straits, what did Madam do?"

"She came for us. Herself," Piers answered. "She risked everything." Piers glanced at Oliver uneasily. "For Cecily, she apprehended the villain who would have seen her dead. For Alys and me, she breached the king's home herself."

Oliver nodded, not liking the direction this conversation was taking. "Are you telling us that we need to go directly to the source of Sybilla's trouble?"

"Why would you need to go to the king?" Graves asked mildly.

"Wait," Piers interjected, then paused, obviously working out the situation in his head. "Julian Griffin was also arrested. You indicated that Sybilla might have gone willingly, and Lord Griffin's child has remained behind at Fallstowe." Piers looked to Oliver.

"Sybilla said she is in love with him," Oliver said.

Piers nodded and then looked back to Graves. "She's going to confess, isn't she?"

"She can't do that, though," Oliver nearly shouted. "She'll be put to death." He looked at Piers. "We must go. I don't know what we shall do when we get there, but Cecily and Alys will never forgive us if we don't."

"Again I ask you, why would *you* need to go to the king?" Graves repeated. "What skills would you add to Madam's defense?"

"Skills?" Piers asked this time, nonplussed. "If you mean skills in the way Lady Sybilla and our wives possess skills, then I don't—"

"Yes, where *are* Ladies Cecily and Alys?" Graves interjected musingly.

"They're safe at Bellemont," Oliver answered, but even as he did, a rock seemed to drop into his stomach.

"Are they?" Graves wondered.

Piers kicked a nearby chair. "Shit!"

Oliver grabbed Piers's elbow. "Let's go. If we ride hard, we should be able to meet them. They surely aren't traveling very fast."

After the two men ran from the kitchens, Lady Lucy gave a most satisfactory belch, and Graves praised her with a smile.

"Can't have the pair of them mucking things up, can we?"

"This is a terrible idea," Alys moaned.

Cecily shot her a reproving look as she jerked on the

horse's reins, navigating their cart into the grass to avoid a series of particularly deep ruts in the road.

"It's a fantastic idea," Cecily argued. "Whatever has happened to your sense of adventure, Lady Alys?"

"I believe I forgot to pack it and left it behind at Gillwick," Alys muttered. "Of all people, I would think you to be more prudent at a time like this."

"Prudence will not save Sybilla," Cecily said firmly, and felt a strange feeling of empowerment come over her, bringing a bright smile to her face. "I do believe marriage and motherhood have effectively dampened your penchant for mischief."

"Mischief?" Alys exclaimed. "Our sister is, at this moment, under arrest and en route to London, where she will be tried for treason. I hardly think *mischief* is an apt term to describe what we're getting ourselves into."

"Would you rather have—oh my! Hold on!" The cart's rear wheels caught the tail end of a gully as they were pulling back onto the road, and the conveyance tipped precariously, causing Alys to shriek and grasp at the bench. Cecily stood from her seat and guided the struggling horse without diving headfirst into panic.

Once they were righted and traveling smoothly once again, Cecily sat down and continued where she'd left off, glancing at Alys's pale face.

"Would you rather have waited, useless, at Bellemont, not knowing what was happening?"

"Of course not, no," Alys said. "But I don't see what we will be able to accomplish on our own. And Piers and Oliver will be so angry."

"Then they should have taken us along in the first place," Cecily said. "It's their own fault. They should have expected it."

"Expected it from me, perhaps, yes. But not you. It

seems I'm not the only one whose personality has been affected by motherhood."

Cecily pursed her lips. "True," she conceded. "Any matter, I'm sure that when Sybilla stormed the king's castle for you, and when she came to save me from wicked Joan Barleg, she had no idea what she would come across, nor exactly what she would do. We'll figure it out."

"This is the stupidest thing we've ever done," Alys muttered.

"No, it's not," Cecily said, enjoying the bright warmth of the sun on her face. "Your running off to the Foxe Ring and then to London with Piers Mallory, and my seducing Oliver Bellecote at the old ruins were the stupidest things we've ever done. This"—Cecily waved one hand in the air, as if searching for the words—"this is positively mundane. Two women on a ride through the countryside. Bland."

"You're mad," Alys accused her.

Cecily smiled down at her sister. "You agreed to come."

Alys brooded for several moments, her chin on her fist. "Besides," she said at last, "I don't know what to make of this revelation about Mother."

"I don't wish to talk about Mother," Cecily said firmly.

"But I don't believe it," Alys argued. "I can't believe that she would orchestrate this entire ruse, place Sybilla in such great danger. Sybilla was her shining star, the child she chose to succeed her, the one she trusted with her secrets. It makes no sense that she would throw her to the wolves as it seems she did, with no real hope of anyone to save her, ever. You have to admit."

"Our mother was obviously full of secrets," Cecily said. "There is likely much that we don't know, and shall never know about what she did or why she did it. It's difficult for you to accept because you are the baby, Alys. You don't want to think anything bad of Mother."

"That's not it, though." Alys brooded some more. "Don't you get the feeling, if you were to stand back and look at things as a whole, that Mother did her best to keep us all isolated from certain facts?"

"She kept us isolated from most all the facts, I daresay."

"Yes, but listen," Alys insisted. "We didn't know anything about the de Lairnes, and from what Sybilla said about what Julian Griffin reported from Lady de Lairne, they knew nothing about us."

"That's not odd," Cecily said, "considering that Mother was posing as a lady of that family for years."

"Yes, but when Mother told Sybilla the supposed truth of her birth, she made Sybilla promise never to contact the de Lairnes. Why would that even be necessary? Why would she ever think that Sybilla would wish to have anything to do with the family that Mother betrayed so? Especially if we weren't actually blood relatives?"

"I don't know. I don't care."

Alys continued, to Cecily's dismay. "Sybil de Lairne loved Mother."

"She was a fool, then."

"*I* loved her," Alys warned her. "And so did you. So did Sybilla. An evil woman would not garner such devotion."

"We were deceived."

"Perhaps," Alys conceded. "But why were we deceived?"

"You are trying to read well of her intentions after the fact, Alys," Cecily said.

"What if—" Alys mused, ignoring Cecily's statement. "What if Mother was not only trying to protect all of us, but Sybil de Lairne, as well?"

Cecily looked aghast at Alys. "That's outrageous. Mother wasn't even of the nobility. What reason would she have—a lady's maid with so much to hide, so much to lose—to protect Sybil de Lairne? And protect her from what?" she demanded.

"I don't know," Alys admitted gloomily.

"Alys," Cecily said, striving for a bit of patience and sympathy for the youngest sister, "I know that the revelation of Mother's true nature has shattered everything you thought you knew about her. But the truth is, we will likely never know why she did what she did. Sybilla is in very real danger now, with very real consequences, and we must focus all of our attention on saving her before she sacrifices herself for us all."

Alys's eyes narrowed as she stared off into the countryside, as if considering Cecily's advice. "Very well, Cee. You drive. I shall think."

Chapter 23

The enormous party of the king's men and his prisoners rolled across the countryside, and Julian kept his eyes on Sybilla's carriage, hoping against hope that something or someone would intervene.

How would he ever vindicate himself to Edward now? How would he ever choose which truths to tell? Telling the whole truth would see Sybilla damned. Telling a partial truth might come round like the curve of a noose to slip over his own head and steal him away from Lucy forever.

What could she possibly be planning? Julian could see no way out for them.

He sighed, staring at the rolling hills, the rarely varying landscape, as the sun sank lower and lower on the horizon, bathing the soldiers in a soft red glow. One of the guards to his right drew his attention to a knoll some distance away.

"Ay, look there," the man said to his friend, pointing to a blocky shadow topping the rise. "Is it wild, you think?"

"Could be," his comrade said. "But I thought they

were all claimed years ago. Looks too big to be Spanish. Probably escaped his stable, is all."

Julian doubted the big grey destrier had escaped his stable, although he was without bridle, without saddle, his mane blowing in the breeze as he solemnly watched the procession of soldiers. The horse *was* wild, Julian well knew, but not without a mistress.

Octavian was following them, and the idea of it caused Julian's heart to pound.

"If it is, I feel sorry for the lord missing that beast," the man said with a laugh in his voice that didn't sound the least bit sorry at all. "I've caught glimpses of him for the past hour. Seems to be followin' us. Per'aps he's wild, and the horses have drawn him out."

His soldier friend shrugged, seeming not in the least bit interested.

"I'd like to have me a horse like that," the first man said, almost to himself. "If he's still at our flank when we camp, I'm going out with a lead."

"You're an idiot," his friend said.

Julian had to agree.

Sybilla felt the carriage slow and then at last come to a rocking halt. Her eardrums throbbed from the incessant thundering of the reinforced cage, and the silence seemed too loud.

No one came to her right away, and so she waited, pulling herself up to peer over the edges of the high-set windows, getting her bearings.

They were setting up camp in a field, opposite a stretch of wood on the other side of the road. Sybilla ascertained that they had positioned her cell in the open, a wide berth of nothing around the carriage.

She acknowledged that as quite inconvenient. Even with her escape route from the carriage itself secured, it was going to prove very difficult to move away from the conveyance in the open, unseen. Nightfall would be her only hope, and she could only trust that what she needed would be provided to her.

There was a crashing knock upon the carriage door, and then the cacophony of what sounded like tens of locks, the rattling of chains on metal.

"Prisoner, step away from the door," a soldier commanded.

Sybilla sat on the bench she had pried loose hours ago and meekly folded her chained hands in her lap.

The door cracked open, and she saw a sword point and a pair of eyes peering through the gap at her. The eyes rolled the limits of their sockets, taking in the interior of the carriage. The door closed for only a moment, and when it reopened, it was only wide enough to toss a battered metal pot and a limp sack of unknown contents onto the floor. Then the door slammed shut again, the sounds of chains and locks heard in reverse order.

Sybilla eyed the grungy, smelly pot distastefully, and kicked it to a corner of the floor. She would wait, as long as she was able, any matter. Then she picked up the light sack by its neck and worked at undoing the knot.

Inside was a crust of hard bread, blackened on one side, and a small root, so shriveled and emaciated with age that Sybilla could not tell if it had at one time been a carrot or a turnip. With a roll of her eyes, she tossed the bag into the disgusting pot. She would have to take Edward to task for his poor hospitality.

The thought made her smirk, but only briefly. She couldn't allow herself to be overcome with despair just yet. Not until she had accomplished what must be done. The lack of adequate cover around the carriage was troubling.

Cover.

Sybilla gained her feet with an obvious clatter of chains and called upward through the window.

"Hello there? Hello?"

After a moment, a wary voice answered. "Shut up. What is it?"

"If you're not going to let me out all the night, might I at least have a blanket to cover myself with?"

"No. Be quiet."

Sybilla frowned, but then heard another voice speaking to her guard.

"Oh, come now—what's the lady to do so sinister with a simple blanket? Have a bit of charity, old chap."

"You mind your own damned business," the man snarled. "She could tear it into strips or something of the like. Hang herself."

"Well, that would save us and the king a spot of trouble, wouldn't it? We wouldn't even need to open the door," the other soldier reasoned. "Simply shove it through the bars there. I can't abide abusing a woman so, prisoner or nay."

Sybilla cleared her throat and called in her most cajoling voice. "Please?"

She didn't hear anything for some time, and so she thought her plea had failed. But then she heard a rustling sound and saw the corner of an impossibly dirty, rough gray cloth being pushed through the bars.

Sybilla grabbed the corner and pulled, wrinkling her nose at the dust and horsehair that was loosed from the rotting material.

Sybilla smiled triumphantly. "I shall certainly remember you to the king."

"Don't do me any favors, mistress," the man grumbled.

Sybilla tossed the blanket to the opposite seat, not looking forward to handling the infested cloth. She climbed back into her corner, drew up her knees and laid her chain across her shins, and waited for night.

She must have dozed, for her eyes snapped open at the soft whinny of sound that tickled her ear. She stilled her breathing and listened.

There it was again. It was him, she was certain.

Sybilla felt down her legs slowly, carefully, and slipped her hand inside the top of her boot. Her fingers found the cincture where the ankle cuff was fastened around the leather, and she checked once more that she could indeed turn her ankle within the metal ring. She reached across the carriage floor for the filthy blanket, draping it over her chains as best she could. Then Sybilla drew in a breath, pointed her toe, and pushed at the sole of her boot while pulling her left leg.

The metal cuff ground against her ankle mercilessly as the bone squeezed through, and Sybilla knew the area would be black afterward. But just as little beads of sweat popped out along her hairline, her left foot slid free of her boot—and the cuff—the chains making little noise as they fell between the leather of her shoe, the blanket, and the upholstered bench.

The cuff around her right ankle was not as perfectly round, nor as big as the one on her left foot had been, and Sybilla panicked briefly when she thought that her escape would be foiled. But then the image of Julian Griffin sleeping in his bed in the tower room at Fallstowe, his daughter's downy head nestled against his bicep, filled her mind, and the skin of her ankle yielded as she kicked the boot free.

Sybilla doubled over her knees, her eyes squeezed shut, and she fought the urge to scream at the burning pain now ringing her right ankle. She didn't dare touch it, as she could feel the wetness running down and under the arch of her foot. She knew her boot was torn, ruined.

She would leave bloody footprints, but they would not be seen in the night, and perhaps would have disappeared with the dew by morning.

She heard the soft whinny again, closer this time, and Sybilla knew she must go now.

She placed her useless boots and the leg chain on the opposite bench and then took up the rotting blanket, again winding it around the chain—this time between her wrists—to dampen the sound. She returned to the seat she had so recently vacated and carefully, slowly, pulled it up.

It creaked at first, and Sybilla froze for several moments, waiting for any sign from beyond the carriage that the sound had been heard. But nothing else stirred, and so she lifted the bench farther.

The square of ground below was marginally brighter than the carriage's interior, and Sybilla leaned her head down, listening for the telltale sounds of a soldier on patrol. She heard nothing. She held the seat aloft and swung her right leg into the narrow opening, reaching with her toes, lowering herself until her left buttock rested on the bench frame. Still, she could not reach the axle with her foot.

She lifted her right leg slightly, adjusting her bottom until she sat rather uneasily on the hard bite of wood. If she slid too fast and missed the axle, she would tumble to the ground conspicuously, the bench seat crashing closed behind her and marking her as a dead woman. The chain between her wrists was not long enough to afford bracing one hand to either side of the opening.

She tried with all her might to bring to mind the image of the axle she'd seen earlier in the day, to gauge how far away from her toes it could be. No more than two feet.

She had no choice.

Sybilla braced as much weight as she dared on the edge of the bench seat in her hands, clenched her buttocks, and slid. It seemed she was going to the ground before her feet struck the wooden axle at an angle, and she quickly bent her knees, turned her feet to cross the cylindrical beam and pushed at the seat above her head just as it was to slam shut on her fingers.

She paused in that most awkward position for several moments, listening, listening. Then she bent her elbows, lowering the seat above her, and leaned into the wooden frame of the underside of the carriage, sliding down into a crouch.

She stepped from the axle slowly, hiding behind the spokes of the iron-rimmed wheel, and looked about her. The camp was quiet, one man on guard beyond the carriage's tongue, perhaps ten paces; one to the rear, the same distance. But the bulk of the camp lay between her and the road and the wood beyond, the soldiers seeming to stretch in either direction as far as she could see in the night.

She heard muffled steps directly behind her and Sybilla slowly, slowly turned her head.

Four massive hooves were just coming to a quiet stop, and then she heard Octavian's gentle breath.

Sybilla did not stop to think of the likelihood that she would be immediately detained upon coming out of the carriage and daring to mount Octavian in that instant. She did not think of the arrows that might chase her and her faithful mount, likely find them both.

Octavian had come for her, and she would go with him. Right . . .

Now!

She scurried from beneath the carriage and stood aright, keeping an eye on the soldier to the fore of the carriage, obviously picking at his nose and examining his findings. She reached up for her horse's mane and heaved herself up with a mighty effort, the blanket tangled in her wrist chains making her mounting all the more awkward. Octavian moved away from the carriage in a strange, sidestepping, backward manner, and then in an instant, reared back on his haunches and leapt into the darkness away from the camp and the road.

The soldier to the rear of the carriage swung around, just as his fellow guard called out, "What was that?"

The soldier chuckled as he saw the moonlit rump disappear in a blink into the shadows of the landscape. "I think it was your wild horse, mate. Missed your chance. Right behind you, it was."

The other guard cursed crossly and then set to digging in his ear with his pinky.

Someone shook Julian's shoulder roughly, as if they thought him to be asleep. Of course, Julian had not so much as closed his eyes since stretching out on the hard ground, his hands and ankles once more bound.

"Yes?" Julian asked, rising up on one elbow and looking over his shoulder where a soldier was bent on one knee. The sun would rise within the hour; already the sky was lightening above the wood. "What is it?"

"Sybilla Foxe has escaped," the man said darkly.

Julian dropped his eyes to the ground for a moment, letting the realization sink in fully. "Did anyone see her? Try to stop her?"

"No, milord. No one saw a thing. We're not even certain how she quit the carriage—it remains quite locked."

"Good. If no one tried to stop her, that means no one is dead. The last thing she needs following her is a charge of murder."

In that moment, Julian and the young soldier were joined by the king's man who had arrested him and Sybilla in Fallstowe's hall. He didn't appear particularly cheerful.

"If you think to follow her lead and escape before gaining London and your just punishment, I hate to disappoint you," the brazen one threatened. "As it is, you'll be taking her place in the carriage to forestall any attempt at flight."

"Because that conveyance is so obviously effective at containing prisoners?" Julian scoffed at the man. "Very well. I accept."

The man looked confused for a moment, but covered his uncertainty quickly. "I'll be sending men back to Fallstowe. She shan't escape for long."

"A piece of advice, soldier," Julian offered. "Your men will not intercept Sybilla Foxe at Fallstowe. But if they would happen to cross paths with her, I would suggest that they not try to apprehend her in any way, lest they long for a hasty death."

"She's but one woman, alone, afoot without even her shoes," the man sneered.

Julian knew a pang of concern at the information that Sybilla was barefoot, but he did not dwell on it.

"She's not afoot," Julian said casually, and then lay

back down on the ground, making a show of adjusting his arms to comfort his head. "And she shall beat us all to London. If I were you, I would not be anticipating the humiliation that awaits you at having your prisoner arrive before you."

"Bollocks, you say," the envoy scoffed from behind him.

Julian shrugged and closed his eyes.

The man said nothing for several moments. Julian feigned disinterest, but his body was rigid with impatience.

"Rally the men. Break camp at once for London. No time to lose—we ride in a quarter hour. Ready a group of men to return to the Castle Fallstowe, on the watch for the prisoner."

Then Julian felt the toe of the envoy's boot nudge him roughly between the shoulder blades.

"If this is some ploy to distract me, to try to buy your little lady traitor some time to further her escape, you would do well to keep in mind that your daughter is alone at Fallstowe, and I have rein to do as I see fit with interferers."

Julian did not so much as flinch. *Come a bit closer, old chap* . . .

He sensed the man crouching behind him now, heard his smug voice close to his head.

"Do you hear me, Griffin? You lead no one any longer. I am in charge."

In a blink, Julian had rolled over, swinging up his arms until the chain suspended between his wrists looped around the odious man's neck. Then he quickly rolled back again, yanking the envoy from his feet, across Julian's body, where Julian held the man on the ground in front of him, his mouth directly over the envoy's ear while the man gasped and kicked and clawed at the chain biting into his windpipe.

"*You hear me*," Julian said in a low voice. "And hear me well: should you even so much as whisper an allusion to the fact that I have a daughter again, I will beat you to death. Chains or no chains, soldiers or no soldiers. I will kill you with my bare hands. That is my solemn vow." He pulled the chain tighter with a little grunt. "And if you dare to touch me again as if you possess some authority over me, I will dismember whatever appendage has offended me and feed it to the king's hounds while you watch. Morsel by bloody morsel, you cowardly piece of dung."

Several of the envoy's soldiers approached now, some of them reaching for their swords.

"This is a man-to-man conversation," Julian warned them. "I have not yet been relieved of my duties, and so I outrank this piece of filth I am defending myself from. Stand down. That's an order!" To the envoy still in his clutches, Julian asked, "Do you understand me?"

The envoy gave a jerky nod.

Julian drew his knees up beneath him and gained his feet awkwardly, dragging the envoy aright with him before quickly releasing the chain from around the man's neck and stepping away.

The envoy whipped around, his hands still at his bruised throat. "I'll kill you for that," he croaked, his eyes wild.

Julian stared back at him, opened his hands slightly to let the chain dangle in a wide arc. "Whenever you're ready."

The envoy hesitated. "Lock him in the carriage," the man shouted hoarsely, and a pair of soldiers reluctantly moved toward Julian. "And keep a closer eye on this one!"

Julian did not resist as the men indicated that he should move toward the reinforced wagon that had until recently interned Sybilla Foxe. In fact he went willingly.

Like the envoy he had just chastised, Julian wished to gain London before Sybilla Foxe did.

Chapter 24

Sybilla felt as though she and Octavian became one in the moonlight, her fingers tangled in his mane as the chains between her wrists clanged with each jarring gallop of the war steed. The flesh of her legs was hot and wet and prickled where it gripped Octavian's sides. She leaned close over his neck, her knees pressed to his heaving flanks, her ankles drawn up behind her, the tops of her feet laid close along the bunched curve of Octavian's rump. She had no need to drive him, lead him—it was as if he knew their destination, knew the urgency. His hooves were solid, sure, his gait steady and untiring.

They were spirits, wraiths, streaking over a dark and shadowed land toward London. Sybilla felt the tears on her cheeks leaving little ghosts of cold as the rushing air dried them. She was racing toward her death, and she couldn't seem to get there quickly enough.

She had not gone back to Fallstowe Castle.

The morning sun was high in the sky when the walls of the great city came into view, and Octavian began to instinctively slow. She let him wander from the road to drink from a rain barrel set against a little cottage, and she tried to smooth back the voluminous tangles of her hair, but it was of no use. The red velvet of her gown was caked with dirt and horse sweat, and she knew her face must be as well.

She would enter Edward's court looking like a common beggar, which was in truth what she was now.

They were back to the road in moments, and through the gates without incident, although as she drew closer to her intended destination, she couldn't help but notice the increasing stares she drew from the citizens of the city. By the time Octavian drew to a halt before the guards, a small crowd had gathered behind her. She dismounted with care, her joints and muscles creaking, and a pair of soldiers rushed forward with concerned looks on their faces as they took in her chains, her hard-traveled appearance.

Before they could approach her, Sybilla reached up with both hands to grasp Octavian's muzzle and pull it to her face. She pressed her lips to the damp, scratchy hair, the warmth of him, squeezing her eyes shut for a moment.

"Thank you, boy," she whispered. "Now go. Go home." Her voice broke on the last word and she pushed his head away roughly. As her horse turned in a quick circle she slapped his rump, sending Octavian galloping through the crowd, which scattered and shrieked at the massive animal racing heedlessly past them.

When Sybilla turned back toward the palace, the guards were upon her.

"Milady, are you injured?" one of the guards asked, taking a quick assessment of her blood-smeared hands.

"I must see the king immediately," Sybilla said, ignoring his query, although her voice sounded odd and faint to her own ears. When the guard took her elbow, Sybilla felt her knees buckle, and she stumbled against the soldier, who took her weight easily. "It's urgent," she managed to whisper. "I have come from Fallstowe Castle."

"Come this way, milady," the soldier directed her, and with his partner taking her other arm, the men commanded the crowd away and half carried Sybilla up the stairs to the ornate doors that marked the threshold to her fate.

A company of men seemed to appear from nowhere, opening the doors, accompanying her swift escorts into the grand entry, shouting orders for a surgeon, for a key to the chains that held her. The antechamber before the king's court was already populated with the nobility who were of a mind to see the monarch, and they made no attempt to hide their shock and morbid curiosity about the woman being escorted across the marble floor.

"The king is not receiving yet this morn, milady," one of the soldiers informed her with the utmost deference, trying to keep his words directed toward her ear. "But due to your state and the urgency of your request, you may await him alone while he is informed of your arrival."

"Thank you," Sybilla whispered, her lips numb as her eyes flicked to each lord and lady, openly staring at her. "Thank you."

"But we must tell him who it is who awaits him," the soldier continued with a slight smile. "Your name, milady?"

Sybilla turned her face up slowly to look at the soldier. "Sybilla Foxe," she breathed, the two words barely stirring the air.

The soldier frowned. "I beg your pardon?" He leaned his ear closer toward her.

"My name is Sybilla Foxe," she said, louder this time, and there was no mistaking that the majority of the persons gathered in the antechamber had heard her that time.

The air came alive with the sound of ringing metal, and as if conjured up, Julian's blond general, Erik, appeared from somewhere deeper in the hall, leading his own group of travel-dirtied soldiers.

"She is a prisoner of the Crown!" Erik said clearly, his face darkened with fury as he stormed toward her, his own weapon drawn.

The hands once so solicitously supporting her elbows withdrew, leaving Sybilla to stagger aright under her own power.

The soldiers stepped away as Eric and his men reached her, joining the perfect circle around her where nothing but sword points lived.

Sybilla felt her shoulders draw up toward her ears, and she grasped her elbows, glancing around her at the handful of armed men, their weapons now trained on her without mercy.

"Seize her," Erik commanded. "And take her immediately to the dungeons."

"Wait," Sybilla said. "I must see the king right away." Her arms were grasped again, but this time there was no kindness in her captors' hands.

"Oh, you'll see him soon enough," Erik promised. Then he stepped toward her, his face a mask of twisted fury. "Where is Lord Griffin?"

"He's still with the king's men," Sybilla answered. "They follow."

Erik glared at her. "You've ruined him, you know."

Sybilla swallowed. "I hope not," she whispered. Dizziness swam around her like hot little whirlpools.

A confused frown creased Erik's brow for only a moment. "Go," he commanded the men around him.

Sybilla was pulled backward from the antechamber, away from Edward's private court, her bare heels skimming over the cold marble floor. In moments, she was in darkness, and yet it would be some time before she was interned properly in her cell.

"My God," Alys breathed as she and Cecily waited in their cart at the crossroads. On the wider London Road before them, only a handful of miles outside the city itself, hundreds of the king's soldiers stirred the brown dust as they passed. Men on horseback, men afoot, wagons carrying battle gear mostly hidden with tarps and covers. In the center of the mob, a lone, barred carriage rattled past, and its purpose was clear: a rolling fortress, a cell meant to contain the most dangerous of criminals.

Cecily stood suddenly on the seat, the reins still in her hands. "Sybilla!" she shouted at the carriage, her voice breaking with volume and emotion. "Sybilla!"

"Cee, sit down!" Alys hissed, and yanked hard on her sister's hand even while one of the mounted guards blocking the narrow throat of their smaller path swung his horse around to face them with a suspicious glare. "Do you want us both arrested as well?"

"But what if she's in there, Alys?" Cecily demanded. "I can't just sit here and watch her pass!"

"There is naught we could do to aid her now, any matter. Keep your seat lest we find ourselves in our own metal box. We shall gain the city soon enough." Then Alys groaned. "Oh, damn. Too late. Here he comes."

The soldier kicked his horse lightly and trotted up to the sisters' cart, his eyes keenly taking in the bed of the conveyance, the blankets, the limp sacks.

"Ladies," he said dubiously, eyeing Alys's obviously rounded shape. "What business have you on the London Road?"

"I don't see how it's any concern of yours," Cecily bristled. "What are you now, a toll collector?"

Alys gave Cecily a sharp pinch on the back of her arm before saying, "We're on our way to London, good sir." Her face glowed with sweetness.

"Is that so?" the soldier challenged them. "What is your purpose?"

"We're to see the king, if you must know," Cecily informed him straightaway.

Even as the guard became obviously wary, Alys gave a merry laugh. "Isn't my sister funny? Of course we're not meant to see the king. What would two lone women, in a cart, have need to press the king for? Only a jest."

The man didn't look convinced. "You wouldn't be following a royal caravan containing a dangerous prisoner of the Crown now, would you? Having a little looky? Thinking of making a little mischief?" He looked them both in their eyes, in turn. "For if you were, that could turn out very badly for you."

"Oh really?" Cecily demanded. "And just who are you to—"

"We're going into the city to sell our wares, of course," Alys interrupted her. "Not very much business in the village lately. Thought we'd try our luck with a larger market."

Alys could feel Cecily fuming at her side.

The soldier looked pointedly into their empty cart once more. "I don't see any wares," he accused them. "Only some old blankets."

Alys swallowed with a gulp. She hadn't thought this particular charade through.

Then Cecily rescued them both, in a most shocking way. "Our wares are of a . . . feminine nature, you understand."

A sly, nasty smile grew across the soldier's bristly face. "I see." The tail end of the royal caravan was now rolling away in a cloud of dust, leaving the soldier alone at the crossroads with Cecily and Alys. "And where had you been plying your . . . wares?"

"Bellemont," said Alys, in the same instant that Cecily offered, "Gillwick."

The man's eyes narrowed.

Alys laughed again, but this time even she could detect the quiver of uncertainty in her tone. "We do tend to get around."

"Like the clap, I'm sure," the soldier said. He eyed Alys's rounded stomach again. "I can't see how *your* services would be much in demand."

"You'd be surprised," Cecily quipped. "Farmers adore her."

The man's eyes flicked to the road, cloaked in a storm of dust as substantial as an earthen wall, then back to Cecily. He didn't look closely enough.

"Perhaps *you* could give me a little sample then. A *toll* for using the road." He grinned.

Alys's hand went to her mouth to cover her own smile as Cecily leaned slightly forward on the seat.

"You'd need to ask my employer first," she said coyly.

"Really?" the soldier said, leaning forward to brace his forearm on the pommel of his saddle. "And where might I find that old bloke on a deserted road such as this?"

Cecily waggled her index finger over the soldier's shoulder. "It must be your lucky day, for he's right behind you."

* * *

"Prostitutes!" Oliver shouted for what had to have been the twentieth time. He glared down at Cecily from his perch on his horse. Piers Mallory's mount followed meekly on its lead.

"I couldn't very well tell him that we were Sybilla Foxe's sisters, come to aid her," Cecily said in their defense. "We'd have been arrested straightaway!"

"Why did you have to be seen at all?" Oliver said. "You could have stayed back off the road until they passed. It wasn't a holiday parade, Cecily."

"If you would have taken us with you in the first place, we wouldn't have been here on our own at all, would we?"

"I told you Piers and I would do all we could to help Sybilla. You don't trust me."

"You're not us, Oliver," Cecily said simply.

"She's right," Piers said calmly. Then he turned to look at Alys over his shoulder as he drove the cart. "I'm sorry, love. I'm only glad that you are unharmed."

"You're apologizing?" Oliver said in a strangled voice.

Alys reached up and patted her husband's broad back from her seat in the cart bed. She looked rather mollified. "It's quite all right, darling. I daresay that soldier is going to have a fantastic ache in his skull when he awakens, thanks to you. You're such a wonderful protector."

Cecily looked up at Oliver expectantly and batted her eyelashes.

"I think not," he grumbled. "Once we return to Bellemont, you are not to leave the grounds—nay, the keep—nay! Our chamber, until after this child is born."

Cecily sighed and rolled her eyes toward her sister.

Alys spoke up again. "Since we are nearly to London, can we please talk about what is going on with Sybilla?

What did the two of you learn at Fallstowe? Was that indeed Sybilla in the midst of the king's men?"

Oliver was still too befuddled to speak, and so Piers added his calm commentary. "We think so. Graves is tending to Lord Griffin's child at Fallstowe. Sybilla went willingly."

"Why is Graves tending to Julian Griffin's infant?" Cecily asked. "Where is Lord Griffin?"

"He is also under arrest," Oliver said. "Apparently he is being accused of collusion with Sybilla in treason against the Crown."

"What?" Alys gasped.

"Graves hinted to the fact that any tender feelings your sister held for Lord Griffin were reciprocated."

"I don't understand," Alys said. "Then why would Sybilla willingly go to the king if it meant her certain trial and possible death?"

Cecily nodded slowly as she spoke. "Because she is doing what Sybilla does best. Protecting. Defending. She is going to confess to save Julian Griffin. It's why the child was left behind—because Sybilla has every intention of Julian Griffin returning to claim both his daughter and Fallstowe." She looked up at Oliver. "I'm right, aren't I?"

There was no trace of anger left on her husband's face. "I fear you are, my dear."

Chapter 25

Julian was treated with slightly more deference once released from his conveyance into a rear entrance of the king's home, but he paid it little heed. His mind raced with the idea of Sybilla already inside, already in the midst of a terrible interrogation.

What had she told the king?

What would Julian tell him?

He was snaking through the underground corridors, a handful of the king's men buffering him fore and aft; from what, Julian could not say. Escape was the last thing on his mind while Sybilla was locked away somewhere inside the palace, and Lucy leagues away at Fallstowe. So many lives depended on his being exactly where he was at precisely that moment.

The corridor opened up into a wider hall, and as the party accompanying him spread out, Julian spied young Erik, advancing toward him like a squall on the horizon.

One of the king's men stepped in front of Julian's protégé, and Julian could not have been prouder when Erik shoved the man aside as one might swat at a persistent fly.

"Lord Griffin," Erik said. He stood there expectantly, his brows drawn down over his youthful face, his eyes sparkling with anger and confusion.

"Have you seen her, Erik?" Julian asked.

The man nodded succinctly. "It was I who encountered her upon her arrival."

"Is she well?"

"I cannot say," Erik replied, his face taking on a deeper expression of frustration. "Is it true?"

"Where is she?" Julian was forced to begin walking forward once more as the king's man gave the command, but Erik fell into step beside him. "Has she seen Edward?"

"She's under lock and key, of course," the blond man said, as if shocked that Julian would think otherwise. "The king was engaged when the traitor arrived."

"I would think there would be naught more important to him at this point," Julian muttered, and then flashed Erik a warning look. "Don't call her that."

Erik suddenly seized Julian's bicep with strong fingers, drawing the party of men to an unwilling halt around them both. "Julian, again I ask you: Is it true?"

"Is what true?" Julian demanded, shaking his arm free of the younger man's grip.

"That you've fallen in league with a traitor," Erik said. "That you are now against the king."

Julian paused. Yes, no—he was unsure of the answer himself. "It's complicated," was all he could say.

From ahead, a soldier called back, "Move it along—the king awaits."

Erik shook his head slowly as a look of disgust came over his face, hardening it. He began backing out of the midst of the men surrounding Julian.

Julian was forced to once more begin walking forward,

away from his friend, who stood in the empty stone hall, alone.

"I thought better of you, Julian," Erik called to him a moment later, his words echoing off the walls and floor.

Julian tried to look back over his shoulder at the young man, but his view was blocked as the group funneled around a wide cylindrical column and into a different, narrower corridor. In another moment, the king's soldiers divided to either side of a plain door, and Julian realized that they had arrived at the private entrance to the king's court.

Julian took it as a positive sign that he wasn't led straight to the gallows.

The king's odious man opened the door for Julian and motioned him inside. Julian wanted to take hold of the edge of the wooden slab and slam it back into the man's face as he entered the king's private chamber, but he restrained himself, his eyes taking in the scene before him.

The king was standing at the side of his table, his profile outlined by the bright sunlight pouring in from the high-set windows on the far side of the chamber. His long, lean frame was bent over sheaves of parchment, snippets of notes—the contents of Julian's leather portfolio, which now lay limp and emaciated on the corner of the table.

A woman joined him, seated at the narrow end of the table closest to Julian's entrance, her back to him. He could see nothing of her save for the sleeve of her right arm, the swell of her skirts around the chair legs, and the veil covering her head, but he knew at once that it was not Sybilla.

Edward turned his head and his narrow face regarded Julian with expected disappointment.

Julian folded himself into a deep bow. "My liege. You sent for me?"

Edward gave a humorless snort. The long fingers of his right hand drummed for a moment on a stack of papers upon which his arm was braced, then he straightened somewhat.

"What in the bloody hell has been going on at Fallstowe, Julian?" he asked in an almost pensive manner.

"My liege, I—"

"I sent you," Edward interrupted firmly, yet still reserved in tone, "to finish gathering the information I sought, and then to bring Sybilla Foxe to me. Imagine my surprise—nay, my shock—when none other than your nurse flies back to me reporting your defection."

"There were facts that—"

"*Here! Are! The facts!*" Edward shouted, and slammed his right fist atop the stack of papers. "I told you—I warned you—that she was cunning, did I not? I wanted you to succeed. Was prepared to reward you outrageously— unlike any other under my command. As my cousin. As my friend." Edward straightened and swept his hand over the table, laden like a damning buffet.

"She's here, isn't she?" Julian dared, and regretted the words as soon as they had left his mouth.

"By my own warrant!" Edward roared, and the woman still seated at the table jumped at the ferocity of his tone. He calmed somewhat and then pointed a long finger at Julian. "I trusted you."

"I was preparing to send you the very information you sought when your men arrived at Fallstowe," Julian offered. "All of it there before you. You would have had it in hand by nightfall tonight, any matter."

"But not you, eh?" the king asked, his eyes sharp. "And not Sybilla Foxe."

Julian could not have imagined the pain the look of betrayal in his king's eyes would have caused him. "I cannot say at this point, my liege."

"You cannot say." Edward sounded unimpressed. "Did she bewitch you? Blackmail you? Threaten Lucy? I beg you, save yourself, Julian. If not for you, then for me."

"She did not blackmail me. And she would never do anything to harm Lucy," Julian said. "As for bewitching me—perhaps. It certainly feels as though I've had a charm plied against me. But I can assure you, my liege, that nothing I have done was forced upon me against my will. I take full responsibility for my actions."

Edward shook his head, much in the same manner as the young Erik had only a half hour ago. "You're in love with her. Of course. Half the men in England are, but I thought you would be impervious to her wiles."

"She escaped your men to come to you herself," Julian pointed out. "I believe she has every intention of honoring your trial."

"She has no choice," Edward hissed. "I will hold court this day, and her fate—as well as your own—will be cast. The law will no longer be denied, and neither will I!"

Julian dropped his head in deference. When he looked up again, he noticed the woman seated at the table was leafing through the parchments, discarding this one or that, murmuring softly to herself as she seemingly searched for something. Julian frowned at the woman's back.

Edward chuckled darkly. "Worried that some information will get out to taint your beloved?" he taunted. "Have no fear, Julian—she's already seen most of what you have compiled, long before even I had."

Finally the woman turned slightly in her chair; delicate

knuckles covered by papery, veined skin curved over the arm of the chair. Her kind and noble face regarded him.

"Good day, Lord Griffin," she said in her lilting accent. "I cannot express my delight at our meeting again."

Julian felt his mouth fall open as he stared at the wizened, gamine figure in the king's own chair.

"Lady de Lairne?"

Sybilla's cell was what she would have expected from a dungeon: dark, dank, smelling of old water, wet rock, and despair. The filthy pot in the corner was the only furnishing, and so she had seated herself on the rough stones against the wall directly across from the iron-barred door.

She assumed she was in the oldest part of the palace. The four walls of her prison were solid gray rock, as were the walls comprising the wide corridor beyond the bars. There had been no allowance for light into her cell, but as her eyes became adjusted to the darkness, she could see the flicker of wall torches down the corridor, causing the shadows cast by the crags of rock to dance and flutter like tiny, curious spirits peeking into her captivity. The doors of the other cells were staggered so that she could see only more unyielding rock through the bars.

She thought she could escape the cell easily enough. But she knew that she would never emerge from the corridor alive, much less make her way undetected to the king's side somewhere far above her head. As it was, a guard came down the long passage every quarter of an hour, Sybilla guessed, and held his torch close to the bars to assure himself that she was still within. Sybilla would simply have to wait until she was summoned.

She went over her confession in her head once more,

making certain she had recalled all that she would tell, and the manner in which she would tell it. Hopefully, it would absolve Julian of any wrongdoing and ensure that he and Lucy would still gain Fallstowe. Alys and Piers would be close by to them, as would Cee and Oliver. They could help him as he learned his way through the vast workings of the castle. They would smooth the way for him.

Her cell suddenly seemed lighter and Sybilla looked up from the dark floor that she had been staring at. The corner of her cell to the right of the door seemed to have been taken over by a small, iridescent blob of white mold. Sybilla stared at it as the edges seemed to ripple, the blob to elongate, form. Her ears popped and she opened her mouth to relieve the uncomfortable sensation.

Sybilla, her mother's voice called.

She stared at the transparent mist for a moment, unsure as to whether she was actually seeing what she thought she was, or if it was only a trick of her fatigued mind, her frayed conscience. Regardless, she turned her head away and looked through the bars of the door. She had no desire to entertain her mother's ghost, or even what her befuddled mind might imagine was her mother's ghost.

Don't confess, the voice said. *Wait.*

Sybilla stared hard through the bars, feeling her jaw set, her eyes water. It did sound remarkably like her mother, only it was the sound of Amicia before she had been stricken, her words refined, unslurred, melodic.

There is no need for it. You must continue to trust me. It's why I begged you and begged you to keep the secrets I shared with you.

Sybilla's head whipped around without hesitation.

"You wanted me to keep your secrets to save your own reputation," she accused her in a whisper. "Even as you swore to me that the truth would come out."

And it will come out. But it need not be through your own admission.

"I don't trust you. I was a fool to have ever trusted you. I was nothing to you but your automaton. Your sacrificial lamb. Your illegitimate and expendable, if very capable, offspring. You used me."

You will be saved.

"You named me after a woman you hated!" Sybilla said on a wretched breath.

No. You don't know everything.

"I know that your entire life was a lie. *My* entire life was a lie! And now it will be I who pays the price for your deceit. Are you happy now, Mother? Are you? Does it please you to know that you have lied to everyone you ever claimed to love? Who ever loved you?"

The white mist was silent.

"Just go away," Sybilla sniffed, wiping roughly at her nose with the heel of her hand. "Leave me alone to do what I must do. You were always so good about that."

You were never alone. And you are not alone now.

Sybilla felt her breath catch in her chest as a sob threatened to break free from her throat.

The mist disappeared even more quickly than it had coalesced, leaving Sybilla in a cell more pitch-black than before. She crossed one arm over her bosom and then brought her other hand to cover her mouth, squeezing her eyes shut as she tried to halt her tears.

She sensed the room brightening behind her eyelids once more, only this time the light was more substantial, yellow, and Sybilla opened her eyes to see the dark, shadowed figure holding a torch beyond her bars. It was only one of the guards. He waved the torch back and forth, seeming to search the corners of her cell, for what Sybilla could only guess, and then his head turned to address someone just out of her sight beyond the rock walls of her cell.

"Are you certain you wish to enter, Father? I could pass your things right through the bars. I've explicit orders that this one is dangerous, no matter her fragile appearance."

"It's quite all right," a man's voice answered. "I have no fear, and I would do what I can for this poor creature."

Sybilla's breath caught in her chest and she quickly swiped at her eyes before struggling to shove up the wall behind her to stand.

The guard was not amused. "*Sit down!*" he roared, pointing the torch through the bars at her.

Sybilla inched back down on the stones.

"I see you so much as twitch while I'm openin' this door, you're dead. Understand?"

Sybilla nodded. "I understand."

The guard fished a ring of keys from his side and fit the one he sought into the square plate on the corridor side of her door. The hinges squealed as he pushed the door inward. A lithe shadow moved around the man's back.

"Go ahead, Father," the guard said, never taking his eyes from Sybilla. "I shall remain right here until you're ready to take your leave."

"Thank you."

The light from the guard's torch was behind him as he entered the cell and made his way toward where Sybilla still crouched, but Sybilla knew the set of his shoulders, the swing of his hair, the sureness of his footsteps.

He sank into a crouch before her, and then moved a bundle to under his left arm before laying his right hand atop Sybilla's head. His blessing was clearly for the benefit of the guard, Sybilla was certain.

After his "amen" she reached up with both hands, grasped John Grey's wrist and brought his palm to the side of her face.

"John," she choked.

"How has it come to this so quickly, Sybilla?" John Grey asked in an urgent whisper.

She shook her head, so glad to feel his warmth against her skin. To have someone in the cell who knew her, who had loved her family, had loved Fallstowe, even if he had never loved her.

"You're to have your trial today—in only an hour," John said, keeping his voice barely above a breath and his back turned to the door. "If you're found guilty on all counts . . . Sybilla, the king will put you to death."

"I know," she said on a watery sigh and then raised her eyes to try to make out his features in the gloom. "Are you here to give me my last rites?"

She heard his faint huff of laughter. "You know I can't do that. It's only—"

"A courtesy title," they both finished, and it felt so good to Sybilla's mouth to smile, even if it was only melancholic.

"But the guard doesn't know that, does he?" Sybilla guessed.

"No. I'm here supposedly to hear your confession before God, to give you religious instruction before you make your oath to the king, and to bring you these." He withdrew the bundle from under his arm and placed it in the narrow V made from her chest and drawn-up knees.

"What is it?" Sybilla asked, feeling the bundle of cloth wrapped around something slightly more substantial.

"Clean garments for your trial," John Grey said. "A simple gown and some linen slippers—they're made by the novices at the local house for the prisoners who come to their fate in less than suitable clothing. There is a comb in there as well."

"Thank you," Sybilla whispered.

"Here," John said, fumbling inside his robes for an instant before drawing out a fine piece of what felt like silk as he pressed it into her hand. "My kerchief. Perhaps you can make some use of it if you can find some clean water. I'm sorry. It's the best I can do, I'm afraid."

"Why are you being so kind to me, John?" Sybilla asked. "After all that has happened, how could you?"

His right hand covered both of hers and squeezed. "Because I realize who you are now, Sybilla. The weeks away from . . . from Fallstowe, that whole terrible, nightmarish mess. It's made me realize that everything you do, you do for love. And although you may not want to accept it as true, you are loved in return by many, many people. Fallstowe's citizens; your family; me, at last, although not in a way that one might expect after our shared history. Even those who claim to hate you admire you, against their will perhaps. You are a remarkable woman. A woman formed by God's own hand."

Sybilla laid her forehead on John Grey's knuckles, unable to speak.

"But now you must tell me," John insisted gently, "why you are doing what you are. Why you will not save yourself."

Sybilla raised her head. "How do you—"

"I've seen Cecily," John interrupted her.

"Cee is here? In London?"

"Yes. Along with Lord Bellecote, and Lord and Lady Mallory."

Sybilla was speechless. How had they gotten here so quickly? She didn't want them to see the end of her this way.

"Sybilla?" John prompted.

She tried to find John Grey's eyes within the deep shadows of his face. "I love him, John. I love Julian Griffin. I love him how a woman is meant to love a man. A lord, a husband, a master of the hold. In a way that I have never and never intended to love a man in all my life."

"But, Sybilla, tender feelings aren't—"

"Listen, please," Sybilla whispered. "Julian was sent to the king to apprehend me, and his reward was to be Fallstowe. He didn't have to love me. He didn't have to believe me. But he did. He does. He knew the facts of my family through his own investigation. He was willing to give up everything he had earned—his honored place among Edward's court, unimaginable wealth for him and his daughter, the ultimate prize of Fallstowe itself—that the three of us might have some sort of a life together. He has loved me, as I am, for who I am. The only one who ever has, I suppose."

"And you would reward him with your death?" John asked incredulously.

Sybilla shook her head in the darkness. "If I do not tell the king what he wants to hear, Julian will be implicated along with me. Stripped of his rank. Possibly imprisoned. Lucy will go to noble strangers at the king's whim, separated from her father for who knows how long. Perhaps forever. Fallstowe and its people will fall to the Crown. I am damned either way. But I would go knowing that those whom I have loved most in this world are safe." Her voice cracked on the last word.

"I don't know, Sybilla," John said. "What if Lord Griffin refutes you? Denies your acceptance of guilt even as he thinks he is saving you?"

"He is not a foolish man, John. I can only hope that he will not, if he but thinks of his daughter."

John Grey said nothing to counter her this time. Only squeezed her hands.

"Father," the guard called from beyond the bars.

John looked over his shoulder. "Only a moment longer." Then he turned back to Sybilla. "I will try my best to be present at the trial, if it is allowed. Perhaps I can vouch for you in some way that neither of us can yet know."

"John," Sybilla breathed.

"Yes?"

"Do you think I will go to hell?" To her own ears, her voice sounded like that of a very young child.

As if he heard it, too, John Grey cupped the back of Sybilla's head and pulled her face toward his to place his lips on her forehead.

"No," he whispered against her skin. He drew away slightly but kept his face near hers. "But I think there is a chance that you may go to heaven. I'm so sorry. Be steadfast. Stand before your king and speak with the power of your love behind your words in the face of the law. Love is the law, above all else, and God will not fault you for that." He drew his hand from behind her head to cup her cheek gently and then stood. "I will wait outside the door while you change. God bless you, Sybilla Foxe."

"God bless you, John Grey."

Sybilla waited until the barred door creaked shut, the lock jangled, and she saw John's slender back silhouetted by the guard's torchlight before she rose to her feet on shaking legs.

She fished out the thin, floppy sandals and rough, wooden comb wrapped inside the light linen garment and laid them on the stones at her feet, placing John Grey's fine silk kerchief atop one of the shoes. Then she draped the simple gown over one shoulder as she worked to free the bodice of her gown, slipping her arms from it carefully so as not to drop the linen dress on the stones and soil it. She worked the ruined red velvet to her waist and then slipped the scratchy gown over her head.

Then she pushed the red gown over her hips to puddle on the floor before stepping both feet on it as if it were a rug. She bent at the waist to retrieve the kerchief and then turned to the wall behind her, feeling the stones with her fingertips for a trickle of wetness, dabbing the silk there, and then slowly, solemnly wiping her face. She stared at the nothingness of black before her, her eyes dry now, her mind already away beyond the cell.

Chapter 26

The king had dismissed Julian with a disgusted wave of his hand, sending him from the chamber as if he could no longer stand the sight of him. It hurt Julian. Edward was more than his king. Julian had saved the monarch's life, married into his bloodline, taken a vested interest in the security of the realm. Julian considered Edward his friend.

And now that friend had sent Julian from him like a disobedient dog. And Julian could not readily fault him, for if Julian had had his own way, he and Lucy and Sybilla would at this moment be in the process of leaving England forever, forsaking his king, his friends, his country, the law. Edward must take into consideration the interests of the realm first; Julian understood that.

What he did not understand, however, was the unexpected presence of Lady Sybil de Lairne. Why had she traveled from her home in France to the king's court, now of all times? Why was she being given leave to plunder Julian's findings, at Edward's side? What did she want? Whose side was she on?

The questions, the possibilities, made his head ache, and he was glad when the surly man showed him into a small, spartan chamber and left him alone with his thoughts. The door locked soundly after the man left, and Julian knew it would be guarded, but it mattered not. He did not want to escape.

The room was more than he could have hoped for: a narrow cot pushed against the wall, bearing a tray of bread and cheese and smoked fish, and a flagon of wine on its rough-looking coverlet. A bowl of water and a cloth rested on the shallow stone sill of the small, high-set window. He would have liked to change his clothing, but could not hope for such a luxury.

He sat on the side of the cot, bracing his forearms on his thighs, staring at the floor between his dirt-caked boots. After several moments, he sighed and turned to the flagon to minister to his parched throat. He had not finished half of the wine when the sounds of locks being breached echoed in the small chamber and the door swung inward.

Erik stepped inside, bearing a stack of what Julian immediately recognized as his own clothing, and his long-confiscated belt and sword. The young blond man walked to the center of the floor and then stopped as unseen hands closed the door once more.

Julian took another long drink, watching his friend—was Erik still his friend?—over the curve of the container. Holding the flagon by its neck, he lowered it and let it dangle between his knees.

"Good day, Erik. Have you come to harangue me some more?"

The young man's jaw was set, his eyes cold. He tossed the stack of clothing onto the bed. It came unfolded, and Julian's tunic and hose slid onto the floor. Neither man moved to retrieve them. Julian noted that Erik still retained the sword.

"My thanks," Julian said.

"How could you do this to the king? To Lucy?" Erik demanded. "How could you do this to me?"

Julian sighed, placed the flagon back on the tray, and then stood, making his way toward the window while shrugging out of his shirt. "Sybilla Foxe has been very wronged, Erik."

"Wronged? Was it she who conspired with de Montfort to ambush the king's men at Lewes?"

Julian tossed his wadded shirt to the floor and picked up the cloth, dunking it in the icy water and then wringing it out. "Yes." He began wiping his face.

"Then she is a traitor to the Crown!"

"Her own father led the king's men that night," Julian offered, scrubbing at his arms and shoulders. "He lost his life. Sybilla Foxe did not know what she was being sent to do."

"Bullshit, she didn't know," Erik spat.

Julian paused to glance over his shoulder at his young friend. "She was no more than a girl. She didn't know."

"Even if that is true," Erik conceded, "she held the castle unlawfully, denied the king's every summons. What of her lineage? Is it true that her mother was not noble?"

Julian swiped the cloth over his stomach and then rinsed the rag. "There are . . . questions."

Erik gave a frustrated growl. "Which you were supposed to answer, and my intuition tells me that you did. Edward didn't send you to Fallstowe to be Sybilla Foxe's judge or jury, and he certainly didn't send you to rescue her. You were to secure the castle and—"

"I understood my obligation to the king perfectly well," Julian shouted. He calmed himself with an effort after a moment. "I require no clarification of my orders from you."

"Well, I suppose it's somewhat comforting to know that your conscience troubles you," Erik snapped.

Julian ignored the goad and crossed back to the cot to shake his clean shirt from the floor. He pulled it over his head and attended to the laces, glancing up first at his sword and then at the face of the man who held it.

"Are you going to give me that or slay me with it?"

"I haven't yet decided," Erik replied. "Perhaps the latter would be more merciful. Who's the old French woman?"

"Lady Sybil de Lairne." Julian sat on the cot and worked at removing his boots.

"What's she doing here?"

"That's a very good question." He kicked one boot free and raised his other foot to his knee. "I met with her in France before Lucy was born. She gave no indication at that time that she was willing to come to England for her testimony. Her mother was very old, very ill, and needed constant care."

"Perhaps her mother has since died," Erik offered grudgingly.

Julian kicked off his other boot and paused, thinking. "Yes. Perhaps she has."

"Julian, I can't support you if you insist on witnessing for a known traitor against our king."

"I understand," Julian said, standing and untying his breeches.

"For one," Erik continued as if Julian had not spoken, "my first loyalty must be to Edward and England. I was to take your place here after you were rewarded with Fallstowe."

"I remember well," Julian said, sitting once more to don his hose. "Alliance with me could damage your future in the king's employ."

"Yes. But more than that, I cannot support your defection. It's not in your nature, Julian, for as long and as well as we have known each other. Or, as well as I thought I knew you, I suppose."

Julian stood, picked up his tunic and shrugged into it, fastening the ornate closures which began below his hips. It took him several minutes before the chore was complete, and then he raised his eyes to Erik and sighed.

"You may choose to believe what I am about to say or not, but I swear to you, it is the truth. I believe everything Sybilla Foxe has told me. Not because I am a fool, or because she has cast some sort of spell on me, or promised me all the riches of Fallstowe. I believe her because what she has told me fits, in light of the information I have gathered myself. It's the truth. She has been wronged."

Julian retrieved the cloth from the bowl and walked back to the cot to sit on the side and wipe at his boots. "It was never my intention to lie to the king, or even to withhold information from him. Yes, I was going to see Sybilla Foxe away from England without trial. Yes, Lucy and I were going with her." Julian held one boot before him, inspecting his handiwork. It would have to do.

"But in lieu of that part of my duty, I was willingly giving up my employ with the king, willingly giving up the prize of Fallstowe that he had so generously offered me. And I had already made arrangements to have the results of my full investigation—as well as my honest conclusions—sent to him. The king was to know the truth—all of it." He paused to look up at Erik. "It was the best I could think of, to assuage my sense of duty as well as my conscience. I could not let her be unfairly damned, Erik. I will not."

"What will you say at the trial, though?" Erik pressed.

"The truth," Julian said, and began to once more don his boots. "I will not lie to the king."

"She'll sacrifice you if she can," Erik warned him.

Julian shook his head. "No. You're wrong."

"She was prepared to fight me and the other guards to get to the king before you."

Julian felt a melancholy smile at his mouth. "Of course she was. You're very lucky she was so fatigued." He looked up at his young friend, but Erik did not seem amused. "You will see at the trial that what I say is true."

"How can you trust her so?" Erik demanded.

Julian stood and faced his friend, looking at him levelly. "She loves me."

"Of course she would tell you she loves you," Erik began.

Julian shook his head. "I know that she loves me. I know that she loves Lucy. And I know that Sybilla Foxe protects those she loves. I can only hope that she knows how very much I love her."

Erik's brows drew together as if Julian had just spoken in some strange, foreign language. "It's *Sybilla Foxe*, Julian."

Julian felt another smile come to his mouth, but this time it was warm. "Yes. I'm very lucky, am I not?"

"You're mad." Erik shook his head and then looked

down at the sword still in his hands. After a moment, he thrust it and the belt toward Julian. "Here. If you draw it at any time, they will cut you down. I will cut you down myself," he clarified.

Julian stepped forward to take his weapon and strap it on. "I understand. Thank you." When he was properly dressed, he looked up at Erik again. "You will be at the trial, then?"

"I wouldn't miss it," Erik answered solemnly. "It's my duty to bring in the prisoner."

Julian paused. "Be kind to her if you can," he requested quietly.

"I shall do my duty," was all Erik would promise. "If she wishes for a theatrical display, she shall have it and I shall oblige her—the trial is to be public."

Julian frowned, feeling a bitterness in his heart. "He wants to humiliate her," he murmured to himself. Then he looked once more at Erik. "Thank you. For the clothes and for your ear." He held out his hand.

Erik stared at it for a long moment and then seized Julian's forearm. "I certainly hope you are right," he said. "But if you are wrong, may God have mercy on you, because the king will not."

It was only perhaps a half hour after Erik departed Julian's chamber that he was summoned forth by the king's man. The man said not a word and Julian had no comment to offer, as he was once more enveloped by a rank of soldiers and escorted to the large and lavish hall that held the king's court. They brought him to the wide, public doors where Julian had first come into direct contact with the Foxe sisters, through Piers Mallory, so many months ago. Julian heard the muffled murmurings of the crowd gathered beyond. He steeled himself for the scrutiny of the people, as a pair of guards swung open the ornate closures.

He could not have prepared himself for the sight that greeted him, nor the intensified roar of the hushed and not-so-hushed conversations. The court was a sea of heads, a wall of skirts and gilded hilts, as Julian was led down the unusually narrowed center aisle to the dais, which seemed a mile away. He had never seen such a crowd gathered for a weekday court, not even by half. The air was already warm and humid, reeking of cologne and sour curiosity. Julian kept his eyes straight ahead, on the monarch who was already seated in his royal throne, watching Julian's entrance as he would the entertainment at a feast. Lady Sybil de Lairne was seated on the dais as well, ten feet from the king's left side. She smiled at him, and although she looked old and tired, hers was the only kind face in the room.

The guards came to a halt perhaps twenty feet before the dais, but Julian took two more steps before stopping and dropping to one knee. The mustachioed old barrister stepped forward, a scroll in his hands. He cleared his throat loudly, and the line of guards ringing the room beat their short swords on their shields twice to call to order the rumbling spectators.

He unfurled the scroll and read, "'Hear ye, hear ye, let it be known to all who witness, today before our royal sovereign, King Edward, the trial of Julian Griffin, a general of the king's army, and Sybilla Foxe, of Fallstowe Castle, to answer for charges of treason, espionage, and insubordination to the Crown.'"

With the announcement of each charge, the crowd behind Julian gasped.

The barrister continued, looking directly at Julian.

"Do you swear that you are General Lord Julian Ignatius Alphonse Griffin, formerly of London and of the king's first rank?"

Julian nodded. "I do."

"Do you swear that your testimony today, before God and before your king, will be only true and accurate to your best ability?"

"I do."

The barrister stepped slightly to the side and lowered his scroll. Edward's eyes seemed to burn across Julian's face.

"My liege," Julian acknowledged.

Edward lifted his right index finger in the slightest movement, indicating the vacant chair ten paces to his right on the dais.

Julian rose and gained the raised platform, sitting in his chair. He was now on display for the hundreds of people gathered before him, and they stared at him unabashedly. Julian did not care. He ignored them all, keeping his eyes on the double doors so far away, waiting for the moment when the guards would swing them wide once more and he would see Sybilla again.

From his left, Julian heard the king warn, for his ears alone, "I hope you know what you're doing, Lord Griffin." Then he nodded almost imperceptibly to the barrister.

"Bring in the prisoner," the mustachioed man called.

The doors opened, too slowly it seemed to Julian. And every head in the crowd below swiveled to the rear of the chamber. No one made even a sound as the first soldiers appeared. Julian caught a glimpse of Erik's blond head near the center of the cluster and looked instinctively in front of it.

There, there she was. And the chamber was a vacuum as they led her in, the loud silence pressing against Julian's ears until he thought they would burst. The soldiers fanned out around Sybilla as a buffer against the crowd.

Her proud dark head was bowed, her hair long and unbound down her back, around her shoulders. She wore a poor, thin, white linen dress, the narrow lace of her underdress visible at the rough neckline, the bodice nothing more than a plain seam under her breasts, the hem hanging limp just above her bare ankles, which were bruised and dirty above the tops of her pale feet where they disappeared into plain, white, peasant slippers.

She looked so slight, so pale, so . . . transparent, that Julian's heart squeezed painfully. What had they brought her to, this proud, beautiful, powerful woman? This white shadow of herself.

And then, as if a signal had sounded, the crowd on the floor erupted with their loud judgments. Shouts of "Boo!" mixed with hissing epithets, vulgar name-calling, and accusations.

"Witch!"

"Traitor!"

"Whore!"

The individual accusations were soon lost in the roar of foul voices, and yet Edward let the humiliation continue until Sybilla had been brought to a chair just below the dais, at the head of the center aisle. Placing her below the common folk.

"Look at me, Sybilla," Julian whispered, longing for just the slightest glimpse of her face, wanting her to see that he was here.

But she did not. She only came to stand on the left

side of the chair set in the aisle for her, her head still bowed, her hands clasped in front of her.

The barrister signaled to the guards again, and this time it took several blows of sword on shield before the crowd was subdued.

"Sybilla Foxe, you are present in the king's court to answer for charges of treason, espionage, and insubordination to the Crown. Do you swear that you are in fact the woman known as Lady Sybilla Foxe, presently of Fallstowe Castle?"

"I do." Her voice was quiet but clear, and held no tremble.

"Do you swear that your testimony today, before God and before your king, will be only true and accurate to your best ability?"

"I do," she said again.

"Sit down," the barrister commanded.

After a long moment filled with coughs from the audience, the shuffling of booted feet, the king spoke.

"Sybilla Foxe," he mused. "Sybilla Foxe. At last we meet." The small figure on the chair was absolutely still. "Nothing to say for yourself? I hear you were in quite a rush to see me after escaping my guards and riding to London through the night, on your own."

The crowd rippled as heads bowed together in a collective hush.

"No, my liege," Sybilla replied.

"No?" Edward sounded surprised. "Very well. Let's get on with it then, shall we?" He turned to Julian quite unexpectedly. "Lord Griffin has been, for the last two years, charged with the task of investigating your mother, now deceased. Amicia Foxe, purportedly of the de Lairne family of Gascony before coming to England. Lord

Griffin traveled to the de Lairne family home. All this is true, Lord Griffin?"

"Yes, my liege."

"Tell the court of your findings regarding Amicia Foxe's birth."

Julian swallowed, shifting in his seat. "I was informed that the de Lairne family was home to two young girls. One was a daughter of the Lord and Lady de Lairne."

"And the other?" Edward prompted.

"An orphan, taken in by Lady de Lairne to be a companion to the de Lairne daughter until the girl was old enough to become a lady's maid."

"And this lady's maid," Edward hedged, "did she live out her days as a faithful servant in the de Lairne household?"

"No, my liege. It was told to me by Lady de Lairne that she conspired with Lord Simon de Montfort against her family, in order to bring the French barons to heel under your father, King Henry."

"And she was rewarded with this treachery against her family in what way?" Edward prompted.

"Her family turned her out," Julian admitted. "She begged mercy from Simon de Montfort, and in December 1248, she traveled to England under a title assumed from the de Lairne family."

The crowd in the hall erupted in shocked chatter.

"Silence!" the barrister commanded.

"So," Edward said at length, "it is your conclusion that Amicia Foxe was not of noble birth at all, and that she lied to her future husband, Lord Morys Foxe of Fallstowe, now deceased, in order to secure her station as lady of Fallstowe Castle."

"That is what the evidence has shown, my liege,"

Julian agreed quietly, and each word was like a stab to his chest.

"Sybilla Foxe, if this is true, it would mean that your mother impersonated a peer in order to hold lands after the death of her husband. That she was never Amicia de Lairne at all. How do you answer to these accusations?"

Tell him you don't know, Julian screamed in his mind. *Tell him you never had the slightest idea about any of it.*

"I am aware of the tale, my liege," Sybilla said.

Again, the crowd in the court bubbled with shocked talk.

"Very well," the king said in a voice that sounded almost pleased, nodding at Sybilla's bowed head. "Then there is only one more witness we have yet to hear testimony from, which should certainly put those particular charges to rest once and for all." Edward turned to where Lady Sybil de Lairne sat, heretofore silent. He held his palm out deferentially. "Lady de Lairne herself."

Sybilla's head shot up, her eyes wide, her bloodred lips parted. Julian drank in the brief sight of her face like a tonic as she gaped up at the tiny old Frenchwoman. Julian didn't think he had ever seen Sybilla so openly surprised.

"Hello, Sybilla," Lady de Lairne said quietly. "It is lovely to meet you at last."

Sybilla turned her face down into her hands, shaking her head as Edward looked down at her once more, a knowing look on his face.

"Lady de Lairne," Edward said, "is it your witness that the information gathered by Lord Griffin while at your home late last year is accurate? That the woman known as Amicia de Lairne was, in truth, an imposter?"

"Yes, it is accurate," Lady de Lairne said sadly. "Lady Foxe was not Amicia de Lairne."

Edward nodded, and Julian thought for a moment that he looked down on Sybilla with something akin to sympathy on his face.

"She could never have been Amicia de Lairne," Lady de Lairne said succinctly, holding aloft a gnarled index finger. Her smile seemed oddly triumphant. "Because *I* am Amicia de Lairne."

Chapter 27

Sybilla could not raise her head. It felt as though all the muscles in her neck had come unbound, the weight of the words now flying around inside her skull too heavy to be moved.

I am Amicia de Lairne, the old woman had said.

Even while the king shouted his command for the hall to be emptied; even amidst the deafening roar of protest from the crowd as they were herded to the doors; even as she was jostled roughly in her chair, some spectators even going so far as to snatch at her hair or pull at her gown before the guards shoved them away; even through all the commotion and turmoil of her physical presence in the king's court, her mother's voice whispered in her ear. Words from years ago, months ago; different times, different locations.

An orphaned child was found in the kitchens. She was given the name Amicia.

She was not my sister.

She sent me away.

I can never go back.

When you love someone, you don't care what happens to you, so long as they are safe.

The truth will come out, but it need not be by your own admission.

You don't know everything.

The hall was now silent as a tomb, as if it had been recently rocked by a tremor of the very earth. Sybilla supposed that in a way, it had. As if to emphasize this idea, a low rumble of thunder sounded from beyond the stone walls. A storm was coming.

"Lady de Lairne," Edward said slowly, deliberately. "Perhaps you had better explain yourself."

"I'm sorry, Your Majesty. I am sure that this is a terrible shock to you. You should be pleased, though, that all the information gathered by the very capable and thorough Lord Griffin is most certainly accurate," Lady de Lairne said. "At least, accurate from my mother, Colette de Lairne's, point of view.

"An orphaned infant girl was found in the de Lairne kitchens and brought to the lady of the house. The child was retained in the home as a companion to the de Lairne daughter, and groomed to be her lady's maid. All that is most certainly true. What Colette failed to mention—deliberately, I'm sure—is that the infant was not an orphan in the true sense of the word. She—I— was the illegitimate daughter of Lord Volan de Lairne, born to a poor village girl. Colette thought only she and her husband were aware of this black little secret, but of course, everyone knew."

"How is it then that the de Lairne family would claim you as their daughter then, and denounce their true offspring?" the king inquired.

"It was the betrayal," Lady de Lairne whispered bitterly. "The nightmare that preceded Amicia's final days in Gascony. And the fact that we so resembled each other, we could have been full sisters. I was in the village, purchasing supplies for my sister, when I was spotted by some of Simon de Montfort's men. They seized me, thinking me to be the true daughter of the powerful baron giving them so much resistance. They thought to torture me into giving them information that would help them bring the de Lairne hold to heel." The old woman paused. "They were going to . . . to violate me. But I had been so long away, Amicia came to the village searching for me. She found me, just as the villains were about to do their worst. And she fought them. She drew her small, jeweled dagger on a brace of large and vicious men, intending fully to defend me to her own death."

Sybilla heard Julian's rapt voice. "What happened?"

"They realized they had stolen the wrong girl," Lady de Lairne said sadly. "They took her up right away, though not without some bloodshed from Amicia's blade first. They turned me loose as if I were some farm beast, shooing me away. But I would not leave her.

"She would tell them nothing, even as they beat her. They stripped her bare. Whipped her. She couldn't see, her eyes were so swollen. They would have killed her." The old woman's voice was faint, quivering, as if once more she saw the vision of her sister being beaten. "And so I did what Amicia would not. I told them what they wanted to know.

"They left us both then, and it was I who helped dress her and took her back to the château. We were discovered right away, and an uproar overtook the castle as it was learned who had done such a vicious thing. But then Colette asked Amicia what the soldiers had learned. It was important, you see, for them to know what information had been divulged. But before I could confess to telling the men what I had to, in order to save Amicia's life, Amicia herself confessed to the treachery. She said . . . she said they had beat it out of her. She had no choice or else she would have died. Colette's face became very cold, and she said—I shall never, ever forget—'You should have chosen death.'"

"But why would your sister admit to such a thing?"

"Because she thought my mother still recognized her for who she was, her true daughter. And she thought that if I, an illegitimate orphan, confessed, the family would have me put to death. But the truth of the matter was that, by the time Amicia and I were ten and two, Colette could not discern which girl was which, save to look at our manner of dress. She was not maternal in the least, and growing up, we rarely saw her. And, as I said, we did resemble each other greatly.

"I can only assume that when she saw Amicia, beaten to the point that her features were unrecognizable, her clothing and body dirty and bloody, her ready confession of treachery on her lips, Colette thought she was I."

Lady de Lairne paused. "May I please have a drink? I've not spoken at such length in years."

While a court servant rushed to bring the lady a refreshment, Edward waited patiently, saying nothing.

"Colette cursed Amicia for a spineless commoner. A traitor. A whore. She had her sent from the house that very night, even as injured and abused as she was. I tried to refute what Amicia had said. I admitted all. I screamed the truth until I was hoarse. But Colette thought I was simply upset at the idea that my only friend would be taken from me. They had me locked in my—in Amicia's—rooms. And by nightfall, everyone in the village knew that the orphan, the lady's maid of the de Lairne hold, was a traitor, persona non grata. Anathema.

"By the time they let me out of my rooms, she was gone."

"So you just assumed her position?" Edward queried.

Lady de Lairne shook her gray head. "No. I was frantic about what had happened to Amicia. Where she had gone, who had taken her. I confessed once again, to Colette. She said—oh, that coldhearted bitch!—she said, 'Fear not, I will find you another maid.' And she refused to speak of it—or of Amicia—again."

"Did you ever hear from her again?"

Lady de Lairne smiled. "Yes. Months later, an English soldier sought me when de Montfort's outfit returned to Bordeaux. He had been Amicia's protector en route to England. He told me she had even stayed with Lady de Montfort at Kenilworth Castle. He seemed to be very much in love with her, but said she had taken up with a wealthy English lord and was to be married."

"Morys Foxe," Edward mused.

Lady de Lairne nodded. "Indeed."

"What of the soldier?" Sybilla asked suddenly, glancing up at the old woman, who indeed looked so much like her mother. "What was his name? Where was he from?"

Sybil de Lairne shook her head slightly. "I never saw him again."

Sybilla's heart pounded in her chest. That soldier, she knew, had been her father. The man Amicia had said had kept her from the other soldiers, nursed her, cared for her. He had loved her mother. The idea made her breath catch in her throat.

"And then, years later and quite suddenly," Lady de Lairne continued, "a letter arrived from my sister. Her husband was dead, leaving her alone with three young daughters. She was in some sort of trouble. Amicia at last admitted her protection of me, in hopes that the years had softened her mother, and that Colette would welcome her back home. But instead Colette was furious. She would never admit the horror of what she had done, even though her actions could have saved Amicia and you girls. She said that there was little sense in two victims. And that what was done was done, and Amicia had made her choice long ago. She sent back a letter telling her never to contact her again."

Sybilla remembered vividly the day that letter had arrived, after the battle of Lewes. She remembered her mother's bitter tears.

"And so when Lord Griffin came to our home with his investigation, my mother told him the truth as she had used it to soothe her own conscience. She perpetuated the lie. Reinforced it. And shed not a tear that her only daughter was now dead, and her only grandchildren were in jeopardy." Lady de Lairne paused. "She was an evil, heartless woman. And I am most terribly glad that she is at last dead."

"Why do you now confess this?" Edward asked. "Why not long ago? And how do I know that it is true? Your own king may not be pleased."

Lady de Lairne shrugged. "What do I care now? Why would King Philip III care? I am old. I can't inherit anything. My family estate has fallen now to the hands of a distant male cousin, who could not care less if I live or die, if only that he does not have to support an old woman in one of his houses.

"I knew I would come to England after Julian Griffin departed my home. I have missed that girl for thirty years. Every day. Every night. She does not deserve the reputation these vicious rumors have given her, and I will not allow for it. She is still my sister." Lady de Lairne looked at Sybilla. "And you are my niece. I will protect you now, as Amicia would want." Her next words were spoken clearly, emphatically. *"As she protected me."*

Sybilla could still not bring herself to look at the old woman. She didn't know if she was grateful or furious. But she was desperately confused, and suddenly very afraid now. What did this all mean for her fate?

"This is all very extraordinary," Edward said quietly. "Lady de Lairne, I will have more questions, of course."

"Of course," she deferred quietly. "But now I must ask to be excused, Your Majesty. I fear I am not as young as I once was, and the excitement of my journey and then reliving such memories has fatigued me greatly. May I rejoin you later, upon your request?"

"Of course," Edward said. "And I thank you for your bravery."

Lady de Lairne did not speak to Sybilla as she shuffled from the dais on the arm of a court servant. The king was silent. Sybilla wondered if Julian was indeed still in the cavernous chamber, which echoed only with the loud scratches of the scribe's quill and the muffled rattles of the soldiers' armor. She sat in her wooden chair, the hardness of it seeming to bruise her bones, her flesh being overtaken by the creeping coldness of the floor, her skin covered in gooseflesh beneath the pitifully thin linen garment she wore. She could no longer feel her toes. But there was a vibration in her now, and energy born of—not hope, exactly, but perhaps more of conviction. She was who she was. She was right in what she was doing this day, in this room, before this man.

She would not be swayed.

"So," Edward said at last, pensively, as if still turning his thoughts over in his own head, examining them in this new light. "So, perhaps we have come down to the truth of your mother's birth. Perhaps we have. But as for you . . . well, it's not so simple as that, is it? There is no one to vouch for the circumstances of your birth, is there?"

"No, my lord. There is not," Sybilla said. "Although I was indeed present on that day, I fear I have little remembrance of it."

To her surprise, Edward snorted. Then he said, "Were you under the impression that Morys Foxe was indeed your true father?"

"The whole of my life," Sybilla said, knowing that this tiny detail could neither save nor damn her. The truth would suffice because it was irrelevant.

"It is no secret that he claimed you," Edward conceded. "And without proof to the contrary, I cannot in good conscience contradict your patronage. Lord Griffin, have you any evidence that Sybilla Foxe was not indeed the offspring of the late Lord of Fallstowe?"

"None at all, my liege," Julian said at once.

"So be it, then," Edward said. He was quiet for a moment. "The more arduous task lies yet ahead, any matter. The one that will decide your fate, Lady Sybilla. Although I have my own theories, I would hear it from your lips: Why is it that you and your mother repeatedly ignored all royal summonses, even after Evesham, when my father readily welcomed even the widows of the men felled under him?"

Sybilla swallowed. "It is because she—because my mother feared that . . . we would be recognized."

"Recognized. Hmm," Edward said. "Recognized would imply that someone important at court had met one of you previously, or had occasion to see you. Perhaps at some task you wished to keep secret?"

"Yes, my lord," Sybilla said.

"Perhaps someone would have seen you at Lewes, you think?"

"Sybilla," Julian warned.

"Let her answer," Edward cut in sharply.

"Yes, my lord. At Lewes, precisely."

"That's what I thought. Do you know what a terrible spot of bad luck that battle was? Not only for my father's men, but for you?"

Sybilla hesitated. "My lord?"

"The men were never supposed to reach Lewes that night," Edward informed her quietly. "They were to remain at their camp, some miles away. Had they done so, Simon de Montfort's men would have been in a very vulnerable location and been overtaken by the king's troops the next day."

Sybilla felt the vibration in her bones increase, even as Julian spoke.

"My liege, do you mean to say that the battle of Lewes should never have happened?"

"Not in the manner in which it took place—yes, that is exactly what I mean to say," Edward said morosely. "Morys Foxe was killed that night. I am most certain that was not in your mother's plans, was it, Sybilla?"

Tears welled heavy in her downcast, unblinking eyes and fell onto her thighs.

It was why her mother had been so shocked, so devastated. Morys was not supposed to have been where he was—none of the king's men were. She had been pretending to cow to Simon de Montfort's demand for information, when in reality, it was he she was setting up for an ambush.

How Sybilla had hated her mother for that ill-fated night! And how misplaced her fury had been!

"No, my liege. That was not in her plans. She . . . she loved my father very much." Sybilla's voice broke and she paused. "We all did."

"I am not an unfair man, Sybilla," Edward said. "And regardless of what you or the love-struck Lord Griffin may think, I have read the results of his investigation thoroughly. I realize now that it was not your mother who went to Simon de Montfort's camp that night. She sent you, did she not?"

Sybilla could only nod.

"And I understand in hindsight her probable intentions. But her intentions cannot be proven, and she cannot be questioned. The fact remains that you were sent to aid an enemy of the Crown, with disastrous results for the king's men, for England, and for your own father. The act in itself was traitorous. And I must uphold the law."

"Before you judge me, my liege," Sybilla said suddenly, but calmly, "I would ask you only one mercy."

"Yes? Sybilla Foxe asking for mercy?" Intrigue was high in the king's voice. "You will wish for a stay of execution, certainly, and—"

"No," Sybilla interrupted sharply. "I would not live out my days as a prisoner, of you or anyone else on this earth." As she continued to speak in the space left by the king's shocked silence, she slowly raised her head to at last look at Edward directly. "I ask that for my cooperation and full admission of guilt, you absolve Lord Griffin of the charges against him and grant him Fallstowe Castle and all its privileges as you previously warranted. The only crime Julian Griffin is guilty of is mercy. He had no choice but to become my accomplice."

"That is a lie, Sybilla, and well you know it," Julian shouted. "I have made my choices according to my own wishes—not yours, not anyone else's! How dare you try to manipulate—"

"He had no choice," Sybilla interrupted, not daring to look at Julian. "I took him to the Foxe Ring not long after his arrival at Fallstowe. On the last night of the full moon."

Edward's eyebrows rose and then lowered quickly. He stared at Sybilla in a queer manner, as if he had not heard her correctly, or not heard her at all.

Julian gripped the arms of his chair as if he would stand. "What has that to do with anything? You think I would be swayed by some old tale? That I would be taken in by whispers of legend or witchcraft? My actions are based on history, on fact, not a superstitious pile of rock!"

"His support and . . . affections became apparent after we had both visited the Foxe Ring," Sybilla said to Edward, somewhat concerned at the way he was still looking at her from his place on the dais, some thirty feet away.

"I was in love with you before I ever laid eyes on the Foxe Ring!" Julian shouted, and then Sybilla couldn't help but turn her head to look at him, his blatant admission still echoing in the air of the hall. "As you were with me," he finished in a quieter voice. "I'll not let you martyr yourself at the expense of my dignity, Sybilla."

Sybilla swallowed the emotion lodged in her throat to turn stoically back to the king. "Of course I cannot force His Majesty to agree to any such demands I might make. But let history reflect that the following is my testimony."

"Sybilla, no!" Julian shouted.

"I admit that it was I who aided Simon de Montfort in finding the king's men at Lewes in the year 1264. The treason is mine, and I admit my guilt." The scribes recorded her words furiously.

The king however, did not move.

Sybilla felt her chin lift as she continued this game of watchfulness with the monarch who for so long had sought her, and now had her in his clutches, her ready confession still wet on his scrolls.

"That's not all you've done, though, is it?" Julian challenged her. "If you're going to confess, let's have all of it, shall we?"

Her eyes flicked to his. "Julian, don't."

"Look at her, my liege," Julian said, moving forward to the edge of his chair and turning toward Edward, holding out an upturned palm to indicate where Sybilla sat. "Only look at her! Why do you think she would not want to be recognized? No one in this room today was present at Lewes to have remembered her! Look at her!"

And Edward did look. And then he brought his hands to the arms of his own chair and pushed himself to stand. "You," he said. His hand went to the long, ornate hilt of the sword at his side.

"You," he repeated, then suddenly walked to the edge of the dais and, in a spry manner, hopped down from it, landing surely on both feet, his eyes never leaving Sybilla. He began to stride toward her purposefully.

"No," Julian shouted, and shot from his own chair, but in an instant his pursuit was arrested by a trio of guards, one of them Erik. They held him, forcing him back into his chair while Julian struggled, shouting, "Edward, don't!"

Edward was nearly upon her now, his hand still laid upon his sword.

One last fight then, she said to herself, and rose from

the chair to stand defiantly before the tall, lean menace that was the king of England.

He towered over her, his eyes searching her face. "You," he whispered now, and his brows lowered menacingly.

Then the king raised his hand.

Chapter 28

Julian let out a terrible roar from somewhere deep inside of him as he watched Edward's hand rise and then disappear below him. The slap echoed in the chamber and was still chasing its own tail when he threw off the men who held him and leapt from the dais.

He ran at the pair, even amidst the sounds of guards converging on the aisle, their swords ringing as they cleared their scabbards. He didn't care. His fingertips found his own hilt, his arm pulled as he ran, prepared to commit the greatest crime imaginable of a trusted soldier of the king.

No one would ever harm Sybilla again.

But as he came upon them, he saw not a broken woman, a furious man, but two people locked in a tight embrace. The king's arms were around Sybilla's back, the thin linen bunched against the lavish embroidery of the royal tunic, her dark hair cascading over golden thread like an ebony river.

Julian skidded to a halt as a score of soldiers ringed the three of them, their swords drawn, their intentions obvious. But Julian ignored them, his sword hanging from his arm, its point touching the grand floor. He didn't think he would have the strength to lift it now, even to save his own life.

Sybilla's pale, delicate hands pressed against Edward's back, her forehead was laid against his chest, and even in the confusion that was so thick as to lend an audible buzz of nerves to the air, Julian could hear her plea.

"Forgive me, forgive me."

Edward angled his chin toward Julian, although he did not look directly at him. "I'd put your weapon away now, Lord Griffin, were I you. I'd hate to have something unfortunate happen to you at this late date."

Julian looked down at his sword as if just realizing he still held it, and then slid it back into its home slowly.

Edward took hold of Sybilla's upper arms and held her away from him, but his first words were for his men. "Stand down. There is no danger to me here, from either of them." As the men grudgingly backed away, he looked down into Sybilla's face. "Indeed, perhaps I am in the presence of the greatest patriot England has ever known. It was you, wasn't it? It was you who came into my tent and led me to de Montfort's unready men. Urged me on to the surprise attack at Kenilworth Castle."

Sybilla nodded. "Yes. It was I."

Julian felt his legs go weak.

"Why did you not come to me? I would have protected you myself. Sybilla—you saved England, you saved my legacy."

And then Sybilla Foxe said words that Julian would never have wagered in a hundred years would fall from her lips.

"I was so afraid." And then she began to weep.

Edward drew her to him briefly once more, shaking

his head. And then he released her, pushing her gently back into her chair and turning away from her.

Julian stepped toward her, fully intending to kneel at her side, but he was stopped short by Edward's hand on his chest.

"No," the king said, a disapproving frown on his long face. "This trial is still in order. I will have no more deviations. Go back to your seat, Lord Griffin."

"But, my liege—"

"Now, Julian," Edward commanded, giving him a little push and then walking toward the short steps that led to the dais.

"Come on." Someone pulled sharply on his elbow, and Julian turned to see that it was Erik. "Don't be any more of a fool than you have been, Julian. It's almost over."

Julian walked backward a pair of steps, his eyes on Sybilla's pale face. She did not look at him.

Then he nodded, to no one but himself, it seemed, and turned to gain the dais once more.

Edward had gone to the scribe's table and was leafing through sheaves of parchment, his long left arm braced at his side. The king spoke with the man at length and then turned away. Julian frowned as the scribe immediately took up several of the pages and then lifted the glass globe of the lantern to his left. He touched the corners of the pages to the flame and slid them into a wide-mouth brazier at his feet. The burst of flame was white as the pages disappeared.

Edward settled himself heavily into his throne in his typical posture: a sideways slouch, his previously broken leg stretched out before him, one elbow holding him aright in the seat. He stared at Sybilla for several moments.

"Sybilla Foxe," he said at last. "Is it your admission that you sneaked into the royal camp in the year 1265 and informed me of the unguarded state of Simon de Montfort's son's army, leading to the siege at Kenilworth Castle, and later, the death of Lord de Montfort himself at Evesham?"

"It is, my lord," Sybilla answered.

"And is it also your testimony that you have repeatedly and knowingly ignored royal summonses, resulting in several acts of outright disobedience to the Crown?"

"Yes, my lord."

"How do you plead to these accusations, then?"

"I am guilty," Sybilla said, with a lift of her chin. Julian thought she had never looked so beautiful.

"Very well," Edward said. "Stand for your sentencing."

Sybilla gained her feet, and even at that distance, Julian could see her swallow.

"For your crimes, Fallstowe Castle shall be fined one quarter of its wealth, payable in one fortnight."

Julian felt his mouth fall open, but below him, Sybilla only blinked.

But Edward was not done. "In addition, you shall supply the Crown with half of Fallstowe's armed men, fully outfitted and paid, mustering at Midsummer for a campaign of unknown duration. How do you answer?"

Sybilla nodded. "As my king wishes. It will be done."

"Very well," Edward said. "All other charges against you are hereby dropped, found to be without cause."

Julian felt the breath go out of him, but he had no real time for relief, for Edward then turned to him.

"Lord Julian Griffin, stand," the king ordered.

Julian steadied his sword and gained his feet before bowing once to the monarch.

"You have also been insubordinate in the duties set

upon you some months ago by my own word. How do you plead?"

"I am guilty, my liege," Julian said, then added quietly, "and I am very sorry, friend."

"Let it be recorded as such," Edward said. "As of this day, you are hereby charged with the demesne of Fallstowe Castle, as vassal to the Crown. What you do with its current occupants"—Edward glanced at Sybilla—"is at your complete discretion. How do you answer?"

"I would—" Julian was forced to stop and look down at his feet while he cleared his throat. At last he was able to look at Edward again. "I would marry the current occupant, my liege, if it pleases you."

Edward nodded slowly. "I think that it does please me, Lord Griffin. Someone must keep that woman in check, and obviously I am not up to the task."

Julian smiled at his king. "It shall be done right away, my liege."

"Very well. Lord Griffin, the other charges levied against you are hereby dismissed." The king held up his hands briefly before slapping them back onto the arms of his chair and rising. "I'm finished here."

The king made his way from the dais through his private door, prompting the mustachioed barrister to step forth.

"Court is adjourned," he called out solemnly, to no one but Julian, Sybilla, and the soldiers still ringing the room.

Julian looked down at Sybilla where she still stood, her arms hanging at her sides, and smiled. Then, too late, he remembered the protocol after a private court was held, as the soldiers threw open the double public doors, and the droves of nobles and commoners ejected from the room earlier flooded the chamber like a tempest at sea. In moments, Sybilla was surrounded by the angry whirlpool, Julian stranded helplessly on the island of the dais.

Sybilla spun on her heel to face the crush of people who were roaring toward her like a rogue wave. The soldiers had obviously not expected such a response in a usually civilized venue, and so their shouts of restraint toward the bloodthirsty crowd were late, and nearly lost beneath the thunderous footfalls and voices.

But Sybilla was not afraid. She lifted her chin and stared boldly at the first wave of common and noble gawkers. And as they drew impossibly nearer, when from the outside it would seem that they would overtake her with her next breath, trample the life from her, Sybilla held up her right hand.

As if a wall had been thrown up, the crowd stopped short, the sudden cessation of motion causing a silvery ripple to race back through the crowd still pushing their way forward, even as a musical sound, like the tinkling of small, crystal bells fell upon the hall from the rafters.

And then the crowd was completely, utterly silent, staring at her wide-eyed, some with a furious look of impotence and others with a sort of confusion. The footfalls of the soldiers increased in volume as they at last reached her, and as they placed themselves between Sybilla and the would-be vigilantes, she lowered her hand.

No sooner had her arm reached her side than it was seized from behind, and Sybilla found herself turned round in a sudden, forceful fashion, to face the intense expression on Julian Griffin's face.

"Sybilla," he whispered. "We've won."

She felt a smile trying to come to her mouth, the

muscles creaking, the expression hesitant to show itself. "Have we?"

"Have we?" he repeated incredulously. "You can't be serious!"

"It only seems so . . . unfinished. Incomplete," she said with a slight frown.

"You have retained Fallstowe," Julian insisted.

Sybilla quirked an eyebrow at him. "If I agree to become your wife."

Julian Griffin took on a pained expression of forced patience. "Do you wish to become my wife?"

Sybilla blinked coolly.

Julian sighed, rolled his eyes, and tried again. "Sybilla Foxe, will you marry me?"

And then the smile did come to her mouth, and although slight, Sybilla felt the sincerity of her happiness all the way to the core of her soul.

"Yes," she said quietly, simply.

His smile matched hers, and he began to draw her closer to him.

"Sybilla!" a woman shouted. "Sybilla!"

Sybilla turned from Julian's arms to try to locate Alys's form in the pressing crush still being held off by the king's soldiers. She spotted her youngest sister's blond hair and round form on the fringe of the crowd near the wall, being blocked by a guard. Piers was beside her, and behind them both, Sybilla saw Cee and Oliver. She held up a hand toward them, signaling that she had seen them.

She turned back to Julian. "I have to go to my sisters," she explained. "I need them to meet Lady de Lairne. Right away, I feel."

Julian stared at her for a moment. "I understand," he said. "But Sybilla, I must—"

"Lucy. I know," she interrupted. "I don't know when I will get away. Not tonight, at any rate. I would try to convince Lady de—my aunt," she corrected herself, "to come back to Fallstowe with me. To see the place where her sister lived, the home where we grew up. Perhaps . . . perhaps she would even stay."

Julian smiled down at her. "I think that is a most wonderful idea. I will have Erik accompany you back when you are ready to depart."

Sybilla looked askance at him. "He'll not try to murder me for corrupting you?"

Julian laughed and shook his head. "He is the only one I would trust with your life, save me."

"Very well," Sybilla said, anxious suddenly to be away, not from Julian but . . . away to somewhere very important.

He saw her impatience, and Sybilla could not help but notice the way his eyes lingered on her mouth, as if he wanted to kiss her but was hesitant.

"Yes, well . . . we shall be waiting for you at Fallstowe." He touched her face gently. "Safe journey."

Sybilla's heart melted inside her chest at the tenderness showing through his stoic reserve. Julian should know by now that she did not give a damn what anyone thought of her. She reached up with her right hand to grasp his neck and then rose on her toes even as his arms went around her back.

And she kissed him before all those who were gathered in the king's court. Thoroughly. It would be talked about for years.

Sybilla had made her wishes known immediately to the guard holding her sisters and brothers-in-law in check, and now, with Piers and Oliver having gone to help Julian outfit for the return journey to Fallstowe, Sybilla, Cecily, and Alys raced through hidden corridors, on the heels of the soldier, to the section of rooms where Lady de Lairne stayed.

"But how did she know to come?" Cecily was asking, even atop Alys's own questions.

"Is it truly over, Sybilla? Are you free?"

"It's over, and yes, I'm free," she said absently, her eyes on the soldier's back in the shadowy corridor. "I don't know how she knew. It's one of the many questions I hope to have answered shortly."

"But what of Evesham?" Alys insisted. "You must tell us! We don't know anything."

"I will tell you," Sybilla promised. "I'll tell you everything very soon. But now we must hurry."

"Why?" Cecily asked. "Sybilla, slow down, please!"

Sybilla didn't answer, only chased the soldier around a sharp corner, her slippers hissing against the stone. The man stopped suddenly and stood to the side of a nondescript door.

"Lady de Lairne's rooms, my lady," he said solicitously.

"Thank you," Sybilla breathed, although her eyes were on the thick wood of the door as her sisters came to a breathless halt to either side of her.

"At His Majesty's request, I shall wait for you to emerge to lead you on to a guest chamber."

"We might be a while," Sybilla said faintly, raising her right hand to let her fingertips lightly graze the door.

"No matter," the guard said, stepping a respectable distance away to give the room's occupant privacy when the ladies entered. "This is my duty."

"Sybilla, Cee," Alys whispered suddenly. "Listen!"

All three women inclined their heads toward the door

to better hear the faint notes wafting weakly through the thick wood.

It was a woman's voice, singing a song the sisters were familiar with from their childhood.

Cecily turned to look at Sybilla and Alys, her eyes wide with surprised pleasure. "She sounds just like Mother!"

"Exactly like Mother," Sybilla said faintly, and felt the frown crease her brow. She raised her fist and rapped on the door.

There was no answer after several heartbeats, and yet the singing continued. Sybilla reached for the door latch.

"Sybilla," Cecily hissed, disapproval clear in her tone.

But Sybilla did not heed her sister, engaging the mechanism that held the door shut and pushing. It was unbolted and swung open soundlessly.

The volume of the tune increased minutely as the three women stepped inside the chamber. They were faced with a curtained bed jutting into the room, perpendicular to the door. The side drapes were closed, but Sybilla could see one footpost, indicating that the end of the bed had been left open to the hearth ablaze before it.

"I've got gooseflesh," Alys whispered, rubbing briskly at her arms. "Is she hard of hearing?"

Sybilla led the way slowly, cautiously, toward the foot of the bed. "Lady de Lairne?" she called calmly, although inside her chest her heart thrashed against her ribs like the splintering of a great tree. "It's Sybilla Foxe. I've brought my sisters, Cecily and Alys, to meet you, and to talk with you."

"Should you really be calling her Lady de Lairne, though?" Cecily wondered aloud on a whisper.

Sybilla paused to look down at her usually meek younger sister. "Would you rather I shout 'old woman'?"

"I see your point," Cecily conceded.

They rounded the bedpost then, and no one was prepared for the sight that greeted them on the mattress. Sybilla reached out instinctively and found the hands of her sisters, just as they in turn were reaching for hers.

Lady de Lairne lay on her side facing the middle of the mattress, her elegant and matronly skirts arranged just so on the coverlet. Her soft gray hair was uncovered, caught at her nape in a short plait. Her eyes were closed in her pale, still, wrinkled face. Her hands lay slightly away from her chest on the bed.

And she was not alone. A silvery mist mirrored the old woman on the bed, and as the sisters stood and stared in the gloom of the chamber, the mist began to take clearer shape: a young woman in a long, plain gown, with hair the color of old, well-oiled wood. She was holding both of the old woman's hands in her own, smiling at the still countenance, and singing so quietly that it would not have disturbed the flame of a candle.

"Mother?" Alys said in a choked whisper.

Sybilla's body went ice-cold.

The child was of the village wise woman.

We looked enough alike that no one could tell us apart.

What do I care now? I am an old woman. I have no family save you to know the truth.

I will save you, as your mother saved me.

"Mother?" Alys asked again, still quietly but with a hint of desperation in her voice as the song finally came to an end.

The sparkling young woman at last turned her head

slightly on the pillow to acknowledge the three sisters standing at the foot of the bed, peering in.

"Shh, girls," she said with a smile. "My lady sleeps."

Sybilla felt her knees twitch as if they would buckle, while at her side, Cecily gasped.

"Forgive me," Cecily pleaded quietly. "Forgive me the terrible things I have said and thought of you."

"I miss you so, Mother," Alys wept quietly.

"Shh, shh, girls," Amicia Foxe admonished again gently. She looked to Sybilla. "Well done, my own." Her voice had an echoey quality, as if coming up—or down—from a great distance. And then her eyes landed on all three sisters in turn. "Take care of each other."

And then Amicia Foxe sparkled away into nothing in the quiet room, to be followed in only an instant by the sound of the chamber door swinging open behind them.

All three women turned, realizing that none had closed the door behind them upon entering. And yet they had heard the click of the latch, a squeaking of old hinges, and now the giggling of what could have been two very young girls sneaking out of the chamber to find a bit of mischief. A door slammed, causing them all to jump, and yet they could still see the corridor clearly through the doorway.

Sybilla looked back at the bed once, and the figure on the mattress seemed somehow hollow now, deflated. And on the coverlet next to Sybil de Lairne, directly where Amicia Foxe's ghost had sparkled only a moment ago, lay the missing miniature portrait.

"One of you fetch the guard," Sybilla said, telling herself that her voice was firm, not at all shaky, as her eyes found the corpse of Sybil de Lairne once more. "Hurry."

Chapter 29

He rode from London alone, through the night, and had stopped only once for a short meal and to change horses.

Now, Julian forced himself to pause some distance away from Fallstowe's great drawbridge, giving his mount a chance to catch its breath, and taking the time himself to look at the imposing stone castle with new eyes. Inside those formidable walls, Lucy waited for him—the rest of his life waited for him.

And everyone would be waiting for Sybilla. It seemed to Julian that the castle itself was poised in anticipation of her mistress's return, the stones sparkling bright enough in the midday sun to guide Sybilla all the way from London, if need be. Julian fancied he could even feel the physical pull of the castle on his own body, and he realized that although the stewardship of Fallstowe now belonged to him, by the king's own hand on the parchment tucked over his heart inside his tunic, Fallstowe did not belong to Julian.

Julian belonged to Fallstowe. He understood now,

watching the banners flap and hearing their sharp snap in the breeze, smelling the sweetness of spring emanating from the earth like steam, witnessing the ring of thin clouds like a wispy crown above the tall towers—Fallstowe was more than a hold. It was a legacy rich and dripping with history and emotion, strife and danger, magic and love. It had called to Julian two years ago when he'd begun his investigation of the Foxe family, and once it had gotten its toothed battlements into his flesh, it had never let go.

Now, it protected the most precious thing in Julian's life: Lucy. And Julian knew that Lucy had belonged to Fallstowe from the very beginning, when he had imagined her so vividly as a little girl in long skirts, running over the rolling hills, playing at the fringe of the wood, her soft little slippers slapping against the tower stairs as she came up to visit her father at his ledgers. She would forever know this castle as her home. She would forever see it as a place of security and comfort, where she would be surrounded by those who loved her most in this world.

Julian took a moment to look up into the sky above the castle. "Thank you, Cateline. I swear to you that Lucy will know of you. And I hope that you are still proud of me."

He looked back down at his horse's neck, blinking the brightness away. When he raised his head, he saw one of the soldiers on horseback now, riding toward him.

Julian spurred his horse, happy to meet the man more than halfway.

Julian's reunion with Lucy was one of the sweetest things he'd ever known. Seeing her little face, looking older somehow even in only four days—the longest he'd ever been away from her—caused a wrenching of his heart and a thickening of his throat that made words impossible things for him. Her big, toothless smile and squeal of surprise and delight as she'd lunged from old Graves's arms, elicited a feeling of love so sharp as to be painful.

Now it was evening, after a long and much-needed nap for both father and daughter. Julian sat at the lord's table with Lucy on his knee as a feast of ridiculous portions was served to them. Sybilla's ornate chair to Julian's right was conspicuously empty, and so, after some thought and assistance from Graves in fetching a thick coverlet, Lucy now presided over Sybilla's table in her stead. The baby pounded regally on the table with an empty wooden cup and screeched her demands, the servants doting on her with little coos and words of praise. Julian could scarcely take his eyes from her, even to glance periodically toward the arch leading from the great hall, hoping with the sound of each footfall that it would be Sybilla come home to join them.

It was near the end of the meal when the king's messenger arrived with a missive for Julian, as well as one for Graves, who was standing, ever ready, behind Lucy's chair. Julian could not help the frown on his face as he split the seal and unfolded his own small square.

Lord Griffin,

Lady de Lairne is dead. I shall remain in London while she is readied to accompany me to Fallstowe. Graves will see to the details of her interment. Any plans for the future must be postponed indefinitely.

S—

Julian's frown increased, and he was at once seized by a sadness for Sybilla's loss, when the de Lairne woman had only just been found to her. But he was also unsettled by her statement referring to future plans. Certainly she was alluding to their wedding. But, postponed indefinitely? He looked over his shoulder to find Graves, but the man had already slipped from the dais unnoticed. Julian wondered what the old steward's message had said.

He read the missive through twice more before folding it away inside his tunic. Then he stood, waving away the servants with an apologetic thank-you as they approached the table with dessert. He disentangled Lucy from her throne and left the hall, intent on seeking his tower chamber once more.

Sybilla was not coming home tonight.

She had not been so long and so far away from Fallstowe in years. It was such an odd feeling, Sybilla considered not going back at all as she stared out the carriage window, her head rocking on her fist as the large wheels rolled over the rutted road. People whom she passed in the conveyance, and those who passed her, did not know her identity. They didn't know who she was or where she was from. Even if she chanced to meet other travelers face-to-face, the likelihood that they would recognize her was almost nonexistent. On this road, she was just a nameless, homeless woman.

Perhaps that's what she was, any matter.

Sybil de Lairne's wooden coffin followed Sybilla's hired carriage in a tarp-covered wagon. Sybilla had encouraged both Cee and Alys to return to their homes at their husbands' sides, although both of her sisters had

protested vehemently and Sybilla thought it possible that
Alys was entertaining the idea of a physical altercation in
order to personally accompany Sybilla to Fallstowe. In
the end, though, Sybilla had flatly stated she did not
want their company, no matter how much she loved and
treasured them. She did not want anyone's company.
She needed time to think, and think she could not do
with Cee's fretting or Alys's endless questions, Piers's sto-
icism and Oliver's outright discomfort with the whole lot
of them. She couldn't fault any of them.

Cee and Alys would first go on to Bellemont and
Gillwick, respectively. But they would likely arrive
at Fallstowe only shortly after Sybilla, as she had instructed the drivers to travel at an easy pace, with orders
to overnight at two inns between London and Fallstowe.
The leisurely journey would give her more time to think.

All the questions she thought had been answered remained unanswered. And more questions had grown in
the compost of convoluted facts and allusions between
the time of Sybilla's trial and the moment the ghosts of
Amicia and Sybil de Lairne had departed the royal guest
apartment. Alys and Cecily had questions, and Sybilla
had her own, of course. But no one had any answers.
Least of all the woman who was slated to marry Julian
Griffin.

The vision of her mother's spirit upon Sybil de Lairne's
bed haunted her still—the plain woolen gown, her simple,
unadorned plait alongside a youthful and scrubbed-clean
cheek. The look of love and protectiveness on her face.

My lady sleeps.

Sybilla had known in that very instant that Lady Sybil de
Lairne had perjured herself before the king of England.

And so Sybilla was still the illegitimate daughter of an
illegitimate daughter.

She was still a traitor.

She was also now a patriot.

A coldhearted matriarch.

A stepmother.

A sister.

The mistress of Fallstowe, but entitled to nothing.

Who was the woman Julian Griffin wanted for his wife? Sybilla did not know, and so she was certain that Julian could have no inkling. How could she ever agree to marry him, to undertake those roles so foreign to her—the roles of mother and wife—when she had not yet come to a polite agreement with who she had been her entire life?

Who was she? What was she?

The carriage rumbled over the road, drawing ever nearer to that place which had for so long been her reason for existence, and which now seemed a stone enigma, housing the whole of the riddle of the woman who had once been Sybilla Foxe.

On the fourth morning, Julian knew that Sybilla had returned when he saw the packages on the lord's table as he and Lucy came down to break their fast. A small, cloth-wrapped bundle tied with flaxen string and decorated with a tiny brass bell, the little vellum tag reading simply L in Sybilla's light, flowing script. Next to it sat an even smaller wooden box with a similar tag labeled J.

He frowned at the gifts, and at the realization that he'd not seen Graves all the morn. Sybilla had likely returned in the night or the small hours of the morning then, but no one had alerted him, and it made him quite cross all around.

Lucy had already voiced her desire for the bell, and was now leaning down to the table even as Julian seated himself. The baby flicked her chubby fingers back and forth over the delicate fixture, letting its dulled tinkle echo in the strangely vacant hall. He pulled the package toward her and slipped the tie from the cloth.

Inside was a gorgeous miniature sleeveless robe in scarlet velvet, the full length of it and also the hood lined with white rabbit. Ornate silver clasps laddered up the front of the white fur trim. It was an outrageous gift for the child, but Julian couldn't help his smile as he slipped Lucy's little arms through the embroidered side slits and fastened the closures. It fit her perfectly and suited her more than humility warranted.

As his daughter continued to play with the little bell, Julian pulled his own gift toward him. He unhooked the little leather strip wrapped around a bone peg and lifted the lid of the box. Inside on a bed of boiled wool lay a silvered quill and ink pot, with an additional slip of vellum.

For your accounts.

The gifts were thoughtful, and in Sybilla's generous mind, likely highly practical. But why had she not waited to give them in person? Had she not missed Lucy?

Had she not missed Julian?

His troubled thoughts were interrupted by a smiling kitchen maid who brought a tray of food and warmed, spiced wine, as well as a bladder of milk for Lucy.

"Good morrow, milord," the girl chirped as she set the offerings in their precise place on the table. "Lady Lucy."

Julian did not mince words. "Where is Lady Sybilla?"

The girl paused in her chore, giving him a kind if curious glance. "Madam doesn't take breakf—"

"I know Madam doesn't take breakfast," Julian said with as much patience as he could muster.

"Of course, milord," the girl apologized. "Madam arrived very late in the night. I would think her still at her rest."

Julian's temper darkened even further. As far as he knew, Sybilla did not have a bed to rest in any longer, as the splintered remains of the black monstrosity that took up the surface of her chamber still lay in ruined pieces on the floor.

And she certainly hadn't sought the tower room in the night.

"Where is Graves, then?" he barked.

The serving girl blinked, and then crossed herself, owl-eyed. "Seeing to her ladyship's grave, I believe, milord. Shall I have him fetched for you?"

Julian shook his head as he sat Lucy back against his chest in her luxurious robe and settled in to feeding her her breakfast.

"No. I shall find them myself."

The serving girl bobbed a nervous curtsy before turning quickly away from the table.

Julian was not completely sure, but he thought he'd heard her whisper, "God be with you, milord," as she'd scurried back toward the safety of the kitchen doorway.

Chapter 30

Everything was the same. And yet nothing was the same.

Sybilla sat at her wide table before the bank of windows in her chamber, her knees drawn up to her chest, her toes curled into the cushion. Her tray of tea and bread sat untouched off to the side, and she had quietly dismissed her maids soon after their enthusiastic arrival. Sybilla would attend to no business today besides the burial of one enigmatic old woman next to another. The impending funeral was all she could handle today, and that made her both angry and sad. Tomorrow, perhaps, she would approach the idea of her future.

Or perhaps not.

She heard the creaking of what was left of her chamber door—it had never creaked before Julian Griffin's violent attack on it, and she had not ordered it repaired.

"Welcome home." Julian Griffin's voice was low and easy, as if he was approaching a skittish animal that might become spooked at any moment.

The analogy was quite fitting, she thought.

She turned her head slightly to look over her shoulder at him. "Thank you." He was standing on the far side of the ruin of her bed, holding Lucy high on his chest. The sight of the infant caused Sybilla's heart to skip. She seemed a little queen in her velvet robe, and Sybilla was pleased that it fit her so well. "Good morrow, Lucy."

The baby squealed and waved her fist excitedly, as if she would direct her father.

"I believe she's missed you as much as me."

Sybilla was not certain of Julian's meaning, and so she let the comment pass unanswered, turning her gaze back to the hills beyond the bailey.

"I'd hoped you would find me upon your return," Julian continued.

"It was late," she answered. "I didn't wish to wake you. I see you found the gifts I left for you both."

"Yes. It was very kind of you to think of us. Thank you."

The air in the chamber grew exponentially thicker with awkward tension, as if the two adults not looking at each other had never entertained more than tolerable company for each other.

"I was very sorry to hear of Lady de Lairne's passing."

Sybilla had nothing to say.

Lucy gave an impatient squawk.

"Are you not going to speak to us at all?" Julian finally asked.

Sybilla swallowed, unable to bring herself to look at them again. "Forgive me, Lord Griffin. I've a lot on my mind. Perhaps later this evening . . ." The excuse trailed away into nothing.

"You are not alone any longer, Sybilla," Julian reasoned in a quiet voice. "Let me help you with whatever it is that's troubling you. Your burdens are to be mine once we are married."

"We are not yet married, Lord Griffin."

There was a heavy pause in which not even small Lucy dared breach the silence. "Will we ever be married?" he asked finally.

"I don't know," Sybilla whispered. Then she blinked away the sudden wetness in her eyes and drew upon her vast stores of cool experience. "After Lady de Lairne's burial, I shall arrange with the clerk to have my fine separated from Fallstowe's accounts and readied to send to the king. I've already ordered a draft of service for the men owed under my obligation at Midsummer. Once I've put my signature to those tasks, I do believe the running of the hold will be officially at your command." She paused again to swallow. "Congratulations, Lord Griffin."

"Sybilla—" Julian began.

"I'm really quite harried this morn, Lord Griffin," Sybilla interrupted stridently. "If we could please continue our conversation later this evening as I've requested, I would be grateful."

"Very well," Julian said, and the wounded tension in his tone was clear. "I shall seek you after the ceremony."

"Good day," Sybilla said crisply.

Julian did not reply, but as his crunching footfalls retreated from the chamber at her back, Lucy began to cry.

Once they were gone, so did Sybilla.

Julian saw Lucy to a maid in the small chamber at the bottom of the tower steps for her morning nap before carrying on to the great hall once more. He could barely contain his frustration long enough to see his daughter lovingly to sleep.

He was angry. He was hurt. He was confused.

What had happened in the short time of his and

Sybilla's separation, besides the death of the de Lairne woman, to have so radically changed Sybilla's demeanor?

It's not really changed, though, has it? a voice spoke inside him. *This is the Sybilla who greeted you upon your initial arrival at Fallstowe. It seems only that the woman has returned after her holiday.*

No, Julian would not allow that. He loved her. He knew she loved him, and Lucy. They were to be married. They had survived royal condemnation by the skin of their teeth, had come through a tempering fire to have the fantastic dream of Fallstowe within both of their grasps. He would not let her throw it away in some pique of melancholic mourning for an old woman she hadn't ever known.

He arrived in the hall on stomping boots, in the back of his mind seeking Graves for whatever insight the old man might offer. He should not have been surprised to find Sybilla's sisters and brothers-in-law just arriving in the cavernous room, but he was.

The youngest, blond Alys, wasted no time, striding through the hall leading the quartet. "Lord Griffin, good day. How is Sybilla?"

Julian stopped in the center of the hall. "What the bloody hell happened in London after I left?"

The two sisters exchanged looks as they came to a halt before him.

"She's not well then," Cecily sighed.

"The three of us were present at the moment of Lady de Lairne's passing," Alys supplied. "Some rather . . . strange events transpired, which we think have led Sybilla to call into question the truthfulness of Lady de Lairne's testimony."

Julian was still frowning. "I don't understand."

The sisters exchanged looks again before Cecily

explained. "Sybilla believes that our mother was not a titled lady of the de Lairne hold, as Lady de Lairne attested. She thinks perhaps that everything Mother confessed to was the truth."

Julian looked to the heretofore quiet men standing behind their wives, in the hope that they would be able to translate this feminine explanation into something he could understand.

"So?" Julian prompted. "The king's ruling still stands, does it not? Sybilla is cleared of all charges. The records will forevermore reflect Sybilla's right to Fallstowe and to the title of lady."

No one said anything, but the sisters looked at each other meaningfully once more.

"Why do they keep doing that?" Julian pleaded with the men.

Oliver Bellecote quirked an eyebrow. "Vexing, isn't it?"

Julian rubbed a hand across his forehead and then placed his fists on his hips. "She won't talk to me. And when she does . . . she's giving me reason to think she has reconsidered our marriage. She's so . . . so cold."

Alys shrugged. "I'm sorry, Lord Griffin. But that's Sybilla."

"No," Julian snapped. "No, it's not. Perhaps it is who she has played to be to the majority of persons, but I know her better than that. I have seen her caring and vulnerable. I have seen her in weakness. I know how kind she is."

"We all do," Cecily said, trying to console him. "But Sybilla has always been very . . . solitary. The last several years, that has been of necessity. She has always had something to fight for, something to prove or defend. And now, well . . . now the fighting is all over, and yet there is still some question about her role in it all. I think she feels rather at a loss. And so she is behaving how Sybilla always behaves. She fortifies her defenses and battles her demons. Alone." Cecily's face was sad.

Julian shook his head. "I don't understand why she can't simply let the past be over."

Alys laid her hand on his arm lightly. "Sybilla's very survival has depended on the past for a very long time," she explained. "It's the essence of who she is. In her mind, her history defines her."

Something in Alys's statement tickled at Julian's brain, but he was too frustrated to flesh out the meaning thoroughly just then.

"We are to discuss our future after Lady de Lairne is laid to rest," Julian said on a sigh. "I do hope I have something encouraging to report to you all on the morrow. I won't be so pompous as to invite you ladies to make yourselves at home—you have greater privilege here than I."

"Oh, I don't think that's true anymore," Cecily said with a kind smile. "Good luck, Lord Griffin."

Alys suddenly brightened. "May we see the baby now, please?"

It drizzled softly while Sybil de Lairne was laid in the deep, rich dirt of Fallstowe. Sybilla was barely present, and she could not have recounted the majority of the short, solemn ceremony, either in Fallstowe's chapel or now, on the knoll. She did know that Julian Griffin had stood at her side throughout. Lucy was conspicuously absent, likely for the damp chill, and Sybilla told herself it was just as well. The child would have demanded that Sybilla hold her, and she did not think that was in either of their best interests at present.

She barely noticed that the few gathered had begun to move away in the gloomy rain, signaling that the ceremony was over. Then Julian Griffin leaned close to her ear.

"In the solar," was all he said, and then he turned and left her in the cold drizzle.

She remained there for quite some time, Graves silent at her side. She knew she made the burly men charged with the task of lowering the box and filling in the hole uncomfortable, but she didn't care. She needed to see the end of this. The very end. By the time she parted company from Graves in the hall and found herself walking down the corridor and pushing at the solar door, she was thoroughly damp. But she didn't care about that, either.

Julian Griffin stood at the hearth, his back to the door. By the way his elbow was cocked, Sybilla guessed him to be partaking of strong drink.

She longed for a cup of her own.

He turned as the door latch clicked shut. "I wasn't certain you'd come."

"I told you I would."

"No, you didn't," he argued as he slowly ambled around the low couch toward her, chalice in his hand. "You didn't say anything." He handed the cup to her. "I thought you might need this."

Sybilla stared at the chalice and frowned, before taking it hesitantly. "Thank you." She took a sip and found greater pleasure in the warmed honey liqueur than she would have thought herself capable of at the moment. It seemed to seep into her frozen, brittle bones and glow. Much like the sensation she had felt after making love with Julian in the tower room. She missed that feeling.

"I miss you, Sybilla," Julian said.

The tender words caught her so thoroughly off guard that she turned and walked to the hearth so as not to face him.

"The monies and the soldiers' orders are finalized," she said instead.

"Are we going to talk about what happened in London?"

She took another long drink and then licked her lips, staring at the flames for a moment. "I don't think I can marry you, Lord Griffin."

He was quiet for a moment, and when he did speak, he did not sound angry. "Why not?"

"Because it seems I don't know who I am after all." She gave a dark chuckle. "You can't marry a stranger."

"You're not a stranger to me, Sybilla," he said easily. "I might even go so far as to say that I know you better than you know yourself. In fact, I'm certain of it."

"You think a lot of yourself. Fallstowe gone to your head, has it?"

"I've heard it has that effect on those at its helm," he quipped, not unkindly. "And yes, I think a lot of myself. Of you, as well. I know what we are capable of as individuals—what we've already accomplished. I shiver for the world at large once we are united."

He meant it as a joke, and perhaps at another time Sybilla would have found it funny.

"Your confidence is self-made, Lord Griffin," she said. "And that is to your benefit, because that means it is proven and true. My confidence . . . was based on nothing more than duty and survival."

"I don't believe that's true at all," Julian countered. "And it seems you have forgotten my given name."

"I don't care what you believe," Sybilla said, ignoring his allusion to her withdrawal of intimacy.

"I *know* that's not true." He came to stand at her side. "You're hiding from me, and there is no reason for it."

"I'm not hiding from anyone."

"That's all you've ever done!" Julian said. "You hid from your mother's past behind a desperate facade of aloofness. You hid from the king. You hid from love. The great and frightening Sybilla Foxe hides from herself because she feels she must be defined by other people! Are you a coward?"

She tossed the contents of her drink at him, and then in the next instant threw the cup itself, aiming for his handsome, rugged face.

He deflected the projectile easily, and then moved in on her faster than a lightning strike, seizing her upper arms and dragging her to him. The liqueur dripped from his hair and stained his rich tunic.

"Quit behaving like a child, or I shall be forced to turn you across my knee."

"I will break both your arms with a toss of my head," she warned, putting her nose close to his. She could feel her flesh pulsing toward his body.

He moved in even closer, so that their breaths mingled and then reached for the closure pin at the crown of her head. He yanked the crispinette free. "Let me loosen your hair for you first."

Then he kissed her.

They fell to the floor between the hearth and the back of the low couch.

She heard her gown rip.

And for a little while, Sybilla was alive again.

* * *

Julian stood over Sybilla, where she still lay on the thick rug with her gown about her hips. Her head was turned to stare at the flames, and she seemed oblivious to the fact that she remained mostly uncovered. Julian's knees were trembling, but he would not let her know how moved he was at that moment.

"You have one week, Sybilla," he said, relacing the placard over his manhood.

She turned her head to him at last, and the odd combination of red flames reflected in her icy eyes nearly made him stagger on his feet.

"We will meet again in one week, and you will give me your decision as to whether you will be my wife or not," he reiterated. "In that time, you need not see me, speak to me, or to Lucy. You are free to do as you will. But I am lord here now, and one week from today, I will have your answer."

"All right, Julian," she whispered. "One week."

He hesitated then, but only for a heartbeat. "Good evening."

Then he turned and left her there alone in the solar, and Julian thought it might have been the hardest thing he'd ever done.

Chapter 31

Julian was true to his word.

For the next seven days, he neither sought out Sybilla nor made any overtures toward her on the scant occasions of their passing. She did not take any meals in the hall, that he was aware of. He wasn't certain where she was sleeping or spending the majority of her days, although he had seen her about the grounds from afar on several occasions.

Once, he had caught sight of her as she descended the tower steps, and he had ducked behind a thick, round column so that he might observe her without incident. She had come to the bottom of the stairs and paused at the half-open door of what had been, until the day before, Lucy's chamber. Sybilla peered through the opening a bit, and then moved down the corridor quickly.

He wondered if she had been seeking him for a purpose. He wondered what she had thought of seeing the tower room, emptied of bed and table and replaced with a large work surface and several chairs and trunks of his belongings that had just arrived from London. He wondered if she noticed the quill she'd given him, poised for action near his crisp new ledger.

He had scrambled madly to get things in order before this night, and now all was ready. He looked about his new chamber, recently outfitted for the Lord of Fallstowe, and was pleased. He looked down at his costume again, his finest suit of clothes, and resigned himself to the fact that this was as presentable as he could make himself.

He was nervous.

He quit the chamber, making his way to the great hall, and was pleased to note that he passed not a single person en route. Indeed, even the hall itself was conspicuously deserted.

Save for the lone woman seated at the end of one of the common tables on the floor, facing the dais. She wore a gown of midnight blue, the deepest sapphire against her cloud-white décolleté. Her hair was twisted and curled atop her head, wrapped in a gilded cage of delicate metal flecked with tiny jewels.

He was glad she had dressed for the occasion.

"Good evening, Lady Foxe," he said as he came to stand a pair of paces from her, then bowed rather formally.

"Hello, Julian," she said softly, looking up at him. Her face looked leaner, her collarbones as delicate as the framework of a swallow's wing. Her eyes sparkled in the candlelight.

Julian was speechless for a moment, in the face of her beauty and of his own anxiety.

"I thought perhaps we might conduct our discussion elsewhere this night," he said. "Would you care to accompany me on a ride?"

She frowned only slightly. "All right. Where are we going?"

He assisted her to stand by lightly taking her elbow. "I thought we might visit the Foxe Ring." He led her down the aisle toward the entry stairs.

She didn't hesitate but only chuckled quietly, and glanced up at him as they neared the top of the stairs. "At the full moon, no less."

"Don't worry," he confided, liking the way she seemed more at peace and wondering at the reason behind it. "It's not yet near midnight, so your will shall remain your own."

"I'm not overly concerned, as its magic obviously failed us the only other time we met there," she said.

"Don't discount it yet," Julian chided. "The old rocks may have a few tricks yet left to play."

They exited through the doors, and Julian was pleased to see their mounts waiting for them, as he'd instructed. Octavian looked rather distinguished with a spray of flowers across his bold, dark saddle, and in the moonlight he glowed silver.

Sybilla's gasp was nearly inaudible, but he'd been listening for it. "Julian, what is this?"

"You don't like flowers?" he asked, tugging on her arm to once more force her to move. "I picked them myself."

She looked askance at him.

"All right, I didn't. But it's a romantic gesture nonetheless."

"Thank you," she said, and made use of the mounting stool at Octavian's side.

He handed her Octavian's reins and then moved to his own mount, a black Spanish beast, lean and wiry. Julian and Sybilla rode the horses at a walk through the bailey and over the lowered drawbridge. As they turned their horses west and then north, to ride around the backside of Fallstowe, Julian at once saw the tiny glow on a faraway hillock. It looked like a star lying atop the hill.

But Sybilla had not seen it, and he sought to distract her until they were down in the valley and separated from the knoll by a stand of trees now in full greenery.

"I've moved my chamber," he stated.

"I know."

"You've been spying on me?" he teased.

She smiled up at him for only a moment. "I'm certain you are much more comfortable. Lucy's rooms are lovely. How do you find the tower room for working?"

"It's quite ideal," he replied honestly. "Remote, perfect for contemplation, planning."

"Yes. My . . . Morys, it was his favorite room in the castle, I believe."

"Sybilla," Julian said quietly. "You can call him Father. How hurt would he be if you did not?"

She was quiet for a long time as their horses meandered up the final rise. Julian didn't know how Sybilla had not noticed the glow by now, lighting the night sky above them, or the faint buzz of voices.

"You're right, of course," she said at last. "You've been right about a lot of things, actually. And I—what the bloody hell is this?"

They had reached the top of the rise at last, and the glow lit upon them like sunbeams. The dirt path before them was lined with tall standing torches, and among them were gathered the villagers of Fallstowe, all dressed in their finest: women, men, children—Julian even saw a handful of mongrel dogs with festive bows tied round their necks. The audience stretched the length of the road, down into the valley and up the opposite hillock, where the brightness was intensified.

The Foxe Ring stood directly across from them, its stones lit up like midday by torches strapped to the standing monoliths and scores of candles on the fallen stones still too far away to be seen individually. The crowd skirted the ring, and as Julian and Sybilla appeared on the rise, a collective shout of joy rose up.

Sybilla turned to look at Julian, surprise and perhaps a bit of fear in her eyes. "What is this?" she repeated.

He smiled at her, and hoped it was reassuring. "You told me when last we spoke that you couldn't marry me because you didn't know who you were. That I didn't know who you were. I am here"—he swept an arm to indicate the hundreds of folk spread out before them—"*they* are here, to educate you."

One of her slender eyebrows rose. "Educate me?"

He nodded. "Come on, then." He made to urge his horse forward, but Sybilla reached out a hand to grasp at his arm.

"Julian, I . . . I can't."

Julian turned his arm to reach back with his own hand and grasp hers. "Yes, you can. Come on." He refused to release her until she at last kicked at Octavian's sides lightly.

As they passed through the living corridor of the folk who had flourished under Sybilla's care, each person bowed or curtsied, calling out respectfully, "My lady."

Sybilla looked around at them all, nodding to some absently as they rode by.

"To these people," Julian said quietly, "you are their livelihood. The difference between prosperity and poverty. You have made them something more than just a man who drives oxen, or a woman who threshes grain.

They are living parts of the greatest demesne in all of England. They are proud of that. You have made each of them important in their own role."

Julian saw Sybilla swallow, but she said nothing.

They started up the hillock to the ring itself, and the audience gradually shifted from village folk to people of the manor itself: the butcher's family, the brewer, the dairymen, Father Perry; and now the house servants, the cook and her minions, the chambermaids.

"To *these* people you have given their own kingdom," Julian continued. "A country more dear to them than England itself, a ruler more worthy to defend than their king. They are a clan, a family, along with you, your sisters, your parents. The history of all of Fallstowe is written not by their hands in some record, but on their hearts, where it can never be scratched away or burned out."

The calls of "my lady" had now changed to the more intimate term of "Madam" by those employed within the keep proper, and Julian could see how affected Sybilla was by their presence.

"You *are* their lady. Their Madam," Julian insisted. "You always have been. You always will be. And nothing that has happened in the past, nothing that might happen in the future could ever change that. The past, to them, is all the years of your guidance, your protection. The future is only the morn, when they awaken to proudly assist in the continuing success that is Fallstowe. If that is not validating to you, then I fear that nothing in this world is."

They were nearly upon the ring now, and so they stopped their horses. Sybilla stared at the innermost circle of guests that Julian had invited with the help of Sybilla's sisters. It seemed everyone in the land had come: Clement Cobb, his new bride, and his mother, Etheldred; Vicar John Grey and his bishop, accompanied by a gaggle of religious from nearby Hallowshire Abbey; Piers Mallory's grandfather tending a monkey; a host of strange people who seemed to be clothed for a primitive pagan feast; Julian's own friend, Erik; and Sybilla's general, Wigmund.

And inside the ring, bathed in the pure white glow of candlelight, stood Alys and Piers, Cecily and Oliver, and at last, old Graves, holding Lucy in her fine velvet robes and the jeweled tiara Sybilla had gifted her with weeks ago, recently refashioned to fit correctly upon her head, with a small veil.

Sybilla looked at Julian at last, her face pale, her eyes wide and sparkling with confused emotion.

"And those people you see there," he said quietly, indicating the inner circle of the ring with a flick of his eyes, "are the ones who love you most in this world. The only one missing from the group is I." Then Julian dismounted, walked around the heads of both his and Sybilla's mounts, and held his hand up to her.

"Let us join them," he said.

Sybilla realized she was trembling as she let Julian lead her into the Foxe Ring, toward her smiling family. She felt so exposed here, in this place that for so long had been a den of secrets and mystery and rumor.

She felt self-conscious and, for once, at a complete loss for words for these people who indeed knew her more intimately than anyone on earth. What would she say to them?

But she had no need to speak, for Piers stepped forward, dropping Alys's hand and giving Sybilla a stiff and shallow bow, so much like his cantankerous grandfather would have done.

"Lady Sybilla," he said in his quiet, humble way. "You have given me so much in the short time we have known each other. Besides providing so well for Alys, you risked your own life to bring my only blood family to me in London, when I was at my most desperate. You gave Alys leave to choose me, and she is the most wondrous thing in my life. I could never have hoped for such gaiety and . . . sunshine." He cleared his throat, and Sybilla felt her own chin tremble as she swallowed.

Piers continued. "Because of your support and generosity, Gillwick prospers. I owe you my life, and that of the family your sister and I will make together. You will always be part of that family."

Then Oliver stepped forward, clearing his throat. "I guess I shall be next then. Right." Oliver rubbed his palms together briskly and then grinned at Sybilla in his roguish way. "Well. We have known each other for quite some time, you and I. You've sheltered me in injury through my own idiocy. You looked out for my welfare even when I had no idea you did so. Sorry about that bit with the king, of course." Everyone chuckled, including Sybilla. "You gave my brother a great deal of joy. You saved Cecily's life. I suppose you were going to be my sister-in-law one way or the other, eh?"

Oliver looked down at the ground for a moment, and when his eyes met hers again, his face was completely solemn and he gave an affirmative nod. "I thank God for that."

Sybilla had to close her eyes and turn her face away for a moment, and then she felt Oliver's arms around her. She returned his embrace. He rejoined his wife.

"Sybilla," Alys said next, "you were a terrible, horrid, wretched replacement for my mother. But you were the best sister, friend, and protector I could ever have asked for. It was because of your example that I could justify standing up against iniquities. I fought for what was right because I knew it was what *you* would do. You were my guiding light, even when I denounced you for the harridan I thought you to be. I know that it was because of your deep love that you demanded so much of me. And I can only pray that I show my own husband and children such devotion and confidence in what they are capable of. I love you."

Alys's speech did not bring Sybilla to tears, and for that she was grateful, but at that moment, her youngest sister seemed so mature, Sybilla felt a pride that could only be described as maternal.

"My turn," Cecily said, and stepped forward before Sybilla could respond. "Sybilla, you saved my life. Both literally and figuratively. You saw in me my deepest desires, desires I denied for too long. You encouraged me, pushed me into uncomfortable situations, made me look at myself and my actions and be accountable for my future. I suppose you rather pushed me from the nest, knowing before even I did that I could fly. You looked out for my safety, even as soldiers bore down on you alone. You gave no thought to your own happiness while those around you needed you. You are the greatest friend I have ever known, and I love you very much."

Sybilla felt Julian's hand on her lower back. Should she tell him now that it was her intention to marry him? That she had decided it a week ago in the solar? What he had done for her here, it was beyond her wildest imaginings of love. Her heart was so full, it felt as though it might burst if she did not tell him.

She turned to him. "Julian, I—"

But someone cleared his throat pointedly and Sybilla and Julian turned to see that Graves had stepped forward.

"Might I say something, Lord Griffin?"

Oliver quipped under his breath, "Don't you mean, might you ask something?"

Graves's head turned toward the young lord with a haughty stare.

"That's not what I mean at all, Lord Oliver."

Everyone within earshot gasped. Sybilla felt her mouth fall open.

"Go on, Graves. Please," Julian encouraged him respectfully.

Graves stepped toward them and handed Lucy to Julian. Then he turned to Sybilla.

"Madam. The day you were born, there had never been such rejoicing at Fallstowe, in all my many days here since my own birth. Never has a child brought a man such joy as you did your father. He delighted in you beyond anything of this mortal world, and he and I spent many an hour discussing your future, your talents, your inevitable success. And your mother—" Graves paused for a moment and his thin, wrinkled lips pursed, twitched. "She perhaps made some missteps. But what she did, she did to protect your father, your sisters, and you. She tried to do it all on her own, until it became clear that she would not live long enough to see its end.

"Everything she ever told you is absolutely true," Graves said in a voice just above a whisper. Then he stepped forward, grasped her shoulders with his bony hands and leaned his papery cheek against hers to speak in her ear. "*And it does not . . . bloody . . . matter . . . anymore.*"

He pressed his cool, dry lips to her cheek before he drew away and took a courteous step back.

"I long for your happiness above all else. Above even Fallstowe's continuation. I can't bear—" He broke off, and when he recovered, his haughty voice was choked, his rheumy eyes glistened. "I can't bear the thought of you alone, when I am no longer here to look after you."

Sybilla broke then, rushing to Graves and embracing him, her tears staining his shoulders as they clung to each other.

"I love you, Graves," Sybilla said.

"And I you, Madam."

At last they released each other, and then Sybilla turned to Julian once more, who now held a solemn-looking and wide-eyed Lucy, little dark shadows under her eyes from the late hour.

She still had no chance to speak, though.

"Now," Julian said, "it's my turn."

Chapter 32

Julian looked down into Sybilla's eyes as he held his daughter. He could see the overwhelming emotion on her face, how it had confused her, shaken her, and that was exactly what Julian had hoped for.

Sometimes the truth was a difficult thing to hear. And sometimes it was only difficult to accept.

"Until the day I heard the king speak your name, I thought you were a fable," he said. "And when I discovered that not only were you a fact, but I would be responsible for investigating your life, I was charged with anticipation. The more I learned about you, the more intrigued I became, and the more I craved to know.

"Then I met you. And you tried to kill me straightaway. Repeatedly, I still suspect." He smiled at her and she returned the gesture as everyone within earshot chuckled. "And I discovered that everything I'd heard about you was true, only worse." At that, the guests laughed out loud, even Sybilla.

"And it was the most lovely experience," he said quietly. "Before coming to Fallstowe, I had memorized dates, names, facts about your life. But it was only as I came to know you as a woman that I realized how phenomenal, how amazing, you actually are to have done the impossible things you have. It was only after coming here and being in this magical place—not just the Foxe Ring, but all that comprises Fallstowe, that I understood loyalty, devotion, the deep kind of love that spans castles, countries, continents . . . generations. Even death."

"Julian," Sybilla said.

"Not yet," he insisted softly. "So who is Sybilla Foxe to me now? She is the bravest, most beautiful, honest, passionate woman that God has ever formed. I hope she will be my wife. The woman who will continue to guard and protect Fallstowe and its people, at my side." He looked down at Lucy, who had nestled her head under his chin but was still regarding Sybilla hesitantly from the safety of his chest.

"To Lucy?" he said, giving his daughter a squeeze and a little bounce on his arms before holding her slightly away from his chest. "You are her mother. All you need do is take her, Sybilla. Take her, and we are yours forever."

Sybilla smiled gently up at him and stepped forward, her hands at her sides. "If you had only asked me once more in the solar last week, I would have said yes, Julian." Then she took hold of Lucy and brought her to her chest, closing her eyes with a sigh. "My darling girl," she whispered.

Julian enveloped them both as a cheer rang out through the valley, echoing up to the sparkling sky and glowing moon. He leaned down and spoke into her ear.

"You shall be turned across my knee for certain now."

"Let me take my own hair down this time," she replied.

Julian threw his head back and laughed for a moment. And then he looked over his shoulder, seeking his accomplice.

"Father Perry?"

"At your side, young man." The slender priest stepped to a spot just before the fallen down center stone, in front of Julian and Sybilla, who still snuggled Lucy.

Sybilla looked at Julian with surprise. "Now?"

"You don't think I went to all this trouble just for a heartfelt chat, do you?" he teased. "Yes, now. Not a moment later. Yes, Sybilla?"

She kissed Lucy's forehead. "Yes."

She would have handed the baby to Graves, but Lucy was having none of it. And so perhaps it was fitting that the three of them were joined together as a family at the Foxe Ring as the hour courted midnight beneath that ripe moon that knew so much of the place.

At the end of the formalities, when Julian and Sybilla had kissed each other sweetly, and then both kissed Lucy for good measure, Sybilla was surprised to see the inside of the old ruins light up like a fair. Julian grinned mischievously as he led her to the old arched doorway where, inside the ruins, Fallstowe's capable servants were bustling about.

A newly sawed, pale wood floor covered the dark, dreadful circle that had once been the dungeon, and atop it was a U-shaped configuration of rough-hewn tables bearing all manner of fresh spring berries and cheeses and cakes. There were casks of ale and cider and a special display of apple tarts. Musicians had set up near where the old stair snaked up the wall of the keep, and within moments, the old Foxe ruins knew life and music and joy once more as the hundreds of guests milled in and out and around the stones.

Many young people tried their luck with the legend that night. Perhaps the resulting population surge at Fallstowe the following winter's end was only a coincidence. But perhaps not.

It was nearly dawn when Sybilla and Julian and Lucy made their way back to Fallstowe. They saw their already sleeping daughter to a clean nappy and her own bed and then Sybilla followed her husband into their new chamber. Nothing was familiar here, and that suited her greatly as they both undressed and crawled beneath the coverlet, each feeling the effects of the wine and the emotions of the evening. They reached for each other in the still, pale light, and were instantly asleep.

They consummated their marriage much later in the morning, upon waking in the quiet; alone together. It was a slow, joyful union that deliberately erased the worst of the past, the unknown, for them both.

After dressing and breaking the fast as a family, Lucy was off for a late lie-down, and Julian had neglected several important messages that needed addressing. And so Sybilla donned a cloak for the chilly rain that had enveloped the land once more and, after retrieving the item she'd brought back from London, set out across bright green fields.

The dirt was still tawny over Sybil de Lairne's grave. Sybilla stood for a long time in the drizzle, saying nothing, hearing nothing, simply experiencing the feeling of standing on the edge of a very high precipice. She had been here before, she felt, but this time she had no desire to take that step.

"Good-bye, Mother," Sybilla whispered. "Good-bye, Sybil."

Sybilla bent at her knees and placed the miniature portrait of the two girls in the grass, one edge of the frame just touching the recently turned earth. She stood aright.

And then Sybilla turned on her heel, her head held high, and walked through the rain back to her husband and daughter. Back to her family. Back to her heart, her future.

And Fallstowe welcomed her.

AUTHOR'S NOTE

I hope you have enjoyed spending time with the Foxe sisters throughout their adventures. Each heroine was special to me in her own way, and each gave me her own unique sort of trouble.

Although the characters and events in all three stories are completely fictional, obviously there was a King Edward I of England during that time period. My interpretation of Longshanks is purely of my own imagination, I assure you, and nothing *this* king does or says throughout the Foxe Sisters trilogy is anything but fantasy.

However, the stories of Simon de Montfort and his troubles with the Gascon barons, and later with Edward's father, King Henry III, are all based on historical events and depict a rather tumultuous time in English history. There are conflicting opinions to this day about the motives and intentions of both Simon de Montfort and Edward I in the baronial revolts. The battle of Lewes did indeed take place, although I invented my own details. And Edward did take back the power of his father's throne by triumphing over Simon de Montfort in 1265 at Evesham with the assistance of a woman spy.

Her identity remains unknown.

GREAT BOOKS,
GREAT SAVINGS!

When You Visit Our Website:
www.kensingtonbooks.com
You Can Save Money Off The Retail Price
Of Any Book You Purchase!

- **All Your Favorite Kensington Authors**
- **New Releases & Timeless Classics**
- **Overnight Shipping Available**
- **eBooks Available For Many Titles**
- **All Major Credit Cards Accepted**

Visit Us Today To Start Saving!
www.kensingtonbooks.com

All Orders Are Subject To Availability.
Shipping and Handling Charges Apply.
Offers and Prices Subject To Change Without Notice.